Being an author has always been **Therese Beharrie**'s dream. But it was only when the corporate world loomed during her final year at university that she realised how soon she wanted that dream to become a reality. So she got serious about her writing, and now she writes the kind of books she wants to see in the world, featuring people who look like her, for a living. When she's not writing she's spending time with her husband and dogs in Cape Town, South Africa. She admits that this is a perfect life, and is grateful for it.

Brenda Harlen is a former attorney who once had the privilege of appearing before the Supreme Court of Canada. The practice of law taught her a lot about the world and reinforced her determination to become a writer—because in fiction, she could promise a happy ending! Now she is an award-winning, RITA® Award-nominated nationally bestselling author of more than thirty titles for Mills & Boon. You can keep up-to-date with Brenda on Facebook and Twitter, or through her website, brendaharlen.com

Also by Therese Beharrie

Tempted by the Billionaire Next Door
Surprise Baby, Second Chance
Her Festive Flirtation
Island Fling with the Tycoon
Her Twin Baby Secret
Marrying His Runaway Heiress

Billionaires for Heiresses

Second Chance with Her Billionaire
From Heiress to Mum

Also by Brenda Harlen

The Sheriff's Nine-Month Surprise
Her Seven-Day Fiancé
Six Weeks to Catch a Cowboy
Claiming the Cowboy's Heart
Double Duty for the Cowboy
One Night with the Cowboy
Maverick Christmas Surprise
Bring Me a Maverick for Christmas!
The Maverick's Midnight Proposal

Discover more at millsandboon.co.uk

HIS PRINCESS BY CHRISTMAS

THERESE BEHARRIE

MEET ME UNDER THE MISTLETOE

BRENDA HARLEN

MILLS & BOON

First Published in Great Britain 2020
by Mills & Boon, an imprint of HarperCollinsPublishers,
1 London Bridge Street, London, SE1 9GF

His Princess by Christmas © 2020 Therese Beharrie
Meet Me Under the Mistletoe © 2020 Brenda Harlen

ISBN: 978-0-263-27905-4

1120

MIX
Paper from
responsible sources
FSC® C007454

This book is produced from independently certified FSC™
paper to ensure responsible forest management.

For more information visit: www.harpercollins.co.uk/green

Printed and bound in Spain
by CPI, Barcelona

HIS PRINCESS BY CHRISTMAS

THERESE BEHARRIE

To the princes in my life.
I love you all more than I thought possible.

CHAPTER ONE

WHEN THE BELL attached to the door of her store rang, Amari Hayes didn't immediately look up. She had some things to do before she officially opened. But being in a small town meant people didn't pay attention to the rules very well. She had learnt that during the three and a half years she'd been a resident of Swell Valley.

She'd also learnt it was fine for her to make her own rules. She finished what she was doing, *then* she looked up. And stared.

And stared, and stared, and stared.

He was tall. Tall enough that she had to lift her chin to make eye contact, which rarely happened since she herself was tall. That would have been enough to snag her attention, but he was also quite deliciously built. Strong and thick; the kind of body that could easily swoop her into his arms during an emergency.

He was impeccably dressed in a tailored suit. Blue. The suit was blue. Normally, the colour of a suit wouldn't matter. But *this* blue on *this* man was something special. It matched his brown skin perfectly and did something for his dark features. Heavy-set brows, the polite pull of his angular cheekbones, his lush mouth.

It was ridiculous to make such superficial observations about a man, let alone feel a rush of…something, in her body as a result. He was a stranger. He deserved respect, not lust.

It was interesting, that was all. She hadn't had a feeling like this since...since her husband. Her *ex*-husband.

She cleared her throat. 'Hi.'

'Hello.'

She got nothing else.

'The store isn't officially open yet,' she said, trying not to shift her weight. 'If you wait another five minutes—' She broke off. He clearly wasn't from Swell Valley, and it was pointless making him wait five minutes so she could, what? Get herself a cup of coffee? 'What can I help you with?'

'I'd like to speak with the manager.'

'You already are.'

'Oh.' Surprise coloured his expression. 'You're the manager?'

'I'm the owner. But those roles are interchangeable around here.' She tilted her head. 'Did you expect someone else?'

His polite expression returned, but a light blush tinted the skin of his cheeks.

'It was rude of me to show surprise,' he said evenly. 'I'm sorry.'

'For showing surprise, or for feeling it?'

'Both.'

She studied him again, but this time it had nothing to do with his appearance. It was that practised lilt of his voice. His measured tone that didn't waver, even when he was surprised or embarrassed. The politeness that seemed to spill from his pores.

They didn't get many people like this in Swell Valley. The town was a stone's throw away from Cape Town, its population about ten thousand, and everyone knew one another. That meant an authenticity that wasn't practised, measured or polite.

When Amari had first moved to Swell Valley, that level of comfort had bothered her. People had asked her about

May, her daughter, as if May were their own. They would enquire about her well-being, about how she was getting on at day-care, about whether she'd overcome her cold. They would ask Amari if *she* was settling in okay, if she needed help with anything, and when was she going to find a partner to help her with all her responsibilities?

The questions had felt invasive. She came from Cape Town, where people didn't particularly care to ask questions unless they knew her. But the questions about May... those had put her back up. She was sensitive when it came to her daughter, no doubt. Being a single mother did that. Choosing a man who couldn't accept the responsibility of being a father did that.

But she had moved to Swell Valley to give May a different life. If she couldn't give her daughter a family, she would give her a community. Over the past three and a half years, she had learnt to accept what came with having a community. She must have come to expect it, too, if she couldn't understand this man's demeanour.

'I'm here about the advertisement in the window.'

'What about it?'

'I'd like to apply.'

For the third time in fifteen minutes, Amari stared. 'You want to apply to be a festive worker?'

The man lifted his chin. 'I would, yes.'

Her eyes travelled down his expensive suit to his expensive shoes and back up to what would no doubt be an expensive face had he ever thought to insure it.

'You realise it's busy work, right? Helping me stock shelves, assisting customers with their Christmas shopping.' At his nod, she continued. 'People will come in here and ask your opinion on what they should get their partners. Or their in-laws. Or their pets. Are you prepared for that?'

'I'm not sure how to answer that. Am I prepared for the questions? Yes.'

'Are you prepared to *answer*?' This time, she didn't wait for his nod. 'If Mrs Hallow asks what she should get her husband, who works on a farm not far away from here, for Christmas, what would you say?'

He opened his mouth, before closing it with a frown. She shouldn't enjoy it, but it was quite fun to see him emote.

'This store…it sells trinkets?'

Amari looked around, took in the items. To an outsider, they probably did look like trinkets. Along the wall he was closest to there was a glass cabinet with jewellery. Most of it came from locals, as did the crafts that formed the shelf he stood in front of. It was waist high, same as the cabinet, though the shelves behind it, diagonally across the counter where she stood, were higher, and packed with craft materials, knitting material, books, stationery. At the counter, she put the brownies and fudge Mrs Hallow made daily that were delivered by her grandson every morning on his way to work.

Trinkets, she thought again, to someone who didn't understand the workings of a small town. Here, people appreciated being supported by one another. They wanted *to* support one another.

This man wouldn't understand that her business succeeded largely because she carried things locals made and provided things they wanted. He wouldn't know that crafts was one of the most popular activities in Swell Valley, followed closely by knitting, and that many of the items she stocked were a direct result of those activities.

She hadn't expected an outsider to apply for the job. She'd expected a teen on school holiday. But she knew she was late, too. She'd lived in Swell Valley long enough to know that available teens had jobs secured months before Christmas. She had only recently become interested in having a festive helper, or she would have hired someone a long time ago.

If only May had started asking questions about her father in September.

'Sure,' she replied evenly. 'They're trinkets.'

'Then I would ask Mrs Hallow what kind of trinket her husband would like.' He moved forward, stepping right under the air-con. It brought a wave of his cologne towards her. It smelled like power, like control. She shouldn't have liked it. She did. 'If he goes out to the farm, perhaps he'd like…this.'

Amari didn't allow herself the smile. For a second. After that, she couldn't help it.

'A tray?'

'Oh?' He leaned to examine the tray closer. 'I thought it was sun protection of some kind.'

'Sun…' She frowned. 'You're joking, right?'

An emotion she couldn't identify dulled his expression. But a beat later it brightened again, as if someone had flicked a light switch. 'Yes. Yes, of course it was a joke. I know people can't use trays as sun protection.'

Amari bit her lip. Before she could say anything, the door opened.

'We got the Christmas stuff you ordered,' Joe, her delivery man, said by way of greeting. 'Lots of boxes.'

'Oh, I can help,' the man said eagerly.

Amari thought about all the stuff she'd ordered. It was the end of November, and her shelves were barely stocked for Christmas. People would start to do their Christmas shopping soon, and she needed to be ready. And she would need help, too, if she wanted to spend more time with May.

'Do I have a daddy, Mama?'

She closed her eyes against the guilt that still flared days after May had asked the question. It had been innocent, and Amari had known it would come some day. But she still hadn't been prepared. Her solution had been to distract May. She'd given a terribly inadequate answer and had suggested they bake cookies. May had been successfully deterred.

But the more time May spent alone, the more likely she was to think up questions. Unpacking the boxes without help would mean a late night for Amari. May would be sleeping by the time Amari relieved the babysitter and in the morning, May would ask one million questions as was her habit. On the off chance one of those questions was about her father again, Amari needed to find ways to occupy May so it didn't come to that.

It was nowhere near a foolproof plan, but it didn't matter. It made her feel as if she was doing something. Even something stupid, like hire a man who looked like a supermodel to work in her store.

'Fine. You can help me today. We'll use it as a trial period. If it works out, you can have the job.'

She didn't wait for his reaction. Only nodded to Joe to start bringing the boxes in.

Kade didn't know if it was the quaint look of the store or the woman inside it that had made him walk through the door. It was probably neither.

Rather, he'd needed a distraction from the calls that kept coming to his phone. His mother's secretary, the royal communications officer. They knew full well that he was on leave, but that didn't matter when they had the Christmas ball to plan. That was when they would announce the news of his mother's abdication and the date of his coronation. Even walking the quiet streets of Swell Valley couldn't ease the anxiety of all that.

But distraction would.

When he'd had the thought, he'd been right in front of the All and Everything store. His eyes had taken in the advertisement for festive help, then they'd rested on the woman inside. His decision had been made some time after that and he'd walked inside.

He'd put his foot into it when he'd assumed she wasn't the owner, and she'd rightfully called him out for it. His only excuse was that he'd been distracted by her beauty. A pathetic excuse if there was one. His mother would kill him if she knew.

She certainly wouldn't be surprised by the faux pas though. He made them far too often.

Not now.

Yes. He had time before he needed to think about that. Now, he had to deal with his guard, Pete, who he'd managed to convince to hang back when he'd gone inside the store. Of course, Pete had had no idea what Kade intended on doing. When the delivery man had arrived, Pete had appeared in the store, refusing instructions to leave.

'You're under my protection, sir.'

Pete said it in answer to every reason Kade gave as to why Pete should leave him alone.

'Is there a problem?' the owner asked from behind him.

Kade turned. It took him a moment to adjust to her face, which was what had happened the first time he'd seen her, too. Something about it had his breath catching, though her features were relatively unremarkable separately. The light brown eyes and hair of the same hue. The creases around those eyes, between her brows. Her lips weren't full, nor were they thin; her cheekbones neither sharp nor rounded. But somehow all those features together created something quite remarkable.

Even when they were pulled in disapproval.

'None,' Kade said smoothly. 'This is my guard. He'd like to assist us.'

'Your...guard,' she repeated. 'As in—a bodyguard? Why?' She didn't allow him to answer. 'I mean, you do *look* like a man who would have a bodyguard, but I can't quite marry that with a man who applied for a short-term retail position in a trinket store.'

Kade pretended not to notice Pete's surprise.

'I'll take those questions one by one. First, yes, a body-guard. It's part of the law of my kingdom that I have protection with me whenever I'm out in public. For this trip, I managed to negotiate one guard only, which I suppose explains his commitment to the job.' Kade sighed. 'As for the rest, you're remarkably astute. The man who needs the bodyguard is not the same man who'd like to help you in your store. The former is a prince; the latter is just a man who'd like to distract himself until he's needed back home.'

He paused, giving her time to process.

'Did I cover all your questions?'

There was a short period of silence. Then she laughed. At *him*.

CHAPTER TWO

'I'M SORRY.' KADE interrupted the laughter stiffly. 'Did I say something funny?'

'Yes,' she said between giggles. 'You implied you're a prince. Or said it outright, I guess.' She wiped her tears. 'A prince.' She shook her head. 'Wow. Your imagination.'

'I assure you, these are facts, not my imagination.'

The amusement slowly faded from her face. 'You're serious?'

He didn't dignify that question with a verbal answer, only a nod.

'Well, Your Highness, I'm not sure what you're doing in my store. I can't afford to pay royal rates. Or whatever your rate is as an—' she narrowed her eyes '—actor?'

This time he didn't even respond with a nod.

'Okay, I'm not sure what you're looking to accomplish,' she said, serious now. 'I'm the only person who works here. Usually, that's enough. People around here are patient, and that patience extends when they consider you one of their own.' The square of her shoulders told him that was how they considered her. 'Over the holidays though, we get busy. People come from out of town. People in town want nice things. I need help to cater to them, and to get home to my daughter at night at a reasonable time. If this is a joke to you, and you don't intend on helping me, please leave. I'll find someone else.'

It wasn't at all a reasonable response, but Kade's eyes dropped to her hand. She wasn't wearing a ring. Immediately after the observation, he lifted his gaze. He didn't know this woman. Her remarkable face didn't matter. He needed something that would keep his mind busy.

Freedom, he'd realised in the two days he'd spent in the house he was renting, meant time. Time to think, to revisit mistakes, to remember all his mother had done for him and their kingdom. It meant picturing his mother's face when she told him she would be stepping down because her heart condition prevented her from ruling the way the kingdom needed. It meant hearing the plea she didn't have to make verbally: that he not disappoint her.

He needed to focus on that—or *not* focus on it—and not think about the remarkable-looking woman or her marital status.

'This isn't a joke,' he said. 'I'm not an actor. I am the Crown Prince of Daria, a small kingdom off the shore of Africa. You've never heard of it?'

She shook her head, lips pursed.

'That's fair,' he said, surprising himself with a chuckle. 'We're small, much smaller than even South Africa's landlocked kingdoms of Lesotho or Swaziland. We also tend to keep to ourselves.'

Her lips grew thinner.

'If it would make you feel better, you can—'

Her phone interrupted the suggestion of an Internet search. With one last wary glance at him and Pete, she went to answer.

'Hello, you've reached All and Everything, this is Amari.'

Amari. A remarkable name to suit her face.

As soon as Kade thought it, he shoved it out of his brain. He wouldn't indulge the frisson of attraction. He wouldn't even indulge *thoughts* that leaned in the direction of attraction. He wanted to convince her to hire him. It had become a matter of importance, distraction and pride.

'Is she okay?'

The concern in Amari's voice caught his attention. As did the relieved sigh, followed by a frustrated exhalation.

'Yes. Yes, I can pick her up.'

There were a few more minutes of back and forth before she put down the phone.

'Is everything okay?' he asked.

'My daughter... She had a fall at school. I have to pick her up.' Amari exhaled again, looking at her watch. 'Oh! I have another delivery coming in twenty minutes.' She chewed her lip. 'If I'm not here, they probably won't come again until tomorrow. That means another delay in getting Mr Potter that material he ordered, which would be fine, if he wasn't such a pompous—'

She cut off with a heave of a sigh.

'Amari?' Kade said softly, though he knew she wasn't talking to him. She had merely been talking aloud. 'I can stay here. I can wait for your delivery and help ensure Mr Potter doesn't become irate with you.'

Amari looked at him for a long time. He could all but see the questions in her head. He decided to answer them.

'You have no reason to trust me, but I assure you, I am trustworthy.'

'That's what untrustworthy people say, too,' she said darkly.

'What are your alternatives?' he asked, trying a different tactic. 'You could have your neighbour sign for the delivery? The flower store next door?'

'Sheryl's out for the week after an op. She didn't have time to make arrangements so she closed.'

He didn't know if closing a store due to a medical emergency was the usual way of doing things, or perhaps the usual way of doing things in this town. Either way, if he was lucky, this could work in his favour.

'What about your opposite neighbours? The post office?'

'Monday mornings are their busiest. I don't think they'll have time to sign for a delivery and wait for it to be delivered.'

'It's sounding more and more like I'm your only option.'

Her gaze settled on him. 'I'm taking all the cash with me.'

'Fair.'

'And putting up the closed sign. You won't deal with customers.'

He nodded.

'And if you take anything, just know that… I'll find you.'

His mouth lifted. 'You'll find me?'

'Yeah,' she said, going behind the counter and packing up, including taking the cash in the register. 'You don't blend in very well with your fancy suit.'

He didn't know if that was supposed to be an insult.

'You don't approve of my suit? It has plenty of pockets to steal trinkets. And with the quality of your trinkets, I'm sure they'll go quite well together and no one would be the wiser.'

She opened her mouth, but instead of the fire he expected in response to his sarcasm, he got a huff of laughter. 'Yeah, I get it. You probably don't need my trinkets, huh?' She came around the counter and stopped in front of him. 'Please, *please*, don't make me regret this.'

With a nod for both him and Pete, she left.

They stood in silence for a few moments.

'I'm not sure she should trust us,' Pete said.

'No,' Kade replied. 'But clearly there's some desperation. I understand that.' He gave it a moment. 'Why don't you and I try to find something constructive to do, Pete? Maybe something that won't make her regret her choices.'

* * *

Amari had May home and settled within thirty minutes. It was part of the beauty of small-town living. Nothing was far away from anything, and help was easy to find. Like Mrs Green next door, who had eagerly agreed to take care of May for the day while Amari worked.

She had learnt pretty quickly she would have to accept help if she was going to raise May in Swell Valley. Since May only had some bruises from her fall and seemed to be in good spirits, Amari knew this was one of those times. She fussed though, and hoped this incident wouldn't make May ask whether having a daddy would have meant him staying home with her.

Oh, no. She was becoming obsessive. She really needed to get a grip and think about something else. Maybe about how she'd left her store in the care of two men she didn't even know the names of.

She didn't even know their names.

She should have asked. Except knowing their names wouldn't add to their trustworthiness. She had known her ex-husband's name, and he'd let her and their six-month-old daughter down. She had known her mother's name, and the woman had left her to fend for herself for most of her life.

Names didn't mean anything at all.

Get. A. Grip.

She took a deep breath. She had made a choice. A decent one. There was a low probability a man dressed as expensively as that man was—a man who *looked* as expensive as he did—would steal from her store. A man with his imagination would rob a jewellery store, not a bric-à-brac store. And the man who was with him, the man who looked about as dangerous as 'the prince' did expensive... He seemed more capable of crime, yes, but...

What had she done?

By the time she reached the store, she was a complete

mess. She was fully convinced she would return to an empty space but talked herself out of it. It wouldn't be empty; she had only been away for an hour. Half empty, though...

But it was nothing like what she expected when she got there.

The first thing she noticed was her Christmas merchandise. They were packed throughout the store, in no order that she could see, yet somehow still looked festive. Or perhaps the festivity came from the decorations. They'd *decorated*. Two men, one expensive and one dangerous, had put up a ridiculous amount of tinsel on her counters and shelves. Christmas ornaments hung from a small tree set up on the counter. Thankfully, all the ornaments had been confined to that tree.

A Happy Festive Season banner, which was meant to go on sale, not to be used, was currently being pinned to the wall behind the counter.

'Higher, Pete,' the expensive man said to the dangerous man.

Silently, Pete obeyed. Even though he must have known the expensive man was wrong.

'No—not that high.'

Amari watched in amusement as they tried to get the banner straight. It took them an embarrassingly long time, but they managed. Pete noticed her standing there long before Kade did, though he said nothing. She was beginning to like Pete. He seemed like the silent type. Dangerous, but silent.

'Amari,' the man said when he finally noticed she was there. 'You're back.'

The words were a little lame. She pretended not to notice.

'I am. And you've been...busy.'

'Yes.'

He looked around nervously, as if seeing it for the first

time. And perhaps he was. Perhaps he was trying to imagine how she was seeing it. A quick glance at his face confirmed her suspicions. He was checking to see how she was responding.

It warmed her. In a weird, totally nonsensical way, this man checking how she was responding to his efforts warmed her.

'It looks great,' she offered, putting him out of his misery. 'I usually don't put up much decorations at the store.'

'You don't?'

Again, the uncertainty had her taking pity on him.

'I leave most of the decorating for home. For my daughter. She's a huge fan of Christmas.'

The man nodded. 'Is she okay?'

'Yeah. She had a fall. Nothing major, but apparently she was crying a lot, and with any head thing they ask parents to keep the child at home for the day.'

'But you're not with her.'

'I have a babysitter with watchful eyes and strict instructions to call if anything goes wrong.' She paused. 'Thanks for asking.'

'Of course.'

There were a few minutes of silence, where the three of them stood and stared at one another. When Amari couldn't take it any more, she walked towards the two men.

'You know my name. It doesn't seem fair that I don't know yours.'

'It's Pr—Kade,' the expensive man said. 'And this is Pete.'

'Nice to meet you both.' She shook their hands. Ignored that little bit of electricity with Kade. It was probably her imagination. 'Thanks for not stealing anything.'

Kade smiled. The electricity that bounced from that smile to her heart wasn't as easy to ignore.

'It was the worst temptation, yet, somehow, we managed.'

She smiled. It was strange, to be caught smiling at him. To have him smiling at her. It felt like a level of familiarity that she shouldn't have with a man she'd only met an hour and a half ago and had spent less than an hour with. She looked away.

'Look…um…about the prince thing…'

'It doesn't have to be an issue if you don't make it one.'

Somehow, the words were gentle. But they made no sense. He wasn't saying that he was joking or lying and yet, those seemed to be the only logical options.

Or no—the one where he was an actor, committed to playing his part, could be an option, too. Or maybe he was simply running away from something.

She understood the desire to run. She had done the same thing when Hank had left. She had been looking for solace and she'd found it in Swell Valley. If people had asked her for more information than she was prepared to give, or poked around in her history, she would likely not have found a home there. But they hadn't. They'd accepted what she was willing to share. Even the half-truths about May's father. If she wanted to give Kade the same courtesy, it would be kind. Fair.

She wanted to be kind and fair. She could handle 'the prince thing' in the name of kindness and fairness.

'Okay.'

'Okay…what?'

'Okay, I won't make this an issue.' She took a moment to get things right in her head, then she said, 'You're hired. Partly because your effort here today is endearing, even if some of it is a little off.' She pointed to a Christmas mug, which had been placed in between knitted scarves. She made a note to ask him about it later. 'And partly because that advertisement has been up for a few days and nobody's responded. If anybody was available in town, they would have already applied.'

'Your confidence in my abilities is overwhelming.'

She liked his dry wit. If he was going to be an employee, that was important. That she liked him. As a person. Not as a man. Not in any way other than as a person who she employed.

'You also proved yourself quite trustworthy today, and, though it was by no means an extensive test, I'll give you a chance. Your probation will be extended to two weeks. I'll pay you a fair wage, starting from today.' She looked at Pete. 'I can pay you for today, too, but I can't have you working here for two weeks. I don't have the budget for you.'

'You don't have to worry about paying either of us,' Kade said, his shoulders oddly stiff.

'Of course I have to pay you. You're working for me. Work means payment.'

'I don't need it.'

She rolled her eyes. 'Everyone needs to feel valued for their work, and, while I can offer you affirmations, money helps, trust me.'

'Amari—'

'I'll pay you in cash, if you don't want to leave a paper trail,' she offered softly. When he didn't reply, she took it as a sign to move on. 'The store opens at eight-thirty. I'll need you here by eight for the latest. On the odd occasion I can't be here to open, you'll need to be here at seven-thirty. Does that work for you?'

'Perfectly.'

'Great.' She put her hands on her hips and looked at the store again. 'Now—care to tell me what you were thinking when you were unpacking this?'

The day went by quickly. Kade was surprised how tired he was when he got back to his rental. It was a two-storey house on a cliff overlooking the beach. Matilda, his secretary, had arranged for the place when she suggested Swell Valley. Apparently, it was where she and her husband stayed when they came to town to visit his family.

He understood why. It was private, the cliff itself forming the edge of the town so it didn't see a lot of traffic. Most of the homes there were owned by foreigners who rented to people like him. This specific one had a comprehensive security system, which was part of why he'd agreed to the suggestion.

The other part was the view.

The décor of the house itself reminded him of the palace in Daria. Dense with its heavy red carpets, gold statues in random shapes, the black furniture. A place that reminded him of home wasn't exactly what he wanted when he was on holiday, but he could set it aside for the sake of that view.

The side of the house that faced the sea—the lounge, entertainment area and dining room—opened up onto balconies. Each balcony had its own table, chairs and greenery. It was more minimal than he expected, but it seemed even the owner understood the main feature was the ocean.

The water was quieter today, the waves lapping against the cliff even though it was almost high tide. The dark blue colour offset the orange sun at the horizon, the orange the only strip between the ocean and the dark blue-grey of sky above it.

Daria was an island; the sea was no stranger to him. Perhaps that was why he felt such a connection to it. He couldn't imagine anything more beautiful, more powerful. He wished—not for the first time—that he could harness that power. How much easier would his role as King be if he could be calm when he needed to be, angry and assertive at other times? And if he could control his emotions as his mother did, would she feel less helpless in letting go of the crown?

He tried his best to do what he thought his mother would approve of, but it never seemed to work. Somehow he always ate more than the polite portion at important dinners, or said something unroyal at important events. He sympathised too much or too little; he wasn't charming enough or he was too charming. All these things he'd heard about himself over the years. All of it from a public he wanted to serve yet could never please.

No wonder his mother was concerned.

If he'd had her instincts, this wouldn't be a problem. But he had his father's.

He had the instincts of a commoner whose kingdom tolerated him because he made their Queen happy.

His parents hadn't been able to have more than one child. His mother had struggled to fall pregnant. By the time they'd discovered they were having him, they had all but given up. At that time, Queen Winifred was already forty years old and high risk, though they were thrilled to have him. And outside the public eye, they were the best parents he could ask for.

But he was certain his parents wished for more than him as a ruler. Surely they didn't want a son the media called 'the Oops Prince' because of his endless mistakes.

The Oops Prince. They called *him*, the future King of Daria, the *Oops Prince*.

Good heavens, it was embarrassing.

It would become more embarrassing once he became King. The Oops King didn't exactly inspire confidence. There had already been whispers about it. Questions about whether he could lead the kingdom when he made mistakes as often as he did.

In truth, it wasn't entirely fair. He might get it wrong on the small things, but he didn't ever cause any political strife.

But then, that didn't sell papers.

At least today, he hadn't felt incompetent. Even when

his instincts were off—which they were, often—Amari had asked him about his reasoning, tilted her head in acknowledgement, then explained why it was slightly off. She didn't make him feel bad about it. And through her explanations, he had learnt.

If only it were that easy to learn how to be King.

CHAPTER THREE

'CAN I...UM...can I help you?' Amari asked after she watched Kade stand in front of the coffee machine for an inordinate amount of time.

He turned around. She sucked in her breath. He had been working for her for two days. Two whole days, and she still hadn't got over how gorgeous he was. She wanted to blame it on the suits, which he still wore, though she repeatedly told him it wasn't necessary. His response had been to compromise; he took his jacket off. And now she got to see how wonderfully a shirt clung to him.

Kind of like she wanted to.

She shook her head.

But it wasn't the suit or the shirt. It was him. There was something about him that...that she shouldn't think about. No. She wasn't there to ponder all the ways Kade's features came together in a rather magnificent work of art. She was there to help him. No—he was there to help her. Right, yes. Help her, in her store.

She swallowed.

'I thought I would get a start on the coffee since it wasn't on when I got here. It's usually on.'

'Yeah,' she said, leaning against the door to the small kitchen at the back of the store. 'Mrs Hallow came earlier than expected to drop off her baked goods today. She came herself since her daughter's taking her to the city.'

'She was here when I arrived.'

'I know.' Because Mrs Hallow had spent a solid portion of the time enquiring about him. Then commenting on how handsome he was. 'But I couldn't take her stuff and send her off. She expects payment.'

'It takes that long to pay her?'

'No.' Amari laughed, and moved into the kitchen when it was clear he still didn't know what he was doing. 'She gets paid when the goods sell, obviously, but she also expects me to talk to her.'

She manoeuvred around Kade, but it felt as if she was very much in his space. Was it because her kitchen was small? Or was it because he took up so much space that *everything* was in his space?

And what was that smell? Power, she'd thought before, but there was more to it now. There was a softness to it. A tenderness. It made no sense and yet somehow it made perfect sense. She gritted her teeth and breathed through her mouth.

'I've noticed that people here like to talk.'

She laughed, and was rewarded for it with another whiff of his smell. Power, softness, tenderness.

Amari.

'Well, it's because you're new,' she said, trying her best to act normal. 'Not only in town—which would have caused some talk anyway, looking the way you do—but because you're working here. For me.'

She filled a jug with water, poured it into the machine, then reached for the coffee. But Kade was standing in front of it, and when he saw her move towards it, he grabbed it and handed it to her.

It was all fairly innocent, if not for the fact that it brought her closer to him than she had ever been. She'd avoided coming close to him before. A combination of self-preservation and the boundaries of an employer/employee relationship.

And it had been easy before, too. Pete was usually around, and she would use him as a human shield against Kade. Which worked, since Pete was literally meant to be Kade's shield if she believed their prince/guard story.

She didn't, but whatever. They were helping her. And for the last two days, she'd got home early enough to distract May from any unwanted questions.

But now…now she was caught near his chest, in his gaze. Even without those eyes, liquid brown quicksand she could easily fall into without any hopes of resurfacing, there was his chest. Broad, hard. The kind of chest someone could lay their head on, listen to a heartbeat on, trace patterns on. Someone, of course, that wasn't her. This was all hypothetical, and didn't involve her. She was standing outside the quicksand, her head was nowhere near resting on his chest, and his smell wasn't a hypnotic mist designed to pull her in and never let go.

'Thank you,' she said, shaking her head. She took a deliberate step back, tightening her grip on the coffee.

She praised her fingers for holding steady as she put the coffee in the machine. And then she pressed a button, and let the coffee machine fill the silence vibrating with tension.

It would take a while, so she stepped back, out of the kitchen, and tilted her head. A sign for Kade to follow her. But she didn't ask him to join her because of attraction. No. It was because she wasn't impolite. She couldn't just leave him there, waiting for coffee in an empty room. Never mind that she did it almost every day of her life.

'What did you mean?' Kade asked when they reached the counter.

'What?'

'Inside the kitchen. What did you mean when you said, "looking the way you do"?'

She quirked a brow. 'I didn't peg you as someone who fishes for compliments.'

'Not from everyone,' he said with a small smile. Small or big, that smile was dangerous. More so when he was implying he wanted *her* to compliment him. 'But I admit, it is rather forward of me to ask.' She didn't get a chance to comment. 'What did you mean about you, then? When you said that people would be interested in me because I work for you?'

'They're protective,' she said, booting up her laptop. 'I came to town almost four years ago with a baby in tow and no partner to be seen. People tend to be protective when it comes to babies and single mothers.'

'Single?' he enquired gently.

She looked at him, but there didn't seem to be any hidden motive to his question. He genuinely seemed to want to know.

'May's father…is not in the picture.'

It was an understatement. Hank had taken their picture, torn it up, and used it as confetti as he found another hopelessly in love woman to take advantage of. He'd drawn another picture altogether.

She blew out a small breath, hoping Kade wouldn't notice. But she needed to do something to temper her thoughts, which weren't entirely fair. Hank hadn't woven a spell over her. Her eyes had been open when she married him. No—it wasn't her eyes. It was her heart. But whatever the organ, she had chosen to be with him. She'd adored the way he'd looked at her as if she were the only person in the world. She'd loved his spontaneity that had somehow still felt steeped in reliability. He would take her out of town for a night without warning, but he would pack a bag for her, answer all her questions, be there for her while he did it.

She hadn't been used to it. To the attention, to the *male* attention. Her mother was more concerned with her own life, her own relationships for the most part. Sure, she took care of Amari in the most basic of senses, but she didn't raise her. Amari had to learn emotional cues and support and all the things that should have come from a mother in different ways. One of those ways had been Hank. She was a better mother because of Hank. She only wished May hadn't been collateral damage in her lessons.

'I'm sorry.'

'Don't be,' Amari replied. 'We're better off without him.'

'He wasn't a good person?'

'He was…' She trailed off. 'I don't know how to answer that, Kade.'

He was silent for a moment. 'I think that's answer enough.'

She didn't respond, afraid of what she might say. Not only about Hank—she'd rather not let the bitterness ruin her day—but to Kade. To his startling intuition. To the gentle way he asked questions that never made her feel as if she had to answer, but still made her *want* to answer.

'The coffee should be done now,' she said quietly.

'I'll go get us some cups.'

He left before she could stop him. As if he knew she needed a moment to herself. As if he knew she needed it here, in the store she had built. The legacy she had created for her child.

She took a deep breath and told herself to let it go. The anger at Hank; the gratitude for Kade. Neither would make her a better entrepreneur or mother. And those were her priorities. Her only priorities.

He was rather astounded by the number of things he didn't know. Like the fact that there were different-sized knitting needles, different types of glue, subgenres of romance novels, necklaces that choked a neck rather than hung loosely on a chest. He wasn't sure how much of his ignorance came from being royalty and how much came from being isolated from the interests of normal people.

He had been taught chess, not knitting, because it was strategic and he needed to develop his strategic skills. He'd observed construction works and carpenters, not craftspeople, learning from a distance, only occasionally jumping in, should he some day need to assist in rebuilding his kingdom. He'd read philosophers and sociologists, not romance novels, because those were the approved reading list of a prince.

Being exposed to things he hadn't even known existed now made him feel as if he'd lost out on so much. It made him worry that he didn't have time to learn any of it.

But he did. He had nine more days. He would make the most of it.

'Amari,' he said after they closed the store for the day. Pete had agreed to wait outside. He was guarding the door, but that was as much privacy as Kade would get. 'I was wondering if I could ask you a favour.'

Her eyes flickered up from her laptop. 'If you're going to ask for more brownies, I'm going to start taking it out of your pay.'

'No,' he said, ignoring how his mouth watered at even the idea of brownies. 'Though you should take it out of my pay. That way you won't need to pay me.'

'We're not doing this again.'

They had been since Monday. He understood her frustration.

'No, it was a different favour. I was wondering… Would you teach me how to knit?'

'What?'

'To knit. You know—' He gestured to the knitting material on the shelf.

'Yes, I know. I just… Did you ask me to teach you?'

'Yes.'

'Why?'

'Does it matter?'

'I suppose not,' she said after a minute, 'but it would be nice to know. Some people call it having a conversation, but honestly, what do I know about that?'

He sighed. She got snarky sometimes and, while he appreciated the fire, it did make asking for favours a tad awkward.

'I was never taught. The last few days here have made me think that perhaps it might be worth my while to be taught.'

'Do you want me as your teacher though?'

She offered him a smile. It was knowing, a little self-deprecating, a lot genuine. She knew she wasn't the easiest to please, to talk to, to ask. And yet he still found himself wanting to please her, to talk to her, to ask her things. Because somehow, the fact that it wasn't easy made the smile, the teasing worth more. He knew it defied logic—they'd known one another for three days; surely easy would have been preferable—and yet here he was. Valuing her. Wanting her.

Wanting her.

He'd allowed his mind to go rogue. This is what he got for it. There was no situation where wanting Amari would work. He had to go back to Daria in nine days. He had to take over his mother's crown, deal with the emotions of being a king when the successful previous ruler was still around, then deal with being a son to a woman who had to quit her job because she wasn't well. And that summary was simplifying things.

'Do you know how to knit?' he asked through wooden lips.

Her smile sobered, as if she could sense the change in his mood. She *could* sense the change in his mood. Why else would her own mood change so drastically? It was as if she'd pulled on a cloak of some kind. Disapproval, disappointment were woven into that coat, though the material itself was coolness.

'I know the basics,' she answered.

'I only need to know the basics.'

'Again—are you sure you want me as a teacher? I could ask several other more qualified people.'

'If you're looking for a way to say no, you only have to say the words.'

'I'm not—' She broke off. Her frown deepened. 'I should say no. I don't have the time to teach a man who claims to be a prince how to knit. I have a daughter who needs to believe in the magic of Christmas. I have a daughter,' she said again, more deliberately, 'who needs every second of spare time I have.'

'I understand,' Kade replied, though he didn't. Not completely.

He understood responsibility, of course, more than most. He had an entire kingdom, and, though it was possibly naïve, he thought being responsible for one human child might be equivalent to an entire kingdom.

What he didn't understand was why she was repeating it. Why her tone sounded so adamant, and why she seemed to be reminding herself more than she was talking to him. Did she think she needed the reminder? Had she made some kind of mistake, just as he had, and now she thought she needed to make up for it?

It doesn't matter.

It shouldn't matter, he corrected his thoughts. It shouldn't matter, and yet somehow it did.

Unless he stopped it.

'You're right,' he told her. 'You should spend your time with your family. I'll find someone else to help me. Or I'll help myself. It can't be that hard.'

She opened her mouth, but whatever she was about to

say was interrupted by Pete. He flew through the door, slamming it behind him, his back against it.

'What?' Kade asked, alarmed. 'What is it?'

'It's…children.'

Kade rolled his eyes. His bodyguard would save him from a bullet heading his way but heaven forbid that bullet turned into a child. Kade would be dead and he wasn't even sure Pete would mourn him.

'The children's Christmas parade,' Amari offered from behind him. She walked until she was beside Kade and watched Pete with a smile. 'It's a Swell Valley tradition. All the children from the local school participate. They march down Main Road, handing out their letters to Father Christmas on the final day of the school year.'

'But wouldn't that mean they don't believe in Father Christmas? Surely they know they can't hand out their letters to strangers?'

'Ah, but we're not just strangers,' she answered Kade. He noted she'd shifted away from him in the last minutes. 'We're their carrier pigeons. Their postal service.' She narrowed her eyes in thought. 'Come on, take a look.'

'I would rather not,' Pete said, his eyes wide.

'They won't hurt you,' Kade told him.

'So you say,' he replied darkly.

Amari laughed. 'What's your deal with children, Pete?'

It took him a moment, but Pete eventually said, 'Some people get a bite from a dog when they're children and they're scared of dogs for the rest of their lives.'

'Are you saying a child…bit you?'

Now Pete didn't answer, which Amari seemed to take as an answer. She snorted, before looking at Kade. He couldn't help but notice how much more careful her expression had become.

'What about you? Do you have a fear of children?'

'Not at all.'

'Good.'

'Good?'

'You get to see one of our town's best Christmas traditions. Trust me, it's worth it.'

CHAPTER FOUR

SHE REALLY DID think it was worth it. But then, she was biased.

May walked somewhere in the middle of the crowd of children. She preferred not to have attention on her, and she and Amari had agreed the middle was likely the best place for her to be for that.

'But what if you can't see me, Mama?'

It was a real concern. And though Amari had wanted to tell May she would be able to pick her out from the crowd—she was part Amari, after all—she didn't think that would satisfy a four-year-old. Instead, she said, 'Wear your favourite red dress, baby. How can Mama miss you when you're wearing that?'

And that was how Amari came to be staring at a red dress in the middle of the crowd.

'This is great,' Kade said from her side.

Amari stopped herself from jumping just in time. She had forgotten Kade was standing beside her. Or she was trying to forget, since her skin had made gooseflesh its permanent state since they'd come outside.

She was so damn aware of him. Of that broad and strong body, but also of him. His moods. His personality. As if she knew that something had happened when he'd asked her to teach him to knit. She could put it down to her imagination, but she knew that was a lie. Something *had* happened. And she shouldn't care what, but she did.

Focus on your daughter. She needs you.

Yes, May needed her. And she would focus on May. Only on May.

'We do something similar where I'm from,' Kade continued, as if he hadn't made her forget for a second that she wasn't supposed to be indulging thoughts about men she didn't know.

'Where exactly is that now again?'

'Daria,' he answered without a beat. 'It's a small kingdom—'

'I remember.'

'So why did you ask?'

'I was trying to trip you up.'

'I...am not entirely sure I know what that means.'

She turned towards him. 'They don't have colloquial phrases where you're from?'

'Of course they do.' But he was frowning. It was cute. 'I simply...haven't encountered that one.'

'Right. Because you're a prince.'

He sighed. 'I thought we were past this.'

'It's hard to get past royalty.'

'Do you want to hear about our Christmas parade or not?' he asked flatly.

She pursed her lips to hide her smile. He wasn't an easy person to get on the bad side of—it was that damn politeness—but he truly made it worth it.

'Please, tell me.'

He took a deep breath, and when he spoke, it was in his usual measured tone. 'We cordon off the streets of the town and have the oldest families do a procession. People become quite invested. They decorate the stores, the streets, with Christmas decorations. It ends at the palace, where families are invited to offer gifts to the royal family.'

'Your family.'

'Yes.'

She thought about it for a moment. The children's Christmas parade wasn't the only parade they had. It was merely the first, marking the town's official countdown to Christmas. But this one was the most special because it was about the children. Their innocence, their purity, their general excitement for Christmas. It filled the streets much more than the decorations did.

Though lights flickered across the roads, highlighting Christmas reindeers and trees, though almost every storefront was decorated with tinsel and ornaments, though Christmas songs pulsed from large speakers carried by the only float accompanying the parade, it was the children who mattered. The public wanted their letters. They wanted to buy gifts and give them to parents so they'd know what to put under the Christmas tree. They wanted to make Christmas special for the most vulnerable, not the most powerful.

'Are you saying the families of your kingdom bring you and your family gifts?'

'I believe I said that, yes.'

She ignored the dry tone. 'How many families participate in this?'

'I've never counted.'

'Give me an estimate.'

'I'm not sure, Amari. One thousand families? Maybe?'

She blinked. 'Those are a lot of families.' She paused. 'I'm sure those families would benefit more from the royal family providing *them* with gifts, not the other way around.'

May came barrelling towards Amari, preventing Kade from replying. Which was probably a good thing, considering his expression. But soon she had an armful of child and she stopped thinking about it.

'That was real good, baba.'

'Thanks!'

May went on to say a bunch of other stuff and Amari laughed, snuggling her neck and smelling her. She smelled like her baby. Her daughter. She smelled like hope and new life. She smelled like responsibility. May was all those things and more, and Amari was so lucky she could be involved in raising her. And that not only made her angry at Hank, but sad for him. He would never get to experience this.

She had chosen a man who didn't care about experiencing it.

'Amari.'

Amari lowered May to the floor and turned to Kade. 'Sorry. I forgot you were standing there.'

'You had other things on your mind.' He smiled at May, but didn't address her. When he looked at Amari, she realised he was giving her the opportunity to introduce him. He wouldn't do it himself. He wouldn't do it if she didn't want him to. 'I only wanted to say I think it's time for me to leave. Pete's getting anxious.'

For the first time, she realised Pete was standing outside. He had apparently overcome his fear of children to protect his charge. But he stayed on the side, eyes wary. For danger or children, she wasn't sure. Both amused her.

He's so committed to this role.

Just as she was committed to believing it *was* a role.

The alternative was more complicated to consider. If Kade was running from something and needed a bodyguard, he was probably in danger. And that…softened her. Due to a fairly basic level of concern for him, but also because she could relate. For a full year after she left Hank, she had expected him to find her. To demand she come back to him. Or to tell her he wanted May.

There was almost no chance of it happening, but that didn't matter. It wasn't a physical level of danger, but it was the most threatened she had ever felt. She'd even struggled to trust the community around her because of it. What if their concern for her turned into suspicion? What if they looked into her background? What if they hired a private investigator to find out where she came from, what her history was? Fear had made logic irrelevant, so though she knew they probably wouldn't, she still worried.

Perhaps that was why she hadn't looked into Kade's story. There were other factors, of course—looking it up would mean she was indulging someone she was sure was lying; she didn't have time to look up everything people told her that sounded iffy; her gut told her not to—but this was at the core of it. If he was running from something, she would afford him the privacy she'd worried she wouldn't get when she had been running. And because she had got that privacy, and knew how much it meant, she knew he deserved it, too.

'Kade, this is my daughter, May.'

Kade gave May a nod. A nod. As if they were passing one another in the street and were greeting. May giggled, which made Amari smile. It made Kade smile, too.

'It's lovely to meet you, Miss May.'

With another nod, this time at both of them, Kade left.

'He's funny,' May commented after a while.

'He is a bit funny, isn't he?' She stared after Kade for a moment, then pressed a kiss to May's head. 'Why don't we go find something to drink? Maybe we'll get you a cookie, too.'

Kade wasn't prepared for seeing a miniature version of Amari. He wasn't prepared for how it would affect him either.

Protective. It made him feel protective. Little surges of it went through his body the moment he saw that girl in Amari's arms. At first, he couldn't define it. It was a feeling he only had with his parents. And occasionally, with vulnerable people in his kingdom.

But never quite like this.

For all intents and purposes, neither Amari nor her daughter was vulnerable. Of course, children were inherently vulnerable. But Amari was strong. And fierce. With Amari on her daughter's side, that child wasn't nearly as vulnerable as others. And Amari… She was independent. As he'd said, she was strong and fierce, too. There was no reason to feel protective towards them.

And yet he did.

His response was to stay as far away from her as possible. The last thing he needed was to feel protective towards anyone with the responsibilities he had at home.

'I have to collect some things for the store,' she said on Thursday. 'A lot of things. And my car is in the shop today because the battery has a problem of some kind. So I need to walk. And I'd like another set of hands. Would either you or Pete be interested in helping me?'

Amari's tone was hopeful. So was her expression as she turned to look at both him and Pete. It was faintly alarming.

'I have to go where His Highness goes,' Pete said.

'Well, I actually need someone to stay here.' She gave him a smile that was half smile, half grimace. 'I promise you, it'll only be for twenty minutes. Maybe thirty, if Mr Kyle is in a talkative mode. He's almost never in a talkative mode.'

'Mr Kyle?'

'He makes these candle holders.' She gestured to the shelf. 'He has a batch of new ones for Christmas, and I usually fetch them, which isn't a problem when I have a car. Look, I swear Kade'll be safe. Here or there, he'll be safe.'

'I'm sorry—'

'Pete, please. Please. I can't close the store. It's too busy.' As she said it, another customer came in. No one was at the till yet. 'He'll be safe here. Or with me. With me!' she said as if it just occurred to her. 'Let him come with me. I learnt how to protect myself and May. I can protect him.'

'He's a big man.'

Amari laughed. 'Pete, I can protect him.' A customer came to the counter. 'Please? Also because I've been trying to teach Kade how to use the register for the last four days and it has not been going well.'

Mainly because he was trying to spend as little time with her as possible. Trying to hold his breath. Trying not to feel his skin become more aware or his body pulse. It was a lot harder to focus with all that going on. He had no frame of reference for a cash register and learning it from scratch while holding his breath…

No, it had not been going well at all.

'Amari,' Pete began with a pained look in his eyes. He was gearing up to say no, but, because he liked her, it was actually bringing him pain.

'Pete,' she said before he could continue. *'Please.'*

They stood looking at one another for a long while. The customer cleared his throat, but neither of them paid attention. Eventually, Pete said, 'Fine. But if you aren't back in twenty minutes—'

'Make it forty. In case Mr Kyle gets chatty.'

'I thought you said thirty?'

'If we're not back in forty minutes, you can come find us.'

'I will.'

'Thank you!'

In a move that was entirely spontaneous, Amari leaned over the counter. It looked as if she was going to kiss Pete. Kade's fingers curled, his body rippling with anger before he could stop it. But she paused.

'I was going to give you a kiss on the cheek, but I realised that might not be welcome.' She lowered to her feet again with a sheepish smile. 'Sorry. That would have been inappropriate.'

'It would have been fine,' Pete said kindly.

The grip of Kade's fist tightened.

'Yes, well, I should ask these things before I do them.' She straightened and looked at the customer. 'I'm sorry, Kent. We'll throw in a free brownie for the wait.'

While Pete helped Kent, Amari gathered her things. She left the address and phone number of Mr Kyle with Pete, as well as her own phone number. It felt strange that they didn't have it yet. They'd seen one another every day for four days and he wouldn't have been able to get in touch with her if he needed to.

It took him a moment to realise strange was actually jealous. He was jealous. Of Pete, and the easiness he shared with Amari. He was jealous that if Pete wanted to, he could pursue Amari. They could have an entirely healthy and happy relationship, even after he went back to Daria.

Pete had that freedom. Kade didn't.

He couldn't be easy around Amari because he was attracted to her. Attraction hadn't done him any good over the years. He was as clumsy about that as he was his royal duties. At times, he wondered if there was something wrong in his brain. Something that made simple, straightforward things harder. Like the coffee machine. He should have been able to figure out where the water went. Where the coffee went. Why hadn't he?

That might have been a bad example. It was a household appliance that he had no experience with. It was understandable that he struggled. But things like packing shelves? Offering comfort to people in his kingdom? Making a call about what to eat during a cultural visit? Shouldn't those things be easy?

If he led a normal life, if he weren't going to be King, perhaps he would have been able to figure out why his instincts were so off. He might have taken a chance to explore his attraction for Amari, the first attraction he'd felt so fiercely. But he wasn't leading a normal life. He *would* be King. And he couldn't explore feelings, or make choices, or do anything that didn't take his responsibilities into account.

So, yes, he was jealous of Pete.

'You're welcome,' Amari said a few minutes into their walk.

'For what?'

'I freed you from your jailer.'

His lips curved. 'Pete is not my jailer.'

She gave a dramatic sigh. 'It's Stockholm syndrome, isn't it? He's captured you for such a long time, you care about him and feel the need to defend him.'

The smile widened. 'Not quite. He's a little too reluctant to be my type.'

'You have a type?'

'Independent, strong, forthcoming in both traits, and not allowing anyone to get away with anything they shouldn't.'

There was an uncomfortable beat of silence, as if they'd both realised he was describing her.

'Well,' Amari said, giving him a small smile that was slightly tight around the edges, 'I'm sure you'll find that person.'

He thought it best not to reply to that. With his current lack of discretion, he might have said something like, 'I already have'. He would have to pray that the earth opened up and swallowed him then, which might pose a problem for his future reign as King of Daria.

They walked in silence for a bit, Amari leading them through the town paths with the ease of someone who knew where they were going. He took the time to enjoy the town, which he hadn't been able to do since he'd arrived. Then, only a few places had been in the Christmas spirit.

It seemed as if the first week of December was the time the entire town accepted the festive season. Christmas cheer was found on every street, at every corner. Lights flickered on storefronts; Christmas trees shone through windows; wreaths adorned front doors. The bakery on the corner offered them gingerbread biscuits; the convenience store next to them offered small glasses of milk. At the end of the road, two young men stood dressed as elves in front of a gift-wrapping station. They had their phones in their hands, but the moment they saw Amari and Kade, they stuffed both into their pockets and waved.

'Everyone really gets into this, don't they?'

'Yep.'

'What happens if you're not a fan of Christmas?'

She gave him a look out of the corner of her eye, but answered. 'You get used to it.'

'Did you?'

'Oh, yes. May was barely a year old the first time I witnessed the spectacle. I was still so tired, and sad, and… Well, you don't need the details.' Her lips thinned. 'Anyway, I didn't want any part of the festivity. But when the first of December came around, my neighbours started bringing over gingerbread biscuits and mince pies. The day after, I got more substantial dishes. It was like they were using the biscuits and pies as a tester, to check whether I was okay by myself. They were quite invasive, actually.'

'You found that amusing?' he asked, wondering at her.

'Not at the time. At the time, I was spitting angry that these people insisted on coming into my not fully unpacked house with food and cheer. Now though, I realise it was their way.' She shrugged. 'You don't have that at home?'

'No,' he said firmly. 'Where I come from, everyone is very pleased to set boundaries and to respect them. We would never expect anyone to bring us anything, and we certainly wouldn't give anything.'

'It sounds…cold.'

'It can be.' He let it sit for a moment, as that answer didn't entirely feel right. 'We do have a fairly established culture of family though. Extended family, too. So while communities might not be like this, our families are. People take care of their aging parents. If they're faced with tragedy of, say, losing a family member who had a child, that child will be taken care of. It's different from this, certainly, but it's not entirely cold.'

'No,' Amari said, stopping. He stopped with her. 'It doesn't sound cold at all.'

Something danced across her face. It wasn't one of the emotions he had become familiar with the last four days. It was darker than anything he'd seen. If it were a painting, it would be streaks of red and black with barely any glimpses of the canvas.

But there *were* glimpses of the canvas. Small, short, no doubt, but visible. In Amari, it was a vulnerability. It made him step closer to her, as if he could protect her from what she was feeling. Her eyes flickered up to his, rested there. And the red, the black, the darkness, disappeared.

This was a bad idea.

There was no doubt about it. Staring into Kade's eyes, falling into those liquid depths that coated her soul, was a bad idea. That didn't even take into consideration that it felt as if he saw right to her hurt. To her inability to understand the kind of family he was talking about even though it sounded exactly like what she wanted.

Her hand lifted, rested on his chest. She saw it happening. Saw it as if she weren't herself because *she* wasn't doing it. She would never be so forward. She would never let her fingers spread, feeling the ridges of muscles, the strength that she had spent days trying not to think about.

It wasn't her left hand that joined her right, as if it understood the strength of that chest couldn't be held by only one hand.

They were travelling now, down, over his abdomen that was rigid, too, though she didn't know if it was from tension or desire.

She wanted to do more than touch. She wanted to taste. To run her tongue over the plane of his chest, to kiss her way down, over his abs. To trace his muscles. To lick.

She looked up, though she didn't know why. The shock of her desire, of that intensity, should have had her moving away. And yet she was looking at him. In his eyes, which were pools of lust and heat. At the tight lines of his magnificent face, which spoke of a control she should have had over herself.

'I'm sorry,' she whispered, not sure if the apology was for her or for him.

He nodded, accepting it. He covered her hands with his. The heat was as comforting as it was stirring.

Until he moved.

Lowered her hands until they fell between them.

Embarrassed, she tried to pull away, but he tightened his grip.

'Kade,' she said, voice hoarse.

'No,' he replied. 'Don't feel ashamed for what happened.'

'I… I touched you. Without your permission. I… I should be ashamed.'

Gently, he took her chin in his fingers, lifting it so she couldn't keep looking down. So she couldn't keep her shame to herself.

'You had my permission,' he told her. 'I told you with my heart. You must have seen it in my eyes.'

Oh, it was corny. So corny. And yet somehow, she was touched by it. Somehow, she didn't feel it was corny in *her* heart.

'You touched me because we're attracted to one another.'

'No,' she said automatically.

He smiled. 'We'll keep up the pretence, then, shall we?' He nodded. 'You touched me because we're not attracted to one another.'

How he could make her smile in such a torturous moment confused her.

'We can't be attracted to one another.' He wasn't teasing any more. It made sense. This made sense. The tension, the awkwardness. '*I* can't be attracted to you,' he emphasised, letting go of her chin, her hand. 'There is no good that can come from it.'

Of course not. He was running from something. And she…she was running towards something. A life for May that involved stability and reliability. That was all Amari had ever wanted for her daughter. When she'd found out she was pregnant, she had been terrified, but hopeful. That hope came from the determination that her child wouldn't live the life Amari had. Her child wouldn't wonder if her mother cared about her or found her to be a burden. Her child would know that they were loved, unconditionally.

And then Hank had left. Told her he couldn't be a father and left. Amari's dream of giving her daughter more had shattered because she had made a poor choice. She hadn't chosen a good man, a man who could live up to his responsibilities as a husband, a father. Having had a father like that herself—she didn't even know who the man was—Amari had thought herself beyond making that mistake. But Amari had thought herself beyond being like her mother, too.

How was raising a child by herself because of her choices any different from what her mother had done?

Kade was right. Just as much as he couldn't afford to be attracted to Amari, she couldn't be attracted to him. It would distract her from what she wanted to do: make sure May had the life Amari had always wanted for her. Even if Amari had already let her down.

Because Amari had already let her down.

She cleared her throat. 'You were right the first time. We can't be attracted to one another.'

'Amari—'

'We should…um… We should get those things from Mr Kyle before Pete comes looking for you.'

She started walking before he could reply.

CHAPTER FIVE

'AMARI, DEAR, WILL we be seeing you tonight at the beach?'

Kade heard the question from one of Amari's customers. It slipped past his guard, as had most things since that *moment* they'd shared. He had set up the guard with one purpose: to protect himself from whatever was happening between him and Amari. And he thought it would be easy.

After all, she had set up a guard, too.

From the second he'd told her they couldn't indulge their attraction she'd put distance between them. It had come with tension, and awkwardness, which Pete had merely raised an eyebrow at when they'd returned to the store. His bodyguard didn't mention it when they were alone— he was too professional for that—but Kade often got the eyebrows. He used it as another reminder to wear armour around Amari.

Since then, they communicated for store purposes only. She told him what to do and he did it. When he screwed up, she gently told him how he had and he corrected it. And that was the extent of it.

But things filtered through.

For example, he knew May was having a sleepover tonight. Amari had arranged it the day before. May's friend's mother, who was apparently Amari's friend as well, had come into the store that morning and insisted that Amari grab a bottle of wine from the vintner down the road and enjoy her night. He agreed—Amari had looked particu-larly exhausted these last few days—but now this woman was asking Amari about going to the beach, and he really wanted to know whether she would be.

'I'm not sure,' Amari was saying.

He tried to pay attention to the customer he was help-ing. The woman was deciding on whether she wanted the wool that was in stock or whether she wanted to order something from the catalogue. She hadn't made her deci-sion yet. Kade kept listening.

'Lydia has May tonight, doesn't she?'

'Yes, but—'

'Then you should come. We only do the fireworks and wine Christmas evening once a year.'

'But you do a fireworks and wine evening once a month.'

'Those aren't Christmas themed.'

'You mean, you don't wear ridiculous festive attire to those?'

The woman chuckled. 'Exactly. So—I'll see you at seven. I'll keep a seat for you. And—' the woman's voice dropped, though it was quite clear she didn't care who heard her '—bring your two hunky new employees with you.'

'I don't think I'll—'

But a bell rang; the woman had left. At the same time, Kade's customer decided to order from the catalogue. He helped her do so, then went to the front of the store to check for more customers. There were none who wanted help, so he merely looked at Amari.

'You heard that, didn't you?' she asked after a few seconds of silence.

'Yes.'

'I'm so sorry. They've been on about you and Pete for the last week. Wanting to know where you came from and what you were doing here and why I hired you.'

He tensed. He didn't mind Amari knowing the truth, but once more people knew, it would become harder to hide where he was. He had been able to do it until now because his kingdom was small and obscure compared to others. No one cared about a prince from an African kingdom far away. At least, no one here did. But that could easily change. Once people heard the word 'prince' they tended to become more interested. It didn't matter that they hadn't known him before; royalty was the kind of temptation few people could ignore.

His parents had only granted him this leave on the condition that it be kept quiet. It was a short enough trip that they didn't have to make an announcement of any kind. If there were any questions or suspicions about his absence, they would likely be overshadowed by the announcement of his mother's abdication.

Still, he would rather keep his whereabouts private. If the royal reporters knew where he was, he wouldn't have a day of peace. He certainly wouldn't be able to work, and he liked working. He liked the routine of it. He liked feeling useful. More importantly, he liked that it didn't feel as if his mistakes affected thousands of people. He could learn without it being a matter of public interest. He could be corrected without it reflecting poorly on his family, who many believed should have taught him better.

'What did you tell them?' Kade asked.

'That it was none of their business.' She accompanied her answer with a shrewd look, as if to say, *Of course I wouldn't tell them who you are.* 'It doesn't keep them from trying. In fact, I'm sure the only reason they asked me to go was so you two could, too.'

She nodded her head in Pete's direction. He was in the back of the store, fitting a shelf to the back wall. He was proving to be a lot more useful than Kade—unsurprisingly—

including suggesting Amari fill the empty space above the kitchen door with a glass shelf that would hold some books.

'I don't think that's true. They probably do want you there.'

'Maybe,' she allowed. 'But it's mostly an excuse for people to get drunk and have fun.'

'I thought it might be. Wine and fireworks at the beach do tend to encourage that assumption.'

'Exactly. And nothing sounds less appealing to me than spending an evening with drunk people.'

'Unless you're drunk, too.'

She dropped her head. 'Excuse me?'

Well, that was a stupid thing to say. Even if Amari hadn't reacted that way, he probably would have thought so. It was presumptuous, for one. He didn't know if she drank, although her friend insisting she get a bottle of wine did seem to be evidence that she did. Still, that didn't account for the fact that he was saying she should get drunk, which was a terrible thing to say to someone. He knew better.

But this was how it was with him. He realised too late that he was saying something stupid. By the time he did, it was out already, and he'd made a fool of himself, regardless of his intentions.

At least he knew he hadn't changed in the last week.

'I only meant that you look like you might need a relaxing evening.'

'I *look* like it?' she asked, leaning on the counter. The casual stance did nothing to take away from the sharpness in her eyes. 'What does that mean exactly? Bags under my eyes? Wrinkles on my forehead?'

'No.' Though the bags part was correct, he had enough common sense to lie. 'I didn't mean it in terms of your appearance.'

'Hmm. I probably shouldn't have assumed that when you said I *look* like I need a relaxing evening.'

He held his tongue. He was going to retort, so he held his tongue.

'Maybe I should have asked instead of assumed,' he said after a moment. 'Do you think you could do with a relaxing evening?'

She narrowed her eyes, then straightened with a sigh. 'I suppose. But I would have had one tonight anyway. In the privacy of my home. With my own wine.'

'And, if I know you well enough, you'd have the store's books cracked open in front of you.'

Her lips parted, but she only ended up frowning, not replying.

'At least at the beach, you'll have people,' he offered gently.

'People are overrated.'

'Perhaps,' he acknowledged. 'But sometimes they offer the kind of distraction you need to feel like yourself again.'

Their gazes held. It felt as if through the contact, they were having a conversation.

She knew he was saying she had offered him some kind of distraction.

He knew she understood. She might have also said that he was offering her distraction, too.

But then she looked away, her guard back in place. He used the time to erect his own shields.

'Consider it,' was all he said, and went to help Pete with the shelf.

She was there because she had a free night. It had nothing to do with Kade.

It was because her daughter was at a sleepover with her best friend and Amari had the night to herself. It was because she would never hear the end of it from Lydia if she didn't do something with her night. That was it. That was the only reason she was at the beach, making small talk, a wine glass in her hand.

Why are you looking for Kade, then?

She ignored the thought. It was getting easier to do, ignoring her thoughts about Kade. The memories were harder. She could still feel his chest beneath her fingers. Could still remember the clenching of his abdomen when she touched him. And the lust. Oh, the lust. She could still feel it wash over her, coating her skin, her breasts, her core. She could still see it in his eyes, in the way he barely breathed, as if inhaling her perfume would break that control he always, always had.

She emptied her glass. When that didn't help, she decided to go for a walk.

The fireworks wouldn't go off until later, when the sky was fully dark and not this mixture of light and navy blue. The sun was already gone, the waves crashing harder against the sand in preparation for high tide. It was a cheat, really, to set an event somewhere near the beach. People saw the beauty of it and immediately thought they'd have a good time. And when people *thought* they'd have a good time, they generally had a good time.

Not her. She had never been one of those 'have a good time' people. She was too serious, too responsible. That was what happened when a child grew up with an irresponsible parent. They assumed the responsibilities of the parent. They assumed the responsibility for *themselves*, which shouldn't happen until they were much older.

Amari could still remember how she would ask her mother to set aside money for her schoolbooks and stationery. She would ask for them months in advance, before the school year even ended, because she knew her mother might not remember. Every month she would remind her mother. And then, when the time drew near, she'd do so weekly, daily. And her mother would usually wait until the very last minute to do so, as if she enjoyed Amari's anxiety.

Even the memory of it now made her faintly nauseous. As did the thought of May ever having to do that with her. She knew everything May needed and made sure she had it. She read every letter May got sent home and signed every form May needed. She checked in with May's teachers regularly.

She didn't want May to be the daughter she had been. Worried about everything. Concerned. Unhappy.

She didn't want to be the mother her mother had been.

But what if I already am?

'Amari?'

She turned at the voice. When she did, she saw the Christmas decorations that flickered in the distance where the gathering was. She hadn't realised she'd walked that far. Which begged the question of why Kade was there.

'What are you doing here?'

'I live here,' Kade said. 'Well, there.' He pointed at a cliff a few metres away.

Amari gaped. 'You live there?' Shook her head. 'Maybe you *are* a prince. Or a millionaire or billionaire because those are the only people who can afford it.' She let it sit for a second. 'Unless you're lying. Did you follow me from the restaurant? Where's Pete?'

'I'm trying to figure out how best to answer you,' Kade said with a small smile when the silence after her questions stretched out longer than she expected. 'I do live there. I came for a walk on the beach, through that path over there.' He pointed. 'It leads to a private beach, which can't be the case if you're here.'

'It's not…' She trailed off. She realised she had come onto the private beach. There were no demarcations apart for some rocks, which she had neatly sidestepped, but everyone knew this property was out of bounds. 'I am, apparently. Although, if they really wanted it to be private, they would have made more of an effort to conceal it.'

'True enough.'

He put his arms behind his back, clasping them. For the first time she noticed how he looked.

Delicious.

He wasn't wearing a suit. Significant, as she had never seen him outside one. More significant were his arms, which he was showing off as though they were cleavage, what with his short-sleeved shirt. It was a dark blue colour, and the sleeves hugged his biceps. Actually *hugged* them, because *clinging* seemed too inadequate to describe just how tight the material around the curves of his muscles was. Dark hair dusted his forearms, which were, unsurprisingly, as defined as the biceps.

Her eyes lowered, taking in the light brown linen trousers he'd paired the shirt with. It was gorgeous against the darker brown of his skin, fitted perfectly, and rolled up at the ankles. He looked like an advertisement for a beach resort, and damn if she didn't want to book an all-inclusive vacation to that resort as soon as she could.

She blinked. Where had that come from? Surely not from her, the person who repeatedly told herself she needed to focus on her kid, on her store. Surely not from the person who had just *reminded* herself of why she needed to focus on her kid and her store.

'As for Pete,' Kade continued, as if there hadn't been a pause after his last words, 'he's around here somewhere. He goes overboard in these spaces.'

'He's afraid someone is going to hide behind one of those rocks?'

'You tease, but I suspect he does.'

Kade gave a smile. A private smile. As if they were

sharing some inside joke, or perhaps as if he only gave that smile to her. She wasn't foolish enough to believe that, but she wanted to.

It bothered her. She couldn't trust this attraction. She couldn't trust attraction at all. Attraction had been the first step into the situation with Hank. Then had come the tumble, the fall, hard and fast. She'd lost her bearings; she'd lost herself. She couldn't lose herself with Kade. She had more responsibilities now. More important responsibilities than herself.

'I should… I should get back,' she said, because it was the right thing to do.

'Why did you come out this far?'

'Oh. Um… I was thinking.'

'Thinking?'

'Yes.'

'Would you like to share?'

She huffed out a laugh. 'Only if you want to share why you're here and not living in your kingdom.' She paused. 'Only if you want to share why you came up with a story about being a prince. Only if you want to tell me if you're in danger.'

He frowned. 'I can answer the first question. The rest…' She wasn't sure how it was possible, but the frown deepened. 'You haven't looked me up, have you?'

'I was going to, but every time I wanted to…'

She trailed off. She couldn't tell him she wanted him to have his privacy. He would likely ask why, and the prospect of answering that made her feel oddly vulnerable.

'Well, it made me feel like I was buying into the whole prince story and I'm not,' she settled for. 'It's ridiculous. Princes don't just come to small towns in Africa for a holiday.'

'That's true.' He went silent for a bit, then nodded his head towards his house. 'Would you like to come with me for a drink? Pete will be there, and you'll be perfectly safe. I think it might be easier to explain if we're more... comfortable.'

She shouldn't go. She knew that. Which was obviously why she was nodding and walking with Kade to his house.

The waves crashed at their feet, reminding Amari that the tide was coming in. She didn't move away, instead let the water wet her ankles, her shins. It was summer, the evening was warm, the coolness of the water welcome. She wouldn't be swimming in it any time soon—it was much too icy for that—but the ice was a reprieve from the stickiness on her skin.

Strangely, that stickiness had increased when she'd encountered Kade. Almost as if he had some kind of physical effect on her.

Very strange indeed.

'You're right,' Kade said softly.

'I usually am.' The dry remark had him smiling, as she intended. 'But about what, specifically, this time?'

'Princes don't visit small towns in Africa on holiday.' He didn't give her the chance to reply. 'They do it to regroup. They do it to... Well, I suppose they do it to figure out how they're going to rule a kingdom when they're not quite sure they're made to do so.'

She stopped. 'Hang on—you're telling me you're...what? Going to become King or something?'

It was a little annoying that she was asking when she wasn't entirely sure she believed him. Or maybe it was annoying because she was beginning to believe him.

There were a lot of things about him that were princely. He wore those tailored suits, a new one every day. He didn't know how to do simple things, like work the store's alarm or replace the coffee filter. Then there was the power he carried with him, as if it had been something he was born with. Raised with. Not to mention his accent, which was proper and made her wonder what it would be like to hear him whisper dirty things into her ear.

Focus.

'It's a little of both,' Kade answered. 'I am about to become King, but it's also an "or something" situation. My mother… She's the current monarch. She has been for over forty years. But she has a heart condition, and it's been making her weaker. She no longer feels fit to rule, and she's abdicating.'

'Abdicating? Like giving up the throne?'

'Yes.'

'To you?'

'Yes.'

'Wow.' The word slipped from her lips. It seemed to make Kade's shoulders slump forward, before he straightened them.

'Indeed.'

'That must suck.'

His lashes fluttered. 'Excuse me?'

'It must suck that you're going to become King because your mother's sick. Well, it sucks that your mother's sick at all,' she added, 'but it must especially suck that you now have to do her job because she's sick.'

He turned, looked out at the ocean as he stuffed his hands in his pockets. It seemed like an un-Kade thing to do. It spoke of vulnerability and emotion and it had her stepping forward, taking his hand.

He didn't look at her, or down at their hands. He only held on tight. Something warmed in her chest, but she was sure it wasn't her heart. She had, after Hank, dropped her heart into a bucket of ice and vowed to never defrost it again.

It was unlikely that it would warm now simply because she was holding someone's hand. Kade's hand, sure, but it was still just a hand. He hadn't kissed her, or made love with her, though heaven only knew why she would put either of those options in her head.

Holding someone's hand wasn't worthy of defrosting was all that she was saying. And she was saying it to her heart.

Apparently, it needed the reminder.

CHAPTER SIX

'THROUGH ALL OF this I've never heard the situation described quite so succinctly.'

Kade looked at Amari now. It took him a second to register her reply since, once again, his brain skipped on how good she looked.

She wore a red summer dress that fell to her ankles, a section of which was wet from the waves. It was patterned, with white flowers that had yellow middles, which he didn't care about since the dress plunged at her neckline, giving him a clear look at the swell of her breasts. She had, quite unhelpfully, worn a necklace that stopped just before that swell. It was a simple gold chain, though the pendant at the bottom was a circle of different coloured stones, which he noticed matched the dress, including the flowers, perfectly.

He noticed because he spent a significant amount of time looking at the pendant and not her cleavage. He would not look at her cleavage.

Not that it matters. If Amari's noticed, she won't think her pendant is keeping you riveted.

With a shaky breath, he tried to think about the other parts of her. Her hair was loose, the first time he'd seen it as such, the curls of it blowing in the wind. Someone, because he was quite certain it wasn't her, had put a flower in her hair. Her lips were the faintest touch of red, and he wasn't sure if that was because she'd been drinking wine, or because she'd painted them that colour. It mattered to him. He wanted to know whether he would taste wine or simply her if he dipped his head towards her...

'It's my gift.'

He blinked. Her brows knitted, but she clarified.

'Phrasing crappy things in an easily digestible manner.'

'That's a gift?'

'Hmm.' She stayed quiet for a while. 'I suppose that's a valid question. Perhaps it isn't a gift as much as something I taught myself.'

'I... I would like to ask, but I'm not sure whether I'd be pushing if I did.'

Her expression softened. It reminded him that they were still holding hands. It made him feel as if they were the only two people in the world. He knew they weren't. He knew they weren't even the only two people on this beach; Pete was around here somewhere. Yet she made him believe that they were alone. It was...special.

'I appreciate that.' She took a deep breath and looked at the sky. 'My mom...wasn't a queen.' She gave a quick laugh. 'She didn't take a lot of responsibility for me.' She paused. 'It meant that I learnt how to deal with a lot of things myself. She would tell me something...like we were moving, for example. And that was it. No discussion, no reasons. Just the facts. And I had to process it. It helped to talk myself through it, one thing at a time. It helped if I was straightforward and concise about it to myself: *Yes, moving sucks, but you'll still have a roof over your head. Yes, a new school will be hard, but at least no one there will remember you wore the wrong uniform for a month because your mother couldn't be bothered to buy the right one.*'

Her face was tight by the end, her chest moving in and out rapidly. He was about to comfort her when it stopped. All of it just...stopped. She relaxed her face, her lips curving in a self-indulgent manner. Her breathing slowed, the in and out of it deep, careful movements.

And he thought he might be witnessing another side-effect of a negligent mother: self-soothing. Self-control.

It was really quite remarkable, even if it did leave a dull thud of pain in his chest that she had had to do it.

'It sounds difficult.'

'Not as difficult as ruling a kingdom.'

'Probably as difficult as ruling a kingdom.' He turned, taking her other hand. 'You understand that your experiences are valid in themselves? You don't have to explain them to me, or belittle them because mine seem worse. I swear to you, your pain is as valid as mine. And I'm sorry for it.'

Her eyes widened, her breath *swooshing* through her lips.

'Wow,' she said. 'You really have that Prince Charming thing down, don't you?'

He chuckled lightly. Then it was gone. Gone, because something else took its place. Something intense. Desire, perhaps, though not only physical. There was more to it.

It was that she was strong and independent. He had known it before, but it meant more now knowing that she had made herself that way. She was sharp, her humour dry and pointed, her wit uncompromising and smart. He loved that she was honest about not trusting him, and that her trust was harder to get than anyone else's. She didn't seem fazed that he was a prince. Yes, that might be because she only believed him about fifty per cent, but still. Some people responded in worse ways at the mere possibility.

She pulled him in as if she were a spider and he were caught in her web. Except that analogy only worked if the spider didn't particularly care about catching its prey. Or if the prey had gone willingly into the danger of that web. Because he knew Amari didn't want him. At least not in a way that allowed her to admit it. He knew it just as much as he knew cupping her face between his hands, bringing his forehead to hers was the worst idea he'd had in a long time.

Or perhaps the best.

'My charm would exceed even my own expectations if I got this right,' he whispered, knowing his mouth was centimetres from hers. Knowing, when lust flared in her eyes, that his breath mingling with hers was a temptation.

'This?'

'You know what I mean.'

'I want you to say it.'

'Let me kiss you.'

She answered by giving him exactly what he wanted.

He was only aware of the surface things at first. That her lips were on his, that they were soft, that the red of them had been wine. He felt her face between his hands, heard the faint moan coming from her mouth. The vibration of it slipped through the parting of his lips, accompanied by her tongue. A slight lick, a test, a teasing.

It was all perfectly lovely.

And then he fell beneath the surface.

His mouth opened wider, claiming her as if he were a knight claiming his captured bride. He let her explore, welcomed the hardening of his body, welcomed the softness of hers as she pressed against him. Her tongue was a weapon—no, a tool. When something was used that skilfully, it was a tool. Even if it caused destruction, even if he felt whatever guard he had put up with her be destroyed.

He fell deeper when her hands touched his skin. They lay on his chest first, like the day she had touched him, and they moved down lower as they had on that day, too. His tension this time came not from a clutch for control, but from the acknowledgement that control didn't matter. He didn't care if she touched him, if she felt the way he wanted her. He wanted her to know. He wanted her to touch, to feel, to claim.

But he didn't do it passively. He touched her, too. Lowered his hands to her hips, a plush landing after the sharp features of her face. He let his thumbs stroke her belly, allowed his imagination to linger on what she would feel like beneath the material of her dress. Slowly, his hands went higher. Over the cinch of her waist, stopping at her breasts.

She moaned again, though he only touched the side of her, and suddenly her hands were on his, placing them over her breasts, her nipples pressed into his palms.

'Sir,' came a voice. It took him too long to respond, but he did, removing his hands, shifting so that Amari was behind him.

'What?'

'It's not…private here,' Pete said, his face pained.

He could relate. Kade had never experienced an arousal quite this painful. Pete's pain likely didn't come from the same cause.

'Your timing is ridiculous, Pete.'

'I'm sorry, sir.' He glanced at Amari. 'I'm sorry,' he said again, before turning around. It was as much privacy as he and Amari would get.

Kade angled back to her. 'I'm…sorry, for that.'

She pushed her hair out of her face. It allowed him to see the flush of her skin. An intense disappointment swept over him because he knew if Pete hadn't interrupted, that flush would have been the result of more than just a kiss.

'Hey, it happens.'

'Does it?'

She laughed, breaking the tension. 'Well, I don't usually kiss royalty, but I can imagine.'

She tucked her hair behind her ears. Fascinating, he thought. She toyed with her hair when she was nervous. He hadn't expected that. She was just so…steady, in everything that she did. Nerves didn't seem to fit a woman like that.

But then, Amari did seem to contradict everything he thought he knew about women.

He wasn't complaining.

'I'll… I'll see you at the store tomorrow.'

'You don't want to come for that drink?'

She smiled again. 'I can't imagine what a drink would result in if a walk on the beach did this.' She stepped forward, pressed a kiss to his cheek. 'Tomorrow.'

She greeted Pete and walked away.

He watched her for a long time, then directed his attention to Pete. 'They have a name for people like you, you know.'

Pete sighed. 'It didn't bring me any joy.'

'It didn't bring me any joy either,' Kade said bitterly, and turned to his house.

She was still floating on a cloud when she reached the store the next morning.

Perhaps that was why she fell through it.

'Amari? Amari Hayes?' a man asked.

He had been waiting for her. He was older than her, perhaps in his forties, and there was something about him that was…off.

'Who's asking?'

'Me. Reporter for *Daria Daily*. Is this you?'

He pulled out a picture from his pocket. It was grey, grainy, but it sure as hell was her. She distinctly remembered the moment Kade put his hands on her waist like that. She also remembered where his hands went to next. Where she put them.

'Nope,' she said, taking the picture out of his hand. 'Haven't seen either of those people.'

With a calm she didn't feel, she took out her keys, began opening the door. The man was still talking.

'You don't recognise him? Strange, considering my sources have him working here for the past week.'

She ignored him, and thanked the heavens that the door opened easily. When he made to follow her, she closed the door in his face. Pointedly. Then she locked it. Also pointedly. Then she rushed to turn the alarm off so she wouldn't have the armed response at her door.

That might not have been a bad thing.

Her next move alarmed her. Filled her with shame, too. She *hid*. Hid in the kitchen at the back of the store. Pressed her back into the wall and told herself to breathe. She talked herself off the ledge.

No one could know that was her. No one…except the people at that party, who had seen her in that dress. But those people were her community. They wouldn't tell a stranger her name, damn it. They wouldn't send them to her store.

But she knew how easily they talked. How they tried to make anyone coming to their little town feel welcome. If someone asked the right questions, made the right noises, she knew they would let information slip.

Oh, yes, that's Amari Hayes. Sweet girl. She owns All and Everything on Main Road. I used to be worried about her, working all alone in that store, but now she has those two gentlemen. Handsome fellows.

Yeah, she could see it. She could see them talking about her, and Kade and Pete, and letting it slip that she was a single mother and that was probably why she needed help from two people instead of one and oh, no! May! They might have told the reporter about May!

If there were noises about her not knowing who the father was, if the reporter made the leap from kissing on the beach to having a child together…

Oh, no...oh, no...oh, no.

She pushed off the wall and headed straight to the phone. Before she could lift it, Kade knocked at the door. His expression was tight, and Pete was nowhere to be seen, and she thought maybe they'd encountered the reporter, too.

She opened it for him, but turned around before he could speak.

'I should have warned you about the man,' she said over her shoulder, 'but I only got here a few minutes ago.'

'Don't apologise.'

Something about the firm way he spoke eased her panic. Still, she dialled Lydia's number with shaky fingers.

'Maybe you should lock the door or something.' She chewed on her nail as the phone rang. It took long. Too long. What if—?

'Hello?'

'Lydia?' Relief nearly choked her. She took a breath. 'Lydia, is everything okay? Is May okay?'

'Everything's fine.' Lydia's voice, which had been faintly dull when she answered, sharpened. 'What's going on?'

'Nothing. Nothing,' she said again. 'Just...you know... I'm not used to May being away from home. Usually, I have her with me in the store on weekends.' She closed her eyes, wondering how much of the lie Lydia would buy.

'Amari, May's fine. They all are. In fact, they're still sleeping.'

'Oh, crap. I forgot. I'm sorry. I forgot the time.'

'Are you sure you're okay?'

She gave a laugh that sounded false even to her own ears. 'Yeah, yeah. I'm fine. Just... They'll have breakfast and you'll take her to school to the make Christmas decorations for the market?'

'That's the plan.'

'Okay.' She exhaled. 'Okay, great. I'll see you then.'

'Amari, you don't sound okay.'

'I'm fine. I'm fine.'

Lydia didn't sound any less concerned by the time she put down the phone, but Amari had done her best. Then she crumpled. Sank into her chair and lay her head on the counter. She allowed herself a minute of it and straightened.

'Sorry,' she said, standing. 'I just had this moment where I imagined them going after her because they think she's connected to you and… I overreacted. I'm sorry you had to witness that.'

Kade hadn't moved from his spot in front of the door. His expression hadn't changed either. Or it had, considering he had come in concerned and now his face held…nothing. It was curiously empty. Practised. She remembered it from that first day he'd walked into her store, asking about the vacancy. She hadn't realised how much he'd relaxed in the past week.

Somehow, the development didn't make her feel any better.

'It wasn't an overreaction.'

She interpreted it as reassurance initially—until the words sank in. 'Wait… Are you telling me that reporter might go after my kid?'

'Not him specifically, no.' Kade took the slightest step forward. 'But those pictures of us are splashed across every newspaper in my kingdom at the moment.' He gestured to the picture she still held in her hand. She'd forgotten about it. 'They have your name and the town's name. That man was simply the first.'

'Whoa, okay, let's just wait a second. Let's just take a step back.' She looked at the picture. 'This could be anyone. I'm not talking about me; I'm talking about both of us. This could be neither of us. Why…why do they think this is me or you?'

'They've been tracking me the entire trip.'

'Isn't that…? That can't be legal.'

'One would think,' he said darkly. 'Unfortunately, it is, and they've been doing it. Now, we have to act quickly and do damage control.'

It all sounded so foreign to her. Perhaps because now, she had to accept Kade was a prince. Sure, she had begun to, but it still hadn't seemed real. Not even when she was kissing him under the night sky at the beach and his bodyguard had interrupted them.

Stupidly naïve. That was what she was.

No more.

She didn't respond to him, instead taking out her phone and typing 'Prince Kade' and 'Daria'. The results came up quickly. So quickly she thought she should have done it before.

Before would have been easier. It would have prevented this from happening. She could have said no to him working for her. She could have stopped herself from becoming entangled in her attraction to him. She could have protected herself and May from whatever was about to change in her life. Because this Internet search told her things were about to change.

The picture of them kissing was one of the first to come up.

Words like 'mystery woman', 'future King', and 'hideout' popped out at her. But that didn't matter when other words were more pressing. Like her name. Her town. Her store. They mentioned May, but not by name, which was the only source of relief she had from the entire thing.

If she had done this search before all this had happened, she wouldn't be in the papers or on the Internet. May wouldn't be a daughter, four years of age, father unknown.

She regretted giving Kade privacy. She probably shouldn't have—her intentions had been noble—but what did noble matter when her daughter was in danger?

Damn it.

Her heart cracked, emotion all about spilling out of it. But she couldn't give in. She'd have to put on her rainboots, take out her umbrella, and manoeuvre through it.

'What's damage control?'

CHAPTER SEVEN

'YOU'RE NOT GOING to like it,' Kade replied.

She rolled her eyes. 'There's nothing about this situation I like. Why would damage control be any different?' She set the pictures on the counter. 'If it's going to be something I like even less than everything else, I'll need coffee.'

She moved before he could reply. She was keeping busy so she could survive the negative emotions, the reprimanding her mental voice was poised to give. It helped to shut down to the most basic of her functioning. She ignored thoughts, instincts, feelings. She only allowed logic; discussing damage control would require that.

She knew, because she had done it before.

May had been a baby then, and she hadn't known how much her mother's mistakes had affected her. That would change now—but Amari wouldn't think about it. She was May's mother. Yes, she had made another horrific mistake that affected May, but that didn't change that she had to do everything in her power to protect her daughter.

She'd leave processing her emotions about it all until after that.

'Do you want a cup?' she asked, when she felt Kade staring at her.

'No.'

'Okay.'

'Amari, I need you to listen to me.'

'I am. I will. I can listen with coffee in my hand.'

He walked into the kitchen again, and suddenly she was back on that beach, touching him. Other memories—of the awareness prickling through her the first time they were in the small kitchen together; that day on their way to Mr Kyle; countless other times when they'd come too close and were hit with that tension—walked through her mind.

No, she told them, clenching her fists, her jaw. If she shut down her mental processes, she could shut down her physical ones, too.

'I'm concerned you might drop the coffee when I tell you what you're going to have to do. Or worse—that you might throw it at me.'

'Trust me,' she said, giving him a look, 'if I was going to throw something at you, I would have done it already.' With quick movements, she poured herself a cup and took a sip. It burnt her tongue. She didn't care. 'Okay, I'm ready.' He shifted and she shook her head. 'No, wait, not here.'

She pressed past him, ignoring the zing of brushing his body, and only looked at him again when she was safely behind the counter.

'Okay, now I'm ready. Tell me. What am I not going to like?'

'You and May need to come with me to Daria.'

Purposefully, she didn't respond. She had taken another sip of coffee, and she was worried she would spit it out. That kind of thing was much too close to the way Kade had said she was going to react, so she would be stubborn.

She swallowed, gave herself a moment, then said, 'We need to do *what*?'

Kade sighed. He knew this was coming. The moment Pete had woken him with the news, alerting him to the phone call coming from the royal communication officer on how to handle the press. He received several phone calls after that, including from his mother, who informed him in clipped tones that it was time he come home.

The entire time he had been thinking about Amari. And he'd worried her reaction would affect him in the same way his mother's had.

It did.

The annoyance, the faint anger, weren't unfamiliar to him. He had encountered it many times before from his mother. But then, it was *only* his mother. She was the only person who said things to him and he knew they meant something entirely different. Now Amari seemed to share that power.

She was handling this with coolness and control, but he knew she was spitting mad inside. Because of him.

Served him right for going against his gut and kissing her.

'I know it sounds drastic—'

'It doesn't sound drastic,' she interrupted. 'It sounds insane. You want me to go to your kingdom? The one hours away from here? That's quite the commute to work every day.'

'You're not going to be able to work for a while.'

She bared her teeth at him. Bared her teeth as if she were a wild animal being cornered.

Seconds later, it eased into a thin smile.

Maybe he had imagined her snarling at him.

Maybe.

'There's no way in hell I'm not working.'

'Amari.'

He wanted to sigh her name, to convince her what he was about to outline was the best plan. He'd come up with it with Pete, with his advisors, with his mother's advisors. But he knew none of that would work, so instead he merely said her name to give himself a moment to decide how best to present the facts to her.

'What happened this morning with that reporter will be a consistent occurrence for the foreseeable future. It won't only be one. It'll be many. They will wait for you outside the store, outside your home, and once they find out where May goes to school, they'll wait there, too.'

Her face changed, but he didn't give the expression a chance to settle.

'They will go to your friends and ask them about you. It won't matter that they won't want to say anything. They will, eventually. One of them will speak out to defend you and that will become the next story. They will go through your garbage and find another story. They will dig into your history and find out everything about your family. They will…' He hesitated now, because he knew this one would be the worst. 'They will reach out to your family and ask them about you. They will offer a lot of money for those stories. And some of your family members might take it. May's father—' he cleared his throat '—May's father might take it.'

She didn't reply or interject. His gaze lowered to her hand. It was clutching her mug so tightly there was no colour in her skin. Slowly, he met her eyes.

They weren't blank, nor were they overtly emotional. They held a small amount of anger, of frustration, of fear, all coated in indignance. With a lift of her chin, stubbornness joined.

'Seems to me that'll happen whether I'm here or not.'

'Yes,' he agreed. 'But I can't protect you the way I need to here.'

'You can't protect me in the way that matters either way.'

He didn't try to argue. He understood. Her life was about to be picked apart, and she hadn't even known it would happen. There was no way to prepare her; he hadn't even considered it a possibility that he would have to prepare her.

Was it worth it? a voice whispered in his head. *Was the*

taste of her lips, the feel of her body, worth putting that look on her face?

He couldn't answer.

'That might be true, Amari. It *is* true,' he corrected. 'But we have to think about it practically. And fast. Once all this happens, it'll happen fairly quickly. Your store will become invaded. You will be followed. Some of this will be reporters; others will merely be curious people. You are no longer a person to them. You're the woman a prince kissed. And they'll want to know if fairy tales are true, and, if they are, how they can make it happen for themselves.'

He wanted to move closer to offer comfort, but he didn't think she'd want that.

'I know it sounds dramatic, but it's your reality for the next few weeks at least. Until they lose interest in you, which won't happen if you're this easily accessible to them.'

'Or they'll realise, because I'm accessible to them, that I'm very boring and not someone worth reporting on or following.'

'Would you be okay to endure weeks of fear and anxiety on the *chance* that might happen?' he asked softly. When she didn't reply, he continued in the same tone. 'You have no protection in a very real sense, Amari. If you come with me to Daria, we can keep you in the palace while we figure out how to handle this.'

'Why can't you leave Pete here? Let him protect us.'

'He's not enough.'

'So send more.'

'I will,' he promised. 'Once we have better security in place here and at your home.'

'My...why?'

'Doors and alarms won't keep them away.'

'They might break into the house? The store?'

Finally he saw real fear break through. He hated it, but

he needed it. Fear would keep her from doing stupid things. It would keep her safe.

'It's a possibility. We're being overly cautious. I can send people to look after you and May, but people are fallible. Pete is the head of the royal guard and he couldn't stop people from taking pictures of us at a private beach. Guards won't be enough to keep you and May one hundred per cent safe while this blows over.'

Her tongue darted between her lips. She looked down, drew her coffee to her lips. The cup shook and, again, he wanted to comfort her. But he couldn't. Not only because she would despise him for it, but because he needed her to feel those feelings. He needed her to understand the immensity of what was about to happen.

'This is not okay, Kade,' she whispered.

'I know. I'm… I'm sorry.'

She closed her eyes. Shut them tight. Swallowed.

'I'm sorry this is your life,' she replied.

When she opened her eyes again, he saw her strength. And damn if he didn't feel his chest fill with a distinctly uncomfortable warmth.

CHAPTER EIGHT

IT ALL HAPPENED fairly quickly after that.

Amari went back to her house and packed May's clothing into a suitcase. She took May's favourite toys, the blanket she couldn't sleep without, and put that in, too. She grabbed snacks that May loved, just in case they didn't have them in Daria, and ignored the inner voice asking if she was bribing her daughter.

When she went to her own wardrobe, her productivity stalled. She stared. For a long while, she stared, because she didn't know what in her closet was appropriate to wear in a palace. After ten long minutes that didn't help her come up with an answer, she stopped thinking and threw in all her favourites. She grabbed her chargers and electronics. She put in toiletries and a towel.

Then she took a deep breath and went to fetch her kid from school.

There was a lot May had to tell her, ranging from her sleepover to the Christmas decorations she'd made that had been worth going to school on a Saturday for. Amari let her talk. It was the cowardly thing to do when she should have been explaining why they were driving to the airport. But she couldn't bear to shut down May's excitement. She was already taking May from her friends. May wouldn't see her decorations get sold at the market the following week. So she let her daughter have her excitement.

About five minutes away from the airport, May realised they weren't heading home. Amari told her what was going to happen, trying to sound reassuring. They were going to visit the Queen of a far-off land. She wanted to surprise May because Christmas in a palace was the best kind of Christmas. By the end of it, Amari had woven a tale so fantastical about royalty and Christmas that even she wanted to buy it.

But she was too old for fairy tales. The truth was that kissing Kade had been selfish and now May was paying the price for it.

You sure are making your mother proud.

Amari resisted the wince, trading it for a smile that May excitedly returned.

But the excitement quickly changed when they boarded the plane and May saw the cabin crew. She could all but see the panic of encountering strangers on May's face. Amari picked her up and held her close, but she wasn't sure if she was comforting May or herself.

'Miss Hayes, we're happy to get her settled,' a woman said, stepping forward.

'The only way that's going to happen is if she stays with me.'

Her voice was a little harder at the end, making *she stays with me* sound like a threat. Perhaps it was. She was still holding onto her control, but it was tenuous. Threats could slip through.

'That's fine,' Kade said, appearing out of nowhere.

He had the audacity to look good. He wore one of those perfectly fitted suits again, but this time it was black, his shirt white, which gave the entire look a dashing effect. She tried to keep her expression neutral, but when he smiled faintly at her, she wasn't sure she had succeeded.

'You're growling.'

No, she hadn't succeeded.

'It comes with being a parent.'

She stepped further into the plane and the crew scattered, as if Kade's presence had negated the reason for theirs. It probably had. They were likely meant to be the welcoming party. Except their guests didn't want a welcome, so why not allow the prince to take over?

The prince. It was still absolutely ludicrous.

Kade's gaze lowered to May, who had shifted her head so she could peek at him through a curtain of hair.

'Miss May,' he greeted her quietly. 'It's lovely to see you.'

May giggled, pressing her forehead back into Amari's neck.

'Remember the prince I told you about, baby?' Amari whispered into May's ear. 'That's him.'

May leaned back. 'The funny man's a prince?'

'Yes.'

May studied Kade again. 'Hello, Mr Prince.'

Kade smiled. 'Hello, Little Hayes.'

'Why you call me that?'

'Well, your mother's Big Hayes, isn't she?'

May looked at Amari. Amari shrugged. 'I am bigger than you.'

Her daughter gave it a few more seconds, then nodded. 'Okay.'

Then she put her head back into Amari's chest.

'She's not a huge fan of new things,' Amari said to Kade.

'You don't have to explain.'

'Generally, I would agree with you. But since we're imposing on your hospitality for the foreseeable future, I think an explanation is necessary.'

Like earlier, her anger slipped through at the end. Kade's slight nod told her he had picked up on it, but he was too polite to say anything. Or perhaps he was smart enough to know he shouldn't say anything.

They got settled in the plane, which was unlike any other Amari had experienced. It was private, for one, a necessity for safety considering they were outside the kingdom and the press was determined to get to them. For another, it spoke of the kind of decadence Amari had never been comfortable with. It was partly because she'd spent her life being practical instead of decadent, and partly because she wasn't a huge fan of people who were used to decadence. They tended to see people like her as beneath them.

She knew Kade wasn't like that. But Kade had also pulled her into this world. One where all the certainty she had spent her life working for didn't matter.

Her fingers trembled as she did May's seat belt, then her own. When she looked up, Kade was watching her hands. She didn't make a fist as her gut told her to, instead letting him see what all this was doing to her. The anguish in his eyes told her she was punishing him. The satisfaction she felt told her she was trying to.

Shame immediately poured into her and she focused on May. Her daughter was having a hard time balancing her fear of the unknown and her curiosity and excitement of being on her first flight. The exhaustion of it had her asleep before dinner.

Amari ate as much of her food as she could, but that wasn't much. She wasn't hungry; she was tired. It had been a long day, and she had been keeping herself in check the entire time. She would have killed for some alone time, but that didn't happen on planes. Perhaps it didn't happen in palaces either. She sent a wish up to the heavens that that wasn't the case.

'You're not hungry?' Kade asked from his seat across the aisle.

'Not really, no.' The flight attendant took her plate away, and she offered the woman an apologetic smile. 'Please tell whoever prepared it that it isn't their fault.'

Kade waited until the woman had taken his own plate away—empty, Amari noted—before he spoke again.

'I can't imagine how difficult this must be for you.'

'I think you can,' Amari said, slumping a little. They'd put May in the bed at the back of the plane—*a bed in a plane*—so she had a little more space. 'You just don't like it.'

He made a noise of agreement.

She closed her eyes, tried to gather her thoughts. Yet somehow she was speaking before she could do it. 'Tell me what to expect.' She opened her eyes. 'Tell me what to expect when I get to your home. Will your family treat me differently because I'm a commoner who put you in this position? Will they treat me poorly?'

'They will treat you like you're my guest,' Kade said, tone hard. 'That means you'll be treated as well as any other guest.'

'You mean, I'll be treated as well as, say, the president of a country?'

Kade's expression softened. 'Better. I'll make sure of it.'

She wasn't sure why, after everything, she believed him.

'When we arrive,' Kade continued, 'you'll be taken to your room. Food can be brought up for you and May— you might be hungry then—or I can have the staff prepare something for the three of us.'

'I think eating in our room might be easier.'

He nodded. 'Tomorrow morning, you'll have breakfast with my family. We're only three—my parents and me— and they'll be perfectly polite.'

'Perfectly polite,' she repeated. 'How diplomatic of you all.'

'Well,' he said, tilting his head, 'you asked me what to expect. This is what you can expect. My family is polite and diplomatic.'

He didn't sound upset. Maybe he wasn't. Maybe she

only thought he should be because she was projecting her own feelings onto the situation. She had been polite and diplomatic—for her—all day. She hadn't said what was on her mind, hadn't dealt with how she felt about any of this, and she was exhausted. She couldn't imagine what living a lifetime of it would be like.

'You're saying that when you describe your parents to people, you describe them as polite and diplomatic.'

'No,' he said with a small smile. 'But people know who my parents are. I don't have to describe them.'

'You've never spoken about your parents in casual conversation?'

'The only casual conversation I've had in the last thirty years has been with you.'

Confusion jumped from Amari's face at first. Realisation followed, and finally, sympathy.

He wasn't offended by her reaction. He knew his life was different from hers. Even if he hadn't witnessed it the past week, he would have known.

It was a good reminder. Before they reached his home. Before he got sucked into procedure and duty, and she got sucked into the same, and he saw her in the context of his life. No matter how well she did—and he had every belief that she would do well—she would be playing a part. Much as he had been playing a part in her store.

They didn't fit into one another's lives. This entire experience had illustrated that quite well.

'Okay, so you're used to having royal conversations,' Amari said. 'This isn't one of those, so you can be honest. What's your father like?'

He thought about it. 'He's…a lot like me.'

Kade smiled at that, because it was true. His father was slightly socially inept. He usually allowed his wife to take the lead, which she did flawlessly, and that had worked for them over the course of their marriage and Kade's mother's reign. When his father did solo engagements, which was rare, he wouldn't fill silences. He would wait to answer a question so he could make sure he was satisfied with his reply, even if that meant minutes. He was deliberate in a way that society wasn't used to, and he didn't have the desire to make other people feel comfortable.

He was exactly like his father in those ways, except he fought those instincts and tried to be like his mother. The result was awkward chatter, inappropriate observations.

'He's charming? Kind? Completely unable to work a coffee machine?' Amari prodded. 'There are many ways your answer could be interpreted.'

She thought him charming. It wasn't the description people used for him—the *Oops Prince* didn't exactly translate to charming—and yet here she was, using it, and not for the first time.

Perhaps she finds awkwardness charming.

Fair enough, he told that snarky inner voice. But she had also called him kind, and, up until that point, he hadn't realised how much it meant to him that she thought him kind.

'He is kind,' Kade agreed. 'And he probably doesn't know how to work a coffee machine.'

'I understand the comparison now.'

Kade smiled. It faltered as he tried to figure out how to articulate the next part.

'My father is the youngest of five children. His mother was considered nobility in Daria, but his father was a businessman. Theirs was a chance meeting and a romantic union.'

'What did that mean for your father?'

He appreciated her ability to get to the point. 'He didn't have the "pure" nobility rearing most people marrying into the royal family had. He and my mother moved in the same circles, and she found herself drawn to him for reasons that to this day don't make sense to me. But they married.'

'Does that mean you don't have the "pureness"—' she winced as she said the word '—you're supposed to have as royalty?'

'Well.' It was all he said for a moment. 'I have a queen as a mother.'

She studied him. 'I'm struggling to follow this. It's probably because you're being diplomatic, but, unfortunately for you, I've been diplomatic all day and I can't be right now. The way you've told me all this makes you sound like you don't believe you're good enough to be royal. As if somehow being like your "regular" father means you're not like your royal mother and that means you're inadequate. Am I right?'

'I...' He trailed off, unsure how to respond. Eventually, he said, 'It does sound like that. But it's more complicated.'

'I don't think it is,' she said softly. 'You think you're faulty somehow because you're more like your father than your mother.'

He was quite speechless—and then he sighed. 'You asked me what to expect when we get to Daria? Part of it is that my father will treat you kindly. He will speak to you as he would any other, because that's his way. My mother... She will treat you politely because you are my guest. But you will get the feeling that she is not pleased with you. That's not because of you, but me. She... I suppose *she* thinks I'm faulty because I share traits with my father. He's not particularly good at social situations, which, as you might guess, is not ideal for a ruler.'

'Well,' Amari said slowly, 'she probably should have thought about that before she married him and had you. You have absolutely no control over which traits you received, Kade. But she did. It hardly seems fair that she now thinks they're faulty.'

CHAPTER NINE

HE WASN'T USED to people defending him. Certainly not against his mother. But Amari's passion on his behalf made him feel…something. It was strong and powerful and so completely foreign he knew he shouldn't engage with it. It was dangerous, getting used to having someone speak to him—about him—like that. And his mother, too.

'You probably shouldn't say that once we arrive.'

'Of course not,' she said with a roll of her eyes. 'I do have some sense of self-preservation. Even if this situation doesn't make it seem that way.'

He had no response to that. It was rather pointed, as he'd put her in the situation. It was also the truth. She should have stayed away from him; he should have stayed away from her. The fact that neither of them had made them both fools.

Except his punishment would be no different from his others. His mother's disappointment, his kingdom's disapproval. Amari's punishment was being drawn out of her life, forcing her to do the same for her daughter. It was leaving behind her home and her support system. It was leaving her job and her livelihood.

They did not compare and he deserved every pointed statement she cared to make.

They fell into silence after that. Kade imagined Amari was trying to process what had happened over the last twenty-four hours and what was to come. He was doing much the same, though he thought her process had less self-admonishment than his.

He was tired of it. Berating himself for doing the absolute worst thing in every situation. The simple solution was that he needed to stop putting himself in those situations. But that was too simple in most cases.

With Amari, he *had* put himself in the situation. But the other situations... Those were a part of his duty. He couldn't stop speaking with people or going to charity events because he wasn't good at it. He needed to become better at it.

He had been spending his life trying, to no avail.

If he was tired of it, he could only imagine his mother's frustrations. Her fears, too. She had given her entire life to Daria. She worked to establish a parliament that would keep the monarchy's power in check to appease those calling for complete liberation from the royal family. The move was widely praised, and the calls for liberation had become softer since it was clear his mother had no intention of abusing her power or disregarding parliament's decisions. She held a lot of sway in parliament, of course, and Kade had often watched her strategically guide decisions so the result would be best for the kingdom.

Daria was her life, and she must be worried Kade would destroy that.

She had never said so. She would merely chide him about his public appearances. There had been attempts to 'revitalise' his image, but he'd messed those up, too. Such as when his mother had asked him to represent her at the opening ceremony of a biennial rugby tournament. He'd gone, done his photo op, and somehow managed to mistake one of the female players as a spouse. And while he hadn't done it intentionally—she looked exactly like the spouse he had mistaken her for, down to the blue dress she wore—it had been a PR nightmare. The press had called him a misogynist, and he had spent a month wondering if it had been a mistake or if he *was* a misogynist.

His mother hadn't been impressed.

He knew she wasn't impressed with the current situation either. He had drawn attention to the fact that he wasn't in the kingdom. That wasn't entirely his fault, to be fair, but he hadn't exactly made the discovery less controversial. And because of that controversy, the news that he would be taking over from her would likely go down less smoothly in the media.

But he had a plan. The first phase had been to make sure Amari was safe. The second phase was to make things right with his mother. The third was to address the situation publicly. Phase three needed input from his secretary and the royal communications officer. Probably his mother, too.

'Hey—where's Pete?' Amari asked, looking around as if he would magically appear because she'd remembered him.

'He's still in Swell Valley.'

'Why? Shouldn't he be protecting you?'

'We've arranged for other security while he remains behind.' He hesitated, but pushed through. 'Pete is the only person who knows your business well enough to help things run while you're here.'

She gaped at him. 'You left Pete behind to look after the store?'

'He offered,' Kade replied. 'We were trying to find a solution that would be least destructive to your life. It's a good solution. He knows the basics of running the store, although I'm sure you'll hear from him quite often, and he'll get some of the other guards to help when needed. He also knows how to handle any threats should they arise, and he can oversee the security upgrades.'

'Why…why would he offer to do that?'

'He likes you.' He lifted his shoulders. 'More importantly, he respects you. Part of that respect is understanding that your business is important to you and trying to make sure it's harmed as little as possible because of this. If we're lucky, business might actually boom. I trust Pete more than anyone else to ensure that'll happen.'

She didn't speak for a while, though her lips moved, mouthing words he couldn't interpret. It fascinated him. Amari was confident and fierce, rarely stumped, but here she was. Trying to figure out what to say to him because he'd told her he'd made provisions for her business.

'If it makes you feel better, I think he also offered because he dreaded the idea of travelling in a confined space with a child.' He aimed for a light tone, hoping it would amuse her. He got a small smile.

After a moment, he said, 'I wanted to make sure this affects your life as little as possible.'

'I know,' she replied. 'I know. I just thought… I mean, my life's been pretty deeply affected.'

'I know. I'm sorry.'

'This… It doesn't make up for it, but it's pretty damn great, Kade. Thank you.'

He inclined his head in acceptance, and let the silence slip back between them. He didn't care to fill it, knowing that they both needed time to prepare. It was funny how he knew that with her. He could sense it somehow. Yet with other people, he filled the silence with chatter. With idiocy.

It was instinctual, almost, with Amari. He could feel what she wanted and he had no idea if it was because she was special to him. He could acknowledge that without doing anything about it. But he didn't know if that was a factor, or because a week away from his mother, his responsibilities, had allowed him the space to make mistakes. He had, and the world hadn't ended.

It seemed like an important realisation to have. He should remember it.

But even as he thought it, a voice told him he wouldn't.

* * *

May was groggy when Amari woke her up once they landed. She didn't speak much, but then, May rarely did when she woke up. She had inherited her mother's unfortunate morning misery. It wasn't only confined to mornings, but after any nap. It was the one thing Amari wouldn't have minded her daughter inherit from her father.

Hank.

She shouldn't worry about him, surely. She hadn't heard from him in years. Didn't even know where he was. If reporters managed to find him, they probably deserved the story. She hadn't spoken about him to anyone in Swell Valley, and she had almost no ties in Cape Town, certainly none that would lead to him. He didn't pay child support for May, so that would lead nowhere, too. Amari hadn't had the emotional or physical capacity to go after him when he'd left. She was raising a baby alone. That was her number one priority.

Pride might have been number two.

Besides, he likely wouldn't care about what was happening with her and May anyway. But then, what did she know? Not him, that was for sure. The man *she* knew would never leave his family. So, yeah, she hadn't really known him at all.

As for her mother… Amari spoke to her more frequently. Out of that responsibility she'd honed over the years she'd looked out for herself and her mother. It was only when she got older that she realised her mother didn't need her to look out for her. She was simply not interested in living the life Amari thought she should live—she didn't care about signing parent letters or going to meetings or looking at reports. And Amari had misinterpreted that lack of interest as her mother needing help. She didn't. She did just fine without Amari. She did just fine not being a parent.

Amari didn't know if that meant she would sell stories

to reporters. She would make a call to ask her not to, but that was all she could do.

It was a relief when they drove through the thick black gates to the palace. It offered distraction. She was looking at a *real-life palace*, after all.

It surprised her. It was grand, no doubt, but it didn't look like she expected. It was more rectangular, for one. There were less pointy towers, for another. And it was old.

She had expected that, to be fair. The extent did still surprise her. It looked like history itself with the faded or stained outer walls, she couldn't tell, and the vines crawling up the sides. There were statues flanking either side of an entrance that looked like a drawbridge, though there was no water underneath. Instead, there were flowers. Beds of red and white and blue.

The minute she stepped inside the palace, her hold on May tightened. The floor was an old, gorgeous wood that fitted perfectly with the pale gold walls. A carpet of the same gold formed a path to a door to their right, and Amari realised they were merely in a reception hall of some kind. She already felt deeply out of place in the reception hall with its ridiculously large paintings of what she assumed were the kingdom and previous sovereigns.

She didn't get a chance to examine any of the pictures— or anything about the hall beyond her initial observations, really—when Kade strode ahead of her through the doors to their right. She followed, not because she thought she should, but because she didn't know what else to do. No one beyond a tall woman who looked to be a decade or so older than her was there. Kade introduced the woman as his secretary, Matilda, but the older woman didn't say one word to Amari. Amari didn't know if it was a slight or pro- tocol, but she thought it best to stick to the one person who treated her as if she was a person.

For now.

Well, yes, thank you, she told that helpful inner voice.

Because she definitely wanted to think about the fact that she was stepping into an entirely different world with only one ally. And she had to protect May, too. She could have done without her inner voice trying to sabotage her.

The room Kade had entered proved to be even more splendid than the reception hall. This one had actual gold on the walls. It formed frames of two large pictures, both in the same position on either wall. One was of a beautiful woman whose features reminded her of Kade, though there was no one thing Amari could point out that they shared. On the other wall was a picture of a gorgeous man. In him, she could clearly see Kade's lips and eyes.

Glass stretched between the two walls, covered in a gauzy material, though thick blue curtains hung on either side. In the room itself was the most expensive-looking furniture she had ever seen. Not in the middle of the room, but on the sides of a large blue carpet. As if they wanted to highlight the carpet. While she knew the value of a good carpet, and this one looked pretty great, she didn't know if it warranted centrepiece status.

She didn't understand any of it, but as she watched Kade turn to her in the middle of the room, she understood that he fitted here. It suited him as well as the suits tailored for him did.

For the first time, she thought maybe she *didn't* really understand him. Not if he fitted so perfectly in a place she could barely make sense of.

'It's a lot, I know.'

He grimaced as he said it, and she shook her head.

'It's beautiful.'

'Grand.'

'They're not mutually exclusive.'

He smiled, as if saying anything more would be admitting to something he didn't think he should. 'I'll show you to your rooms, and then we'll call down to the kitchen and get food sent up for you.'

'Oh—you don't have to show us to our rooms,' she said. 'I'm sure you have more important things to do. Someone else can do it.'

'I'd like to do it,' he said gently, firmly. Those same things—gentleness, firmness—fluttered in his eyes. He needed this. He needed to do this for them, and, though she shouldn't be trying to make him feel better when her entire life was out of place because of him, she nodded.

'Thank you.'

She followed him, her arms growing weary after carrying May for so long. May let out a little cry every time Amari tried to put her down. She didn't blame her daughter. If someone could carry her around, protect her, comfort her right in this moment, she wouldn't say no.

Eventually, Kade stopped in front of a large door. He pushed it open and gestured for her to go inside. Her feet sank into the carpet when she did, and she barely stopped herself from gasping. The room was gigantic, probably the size of the entire flat she still spent most of her income paying for back home. There was a four-poster bed in the middle of the room, a dresser opposite it, a cupboard along another wall, and a large window opposite that. A window seat had been built below the glass, and it looked as comfortable as the bed did. It also had a much better view— the ocean.

'Wow,' she breathed. She walked to the window, nudged May. 'Look over there, baby.'

May just clung tighter. Amari sighed and turned to Kade. 'It's lovely. Thank you.'

'We thought you might want to sleep with May, but, if that situation changes, we've prepared the adjoining room for her.'

'She'll stay here with me.'

He nodded. 'The bathroom's through there, and you can call down—' he walked to the phone next to the dresser '—whenever you need to and someone will respond. The list of numbers is here.' He tapped a panel next to the phone. 'I've had my number added to the list as well. Any time you need me, night or day, please call.'

'Thank you.'

'I know it's a lot,' he said, stepping forward. 'I… I'm sorry.'

'We're in it now, Kade,' she replied, though her heart was beating fast and she felt as if she needed the apology. As if she deserved it. 'There's no point in doing anything but make the best out of it.'

He studied her, but nodded. 'Would you like me to call down for anything?'

'I know it's not fancy or anything, but we could do with some burgers and fries.' She dipped her head to gesture to May. 'It's her favourite. I think she could do with some comfort.'

'Of course. I'll make sure you get it in the next thirty minutes. It should give you enough time to freshen up.' His brow knitted as he looked at May. 'Is she okay?'

Amari rubbed May's back. 'Like you said, it's a lot. But she'll be fine. We'll both be fine,' she added.

She wasn't sure if she was reassuring Kade or herself.

'Darling,' Queen Winifred said when he eventually joined his parents for a meal.

He wasn't ashamed to admit he'd stalled. He'd arranged for Amari and May's dinner, been to his own rooms to freshen up and had taken his sweet time doing so. But he had needed the space. He wanted to erase the memory of Amari's tight expression as she told him she and May would be fine. He wanted a moment to breathe before he found his mother and that emotion he felt with Amari started to weigh even more.

'Mother,' he said. 'You look lovely.' He brushed a kiss on his mother's cheek, before moving to his father and shaking his hand. 'Father.'

'Son.'

Without saying anything else, he took his seat opposite his mother. It wasn't strange any more that they sat at a small table. A six-seater liberally set to accommodate the three of them. His father sat at the head of the table, his mother at the side, and Kade opposite his mother.

It was late for them to be eating, but Kade knew they'd arranged it this way to talk. He didn't say anything as the waitstaff set his meal in front of him. He waited.

He didn't have to wait for long.

'Quite the mess you've found yourself in, isn't it?' his mother said, swirling around her wine in a glass.

'It isn't the first time,' he answered, since that was what she was implying.

Winifred gave an impatient sigh. 'I wanted you to have the time you asked for to recuperate, Kade. To prepare. I wanted you to have your freedom. But this—'

'Is hardly something we could have anticipated.'

'Are you in love with her?'

Good thing he hadn't started eating. He would have choked, and that would have displeased his mother even more. '*No*, Mother. It was a kiss.'

'It looked to be a little more than a kiss.'

He made a disgusted noise. 'Please, don't.'

'If you can't keep your hands to yourself on a public beach, then you can hardly be upset with me—and the world, for that matter—for reacting to it.'

'I didn't—' He broke off. 'It was a private beach. We're looking into suing the reporter for trespassing.'

His mother snorted. It wasn't something she would have

ever done in public. She rarely did it in front of them. But apparently this situation warranted a snort.

'It won't make a difference.'

'It will to me.' It would give him back some measure of control, even if it was merely the illusion of it. 'Regardless, I couldn't anticipate that a kiss I shared with a woman I respect would make it onto every newspaper in Daria.'

'A woman you respect?' Winifred repeated. 'You're not in love, but you respect her.' He didn't answer. 'That's worse, possibly.'

He didn't speak for a moment. Even after taking a beat, he said, 'I don't think I want to know how you've come to that conclusion.'

'Love is passion,' his mother said, as if he had, indeed, asked. 'It burns hot, but it burns fast. Usually, it fizzles out. Oh, I didn't mean you, dear,' she told her husband, Deacon, when he looked up. 'Sometimes, if you're lucky, it lasts.'

'But if I had been in love with Amari, it wouldn't have been the kind that lasts.'

'Respect,' Winifred continued, and he didn't know if she was ignoring him or agreeing with him, 'is built on a much sturdier foundation. You feel responsible for this woman now, which I already assumed considering she's here in your kingdom, distracting you from the fact that you're about to become King.'

'Nothing could distract me from the fact that I'm about to become King.'

'And that's where you underestimate having this woman here.'

He exhaled. 'Mother, I put her in this situation. She isn't safe in her home because of me. I can hardly have her and her daughter in danger because of something I did.'

'Did you coerce her into kissing you?'

'Of course not.'

'And you were honest about who you are?'

'Yes.'

'Then she's put herself into this situation just as much as you have.'

'You and I both know it isn't as simple as that.'

Winifred sighed, and suddenly looked every inch of her seventy years. It was plausibly because of her illness, but Kade couldn't help but wonder if it was him. Was he making his mother age? Was her concern about him making her feel worse?

It was self-indulgent, and a part of him knew that. But he wished he knew for sure. He wished he knew what it would be like to make his mother proud, and not feel as though she had to coach him through every decision he made.

'I'm not going to claim that this isn't a bad situation,' he said. The least he could do was be honest. 'I know bringing Amari and May here complicates things. But being responsible is part of being King. Making sure people are safe is part of being King.' He paused. 'She might not be a part of this kingdom, but I've inadvertently drawn her into this. She has a right to be offered those things just as much as anyone else in this kingdom.'

His mother opened her mouth to reply, but his father laid a hand over hers. They exchanged a look, before Deacon looked at him. 'You're right. And we're proud of you for it.'

The words would have meant more if they'd come from his mother, but he told himself to take the win. He might not have acted like an adult before, getting himself into this mess, but he was now. And it meant something to him that his father saw it. His mother would get on board or she wouldn't, but there was nothing he could do about that.

That didn't mean he wouldn't try.

Picking up his utensils, he told his parents his plan.

CHAPTER TEN

AMARI DIDN'T DARE slip out of her room as she wanted to that night. She was afraid she would get lost. She was afraid May would wake up, see that she wasn't there, and panic.

But she couldn't sleep, so she spent the night on that wonderful window seat, looking out at the magnificent garden, at the ocean in the distance.

It helped clarify some things. Like the fact that she had been blaming Kade when she, too, had a part in what had happened between them. It was the easier option, blaming him. She didn't have to think too deeply about how she had made the same mistakes he had. They'd kissed and they both knew they shouldn't have. For their own reasons. But they had. Because… Well, for a number of reasons. Including that the moment on the beach had been *magical*.

The sky had slowly been turning to night; stars had begun flickering down on them; waves had crashed at their feet; and Kade had looked every inch the prince he was. Tall and stately, that intensity shining through his eyes, aimed at her, as if she were the only thing he wanted to look at, to see. Anyone could have fallen for that.

Except it hadn't been anyone. It had been her. She was the reason she and May had to move away from the community who had welcomed them with open arms. She was the reason she no longer trusted that community to keep them safe. Someone had told that reporter where to find her. And though she didn't blame whoever it was, she simply couldn't believe that if she'd stayed, people would have protected her. That was on her more than it was them. And she felt as if she had lost something pivotal, something precious, because of it.

She had projected her frustration about it onto Kade, too. She had even used him as the reason May was so quiet. He'd forced them to come to the palace. But Amari had agreed to it. Amari was the reason May's life had been upended, and that was the real reason May was acting like this. She didn't do well with new things. It was something they were working on, as much as one could work on something like that with a four-year-old, but this was…this was too fast. It was throwing her into the deep end of a pool and expecting her to swim.

They had no choice though. Not any more. So Amari would jump in with May and hold her up until she learnt how to swim.

There was a knock on the door.

Amari glanced at May, who was clutching her favourite teddy and looking out of the window. Amari had succeeded in directing her interest to the boats they could see in the distance. May was currently trying to figure out what the boats were doing.

'Hi,' she said when she opened the door to Kade.

'Good morning.'

His voice was smooth and deep and she hated that it soothed something inside her. She hated that he looked as he had that night on the beach; princely and handsome and downright irresistible. She hated that, looking like that, he reminded her that kissing him wasn't as simple as saying she had been irresponsible. There had been more to it. Attraction and a pull she couldn't explain. She hadn't felt anything that strong before. Not even with Hank.

She hated it.

No, you don't.

And that was part of the problem.

'How did you sleep?' he asked, all concern. Really, it made her want to hit him.

Or kiss him.

'As well as expected,' she answered vaguely.

He narrowed his eyes. 'Why do I feel like that means not well at all?'

'Does it matter?'

'To me, very much so.'

She took a shaky breath. *You hate this, remember?* she told herself. She lied to herself.

'I didn't sleep.'

He stepped forward. 'Is there anything I can do?'

'No.' He was in her space, messing with her head with that scent of his. 'There's something I should do though.' She took a deliberate step back. 'Apologise. This situation isn't your fault. Well, not only.'

She gave him a small smile. A controlled smile. It would give her some power back. She would be able to pretend her emotions weren't shifting inside her, trying to get to him.

'I… I appreciate that.'

'You seem surprised.'

'No, no. It's not that. I just… Well, my mother said the same thing last night.'

Amari stared. 'I'm glad she and I will be starting off on the right foot, then.'

He smiled. 'I know you're being sarcastic, but the fact that you agree with her and said so without her prodding bodes well for your relationship.'

She snorted. 'I doubt you can call whatever will happen between your mother and me a relationship.'

He angled his head. 'Don't sound so sure.' Without pausing, he nodded towards May. 'How is she doing?'

Amari sighed. 'She's scared. It's a lot of new, and I...' She trailed off. She was about to say something corny, like she wished she hadn't put May in this situation. Like she should have been a better mother, and that was why she was taking responsibility for this situation. It had nothing to do with him. She settled for, 'I wish I had something to distract her with.'

'I might be able to help with that,' he said mischievously. 'May I?'

'She might not respond, but you're more than welcome to try.'

He walked into the room and sat down on the bed opposite the window seat. Amari thanked the heavens she'd been trained into making up a bed in the mornings. Something about him sitting there already felt intimate. She could only imagine what it would be like if he were sitting on an unmade bed, as if he'd spent the night there.

You need to stop this, she told herself, and tried to listen.

'May, do you remember...?' Amari hesitated. She was about to say Kade, but that felt wrong. Prince Kade sounded too formal, too. 'Do you remember Uncle Kade?' she asked with a grimace.

Kade glanced at her in confusion. She wrinkled her nose. Gave him a shrug. May turned towards them and prevented any further communication.

'The funny man,' May said without any preamble.

Amari walked closer with a smile. 'Yes.'

May nodded.

Kade took over. 'Remember how you gave us letters to send to Father Christmas last week?'

May eyed him suspiciously, but nodded.

'I think if you wrote another one, we could get it to him quicker from here.'

May frowned.

'You should come with me. You and your mom,' Kade added quickly, with a furtive glance her way, 'and see what I mean.'

May looked at Amari. Amari nodded and held out her hand, and after a long pause—during which May studied Kade suspiciously a while longer—she shimmied off the couch and went to Amari, taking her hand.

'Lead the way, Uncle Kade,' Amari said, a lightness she hadn't felt since they'd left Swell Valley dancing inside her chest at the look he gave her.

But he didn't protest, merely leading the way through the door into the gigantic hall. Amari picked up more of it now that she was less afraid, and perhaps because it was daylight, too. It looked a lot like a hotel with the pictures up in frames on the walls and small tables with fresh flowers at different intervals. There were more expensive things on the walls the deeper they got into the palace. Gold accents, expensive artworks, things Amari couldn't entirely wrap her brain around.

It was a bit of a relief when Kade stopped in front of a door. It was larger, stretching over her head. The wood looked ancient.

She lifted her brows. 'Are you taking us to a dungeon?'

He widened his eyes down at May, who looked up at him expectantly. 'No, of course not. Why would you say that?'

She laughed at the nerves. Kade's and her own. She was pretty sure he had taken them to a dungeon. 'It was an innocent question. May's read about dungeons in her fairy-tale books. She knows it's where they keep the princesses.'

She winked. Kade visibly relaxed, then lowered to his haunches. 'There aren't any princesses here,' he said seriously. 'But there is…well…would you like to see?'

May's grip on Amari's hand tightened, but she nodded. Amari tried not to let the little exchange do anything to her heart, and watched as Kade knocked on the door. Seconds later, it opened.

She wasn't sure who gasped louder: she or May.

The room was massive. There was the tallest Christmas tree she had ever seen in one corner. It went up to the roof, which had been covered in snowflakes. They were decorations, but she half expected to feel the ice prickle her skin. An ice slide took up most of the room, and since almost everything leading to the slide, as well as everything around it, was padded, she assumed it had been created with the safety of kids in mind. Near the tree was a table with blank paper and crayons. A man in an elf uniform stood just beyond it with a patient expression, as if his entire purpose in life were to play an elf. There was also an elf on the other side of the tree, which she now noticed had a great number of Christmas presents beneath it, and a few more elves near the start of the slide. Opposite the table was a fairly simple jungle gym, not at all Christmas decorated, though, by being in this Christmas-themed place, it seemed like a Christmas jungle gym.

Amari looked down at May and smiled at the look of awe.

Kade lowered to his haunches again. 'This is where we send our letters to Father Christmas. We write them over there—' he pointed at the table '—before giving them to that elf, who will help us with the address and make sure it's in an envelope. Then, we go over there—' he pointed to the slide '—with them, tuck them into our pockets, and slide down until we get there.' He pointed to the end of the slide.

She hadn't noticed before, but the end of the slide led to a small door with a slot in it.

'We pop the letters in there and trust that the elves on the other side send them to Father Christmas.'

As he said it, fingers in white gloves popped through the slot, wiggling, as if they were looking for something. May gasped and Amari bit down so she didn't laugh. It was simply joyful. It was *wonderful*.

'We write as many letters as we want, but we also use the slide even if we don't have letters.' He dropped his voice. 'We had to get special permission for that, but it was worth it. But don't tell the other Christmas postal stations.'

Christmas postal stations.

Whoever came up with it was brilliant.

'We had a jungle gym set up here in case any of the children didn't feel like using the slide. We don't force anyone to do something they don't want to in Daria,' he continued matter-of-factly. 'And we also have some hot-chocolate stations over there, marshmallows over there, and some Christmas biscuits over there. But first we have breakfast, of course.'

He straightened then, throwing Amari an apologetic look. 'I probably shouldn't have mentioned the hot chocolate before the breakfast part,' he said under his breath.

'Is it possible for that hot chocolate to be served with pancakes?' Amari asked.

'Yes.'

'How about some fruit with those pancakes?'

'That's exactly how the…um…the elves do it here.'

Amari's lips curved, but she kept the smile in. 'Well, then, it sounds like breakfast is all sorted here at the Christmas postal station. What do you say, May?'

May stayed silent for a while, then she looked at them both and gave them the biggest smile Amari had seen.

'Can we write a letter, Mama?' she asked.

Amari laughed. 'After breakfast, honey.'

With a disappointed sigh, May took Amari's hand and led her to the hot-chocolate station. They'd taken a few steps towards it when May turned around and asked Kade, 'Are you coming?'

After several blinks, Kade nodded. 'I would love to.'

'I'm sorry we didn't get to eat with your parents,' Amari said.

It was a while after breakfast, and the two of them had settled in to watch May take her second slide down. The child was having the time of her life. It was such a leap from how she had looked when they'd arrived or when Kade had seen her this morning. He felt no insignificant amount of pride that he'd helped put that smile on her face.

'We should make it in time for tea,' Kade replied.

'Oh?' Amari straightened in her seat. He'd had the adult-sized comfortable chairs brought in for them. Even he was feeling relaxed. 'I can't imagine they're thrilled I didn't make breakfast. Or that I pulled you away from it.'

'You didn't pull me away from anything,' he said. 'I chose to be here.'

Though in some ways, she was right. He was choosing her company rather than that of his parents, or his responsibilities. In the grand scheme of things, carving out a few hours in the morning for himself wouldn't hurt anyone. But he was already on thin ice. He should be out there doing damage control, or strategising, or preparing the press release he'd scheduled for later that day.

Instead, he was sitting in a comfortable chair next to Amari, enjoying the sound of her child's laughter.

'That's probably the truth,' she said quietly, 'but I think you might be choosing me as an excuse.'

He laughed lightly. 'You weren't going to be polite enough to not call me out on it, were you?'

She clucked her tongue. 'When have you ever known me to be polite, Kade?'

'It should be annoying.'

'But it's not.'

'No.'

They smiled at one another. It was a simple smile—until it wasn't. Until it became more. Until it became a bond, a symbol of that pull between them. It flared with attraction, spun with heat, and soon they weren't smiling any more, just staring at one another.

Kade didn't know what was happening in Amari's head, but he was thinking about their kiss. The sweet taste of her lips, the slick heat of her tongue, the gentle curve of her waist. It had tortured him that night, the memory of their kiss. Not because he was thinking about how he shouldn't have done it, but because he was thinking about how much he wanted to do it again. This time, he didn't want to be stopped. He didn't want to stop at all. He wanted to feel the curve of her breasts, her thighs. He wanted her heat, her sighs, her moans until neither of them could breathe.

Amari looked away first, cursing as she did.

'You can't do that,' she said, her voice barely above a whisper.

'What?' His voice was no better.

'You know what I'm talking about.' The words were harsh. 'You can't look at me like you want me in your bed. That's what got us in this situation in the first place.'

'I thought you were taking responsibility for this situation.'

'I am.' She gave him a look. 'I didn't say I don't want to be in that bed. I do. And that's the problem.'

Kade opened his mouth, but found that he didn't have anything to say to that. Largely because she had caused a meltdown in his brain with the image of her in his bed. He hadn't allowed himself to indulge in that fantasy, and knowing she wanted to be there was…a lot to process.

She shook her head. 'There's no future for this. It's best I don't end up there.'

'Why?' he asked.

It was a stupid question. He knew why there was no future. He was about to be King. He had enough on his plate with that, and he wasn't even factoring his mother into the equation. He wanted to make her proud. He wanted her to feel at peace with him being King. He had a plan to get her there, but that plan would mean nothing if he was distracted by a woman.

Yet here he was, distracted by a woman.

'You don't need an answer to that,' Amari said, infinitely wiser than he was. 'But I'm going to answer you anyway. Beyond the fact that you're about to be King, your mother is ill. You probably want to be there for her as much as you can. How will that be possible with me in the mix?'

'My mother has the best healthcare in the world,' he surprised himself by answering. 'I can't do much for her beyond support her and try to make her proud. The former she knows she has. Unwaveringly.'

When he didn't continue, she said, 'And the latter?'

'I've told you my struggles, Amari,' he replied after a moment. 'Our situation hasn't done anything to soothe her fears when it comes to me and ruling this kingdom. I can't imagine the abdication will be easy on her in general, but with this, with me, it must be particularly hard.'

She stayed silent for a while. 'You told me she hasn't said anything about it. About your struggles, I mean. Is that true?'

'She's mentioned it.'

'That she's disappointed in you?'

'That she would like me to try harder.'

'And you've been interpreting that as her disappointment?'

'How else would you interpret it?'

'Well, if I was telling May that, it would probably be

because I see her potential, and I think she's not living up to it.'

'How is that different from disappointment?'

'It's called raising a child, Kade. It's called support. It's knowing that, perhaps, they're not doing what you know they can do and trying to guide them into doing what you know they can do.'

'I…she's… She's not…'

'But how do you know that?' she pressed. 'You've never asked her. You've assumed.'

'I know what I'm—'

'You never truly know what the other person is thinking unless you talk to them,' she interrupted, and something about how she said it made him think she wasn't only talking about him.

It was fair. He could hardly argue with that. It was completely reasonable for him to ask his mother about what she thought about him and his abilities. He had never thought about it before. Now that he did… Well, he wasn't sure he wanted to know the answer.

Would it be easier if she told him she was disappointed in him rather than him assuming it? And what if she didn't say she was disappointed in him? What if…what if she thought he wasn't living up to his potential, as Amari said? Maybe part of living up to that potential meant asking his mother for guidance. Maybe she was waiting for him to acknowledge that he couldn't rule alone. That he needed help.

'I can't believe the children of the palace get to come here every Christmas,' Amari mused out loud.

'They don't,' he replied distractedly, still thinking about whether she was right.

'What do you mean?'

'I had this done when I knew you were coming. It's not a standard thing.'

'You mean…you mean you did this for May?'

Something in her voice had him focusing on her again. 'Yes.'

'All this…for her?'

He was more hesitant this time. 'Yes.'

'Kade…it's…this is…wow.'

'That doesn't sound like a good wow.'

'I'm still trying to figure out whether it is a good wow.' She exhaled shakily.

'Should I apologise?'

'I… I don't know.'

He waited for more.

'I feel like I should be upset with you for this, but I can hardly blame you for this extravagance. I mean, look at your home. It's beautiful and expensive and grand. Of course you're going to make this Christmas postal station as beautiful and expensive and grand as the rest of your home.'

He still didn't say anything.

'But…this is a lot. I'm not saying it's bad. Clearly not.' She gestured to May, laughing as they pushed her down the slide once more. 'But maybe…maybe May shouldn't be the only one enjoying this. Maybe you should let your staff bring their children here, too. Maybe it wouldn't seem so extravagant if it wasn't only for May.'

He almost spoke then, to say that it *was* only for May. He had only been thinking of May's smile, which he had really only seen twice in his life, and yet it seemed quite important to him. Well—fine, he hadn't only been thinking of May. He had been thinking of Amari, too. He had been thinking about seeing her smile. About making her daughter happy so she could be happy, too.

But this was the kind of person she was. She had done the same thing when she'd suggested the royal family offer gifts to their people instead of the people offering them gifts. She thought about how others could benefit. Especially those who weren't in positions of power.

He took a steadying breath. 'You're right. I'll have Matilda inform the staff.'

She sat back with a nod of approval. Then she sighed. 'This life is very different from mine, isn't it?'

He looked up and saw Matilda gesture to him from the door.

'I suspect it is.' He paused. 'And we'll have confirmation of it soon. It's time for tea with my parents.'

CHAPTER ELEVEN

AMARI HAD NEVER met a queen before. She had never thought it an experience she'd want until now, when she was actually meeting a queen and she had no idea what she was doing.

Matilda had told her to curtsy, had shown her how, but Amari still felt as if she'd messed up. Although based on what Kade told her, it was highly possible that Queen Winifred's expression of faint disapproval was one she carried with her wherever she went.

If Amari *had* met a queen before, maybe she would have known that with more certainty. Then again, she had no desire to feel inept twice. So perhaps meeting one, if slightly disapproving, queen was enough.

Kade's father was much more relaxed. Or perhaps she merely felt relaxed with him because Deacon was so much like Kade. That wasn't a good admission, since she shouldn't have felt relaxed with Kade either. He was a prince. He built Christmas stations for her kid. He made sure her store was taken care of and they were safe even though he didn't have to.

He was kind and attractive and insecure mixed with the deepest sincerity and she should not have felt relaxed with him.

Still, she sought his eyes when she sat down. Looked for

his reassurance. When she got it, her heart stopped beating so erratically.

This is not good, a voice in her head whispered.

No, duh, she whispered back, and tried to focus.

'Amari, Kade tells me you have a daughter.'

'Yes, Your Majesty.'

'Oh, please.' Winifred waved her hand. 'Call me ma'am.'

'Mother,' Kade chided, but Amari laughed.

'Ma'am it is.' They shared a smile. Amari had not expected that. She cleared her throat. 'I do have a daughter. She's four years old and the love of my life.'

'Kade seems quite fond of her, too.'

'Mother.'

This time it was a warning. Winifred merely lifted an eyebrow, but she didn't say any more.

'I'd be happy for you to meet her,' Amari said. 'She's at the Christmas station. Kade assures me she's safe, though I am currently resisting the urge to check on her.'

'You can check on her,' Kade said gently.

She offered him a smile. 'She'll be okay. I know she'll be okay. It's just… It's part of being a parent.'

Amari didn't miss the look Winfred and Deacon exchanged. She didn't know what it meant. Or maybe she did, but she didn't want to think about it.

'Tell me about your life in Swell Valley.'

This from Deacon. He looked sincere, and she told him, but she felt uncertain the entire time. It was like meeting the parents of a boyfriend. The parents who apparently didn't like her. Or tolerated her, because she was dating their only son and they had no choice but to support his decision even though they didn't particularly like her. The worst part about it was that she wasn't dating their son. He wasn't her boyfriend, except how were they to know that? The only thing they knew about her for sure was that she'd kissed their son and turned the news of his impending rule into a dating show.

Oh. Yeah. She wouldn't like her either.

'My store is essentially a trinket store,' she continued nervously. 'I source my inventory locally, which involves the community and really garners support from them. It's… um…it's great.'

Yeah, it sounds great.

'It's really quite magnificent,' Kade said. 'The community love her because she supports them. She gets quite a lot of traffic from out-of-town visitors since she's on the edge of town, so both locals and foreigners support her.'

'Oh, I—'

'You're being modest,' he interrupted. 'And while that's a fine quality, you should brag here.'

'Kade,' she said, shifting a little. 'Thank you, but you're making it sound more important than it is.'

'I am not,' he said, rearing back as if she insulted him. 'My parents, out of everyone, understand the value of making the community feel as though they're a part of something.'

There was a beat where no one spoke. It was fine that Amari didn't, but she suspected Kade wanted his parents to jump in and agree with him. Their silence didn't seem like a slight to her, though she was sure it probably was. It felt like a slight to Kade, who was doing his best to make her comfortable and his parents weren't exactly playing along.

'Thank you.' She spoke directly to Kade. 'I believe you, and I'm saying thank you.'

His eyes twinkled back at her. He was saying *thank you*, too, because she was seeing him in a way his parents didn't. Or she was validating him in a way his parents didn't.

Well, he had done the same for her. She had never looked at her store in the way he'd described. Sure, on some level she knew that including local products was something special. But it had made her a part of the community in a way she hadn't expected. She was quite proud of that, even if she hadn't acknowledged it before. Hearing him say it allowed her to say that it was…significant.

'Well, it sounds like you're doing quite well, Amari,' Winifred said, her tone no less cool and distant. But there was something more there. She couldn't put her finger on it, but it was there. 'Which really begs the question as to why you would risk it all by kissing my son.'

Amari sucked in her breath even as Kade snapped a reproach at his mother. But Winifred paid him no mind. Her sharp eyes were on Amari.

She remembered that Kade had said his mother had told him Amari played a part in this, too. It seemed like a strange time to remember it until she realised her brain was trying to tell her something. Seconds later, it clicked.

'You're wondering if I kissed him because he's a prince.'

'Yes.'

'Amari, you don't have to do this.'

'I know,' she told Kade, but she didn't look away from Winifred. 'I didn't believe he was a prince, ma'am. I thought he was in trouble and telling me a story about being a prince so I wouldn't ask questions.'

She debated how honest she wanted to be. Thought about how worried she was about May all the time. If Kade were her son, she'd be worried about her intentions, too. So she went with the entire truth.

'There was a time I was in trouble, too. I was a young mother, abandoned by her husband, with no support system, and I despised the idea of anyone asking me questions. So I didn't ask Kade questions, though he was perfectly upfront about who he really was.'

'You didn't do an Internet search?'

'It felt like a violation,' she replied. 'He told me to, and yet it still felt like a violation. Again, this is likely because of my own experiences.'

The next part would be harder. She took a breath.

'If someone had looked into me in that way, I'm not sure what they would have found. But even the idea of it terrified me. I had irrational fears that it would somehow lead my husband, who'd left May and me, to us. I was afraid he would want us back or that he'd try to take May away.' She avoided Kade's eyes. 'I thought I was affording Kade a privacy and freedom from those fears I would have loved when I was that terrified.' She paused. 'And on top of all this, doing an Internet search felt like an admission that I believed him. It was too ridiculous to even consider.'

She tried to end it on a lighter note, but she didn't think she achieved it.

No one interrupted her, not even to ask a question. She had a rapt audience; she had to continue whether she wanted to or not. But she could make it concise, so she jumped right to the point.

'I wasn't thinking about Kade as a prince when I kissed him, ma'am. I was thinking about him as a man. He's... um... Well, he's an impressive man.' Her face heated, but she continued. 'I was attracted to him, and after a glass of wine there seemed to be fewer reasons to resist that attraction.' She met Kade's eyes. 'He and I both know it was a mistake.' When something flickered in his eyes, she looked back to his mother. 'But making mistakes is human. We handle them. Learn from them. Try to do better.' She exhaled.

The silence this time didn't seem as intimidating as before. Still, it didn't make her feel comfortable. She took her tea, cool now, and drank as much of it as she could. It wasn't polite, she didn't think. She might have even broken a few royal protocols. But she had exposed her soul to royalty and it made her thirsty.

'Seems you have your answer, Mother,' Kade said eventually. 'Any other questions you'd like to ask Amari that you could easily get answers from me for?'

Winifred's expression went from pensive to sharp. 'Don't sass me, son.'

Kade narrowed his eyes. 'I would respectfully request you offer me and Amari the same courtesy.'

She shouldn't have been amused, but she was. Royals even *argued* politely. When things had eventually got bad enough between her and her mother—and her and Hank, for that matter—there wasn't much politeness.

It was new, sitting there, watching them be formal, but something about what she had said, and the fact that she had said it, made her less uncomfortable. When Winifred sat back and asked her about her bestselling product, she answered as she would have with anyone else.

It wasn't right that he found Amari more attractive because of how expertly she handled his mother during tea. The best part was that she wasn't handling his mother at all. She was being honest, treating his mother as she would any other person, and something about it had earned his mother's respect. He saw it the moment his mother looked at him after Amari spoke.

It made him want to kiss Amari until neither of them could speak. Which was a foolish wish, yet he was still devising a plan to make it happen.

He didn't stop to think about the ethics of it. Or he did, but he told himself it would be fine. They were both adults, and it would only be a kiss. And nothing would happen if Amari didn't want it to.

He hoped it wouldn't come to that.

'Aren't there other things for you to do with your time than escort me back and forth?' she asked when she opened her door.

'Yes,' he agreed. 'And I've done them. I have this afternoon to myself.'

She looked over her shoulder, then slipped through the door, closing it behind her. 'We do, too. It was an exhausting day of sliding for May, and she was so testy at my suggestion for a nap. And now she's out like a light.'

'Did I wake her with my knock?'

'What do you think out like a light means?'

He smiled. He hadn't planned this. In fact, he intended on taking May with them. He wasn't proud of it, but he was going to distract her by showing her the swing his parents had put in for him when he was a child. It was magnificent, and had kept him busy for hours. He had already put one of the elves on standby to supervise. And he only needed minutes to steal a kiss.

But this was easier. And less weird, he supposed.

'Why…um…why did you knock?'

'I was wondering if you'd like to take a walk in the garden.'

'Oh.' Genuine surprise. 'Oh. Um… I shouldn't leave May alone.'

'I can have someone come up and stand outside the door. If she wakes up, they'll call me and we'll have you back in a matter of minutes.'

'That's ridiculous. I can't have someone guard the door as if…' She trailed off.

'As if you're in a palace? As if you're royalty? As if we have countless people whose job it is to guard something precious?'

She narrowed her eyes. 'Your snarkiness doesn't mean I'm going to say yes.'

'Maybe not. But it should.'

He grinned. She bit her lower lip, rolled her eyes and said, 'Fine. Do I look okay to go out like this? I feel like I need to watch everything I wear. What if someone sees us and thinks you're hanging out with the help? There's nothing wrong with that, of course,' she added hastily, 'but I can't imagine it'll make things easier for you. First you kiss a shopkeeper who happens to be a divorced single mother, then you stroll in the garden with the help.'

Divorced.

He set the information aside, just as he had when she'd mentioned during tea with his parents that her husband had left her. There was a stack of information about her and her past on the desk in his office, but somehow it felt like a betrayal to look at it. He wanted to know about her past, about her, from *her*. He wanted to get to know her as anyone else would.

'For one, no one will see us. The garden is entirely secure. And second...'

He let his eyes lower, taking her in. It wasn't what she meant when she asked if she looked okay, but he couldn't resist the opportunity. She wore a plain white cotton dress with big brown buttons down the middle. It had capped shoulders, lowering into a respectable V at her chest. The brown of her skin was complemented by the gold necklaces she wore. Three layers: one that hugged her neck, the second lying slightly lower, with the third scooping until the edge of the material of her dress. Her shoes were gold, too, matching the necklace, and her earrings were bright orange mixed with gold, dangling midway down her neck.

It was all very simple, including the curls she had tied up to the top of her head. It created the most alluring picture. Simple and alluring were excellent descriptions of her.

When he met her eyes again, saw the blush at her cheeks, he smiled. 'You look beautiful.'

'You took so long to come up with "beautiful"?' she grumbled, but she pushed a curl behind her ear.

'I have other words, but I'm almost certain you wouldn't want to hear them.'

She muttered something that sounded suspiciously like 'too late', but she was talking after that and he didn't get the chance to ask.

'If you wouldn't mind calling someone you trust to guard the door, I'd appreciate that.'

He did so immediately, and they waited in silence until Matilda came striding towards them.

'Oh, I didn't mean Matilda,' Amari said when she saw the woman.

'You asked for someone I trust.'

'Yes, but I'm sure she has a million things to do.' Amari smiled when Matilda stopped in front of them, no sign of the frustration she'd spoken to him with anywhere. 'Matilda. I'm sorry Kade called you away for this.'

'I work for him,' Matilda said briskly. 'Whatever he needs me to do, I'll do.'

Amari's smile wavered. Kade smiled. 'Thanks, Matilda. We'll be back in less than an hour.'

Amari barely waited until they were around the corner before she hissed, 'An hour? You expect that woman to stand there for an hour?'

'She'll have a table set up within minutes. She's efficient like that.'

'Yeah?'

'Yes.'

'I mean... I guess it's okay if she's productive.' There was a pause. 'But I'm sure having her babysit my child isn't going to make her like me any more.'

'She likes you.'

'She does *not* like me.'

'She's like that with everyone.'

'Not you.'

'I'm her boss.'

'So she said.'

He chuckled. 'You really aren't used to people being curt with you, are you? You prefer being the curt one.'

She angled a look at him. 'I just…' She lingered on that, before rushing into, 'I don't want her to take out her annoyance with me on May.'

Her triumph made him smirk. 'She wouldn't.'

'Good. Then I don't care what she does otherwise.'

When he chuckled again, she glared. He held up his hands, stopped laughing, but didn't bother to hide his smile. They didn't speak much as he led the way to the garden. The few times they did speak, Amari would ask about something on the walls or comment about a piece of art.

'Most of these things were here long before me,' he said, nodding to the guards at the door. 'But when I was young, my father would take me down each passage and tell me about the art.'

'That must have taken a while.'

'It did. But they were some of my favourite memories of growing up.'

'Hmm.' A few seconds later, Amari gasped. 'You've decorated.'

'I was wondering when you'd notice.'

She ran a hand along the garlands that hung from the outside stairs banisters, gently touched the baubles that decorated the wreaths. When they got to the bottom of the staircase, she looked up at the palace, her eyes widening at the lights. They wouldn't go on until later, and he planned to bring both her and May out for that. But even off, they were spectacular. Something about the sheer number.

He liked the Christmas trees that flanked the entrance, too, and the wreath that hung against the usually formal wooden door. Christmas wasn't big in his family. They were usually punctuated by more events, more responsibilities. It meant that he didn't care much about the holiday. Except for this. The decorations, the way his family home looked like something from Father Christmas himself. He particularly loved seeing people's expressions when they saw the decorations. Amari was no different.

Except she was different. He had stopped denying that the moment he'd witnessed her with his parents. It didn't have to mean more than that, he told himself repeatedly, but acknowledging it made it…easier, somehow. Perhaps because it meant he didn't have to concentrate so hard on not thinking about how much she meant to him.

The look on her face now, for example, was much better than the look he'd seen on anyone else's faces when they saw the lights. He couldn't wait to show her the dining hall, once they eventually managed a meal with his parents. Now that his parents had got their questions in—he wanted to speak with them about that, but his mother had been resting after tea, his father out, and he had his own work to do—a meal shouldn't be as contentious as it had been with Amari before.

He was almost looking forward to it.

'When May sees this, she's going to go out of her mind.'

'She likes Christmas, it seems.'

'Loves it,' Amari corrected, still staring up at the palace. 'I don't know what I did to encourage her, since, as you know, I'm a miserable person most days. But somehow, she's managed to drum up a level of excitement for Christmas that I've only seen in children her age.'

'You're doing a good job, then.'

She frowned. 'Why would you say that?'

'Well, if she's excited for Christmas, it means you've allowed her to be. She doesn't have to worry about other things. Money, perhaps. Or whether her parents will be around for Christmas.' He lifted a shoulder. 'I didn't particularly care about Christmas because it came with responsibilities. Engagements.'

'And I didn't care because I was worried about money.

And whether my mother would come home for Christmas.' She slanted a look at him. 'If I didn't know any better, I swear you've dug up some information about me.'

'It's not likely I would know information like that, is it?' He neatly skipped over the insinuation. 'I've inferred it. From the little you have said about your mother.'

'Your powers of inference are quite extraordinary.' She was quiet for a few seconds. 'Christmas wasn't a thing when I grew up. My mother wasn't home a lot. When she was, she was always talking about her relationships. It wasn't bad. I had what I needed. For the most part,' she said as an afterthought.

'It doesn't sound like you were afforded the opportunity to be a child.'

'No,' she agreed sadly. 'I was a burden, and I tried not to be.' She exhaled. 'But I've spent too much time resenting my mother for it. I can't change what happened. I can't change her.'

He offered her his arm. After a brief moment of hesitation, she took it. 'Mothers aren't easy, are they?'

She let out a little laugh. 'As someone who has one, and who is one, I think the only answer to that is no, they aren't.' She paused. 'Yours seems a tad challenging, too.'

He snorted. 'She's impossible. I adore her.'

'That much is clear.'

'I am sorry for the way she treated you at tea today.'

'Don't be. I understood. I would do the same thing for my child.'

'You'd try to ascertain someone's intentions towards May?'

'Absolutely.' She squeezed his arm. 'Besides, it's not only you she has to protect. It's the crown, too. I can't imagine how much that must take from her.'

'Too much,' he said. They arrived at the garden, and Kade was saved from spilling out his concerns, his worries. He would have. Told her things he hadn't told anyone before. He shook it off. 'Here we are.'

'What...?' she breathed, but didn't say much else.

Exactly as he intended.

Green stretched as far as the property went, with a large pond that held different-coloured water lilies in the middle. Trees rose up at various heights around the pond, wildflowers of pink and purple bunched at the bottom. A bridge took them over the pond, which was decorated with garlands and lights, too. Though the sky was only just going dark, he'd had the lights turned on for effect. Amari's face told him it had been the right decision.

'This is your backyard?' she asked, voice filled with awe.

'It's one of the official gardens of the kingdom. We open it to the public on certain days of the year. That's why there was such a convoluted journey to get here. We don't want anyone having easy access to the palace.'

'It's amazing.' She went to the edge of the bridge. 'How sturdy is this?'

'Perfectly. It's in use.'

'May I?'

He nodded and she took a step on the bridge. Tentatively, he noted, despite what he'd said. He didn't take offence. This was her personality. She took each step forward carefully. Now that he knew a bit more about her, he understood she was doing it to protect herself. And her child.

He didn't want to keep her from that. He understood the value of protection. He had been protected his entire life, though he'd grown up in the public. There was a force behind his protection. His family, regardless of whether they approved or disapproved of his actions. The communications team, who made sure he was as prepared as he could be when stories went out. There were so many more forms of protection that he hadn't realised.

Amari only had herself.

She had only had herself, for the longest time. And though he wanted to protect her, he wasn't a part of her life. Not in the way that would allow for that to happen. Sure, he was protecting her now, but that was temporary. As soon as things blew over, she would go back home and he would be here, ruling a kingdom.

Suddenly, his plan to kiss her seemed like the stupidest thing.

'Maybe we should head back to the palace,' he said as he followed her. They were almost at the end of the bridge and the moment they got there, she would discover his idiocy.

'Do we have to? I'd love to see what's on the other side.'

'Well, we should probably get ready for dinner,' he hedged. 'Perhaps we should go back and see if May and Matilda are fine.'

She gave him a strange look. 'Are *you* fine?'

'Yes. Yes, of course.'

'I only ask because dinner's in an hour. I checked when I took May up for a nap. And unless they called you, which I don't think they did, since you still sound relatively calm—'

She broke off when she got to the end of the bridge.

He barely resisted his sigh.

CHAPTER TWELVE

AMARI KNEW IT was magical. She would be a fool not to see it. They were at a palace at Christmas. At almost every direction, she was reminded that royalty did Christmas differently from what she'd grown accustomed to. The magnitude of the decorations, the number of lights, the height of the Christmas trees. The slides, the elves, the letters to Father Christmas.

There was also the fact that she felt as if she had been placed in a fairy tale. The palace was what she expected to find in those fairy tales. The garden looked as if it had been designed with royalty in mind. And the prince... Well, the prince was every bit as delicious as she imagined those animated princes would be if they were real.

And then there was this.

There was a pathway from where she stood down until she couldn't see any more. Greenery exploded around them; flowers and leaves reached through wooden arches above them. It seemed as if those arches had been built to keep nature from collapsing on them, and it was beautiful. On either side of the path at regular intervals were wooden benches. Some held gold plaques on them, others had engravings directly on the wood.

If there weren't a small table right in front of them with a bottle of champagne chilling, she would have asked Kade about those plaques and engravings. But there was a bottle of champagne chilling. And there was music playing softly through hidden speakers.

She turned to him. 'Did you do this for me?'

He sighed. 'Would you believe me if I said no?'

'Yes, actually. Your reaction doesn't seem like someone who's done this.'

'You're right. I did do this.' He stared at the table as if it had challenged him to a duel. When he looked at her, his expression was tight. 'I wanted to seduce you into kissing me.'

Her heart hammered against her chest. It had been beating faster from the moment she'd reached the end of the bridge, but this couldn't simply be described as 'beating faster'.

She took an unsteady breath. 'You've...changed your mind?'

'Logic has returned to my mind,' he corrected. He took the champagne from the bucket and poured them both a glass. She took the one he offered, but only held it as he downed his.

'I don't know what I was thinking,' he admitted. 'Kissing you...would complicate matters even more. We haven't spoken about the last time we kissed, and I have no idea what you think about it. All I know is that it upended your life. And then I go do this.' He gestured wildly. 'As if I didn't know that. As if I don't understand that you need to protect yourself and your daughter. As if I didn't want to help protect you.'

'Kade—'

'You deserve more than this life,' he interrupted. 'You deserve your freedom. You deserve—'

'Is that mistletoe?' she asked, when the wind rustled the leaves and something fell to the ground.

Kade let out another sigh. 'Yes.'

'You were planning on seducing me with champagne and mistletoe?'

'Yes.'

She was oddly impressed. 'It's on the floor now though.'

'I can see that,' he answered, his expression pained.

She let it sit for a second, then asked, 'Why? What happened that made you want to seduce me with champagne and mistletoe?'

'You went head to head with my mother.'

'And that…made you want to kiss me?' She grimaced. 'I understand that we both have issues with our mothers, Kade, but I'll be honest with you—that particular one isn't something I'd like to engage with.'

He gave a quiet laugh. 'No, although that's disgusting and I'm offended you'd say it. No, I meant… You were fierce and strong and honest when you spoke with her. I've seen many other people who've chosen to sacrifice those characteristics with her.'

'Well, she *is* a queen. Perhaps I was foolish for being myself.'

'You could never be foolish for being yourself,' he chided gently. 'And she respects you now because of it.'

'Yeah…well… I suppose…that's fine.'

She put her free hand on her hip, because she had no idea what to do with it. He was flustering her with his compliments. With this entire scene. Yes, there were the champagne and the mistletoe and the garden and the fact that he'd orchestrated the romance and the magic. But it was also his sincerity, the way he looked at her as if he were truly proud of her for being her grumpy old self. It was the way he made her body tingle by simply looking at her. And the way she knew he could make that tingle turn into smoke and fire when he kissed her.

'It's a bad idea,' she said, and not for the first time when it came to him. 'To kiss you. It's a bad idea.'

'But you're looking at me like that,' he said, his voice deepening as he took in the change on her face.

'And I put down my glass. I'm coming closer.'

'You are.'

'It's the mistletoe,' she said, stopping in front of him. 'We don't generally do the mistletoe thing where I'm from, but it doesn't seem like a good thing to ignore. What if I become cursed?'

'It's a possibility.'

'Hmm.'

She ran a finger over his forehead, down his cheek. She brushed his lips with her thumb, feeling the soft heat of his breath when his lips parted. She touched his neck, the veins that ran there. She pressed her hands lightly to his chest, scraping her nails over his nipples. Her fingers pressed against the ridge of his abs, before hooking into the front of his trousers.

'You feel good,' she whispered.

He smiled. 'There's more to feel.'

She laughed. 'I'm sure there is. How about we just start here though?'

She leaned in until she was inches from his lips.

'I'm happy with that,' he replied, and closed the gap.

The first time he'd kissed her, she had been distracted by the sensations. They had been overwhelming. The taste of him mixed with the wine she'd drunk. The feel of the muscles hard against her body. The heat of his mouth, the expertise of his tongue. All of it had been too much at one time and she'd felt as if she had been sinking beneath the ocean beside them, clinging to him as though he were the only source of air.

This was different. Oh, the sensations were still there. He tasted like champagne now, and of him. Seduction on a Sunday morning. Touches beneath the covers before they were fully awake. He felt warm and hard. A body that could pick her up and toss her over his shoulder. Or press her against a wall and have his way with her without losing a breath. His tongue still tortured her. It slipped over hers, coaxing her to open her mouth wider, to allow him deeper.

Desire flooded her body, touched her breasts, hardened her nipples. It caressed her skin, making every hair stand on end. It teased between her thighs, urging her to press into him, to allow him to soothe and torment at the same time.

But still, it was different.

Perhaps because she felt more present now. The taste, the feeling of him, of her desire, of his, were all there, as if at the tips of her fingers. Power mingled with lust as she tested her presence of mind. As she pulled her mouth from his to press a kiss to his neck, to open her mouth and taste his skin. She grabbed hold of his shirt, tugging until it came free of his trousers, and let her hands feel the heat of his body. She smiled at the tremble, the curse when she brushed her thumbs over his nipples. And she kissed him again as she undid the buttons of his shirt, as she moaned her approval when he helped her.

'Let me see you,' she whispered against his mouth, and with a moan of his own, he stepped back.

She pursed her lips as she took him in. The brown skin that covered muscle, that contained his strength. She didn't care much about a man's body. She thought about it much as she thought of hers. If it allowed her the life she wanted to live, she was pleased with it. But she couldn't deny that this was…enjoyable.

'You look like a prince,' she told him. 'One from a book that couldn't possibly exist.'

'I'm not sure that was a compliment, but I'll say thank you nevertheless.'

'You're such a gentleman.'

'No, I'm not.'

He proved the words by closing the distance between them and picking her up. Her legs automatically went around his waist, then adjusted when he lowered them to one of the benches.

'The garden isn't open to the public today, is it?'

'Of course not,' he told her. 'Do you think I would allow this if there was a chance someone else would see us? I've taken precautions.'

'That's an odd way to phrase it, considering I only plan on kissing you this evening.'

'Oh, no, I didn't mean—' He broke off when she started laughing. 'You'll pay for that.'

'Really? How do you…?'

She trailed off when he kissed her neck.

'I know you meant that as a punishment,' she said, angling to give him better access, 'but it's really not as bad as you think.'

'Stop talking,' he said now, and kissed her.

She fell into it. Into the intimacy of having his tongue tangle with hers. Into the familiarity of it despite that they'd only kissed once before. His hands dug into the flesh at her hips, gripping the fullness, before they moved. She felt the trail along her skin though he didn't have access to it because of her dress. She could only imagine what it would be like if he did have access to her skin. She might have become that trail; a mere path for the pleasure of Kade's hands. She was strangely okay with that.

Slowly, he touched her breasts, testing the fullness of them in his palms. She arched almost without realising. When she did realise, she couldn't bring herself to be upset by it. Here, in the magical garden, she had no shame about her body feeling good. Here, in the magical garden, it was only her and Kade.

She chose to ignore when her mind pointed out that they wouldn't stay in the garden for ever. Instead, she merely focused on his touch.

It was the easiest thing to do.

* * *

Something had changed.

It wasn't that they'd made out in the garden he'd spent his childhood running around. Because obviously, that had changed things. Not only between them, but inside him. He couldn't describe how different he felt now that he'd kissed her for more than a few minutes. He didn't know what it meant that the feel of her body in his hands, the taste of her skin against his tongue, felt revelatory.

None of that even touched on how it changed things *between* them. They'd shared private smiles and quiet laughs as they'd righted their clothing after. They'd held hands on their way back to the palace. Amari had insisted on going back to her room alone, which he thought was for the best. She had to focus on May once she got there, and that should be her priority. She didn't need him distracting her with stolen kisses on their way. He didn't want to distract her by pushing her into one of the many dark corners of his home and kissing her all over again.

Yes, it was best that she go to her room by herself.

But now the changes were settling around him in a much less pleasant way. His plan to deal with what had happened in Swell Valley was simple. He'd written a letter to the press explaining that he had taken a short break from duties after a busy year. Because of that short length, they hadn't thought it would be necessary to announce it, as he would be back before any Christmas engagements. While he was there, he'd met a woman he liked and happened to share a kiss with. At this time, he would prefer not to delve into any more than that, especially as the incident had already been a breach of privacy and caused upheaval in both his and the woman's life. He appreciated any respect afforded to this request.

The royal communications team had approved the letter, as had his mother, and though, technically, nothing in the letter was incorrect, it felt disingenuous. Amari wasn't simply 'a woman he liked'. He cared about her. Deeply. That kiss had been a culmination of that. Their kisses today had been an expression of more than attraction. At least for him.

He wanted her at his side when they made the announcement about him being King. His mother wanted to postpone it until after Christmas. She felt that the incident with Amari would cast doubt over his abilities to rule. He didn't agree. At first, he'd thought it was because announcing it now would distract from people's interest in his private life. That would mean Amari could go home, live her life, and move on. Now he wondered if all along it was because he wanted her support. She was the only person he could speak honestly to. He hadn't realised how much he needed that until now.

But that posed another concern. Was he confusing the fact that she was the first person he could talk to with feelings for her? It was feasible. Especially if he threw in the attraction he felt for her. But perhaps that was what relationships were. Feeling a connection with someone he was attracted to. Heaven knew it hadn't ever happened to him before. So maybe he was—

That was what relationships were.

It was a huge step to go from making out with someone to being in a relationship with them. He didn't have to jump to that. He didn't have to have it all figured out.

And that might have been true if he weren't about to become King.

If he were a normal person with normal responsibilities, figuring out whether he wanted to have a relationship with someone would be far simpler. But he wasn't. He'd kissed someone and it had made the front page of every newspaper in the kingdom. How could he explore his feelings, his relationship, in that? Especially when the news that he would be King would intensify the scrutiny he was under?

All of it swirled in his head as he went to dinner that evening. He tried to shake it off, but the looks Amari kept shooting him told him he wasn't quite succeeding. But she didn't get a chance to call him out on it. May had joined them for dinner, and apparently her time in the Christmas station had made the newness of the palace easier to digest. While she wasn't overly chatty—he doubted she was the kind of child who would be—she did say enough to make both Winifred and Deacon laugh in fondness.

He had never thought about his parents' desires for grandchildren. They'd never expressed it, nor had they ever said anything about wanting him to marry. He couldn't believe he hadn't realised that until now. *How* hadn't he realised it until now? He considered his mother's disappointment in him from every angle except this one. Surely she must have wanted him to marry? To have children and continue the line of succession?

But she hadn't said a word about it. And he…he hadn't even thought that she might want him to. Now that he did, he thought she might want him to marry the right person. Someone who could help him rule. Someone who knew the realities of royal life and could raise a child to be aware of those realities, too.

It was another reason Amari wouldn't be right for him. For the family. She hadn't even known he or his kingdom existed before he'd arrived in Swell Valley. She didn't understand royalty and its responsibilities. She was a divorced single mother. Her child was not his child. If he pursued a relationship with her, he couldn't imagine his mother approving of any of these facts. He couldn't imagine the public approving any of these facts.

Did he care?

He wanted to be brave and say no. But he had failed

too many times in the past to make such a naïve assertion. Things were becoming way too real with Amari. He was falling for her. He'd caught himself before he was too far gone, but that was over now.

He needed boundaries. And he would have to set them up.

CHAPTER THIRTEEN

AMARI DIDN'T GIVE men a chance to blow hot and cold. She didn't give men a chance at all. She had kept her focus on raising May and running her store ever since things had broken up between her and Hank. No man had interfered with that focus until Kade. And now, he seemed to be the kind of man who blew hot and cold.

He hadn't shown up at her door to guide her down to breakfast that morning. Matilda had. But the woman didn't join her for breakfast, nor did Kade, so she ended up eating with her daughter and the King and Queen of the Kingdom of Daria.

It wasn't awkward, thankfully. Things had settled between tea and dinner the night before. They had settled even more so at the dinner itself. That was the nice thing about being a parent. Rarely did anyone feel so bent out of shape about something that they ignored a kid. Throw in a cute kid—and May was the cutest—and tension barely existed at all.

Kade seemed to be immune to the May effect though. Well, not immune, but it didn't seem to change his obvious tension at dinner the night before. That had nothing to do with May, she'd soon discovered. He'd spoken to her daughter with patience, in a quiet voice that was neither threatening nor overwhelming. May was warming up to him, too. It was all relative with a child like May, but the fact that she was talking to Kade at all? That she had gently pulled Amari to Kade's side so they could sit together at dinner? It was significant.

Amari hated that that significance would blow up in May's face because Kade couldn't talk to her like an adult.

She set it aside. They had the day free, and Matilda had suggested Amari take May down to the beach. It was a great idea since May didn't get to spend much time at the beach, though she loved to swim. Amari simply didn't have the time to take her. Weekdays were out of the question, even in the holidays, because Amari had to work. Weekends, too. Either because Amari had to work or because she had to prepare for work. She tried not to feel bad about it, but she knew it sucked. May deserved to have someone who took her to the beach.

There was no point in lamenting about it, especially on a day Amari *could* take her to the beach. When they went down to the door, Matilda was waiting with supplies.

'A picnic basket for lunch, sunscreen, and towels. We've already set up a gazebo for you with some beach chairs. You'll be escorted down—' Matilda nodded to a guard hovering nearby '—and find some other guards already there to assist you.'

'Wow, this is…amazing. Thank you.'

'Don't thank me, thank Prince Kade. He arranged for it.'

Of course, Amari thought with a nod at Matilda. There was no way the woman would have done this for her without a push from Kade. And while she wanted to be pleased that he had thought about a way to keep her busy, she suspected that he had done it to keep her busy *away* from him. Something was going on with him. After a fiery make-out session that hadn't been sex, but hadn't been just kisses either, it didn't bode well.

But it was fine. She didn't need him. In fact, it was good. She *didn't* need him. She shouldn't need him. She shouldn't have made out with him, or found him charming, or sweet. Him pulling away actually did them both a favour.

Then why does it feel so damn personal?

She shook her shoulders. Today wasn't about him. It was about her and May and the beach. And it turned out to be an excellent day. They swam, ate the delicious snacks that had been provided, tanned, built sandcastles, destroyed sandcastles, and laughed. Amari hadn't seen May this happy in a long time. And it hadn't only been at the beach. It had been the day before, too, at that Christmas station.

All of it almost made it okay that she didn't see Kade that day. Or the next, or next, though she and May had full itineraries for both days. On day one, they went to the only theme park on the island. It was prepped for Christmas: elves roamed around, tinsel and garlands and fairy lights decorated storefronts, a Christmas village had been created with Father Christmas distributing Christmas cookies and gifts. May didn't want to get too close to Father Christmas, concerned that he might confuse the gift he gave her with what she'd written in her letters.

Matilda had given Amari the letters May had written Father Christmas at the Christmas station. They were more coherent than Amari expected, but she suspected that was because May had had some elven help. In the first few letters, May had written that she had already sent him her own list, and now, she wanted to send some things through for her mother. On there had been some things Amari had mentioned to no one in particular at home. Body wash, honey, oil. It was cute that May thought Father Christmas could help Amari with her groceries.

The other letters weren't as cute. May asked Father Christmas to send someone to help her mama at the store so she wouldn't always be working. She seemed tired, and May just wanted her mother to be happy. They were sweet requests. Simple.

If only they didn't make Amari feel so guilty.

At least they weren't about May's father. Amari knew she couldn't avoid the topic forever—and she wouldn't—but Amari needed more time to think before she dealt with that. Now, all her time was dedicated to her daughter.

With May's letters in mind, during their second day, when Kade sent them to an aquarium that connected to a rehabilitation centre for penguins, Amari tried to be happy. It wasn't a huge stretch. Pete called her regularly to assure her business was doing well and to ask her about stock and any other things she might need him to order. He also told her the security at her house was working fine and things seemed okay there, too. She didn't have any other responsibilities. Only her kid, who was laughing and happy and didn't seem like a responsibility at all.

The only thing that was slightly off were things with Kade. But that was okay.

Until she saw him the next morning at breakfast and his presence just about kicked her in the gut.

'Hi,' she allowed.

May waved to him. With a pull of Amari's hand, she went to sit beside him and very softly began telling him about what she'd been doing.

Amari merely accepted the tea she'd been offered, before trying to find a distraction. Only then did she realise it was just the three of them.

'Where are your parents?' she asked.

Kade looked up from May. 'My mother wasn't up to a formal breakfast this morning. My father's with her.'

'Is she okay?'

'Fine.' He offered her a nod. 'Just a little fatigued. It's been a busy few days strategising. The announcement's coming up.'

He didn't offer any more than that. She tried to ignore it, but it bothered her. She didn't like that he couldn't talk to her like an adult. She didn't like that he'd run away, or made whatever decision he'd made by himself, without her input.

She was aware that this resentment wasn't entirely because of him. She had some residual anger over Hank. He'd made decisions about their relationship for her, too. He hadn't been willing to try. *He'd* decided and he'd expected her to go along with it.

It wasn't an unreasonable expectation, she supposed. She had, after all, gone along with it. But she had been a new mother, hormonal, and fighting to be with someone who didn't want to be with her required energy she hadn't had—and wouldn't have for the foreseeable future. She didn't regret it. Hank had walked away from May, not just her. If he could do that so easily when May had been born, there was little doubt in her mind that he could do it later, too. When May was older and capable of feeling that abandonment in a way that would scar her for ever.

The situation was scarily similar to Amari's own life. Her father had left before she got the chance to know him. And perhaps that had been a blessing—she didn't know what it was like to have a father, so she couldn't really miss him—but her mother had been so uninterested in raising her that she'd had fantasies about having a father who cared.

What if May felt that way, too? What if *that* was where her questions came from? What if she saw her mother busy and tired and unhappy and she wondered if having a father would change things? Would May blame Amari in the same way Amari had blamed her mother? Would she wonder what Amari had done to make Hank walk away?

Amari stilled. It wasn't an unusual thought. She'd had it before. Hell, she'd spent the entire four years of May's life trying to make up for it. But if that thought wasn't going away, she wasn't trying hard enough. If she wasn't as busy, wasn't as tired, wasn't unhappy, surely May wouldn't care about a father?

She couldn't afford to confuse the situation with Kade. May was already getting attached. That could lead to nowhere good when they went back home.

'Amari?'

Amari's head lifted. Kade was looking at her intensely. Her cheeks burned. 'I'm sorry. I got lost in my own thoughts for a second.'

There was the shortest pause. She used it to check on May. Her daughter was picking berries from her plate and stuffing them in her mouth triumphantly.

It made her smile, until Kade said, 'I was wondering if you'd attend an engagement with my parents and me this afternoon?'

'Me?' Amari looked around, as if somewhere she would find a hidden camera. 'Why?'

'We're visiting one of the orphanages in town. It's tradition to go there, do some activities with them, then have lunch and hand out gifts.'

'I still... Well, wouldn't it be better if I weren't with you?' She dropped her head, not believing Kade didn't see the flaw in his plan. 'I imagine any event where you and I are together will garner the kind of attention you don't want.'

'This is different,' Kade said smoothly. 'We only invite a small group of reporters, all from publications we trust. Our instructions this time around will be to picture only official members of the royal family. We'll allow them to mention you were there—not by name, of course—because it might change the public's perception of you.'

'You mean as someone other than the woman who seduced the prince?'

Kade's lips pursed. 'Yes.'

If he got upset by her describing seduction, how did he expect her to feel about him actually seducing her? That she'd allowed him to, and that he seemed to regret it?

'I think it's a bad idea,' Amari said. 'If I'm there and they mention it, it will seem as if we're dating, and we're not,' she added flatly, as if he needed the clarification.

Maybe the clarification was for her.

'The kingdom already knows you're here.' Kade's face was impassive. He was being the Polite Prince again.

'What does that mean, exactly?'

'Nothing.'

'No, it means something. It must mean something or you wouldn't have come up with this.'

Now, Kade looked pained. 'I think… It might change the public's mind about you being here.'

Ah, so that was it. He wanted to make her more palatable. If she helped with a charity event, she would seem less like an evil seductress. But what she couldn't figure out was why. Why did it matter to Kade what his kingdom thought of her?

Or was it because their opinion of her was a reflection of their opinion of him?

'What do you want me to do?' she asked quietly, ignoring the question her inner voice was asking *her.*

Why does his kingdom's opinion of him matter to you?

Something akin to gratitude fluttered in Kade's eyes. It was a pity she didn't want it.

'I thought it would be good to have you lead them in some crafts. It doesn't have to be anything fancy. A simple activity would do.'

'And you believe this will change people's opinions of me?'

'I do.'

'And what about you?'

He was quiet for a moment. 'I'm not sure what you mean.'

'Of course you do,' Amari replied. 'You've come up with this plan to redeem my image, although really it's your image.' She paused. 'I know it doesn't matter what your kingdom thinks of me. When I leave, no one will even remember me. But it matters that the woman you kissed on a beach—currently living in the palace—hasn't manoeuvred her way into a first-class holiday or life.'

She was looking at May by the end of it, speaking as calmly as she could so May wouldn't pick up her tension. She knew it might be futile. Children were good at picking up undercurrents, and she couldn't control those other than her own. But she would try.

She smiled when May looked up at her, and took a bite of the pancake May offered. She didn't look up until she was done chewing. Kade was staring at her with something fierce shining in his eyes. She wanted to say it was respect, and perhaps it was, but it didn't matter.

'I'll do it,' she told him. 'I have no desire to sabotage your reputation, or the reputation of your family.' Her own breakfast was put in front of her and she picked up her utensils. 'Now—shall I speak to Matilda about the details, or do you already have those for me?'

CHAPTER FOURTEEN

AMARI WAS FIRE. Passion. Strength. Kade knew it, of course, so he wasn't sure why he was surprised.

Perhaps he had forgotten. He'd certainly tried to. He'd spent three days avoiding her. Keeping both of them busy separately so he wouldn't think about her and she wouldn't think about him. Her icy look that morning at breakfast told her he might not have succeeded. She had clearly thought about him—and not in good ways.

It was for the best. It would be harder to forget her and the effect she had on him if she still wanted him. After what she had said that morning, he saw he'd made that decision for her. Just as he'd made the decision about the orphanage visit. The shame he felt told him he needed to apologise. But something deeper told him that, too. Not only for making decisions for her, but for avoiding her.

And he had to do it all without mentioning that her fire, passion and strength were exactly why she was such trouble for him.

He found her in the playroom he'd arranged for May. May was currently focusing hard on colouring in. Amari was sitting in the corner near the window, staring out of it. From there, he knew she could see the garden. Was she thinking about what they'd done in there? Was she regretting it? Reliving it?

He shook his head. 'Amari.'

Both she and May looked over. May gave him a shy smile that filled his heart, but she continued colouring. Amari merely stared at him. After a few seconds, she nodded her head. He approached with caution.

'Matilda said the kids at the orphanage are around May's age,' she said when he sat down. She didn't look at him. 'We came up with some great ideas. She's working on one of them. Making Christmas decorations.'

'They'll love it.'

'Your mother thought so, too. I ran the idea by her during tea earlier.'

Neither of them said anything after that for a bit. Kade exhaled. Then he inhaled and said, 'I'm sorry.'

'For what?'

It was just like her to not allow him to be vague. But she deserved the clarity.

'I should have involved you when I came up with this plan.'

'Why?' she asked, pulling her knees up to under her chin. She was looking at him now, and somehow the position made her look so vulnerable, his heart ached. 'You're used to making decisions for others. That's how you run a kingdom, isn't it?'

'It's not supposed to be.' He straightened his shirt sleeves. 'We have a parliament we rule alongside. Whenever there are decisions to be made, we make them with the representatives our people have voted in.'

'Oh.' There was a beat. 'So you just make them for me, then.'

'You don't understand how many things come into play with something like this.'

'Maybe not,' she said evenly, 'but I am both emotionally and intellectually capable. If you'd talked to me about the idea—*talked*, not told—I would have easily agreed. I might have even contributed something valuable. But you didn't give me that opportunity.'

'You're right.' He shook his head. He was getting into an argument for no other reason than his pride. He'd already admitted he needed to apologise. He had already apologised. And now he was defending his actions. 'I'm sorry. This situation is…difficult for me. I want to protect you.'

'Protecting me isn't robbing me of my agency. It's allowing me to choose, to be a part of something, especially when it pertains to me and my actions.' She frowned. 'And you're not protecting me. You're protecting yourself.'

'I know. I know.'

'And I'm not only talking about this thing with the orphanage.'

He cast an eye towards May. She wasn't paying attention to them, but was engrossed in colouring in a Christmas star for a tree.

'That's different.'

'How?'

'It's… There's no future with us.'

'I know that,' she snapped. She looked at May, too. Lowered her voice. 'Do you think I don't understand the complexities of any relationship with you? I do. Which is why I'm not asking for a relationship. A couple of kisses don't mean I want a relationship.'

'They weren't only a couple of kisses,' he told her, as if he needed to defend what they'd shared.

She snorted. 'Oh, so now there's more to it? Didn't you pretend it didn't happen for three days?'

'I…'

'Yeah,' she said when he trailed off. 'There's no real excuse for that.'

'I was protecting myself.'

They were useless words. Empty words. But still, she nodded.

'I understand that. I do. But I wasn't the one who created the perfect magical opportunity to make out outside my home. I didn't pursue you in any way, or seduce you. I didn't ask you for anything more than you were willing to give, and those opportunities you created, that seduction… That made me think you were a willing participant.'

'I…was.'

'Okay, you were. You're not any more. That's perfectly okay. Just don't…' She exhaled and lowered her feet to the floor. 'Look, I've been here before, okay? Deeper in, because I was married to him and had a kid with him. He decided things weren't working for him any more and I had to accept that. And I did. But I still resent him. I resent him because he didn't give me any say. I resent him because my kid doesn't have a father, and likely never will, because he decided he didn't want to be one.'

'That's why he left?'

She snorted lightly. 'He didn't like the responsibility of a newborn. Six months in, when things were the toughest, he decided life was easier without a child. It is,' she acknowledged, 'but that's something you should talk about before you get married. It's a decision you make together. It's not something you discover after you get your wife pregnant and make her think she's lucky because she has you and all your support.'

'He sounds like a jerk.'

'Yeah?' She clucked her tongue. 'That situation was worse than this, no doubt, but I guarantee you when I go home and tell Lydia about all this, she's going to say the same thing about you.'

He stared at first, then he chuckled. 'You're right.'

'I know.'

'I'm sorry.' He took a beat. 'That your husband wasn't good to you either.'

She heaved out a sigh. 'I wish I could tell you that I'm over it, but I'm not. Him and my mom—' She shook her head. 'They hurt me, and I carry that with me all the time.' She looked at him. 'So when you do something like this, it takes me back to the people in my life who didn't consider me. They only thought about themselves. I get that that's on me, I do, but…'

'It's not only on you. Not if…'

He was the one to trail off now. Because he had been about to say, 'Not if we're in a relationship,' and clearly, they weren't. But he cared about her. He cared about not hurting her, and he had been selfish for not even considering it before.

'It's not only on you,' he said again, more firmly. 'I have things that trigger me, too. The reason I tried not to see you for three days is… You mean something to me. I don't know what, and I thought I should. This isn't a world you bring someone into when you're not sure about how you feel. And I was convinced—'

He broke off, ashamed of what he had thought. How could he tell her he was convinced she wasn't right for him? He didn't care about her past for himself. He only thought his family would care. His kingdom. That was a shameful thing to admit out loud.

Luckily, she didn't push him. She merely nodded and stared out of the window again.

'I'm not sure either,' she said eventually. 'And I should know, too. My responsibility might not be a kingdom, but it's as important to me as your kingdom is to you.'

She looked at May. When her gaze rested back on him, she nodded. 'I understand why you don't want to pursue this. And I…agree. You have my permission to avoid me.'

'Amari—'

'No, Kade, you're right. This isn't…we can't do this.

There's too much at stake. Especially when we don't even know what this is.'

Why did it feel so devastating? It was the exact same conclusion that he had come to. But hearing it from her...it felt final. And his heart wasn't entirely ready to handle that.

Did that matter, though?

He stood. 'So—we're okay?'

'We're deciding this together. That's all I wanted.' She stood with him. 'We're okay.'

They were standing close enough that he could feel the heat coming off her body. His body immediately responded. Fingers itched to touch; skin prickled for her touch; his heart pounded so hard it felt as if it wanted to jump out of his chest into hers.

Not touching her felt like a tragedy. All of it did.

Something niggled at his brain, his heart, but he ignored it. It didn't matter. The only thing that mattered was that he made his mother and kingdom proud.

He didn't examine why that felt like a lie.

CHAPTER FIFTEEN

THE TRIP TO the orphanage once again proved Kade had underestimated Amari. He was well aware it reflected poorly on him, and his only consolation was that he would try to do better. He was also immeasurably proud of Amari. She displayed the kind of behaviour he could only describe as grace. It wasn't a term he used often. In fact, it was only a term he used for his mother.

But it suited Amari. Perhaps even more than it did his mother.

She worked with the children easily, not showing the discomfort he usually saw when adults were around kids. She was a mother, which he supposed helped, but he didn't think motherhood had changed her all that much. He could easily see her respond in the same way even if she weren't a mother. She gave them affection, showed them patience, enthusiasm when they called her to show off the tiniest thing. Not once did she look annoyed or frustrated by it, even when a young boy crawled into her lap and clung to her without showing any desire to let go.

May had come with them, and at that, she'd given the boy a long look. But her mother winked at her, and something about it must have made May realise her mother cuddling another child didn't rob her of anything. It was the only explanation he could come up with as to why she merely went back to the task at hand.

The staff were impressed. He didn't have to see the smiles of approval they sent his way to know. They murmured, actually vibrated, as they talked about her. He wanted to tell them it was impolite. It was obvious they were talking about Amari. But she didn't seem to care. She ignored the whispers. Returned the smiles. When she met his eyes, she rolled her own slightly, but seconds later she was speaking to a child and if anyone had seen it, they would doubt they had.

As Amari handled the crafts with the children, he and his parents spoke with some of the beneficiaries of the orphanage. It was more of the usual. Gratitude for their generosity. Patience when they expressed concerns or plans. Kade tried to engage as much as he could, but his eyes kept going back to Amari.

Why was he so surprised she was good at this?

'You're staring,' his mother said under her breath as she lowered into a chair. She seemed tired, but it wasn't unusual for an event to make her feel that way. Besides, they were coming up to the announcement of her abdication, and he couldn't imagine that helped her sleep.

'It's involuntary,' he admitted.

'She is rather magnificent.'

He turned to his mother. 'What?'

'You heard me. Here, take a seat,' she ordered, pointing to one. 'It will seem less suspicious that I'm sitting if you do, too.'

He obeyed, giving his father a nod when Deacon caught his eye. He would stay with his mother while Deacon drew the attention of anyone who might question it. His father didn't like being social, but he would do anything for his wife. It also helped that they were preparing the gifts around Kade and his mother, and it seemed as though they were merely supervising.

'I heard you,' Kade said. 'I suppose I was wondering if you'd really said it or if I was making it up.'

'You can be so dramatic,' Winifred said with a shake of her head.

He smiled. 'Where do you think I get that from?'

She slanted him a look, but didn't address the comment. 'I said it because I believe it. She's surpassed my expectations.'

'What were those expectations?'

'Of a divorced single mother?' She let the question linger for a moment. 'Nothing that wasn't merely prejudice on my part. If I thought she would care, I'd apologise.'

'I don't think she does care.'

'That much is clear. If she cared about what I think, she wouldn't have said any of what she said to me in this last week.'

He smiled. 'I'm pleased she did. What?' he asked when his mother gave him a shrewd look. 'No one is assertive with you. They tend to be too scared.'

'Even you?'

'Especially me.'

His mother was silent for a while. 'In the weeks since you've known her, you've been more assertive and decisive. The decision to bring her here was bold.'

He didn't know how to respond, so he remained quiet.

'I don't think she's changed you,' his mother continued, musing more than anything else. 'But I think she's allowed you to step into yourself. Perhaps that's because she's so unapologetically herself, or because you love her, and thus want to protect her. Either way, I'm pleased it's happened now.' She reached out to take his hand. 'It's all I've ever wanted for you, Kade.'

His silence now wasn't because he couldn't form an answer, but because he was stunned. There were so many parts to this. The fact that his mother approved of Amari, though he'd believed she wouldn't. His mother wanting him to be himself when he'd spent a lifetime believing the opposite. She supported him in a way he hadn't believed possible.

Through all of it, he could only say one thing, 'I don't love Amari.'

'Of course you don't, dear.' His mother patted his hand. 'You've merely stepped into the man I've always believed you could be because of a kiss.' She laughed. 'It must have been some kiss.'

She laughed again.

She was laughing at *him*.

'I've spent my life thinking you didn't believe I could do this job.' His voice was hard.

'I never once thought you couldn't do this job. But I didn't believe you wanted to do this job. You were never interested in the work, Kade. You were more interested in pleasing me. And while I can't fault you for it—I'm your mother and it made me quite happy that you wanted to please me—it's distracted you from your potential.'

'My...? Mother, this is a lot.'

'We can discuss it later,' she said. 'With more privacy, too.' She paused, then dropped his hand and turned to look at him. 'I will say this, as you seem to need to hear it. I've always wanted you to be yourself, Kade. I'd hoped you'd come to the conclusion long before I had to say it.'

'What about all those mistakes I made? What about the disappointment you felt?'

'The mistakes came because you were trying to be like me. I wanted you to be yourself, and I was disappointed that you didn't believe you could be.'

His heart was racing, and it wasn't entirely comfortable. Neither were his thoughts. He knew he needed time to process, and that now, at an event, wasn't the best time to do so.

But he couldn't help but think about how he'd misinterpreted things. How he'd made up this narrative because he was so convinced that he knew his mother, he didn't give her the chance to surprise him.

Because you didn't ever ask her.

Amari had asked him that several times. *'Has your mother ever said she's disappointed in you?'* Each time he'd said no, but dismissed it because he was so sure she was. He'd spent a lifetime believing it, after all. Amari posing a simple question hadn't been enough to undermine that belief. Only this conversation had.

Which made him think about something else Amari had said. About how he made decisions for them, for her. He'd done the same thing with his mother. He'd decided she was disappointed in him. He'd decided he wasn't enough. He'd decided not to engage with his mother about it, or talk to her about what she thought he was doing wrong.

He'd decided all these things without ever once speaking openly with his mother. If he had, it would have saved him so much heartache. If he had known his mother didn't care about him being her, only himself, he would have spent the last years growing into who he could be as King. He wouldn't have messed up trying to be who he thought his mother wanted him to be.

He'd also decided that his mother wouldn't approve of Amari. That he needed to have the right kind of wife for his family and kingdom. But his mother didn't care about that. She cared that Amari was a woman of integrity. She had reflected on her prejudices and faced her mistakes. That was the woman, the ruler, his mother was.

And he had spent a lifetime casting his own fears and opinions onto her.

What the hell did that say about him?

Amari liked helping those children more than she'd expected she would. Some of that was because she hadn't exactly known what *to* expect. In her mind, she had pictured the press clamouring to get pictures of the harlot who had tempted their prince into sin, despite what Kade had told her about which press would be there. She had thought people would judge her, and treat her poorly.

None of that had happened. And once she'd realised it wouldn't, she'd allowed herself to relax. She'd enjoyed it. Speaking with the children. Helping them, watching May interact with them. She imagined that this was what it would be like to volunteer at May's school. She had never had the opportunity to; she was always too busy working. Now, she felt as if she'd missed something valuable. May around children was a delight, and she wished…

Well, she wished she could be in her daughter's life more. Because it wasn't *this* that was delightful. It was spending time with May. It was watching her engage with the world and navigate new experiences. And yes, doing something this meaningful with her somehow felt more significant, but Amari wasn't foolish enough to believe she wouldn't feel the exact same way in other circumstances. This time in Daria had taught her what she had lost with May. And made her wonder if she was willing to keep losing it.

'Are you okay?' Kade asked on the way home. It was only the three of them in the car. His parents had taken their own. 'You've been quiet.'

'As have you,' she countered, because she wasn't in the mood to talk about it. 'I saw you and your mother having an intense conversation. Are *you* okay?'

He looked out of the window before he replied. Amari couldn't help but notice how beautiful his kingdom was. Rolling green hills, bodies of water, flowers everywhere… Somehow, Daria had been blessed with the most beautiful of what nature had to offer. She would miss the simplicity of it when she went home.

Home.

Strange, she hadn't thought about it since they'd arrived. Stranger yet, she hadn't missed it since they'd arrived. She had what she needed with her. Why had it taken her such a long time to see it?

Because you're distracted.

'I am,' Kade replied, interrupting her thoughts, yet somehow proving them as well. 'We had… The conversation was good. It's showed me that a lot of my preconceived ideas were created based on my own fears.'

'That's a deep thing to say.'

He looked at her with a half-smile. 'I'm still working on it, but I've managed to come to that conclusion.'

'It can't have been easy,' she said, studying his face.

'It's not.'

'But it's worth it.' She shrugged at his furrowed brows. 'Whenever you realise your actions come from a place of fear instead of something positive, it propels you in the direction of something positive.'

She ran her hand over May's head. Her little girl was sleeping on her lap. It had been an exhausting day. The simple comfort of it filled her heart.

'Take this, for example. I was so scared of becoming like my mother…' She trailed off when her eyes burned. Looked out of the window. 'I'm trying to be a better mother to May. That fear turned into something beautiful.'

Has it?

She bit her lip. The beauty of raising May hadn't erased any of her fears about being her mother. And it hadn't entirely changed her either. She was still making decisions that reminded her of her mother. She wasn't putting May first. That entailed protecting May and loving her. It entailed giving May the mother she wanted; a mother who wasn't tired and busy. A mother who was happy.

She shook her head. 'But then, what do I know?'

'Not enough, if you're still comparing yourself to your mother.'

She snorted. 'You don't know my mother. She…she's self-centred. Which isn't necessarily a bad thing.'

'Unless you're a parent.'

'Yes.'

They were quiet for a bit.

'She's not a bad person,' she continued softly, loyalty compelling her. 'She agreed not to sell any stories about me to the papers. That's something.'

He nodded. 'I suppose you don't have to be a bad person to be a bad mother.'

Why did it feel as if he was describing her?

But no, she wasn't a bad mother.

Was she?

'What were your fears?' she asked, desperate to get out of her head.

'You're deflecting.'

'Obviously.'

He looked to the sky, as if asking for strength, though his lips twitched. 'I've told you my mother's disappointed in me because I can't rule as she does.'

'You have.'

'As it happens, she's been disappointed in me because I've tried.' The disbelief on his face made her want to reach out. A stronger emotion inside her kept her from doing so. 'She's spent my entire life waiting for me to do *my* best. Not what I think she thinks is my best, but *mine*. She wanted me to be me, and I spent a lifetime trying to be her.'

Amari opened her mouth, but she didn't think what she wanted to say would be welcomed.

'What?' he asked.

'What do you mean?'

'You don't have to feign ignorance. Especially when your face is the most expressive I've seen.'

'I might not have to feign ignorance, but I can check whether you truly want to hear what I'm going to say since it's probably going to sound snarky.'

'And when has that ever stopped you.'

'Hey—I'm trying over here.'

He angled his head. 'Apologies. Would you tell me? I'd like to know.'

She gave him a beat to change his mind. And silently thanked him for drawing her out of her own problems.

'Okay, this is what I've been thinking since you told me your mom's disappointed in you. You're great. Genuinely great. You're kind and thoughtful. You carry yourself in a way I'd expect a prince to, though I'm not completely sure I'm the best judge. You're smart, have a big heart, and you do well under pressure. Working in my store put you under pressure—you and I both know it,' she added to clarify. 'You don't like not knowing things, but you didn't once snap, or make me feel like it was my fault, or do something ridiculous. You listened. You tried your best. I couldn't understand how your mother wouldn't see that in you. I mean, she's known you your entire life and I've known you for weeks.'

'I... I...'

When he kept stammering, this prince who was smooth and rarely speechless, she smiled. 'I know it's hard to get out of your own head. But it's true. This is who you are: a king. And the fact that you couldn't see that only proves how much you deserve to be King. Anyone who wants to do better for their loved ones, for their people? Yeah, they deserve to rule a kingdom.' She lifted a shoulder at his stare. 'All this kingdom can ask for is someone who wants to do their best.' She looked back down at May. 'All anyone can ask for is someone who does their best.'

For a long while, they drove in silence. Amari didn't mind. It gave her the opportunity to get her thoughts in order. She needed to change her life, and she knew that if she didn't do it when she got back, she would get sucked back into routine and it would be harder. This was already going to be the hardest thing she had done.

'Amari.'

The softness of Kade's voice sank into her heart before she saw his expression. It stole her breath even though she didn't allow herself to think about what she was seeing there.

'You're a good mother.'

She swallowed. 'Yeah. Yeah, I know.'

'No, you don't. I can see you're judging yourself. I don't know what the basis of it is, but I know that it's not deserved. You're doing your best. It's all she can ask for, as you just said.'

'Except I'm not,' she replied. 'I'm using motherhood to fight my own demons and she deserves…she deserves more.'

His gaze was intense. 'And you'll give her more.'

'I'm going to try.'

'And that means you're a good mother.'

She blew out a breath, but offered him a smile. 'Thank you.'

'Don't thank me. Believe it.'

If only it were that easy.

CHAPTER SIXTEEN

THE DAYS PASSED in a blur after that first charity event. Amari hadn't expected it to be a first, but Queen Winifred had asked Amari to assist her with some of her festive charity obligations. Amari couldn't say no. Especially when the Queen had made the request because she was 'feeling weak'. She had said those words looking both shrewd and strong, but Amari could hardly point that out.

Queen Winifred was probably counting on that.

The upside was that the work was inspiring. All the events were for charities supporting children. Some assisted those who'd experienced some form of violence by teaching them how to defend themselves. Others supported those without one or both parental figures. Some fed children at foster homes; took children off the street; worked to improve conditions in orphanages.

She didn't know why Queen Winifred had chosen her to help with these charities specifically. Was it because Amari had her own child? Or had she simply done a good job at the orphanage? It certainly couldn't be because the Queen knew Amari felt fulfilled by it. She wasn't even doing that much, merely talking to the children and the staff, helping out where she was needed, yet her heart was filled by it. It felt like…like purpose. She hadn't experienced that in a long time. Not since May was born. Not even with her store.

If she spent too long thinking about that, loyalty speared a lance through her chest and she leaked guilt. Because her store *did* give her purpose. It did. She had built it from the ground up. It belonged to her and would some day belong to May. It provided for them. It meant something to them. To the community.

But it also kept her busy. It kept her from spending time with May. It caused anxiety and fear, neither of which allowed her to be the mother she wanted to be.

The guilt ate at her.

She thought talking about it might make things better, but the only person she wanted to talk to was Kade. And things with him were…complicated. He accompanied them to the charity events—another reason Amari was convinced the Queen didn't need her—and he was splendid.

She had only seen him in his official capacity once before, at the orphanage, but she could tell he was different now. He wasn't as tense any more. He didn't seem to be bracing for something no one else could see. And witnessing him being himself, witnessing everyone see what she saw in him, was special. It did something to her heart. Just as seeing him with May did.

Somehow, they always found their way to one another. They didn't talk much, but it didn't seem to matter to either of them. They looked for each other in a room. May would take his hand; his would swallow hers. And he didn't seem to care one bit that they got curious glances.

Amari wondered if *she* should care. Did it matter that there had already been insinuations on gossip sites about who May was? About what she meant to Kade? There were stories about Amari, too, though she didn't waste her time thinking about those. No, May was her main concern. Except May wasn't hurt by the insinuations. Neither was Amari. But Kade must have been.

Of course, no official media outlet had run with the stories. Kade's case against the newspaper who had taken the picture of them kissing on the beach was still ongoing; no one seemed willing to take the chance that they'd be next. They had even signed legal documents that prevented them from mentioning or taking pictures of her and May at any of the events. Amari could only imagine what Kade had offered them in return. And yet he didn't seem unhappy or worried.

The only time she saw those emotions was when she caught him looking at her.

That mainly happened at the events, as she and Kade barely spoke then. But after, they always seemed to find one another. Sometimes it was in the afternoon; other times, the evening. But every day they found moments to spend together. They either supervised May as she played, or went for a walk after May went to bed. And they talked. About superficial things, mostly. They were careful to stay away from talks of family, of responsibility, of them.

But still, their talks didn't feel superficial. They felt special, as if she were pushing open a door that had been stuck for a long time, letting long-overdue air into a stuffy room.

Somehow, the talking led to handholding. To lingering stares and kisses on the cheek. She ignored the significance of it, of any of it, because there was no point in acknowledging it. Nothing had changed. He was still going to be King; she was still May's mother. They had their responsibilities. Talking, handholding, lingering stares and kisses didn't matter.

Even if teasing him about wanting to knit; feeling his skin as she held his hand; falling into the liquid depths of his eyes; brushing her lips to his cheek made her day.

'What's this?' she said to no one, really, when she reached the door of her room and an envelope was stuck to it. They had just come back from a walk, where she'd made the mistake of mentioning ice cream. Ignoring May's insistence that they needed ice cream *now*, she opened the envelope.

Please be ready at two p.m.
Matilda

That was all.

Frowning, Amari looked at her watch. It was one-thirty. She had thirty minutes to get ready, and she had no real idea what that meant. She shuffled May into the room, distracting her with TV, and took a shower. After, she stared at the closet. Most of the clothes she'd been wearing recently had come from Matilda.

'We need you to look a certain way,' the woman had said, before telling her exactly which outfit to wear to which event. Since there had been no instructions this time around, Amari chose something from her own clothing. A simple black dress that could be dressed up or down depending on the occasion. She decided on down since she probably wouldn't have been given the chance to decide for herself if she needed to dress up.

'Good, you're ready,' Matilda said when Amari opened the door to her knock precisely at two.

'Is this okay?'

'It's fine. I'm only taking you shopping.'

'Oh.' She frowned. 'Is that necessary? The sizes you've got for me have been fine so far.'

'It's easy to pick something for obligations,' Matilda said crisply. 'This is for the ball tomorrow night.'

'Tomorrow...' she trailed off.

They were announcing Queen Winifred's abdication at the ball the following night. They would also be announcing Kade's coronation would take place a few days into the new year. It was a big deal.

'I didn't think I would be going.'

'Both the Queen and Prince Kade have indicated their desire to have you and May present.'

'May—'

'Are we going to the ball, Mama?'

May perked up from where she sat on the bed. Amari narrowed her eyes. She hadn't realised May had been listening.

'No, honey. We're just—'

'It's not advised to ignore an invitation from royalty,' Matilda said blandly.

'Hmm.'

'Mama, we should do it. We can get pretty dresses.'

'Yes,' Matilda said. 'In fact, we're doing that right now.'

May squealed with happiness. Amari gave Matilda a stern look. 'Don't think I don't know I've just been manipulated.'

For the first time since Amari met Matilda, the woman smiled.

Kade couldn't quite describe what it was like walking into that room and seeing Amari in a ball gown. He should have waited until the following night to see her in the full outfit, but he wanted to make sure that she was okay. He also didn't know what the night would look like. He did know most of the attention would be on him, and that his couldn't be consumed by a woman he wasn't supposed to be in love with because she looked gorgeous in a gown.

The fact that she stole his attention completely from the moment he saw her in the gown told him it was good he hadn't waited.

The fact that he was absolutely in love with her seemed almost irrelevant in light of that.

'I asked them to put you in red because it reminded me of that day at the beach,' he said into the room.

Amari whirled around, causing the skirt of her dress to spin around her as if she were a fairy-tale princess. He didn't care for the fairy-tale part, but he wanted her to be a princess. Or a queen. The title suited her better anyway.

Kade.

Right. He needed to rein in his fantasies until after the ball. That had to be his main priority.

But it was just so damn easy to imagine her in his life.

Spending the weeks with her in his kingdom had been amazing. And the last week... Well, that had been something else entirely. She handled each event she attended with grace and poise. It was almost as if she'd been born for it. It was significant, considering she hadn't had any preparation, but that was part of the charm. She spoke with people honestly, relating to them in ways he knew he never could.

His mother's words at the first charity event had stuck with him. Perhaps that was why, when he realised he was in love with her, he wasn't entirely surprised. His feelings for her didn't feel taboo any more either. She would be good for the kingdom. And his mother approved. Hell, she was fond of Amari and May in ways he had never thought possible.

Which was why, after the ball, he was going to propose.

'You're biased,' Amari said, smoothing down the front of her dress. There was no reason for the action to draw his attention to her chest, but it happened anyway. The sweetheart neckline showed off the smooth lines of her clavicle, the expanse of her golden-brown shoulders, the curve of her cleavage.

He forced his eyes up. 'I am. It was a good day.'

'I had to move to a kingdom I never knew existed because of that day,' she chided, but the edges of her mouth pulled up.

'You're happy here though, aren't you?'

It was a loaded question, deliberately so. He wanted to

know what his chances were. She smiled—a private, intimate smile that made him want to chase the designer out of the room so only he could see it. So only he could witness the moment he realised his chances were *good*.

'I have been.' Her eyes twinkled, warming his insides. 'This has been the best Christmas May and I have had. Right, sweetheart?'

Amari winked at him. For a second, he didn't know why. Then she moved, stepping to the side to reveal a miniature version of her.

May had an almost identical dress on to Amari, though hers went higher up at the neck. She looked at him shyly, but expectantly. He hid his smile as he walked to the front of her, before dropping to his knees.

'You, darling May, look like a princess.'

May beamed. 'I look like Mama.'

'Yes,' he agreed. 'And your mother looks like a princess, too.'

He looked at Amari as he said it, hoping she would see through the words to his meaning. He wanted her to be his princess. His queen. He wanted her to rule beside him. She made him a better person. She made him a better king— she had done long before he was even supposed to be King. What effect wouldn't she have once he was?

For a moment, it felt as if she did see his true meaning. Their eyes held, electricity sparked. He remembered what it felt like to have her body against his, the softness of her lips, the teasing of her tongue. It hadn't happened in much too long, but he was a patient man. He would experience it again.

Hopefully, for a lifetime.

She looked away and May started speaking to him as the designer drew Amari to the side, putting pins into the dress and murmuring. The moment was over.

He tried not to project any meaning onto it.

CHAPTER SEVENTEEN

THE MOMENT AMARI walked into the ballroom, she knew she would remember the experience for ever.

Perhaps it would be for a simple reason, like the décor. It was spectacular: the crystals glistening from the roof that looked like ice and snow; the lights dangling down the walls, casting the room with a warm glow. Or perhaps the reason would be more significant. The joy in May's eyes as she took in the Christmas tree, the presents beneath it, the throne that was regal and gold and breathtaking...

Then, of course, there was the way Kade looked at her when he noticed her in the room.

Amari felt it before she saw it. It hit her between her shoulders and she turned, catching his eyes immediately. The rise in her temperature came from a deep, intimate place inside her. Her skin felt sticky even as it turned into gooseflesh as he stared and stared, much as she had the first time she had seen him.

He gave her an almost imperceptible nod an endless amount of time later, just as May pulled at her hand. Amari looked down for a second, then back up, but Kade's attention was already elsewhere and her daughter was dragging her to a Christmas tree.

And that was when the magic stopped.

Because it quickly become obvious that May was the only child there. Amari had assumed, because Kade and his parents had invited them, that that wouldn't be the case. She had assumed they would know people already saw them as outsiders. She had assumed the royal family would protect her and May and not give people any more reason to stare. But apparently that had been too much to hope for.

People *did* stare at them. And they whispered, or ignored them entirely. She hadn't anticipated how awful it would make her feel. She had known that she would only know Kade and his parents there, and that they wouldn't have time to talk with her, but she'd thought she could mingle. She had, at the charity events. She had done fine in those circles. But she was beginning to realise it was because she was like the people at those charity events; it wasn't because she was like Kade.

It twisted inside her. Became an ugly, sharp weapon that pierced into hopes and dreams she hadn't given herself a chance to entertain. Hopes and dreams she'd thought she had discarded when she realised who Kade was.

And yet here she was, devastated because it was clear she didn't fit into his life. Because it was clear that in the last two weeks they had been living in a reality that could never exist.

And she was angry. Angry at Kade for bringing her here and making her believe it could exist. For inviting her to a ball she had no business being at.

It didn't take a genius to know she was really angry at herself. Because once again, she had put her own desires above her daughter's. And once again, it hadn't worked out.

So when May began to complain, to pull at her dress, Amari immediately picked her up. Her heart ached when May hid her face in Amari's shoulder, a clear sign that she had felt the tension in the room, too.

She made the decision quickly: she wasn't staying. She would send Kade an apology for not making it through the announcement or the dinner, but she *couldn't* stay. Even though she wanted to. She wanted to make those people uncomfortable by staring back, whispering back, making them feel as small as they intended on making her feel. But she couldn't do it alone—and she was. Utterly alone. More importantly, trying to prove a point wasn't the best thing for May.

She owed her daughter her best. Even if she kept failing, she still needed to try.

May was quiet when they reached the room, and Amari got her into bed without much of a fuss. She wanted to call down for dinner, but she worried with the event happening that she would be asking for too much. Since she refused to let her daughter go hungry for the night, she called Matilda. She felt as if the woman would have an easier time securing food without being an inconvenience.

The food arrived less than twenty minutes later. They ate, Amari sang May to sleep, and, when she finally succeeded, Amari put off all the lights. She had taken off her dress to convince May to do the same, and wore one of her own. But she hadn't taken off her make-up or undone her hair, and she couldn't bring herself to do either. Instead, she curled up around May, caressing her forehead and silently promising her she would never put her in this position again.

When the knock came hours later, Amari still hadn't fallen asleep. She had expected it, though she only knew that when it was already there. She tiptoed to the door and eased out before she spoke.

'Hey,' she said. 'How did it go?'

'Fine.' It was curt. 'You weren't there.'

'No.'

'Why not?' Kade asked.

'We…left early. It wasn't the right… We shouldn't have been there.'

'Why the hell not?'

She frowned. 'I'm sorry—have I upset you by not attending a ball that has nothing to do with me?'

'Is that why you left? Because you wanted it in your honour?'

'What—?' She exhaled. 'I do not have the energy for this. Let's talk in the morning.'

'You ran,' he said before she could move. The only reason she didn't move was because his voice was…raw. 'You ran away from that ball. I've never seen you run away from anything before.'

'I didn't run, I left. Because in the two hours I was there—*two hours*, Kade—not one person spoke with me. And we were drawing attention because we were clearly the only people who didn't know someone other than you and your parents in that room. While we're on that subject,' she continued, her tongue loose, 'why would you invite May to that ball? There were no children there. It put targets on our back when we already had them.'

'I didn't…' Kade trailed off, brow knitted. 'I didn't realise you would feel that way.'

'How could you not?' she asked softly, though her voice was strong. 'I thought there would be other children. I thought May would be…' She trailed off with a breath. 'I thought you'd want to protect her.'

When her knees suddenly felt weak, she sank down to the floor. Kade looked pained for a moment, but he joined her, back against the wall. They sat like that for a long time. There was no movement in the hall despite the many guests at the palace. For the first time, Amari wondered if that was because they'd been put in a different area from anyone else. Perhaps the other guests, the ones who weren't quite as common as them, got put in a fancier wing.

But even as she thought it, she felt shame. Nothing about the room or the way she'd been treated had made her feel common. Apart from the initial conversation she'd had with Kade's mother, a conversation she understood, she had never been made to feel like an outsider.

This evening had just…hit her harder than expected. And it had nothing to do with the event and everything to do with her feelings.

For Kade.

The ones she had convinced herself she did not have.

'I should have,' Kade said into the silence. 'I should have realised you would feel vulnerable. I should have made more of an effort to be there with you.'

'No, you shouldn't have,' she argued. 'You're about to become *King*, Kade. You can't be my bodyguard.'

'Then what?' he asked. 'What could I have done to make this night easier for you?'

'I don't know,' she said a little helplessly. 'It would have helped if you'd told me May would be the only child there. I could have told you it was a bad idea then.'

'Would you still have come? Without her?'

'I… I don't know.'

He didn't reply for a while. 'Maybe I knew that. Maybe that's why I invited you both.'

'At her expense?' Amari asked, not quite believing what he'd said. 'You had her there, knowing it wasn't appropriate, because you wanted *me* there?'

'I… No.' He shook his head. 'No, that came out wrong.'

'How could it come out right?'

'I care about you,' he blurted out. She looked at him, her heart skipping when she saw the serious look in his eyes. 'I care about you both. I wanted you both there because… because it was important that you be there.'

He was being vague and they both knew it. But then he reached out and cupped her face. The heat was warm and soothing. It went straight to her heart, and it alarmed her. Because he had just revealed he hadn't been thinking about her kid. Or he had, but he hadn't thought about her enough to put his needs aside. He'd made a decision that worked for *him*.

Just like you've been doing.

No, she told that mental voice. It wasn't the same. It *wasn't*.

'I overreacted when I came here. I was upset. I thought...' He dropped his hand, but it fell to her lap and he left it there. 'When my mother made the announcement, the crowd wasn't surprised. It seemed they'd been expecting it these last weeks, especially with me taking more of a leading role in my mother's engagements.'

She wanted to hold his hand. To tangle their fingers together and let the warmth comfort her even more.

She didn't.

'There was applause and general approval, though I suppose that was because they're in my home and any other reaction would be frowned upon.' He paused. 'I didn't care. About any of it. I only cared that you weren't there. That at some point you had disappeared and I hadn't noticed. I worried, and eventually, my mother said something to me that snapped me out of it.'

'I'm sorry,' she breathed, because it was all she could manage. It felt like...like too much.

'I was being selfish,' he said when it became clear she wasn't going to reply. 'I should have thought about you not having anyone to talk to. I should have known May would be the only child there. But I only... I only thought about how much I wanted you both there for the most important moment of my life.'

She shifted away from him, forcing his hand to drop. Hurt flashed in his eyes, as if he knew she was trying to put distance between them.

'Kade—'

'Amari,' he interrupted. 'You can't tell me that you haven't at least thought about it.'

He didn't have to clarify for her to know that by 'it', he meant the two of them.

'What are you doing?' she whispered. 'We've talked about this. I'm not… We're not…'

'You are,' he said. 'We are.'

'No. No. We need to think about May,' she said a little desperately. 'Tonight was the perfect example of why this isn't good for her. She was clinging to my chest because people were staring at her, Kade. She was as quiet when I brought her back tonight as she was the night we first got here.'

'That shouldn't have happened,' he said in his calm way. 'And it won't happen again. If you and I are together—'

She scrambled to stand, pacing so the energy in her body wouldn't turn into screaming.

'Amari,' Kade said, deliberately now. Somehow, he was standing, too. 'If you and I are together, no one will be allowed to make you or May feel that way again.'

'How can you be so sure?' she demanded. 'I've been a parent for *four* years and I haven't been able to guarantee anything for my daughter.' She fought against the burn at her eyes, in her throat. 'People say that when you become a parent, you only think about your child. But that's not really true. Your instinct to do what's best for you is still there. It happened tonight.'

'That's not fair. I didn't want—'

'I'm not talking about you,' she interrupted. 'I'm talking about me. I wanted to be there for you tonight. I wanted to see people's faces when they realised they were getting a damn good king. I should have realised…' her voice dropped to a whisper '…that this wouldn't be good for May. I should have asked whether she would be the only child there. But I didn't because I wanted to be there.'

She waited to catch her breath. Her emotions. When she had them in her hands—precariously, but still—she continued.

'That's what you make me do, Kade. You make me think about myself. About what I want. About…about you.'

'Because you want me.'

'Yes.' What was the point of denying it now? 'But wanting you made me move my child away from the only home she knows. It put her in a situation tonight that she shouldn't have been in.'

'I thought she was happy,' he pointed out quietly. 'Didn't you say being here was the best Christmas she's had?' She couldn't reply, but it didn't matter. He was talking again. 'She was quiet when she got here, but that didn't last. Neither will her discomfort at these events.'

'How do you know?'

'She has us.' The simple way he said it broke her heart. 'We'll be there for her. We'll protect her.'

'We won't.' She shook her head. 'We haven't.'

'We can't anticipate everything we need to protect her from. But we can learn. Now that we know better, we'll do better.'

'I know better,' Amari said with a firmness she didn't feel. 'This is not better.'

He studied her. 'You've already made up your mind, haven't you?'

She forced herself to nod.

Silence stretched before Kade took a step back. 'I'm sorry I bothered you.'

It was the disappointment in his tone that had her blurting out, 'How can I be in a relationship with you and be a good mother to May?'

He paused, his eyes boring into hers in a way that made her feel as if he could see inside her. To that dark hole of feelings her words seemed to be coming from.

'If you wanted an answer,' he said slowly, 'I would have repeated your words to you. About how all anyone could ask for was someone to do their best for them. I believe you're doing that with May. I believe that, together, *we* could do that for May. But then, I believe that your happiness is as important as May's. There's nothing I can do if *you* don't believe that, Amari.' He let the silence linger before continuing. 'It's probably a good thing you don't want an answer, then.'

Seconds later, he was gone, leaving her feeling emptier than she had when she'd left the ballroom.

Kade avoided Amari the next day. He wasn't proud of it, but he kept hearing her words. *'How can I be in a relationship with you and be a good mother to May?'* If she truly believed that—and it was clear that she did—they couldn't be together. If the choice was between him and her child, he knew where he stood. Nowhere. And he couldn't blame her. Not when he understood her insecurities. Not when he knew how much she loved May. How she would do anything for her child. It broke his heart that she couldn't see she was a good mother. Or that she didn't believe she deserved love.

But how could he blame her when he loved May, too? One day without the kid and he already missed her. She was way too serious until she wasn't, and that combination had wormed its way deep into his heart. He hadn't only lost his chance with Amari; he'd lost his chance with May, too. And the double blow meant he needed time.

He hadn't expected them to leave while he took it.

'What?' he asked his mother. 'What do you mean they're gone?'

'I've already told you, Amari asked me to arrange for her and May to return to Swell Valley,' Winifred said, flicking out her wrists as she lay a napkin on her lap.

'And you did it?'

'You dealt with the situation quite well, Kade. The threat has passed.'

'How do you know that?'

'Pete says there hasn't been a single reporter around her home or store in the last week. Interest has died down, especially in light of last night's announcement.'

'That doesn't mean she's safe.'

'No,' his mother agreed. 'But she has state-of-the-art security systems now. We've also allocated guards to remain with her until they're sure no one is following her.' Her eyes flicked up. 'Additionally, I believe your lawsuit has made it clear pursuing her or May in any way will be dealt with severely. I think they've realised your private life is off limits. I suppose we'll see when you start dating again.'

'I won't—' He broke off. Curled his hand into a fist. 'Why didn't you tell me?'

'You would have spent the time trying to convince me they should stay.' Winifred picked up her coffee, took a sip before continuing. 'We've made too many decisions for them, Kade. The least we could do was respect this one.'

Kade stared at the space across from him. Amari used to sit there. May would sometimes sit next to her, sometimes next to him. The fact that they weren't there now made him feel empty. The table felt too big, his chest too hollow. His mind couldn't fully process that they were gone.

But his mother was right. He had realised that the night before, when Amari told him about what happened at the ball. *He* had decided he wanted them there. Both of them. He hadn't thought about how it would be for them. He hadn't even spoken with Amari about it. After the last time he'd made a decision for her, he'd thought he'd learnt his lesson. But apparently he hadn't, and it killed him.

It was why he hadn't proposed. He had made that decision all by himself, too, without talking to her about it.

Without taking her feelings into account. His love for her didn't change that marriage would change her life. Everything she knew would be different. Even if she loved him, too—and he wasn't sure that was the extent of her feelings for him—she needed to have agency in this decision. He wouldn't put her in the situation where she had to decide something this important until he could prepare her for it.

Maybe he had learnt his lesson. It was a pity it was too late.

'I thought you were planning to propose, son,' his father said.

Kade's head lifted. 'How could you possibly know that?'

'We know everything,' his mother said breezily. 'What happened?'

Trying to figure out how he felt about his parents' knowledge of his life took too much energy. He sighed. 'It would be selfish to ask her to marry me. I couldn't do that to her again.'

'What do you mean?'

'I wanted her at the ball for me. I didn't think about how vulnerable it would make her feel, knowing only us. I didn't even consider whether it would be appropriate for May to attend when she would be the only child there.'

His mother glanced at Deacon. 'We should have thought about that. We could have invited some of Amari's friends from home. Maybe we could have planned a mini ball for the children.'

'You would have done that?' Kade asked.

Winifred gave him a shrewd look. 'You know we're fond of Amari and May. The last thing we wanted was to make them feel out of place when we very much want their place to be in this family.'

He blinked. 'Your support here is making me feel rather strange.'

'You're being foolish,' Winifred said. 'We knew you

wanted to marry Amari and we didn't interfere. That must have told you how we feel.'

It took him a moment. 'I tend to need to hear these things.'

Winifred rolled her eyes. 'Tell me you at least told her what she needs to hear, then.'

He stared.

'That you love her, son,' Deacon said.

'Oh. I... No.'

'Why not?'

'I was worried—'

He exhaled. He wasn't sure he wanted to rehash his love life with his parents. But as he looked at them, he saw nothing but love. Well, he saw impatience and curiosity, too, but he knew it was because they loved him. And for the first time in his life, he realised he was loved unconditionally.

All his worries about his mother's expectations of him, all his fears of disappointing her, had blinded him to the fact that she loved him. Both his parents did. And they supported him.

Who might he have been if he'd spent his energy claiming that instead of his anxieties?

He would never know. But realising he was loved unconditionally made him realise he loved unconditionally, too. And if he didn't tell Amari that, she'd spend her energy on the bad instead of the good, too. He needed to give her a chance to claim the good. He owed it to the both of them.

'I have to go,' he said, pushing out from the table.

He didn't miss his parents' smiles of approval as he left the room.

CHAPTER EIGHTEEN

IT WAS CHRISTMAS EVE and Amari was staring at her empty store.

She hadn't been back since she'd got back home from Daria. Pete had been waiting for her when she'd got to her house. When she'd told him her plans to leave the store closed until after Christmas, he'd offered to run things until Christmas Eve. It was only for two days, so she'd accepted. Except she hadn't been accepting because it was only for two days. She'd been accepting because she was a coward who couldn't bear to be in a space she had once shared with the man she loved.

That realisation had hit her the moment her flight from Daria had taken off. The impact was nowhere as severe as she expected. It told her that her heart had been ahead of her brain for a long time.

But it didn't matter. She had chosen to come home and figure out how to be a better parent to May. It didn't matter that every time she thought about it, she heard Kade telling her she was already doing her best. And that she deserved to be happy. That May deserved to see her happy.

And now she was standing in her store on Christmas Eve, trying to figure out whether running the place still made her happy.

'The last two days I've spent at home have been really great,' she said out loud. 'I got to spend time prepping the house for Christmas with May. She loved it, though we did have to work through her feelings about leaving Daria. She wasn't thrilled that she didn't even get to say goodbye to Kade.'

Neither had Amari, but that was for the best.

'But the last two weeks without you has been…eye-opening. It's not you, I don't think. It was more spending time with May. And finding out I really like working with kids who aren't my own. Who would have thought it?' She ran a hand over the shelf in front of her. 'I need to figure out how to balance you with those other things. And I don't know how to do that right now.'

She would have spent longer thinking about it if the bell to the door hadn't rung. She whirled around. Her heart just about stopped.

'Kade.' It came out like some kind of breathy prayer. She cleared her throat. 'Wh-what are you doing here?'

'I don't have a job any more?'

He said the words with his unbearable charm. Oh, she'd missed him. And the thought of it made her want to throw something at him. The thought, and the fact that he was standing in front of her looking so damn handsome in his perfect suit that fitted his perfect body. She could still feel it beneath her fingers.

'You have more important jobs.'

'I love you.'

She stared at him. 'What. The. *Hell?*'

'I didn't get to tell you that before you left.'

'That's why I didn't say goodbye, genius. So you didn't get *to* say it.'

His brow furrowed. 'You knew?'

'No. Not for sure.' She closed her eyes. Maybe it would help silence the echo of his *I love you* in her head. It didn't. She looked at him. 'It doesn't change anything.'

'It does.' He took a small step forward. 'Now you know for sure. And you can make a decision.'

'Kade…' She shook her head. 'I told you that I don't know how to be a good mother to May and be in a relationship with you. That hasn't changed.'

'But you *are* a good mother.' His certainty had longing surging inside her. 'I don't know why you can't see it.'

'Because I do stupid things!' she exclaimed. 'I make mistakes that are selfish and I… I do things that my mother would do.'

'Do you?' he asked. 'When your father left, did your mother change her entire life so that you would have some semblance of family?'

Her lashes fluttered. 'No.'

'Did your mother ever think about your well-being when she took a job? Or when she was in a relationship?'

This time, she couldn't speak. She only shook her head.

'Did your mother berate herself because she didn't think she was doing enough for you? Did she always try to think of you? Did she think about your happiness before her own?'

Her eyes prickled, but she didn't realise she was crying until Kade brushed a thumb across her cheek.

'Those things are selfish, Amari,' he whispered. 'And you haven't done one of those things.'

'I… I…'

'Made mistakes, like we all do. But you do your best to learn from them. Even if you don't always succeed the next time, you try. Trying is the best you can do.'

She pursed her lips. 'Stop using my words against me.'

He chuckled, but the humour quickly faded. 'Wanting to be happy isn't selfish. Being happy isn't selfish. How can it be? You'll be showing May that thinking about other people *and* herself is okay. You'll be showing her that her feelings are every bit as important as anyone else's. You'll be showing her she deserves the life she wants.'

The stubborn side of her wanted to disagree. But she couldn't. She wanted May to have the best life she could possibly have. That meant thinking about her own needs. It meant valuing her happiness. How could she see that if Amari didn't show her?

It wouldn't be easy. She'd had too much practice branding every similarity she had with her mother as selfish. Yes, she made some mistakes, but the way she responded to them wasn't like her mother at all. It had taken Kade to outline the differences, even in those similarities. He could see them because he loved her. It terrified her.

'You seem pretty confident that what I want is you.'

'No.' He said it with a nervous laugh, though it sounded more like a simple burst of air. 'No, Amari.' He took a breath. 'I just… I love you. I love you exactly as you are. I'm not perfect. I will never be. And I'll make mistakes in our relationship and in my relationship with May. But I want to try. I want to be with you and raise May. I love her almost as much as I love you.'

She had never realised her heart wasn't whole until that point. Because now it felt whole. It felt full. He'd done that.

'I don't like your charm. I don't like that it utterly disarms me.'

His eyes widened. Slowly, the ends of his mouth followed.

'But I do like you. I like you exactly as you are. I like that you are a good man who sees the good in me. I like that you try, even when you don't think you are. I like that you can see me when I can't see myself.' She paused there because her throat got thick. 'I like it all so much that I… I might love you.'

He was grinning by the time she was done.

'Might?'

'Small steps.'

His smile somehow got bigger. She felt her own lips twitch.

'You love me,' he said.

She grunted.

'Maybe I need to say this to get you to admit it.' He suddenly got serious. 'I'll protect you. Both of you. As best I can.'

Her heart did the strange filling thing again. Strange because it was already full. Apparently, with him, her heart overflowed.

'I believe you. I trust you.'

'But do you love me?'

He was still trying to get her to say it when she kissed him.

EPILOGUE

One year later

AMARI COULDN'T BELIEVE that she was staring at her kingdom.

They were on the balcony of the palace, a part she hadn't seen when she'd visited the year before, looking out at all the people who had gathered to celebrate her marriage to Kade. A sea of faces she was now responsible for.

It didn't concern her nearly as much as it would have once upon a time. She had her husband by her side. She had her daughter by her side, too. She squeezed both their hands, clasped in hers as they, too, stared out at the crowd.

It hadn't been an easy transition to royal life. And it wasn't the transition *into* royal life that was the problem as much as transitioning *out of* the life she had built for her and May. She had sold the store, a heartbreaking decision that had had to be made. She had given up the lease on her home, said goodbye to her friends—her family—and asked them to visit. And she had tried to make May as comfortable as she could during the shift.

The year had been rough and long. Planning the wedding while finalising things in Swell Valley and learning about what her royal life would entail had seemed endless. But standing there, with their family together, happier than they had ever been, made it worth it. Especially when May had laughed more that day than Amari had heard in a year. It was all worth it.

'Ready?' Kade asked, turning to her.

She squeezed May's hand one last time before nodding at Queen Winifred. Her mother-in-law deftly distracted May, and Amari turned back to her King.

'Ready.'

Their lips touched in the sweetest kiss, though the heat wasn't far behind. It never was when they kissed these days. But today, there was promise in that heat. An acknowledgement that they would have a lifetime to sate it.

Amari smiled, her husband's mouth still against hers, her heart full.

* * * * *

MEET ME UNDER
THE MISTLETOE

BRENDA HARLEN

This book is dedicated to readers everywhere.

Over the past year, there have been far too many headlines and hashtags that made me (and likely everyone else!) feel as if the world had been turned upside down and was spinning out of control. Too many days when I wondered what was the point of sitting down at the computer to write.

Then came the social media posts from readers asking for more stories—because they wanted happy endings. They wanted hope.

Or, at the very least, they wanted to escape from the real world for a few hours.

I hope this story does that for you.

Chapter One

Haylee Gilmore kicked aside her work boots as she hung her coveralls on the hook beside the door, aware that her roommate, who also happened to be her sister, would curse a blue streak if she tripped over them. Finley's shoes, half a dozen pairs of three-inch heels in various styles and colors—and not even a fraction of the number to be found in her bedroom closet, were neatly lined up beneath the deacon's bench on the other side of the door.

"Fin? Are you home?"

"In the kitchen."

Haylee followed her voice—and the mouthwatering scents of tomato and basil—to the kitchen.

When the sisters decided to move out of their parents' Victorian home and into the carriage house apartment together, they agreed to divide the domestic chores equally, alternating cooking duties and sharing the housecleaning and laundry responsibilities. But it was quickly apparent to both that Finley was the much better cook (though Haylee was indisputably the master of baking), so now the younger sister spent more time in the kitchen and less scrubbing toilets.

"Something smells good," Haylee noted.

"I'm making deconstructed lasagna."

Apparently Finley had been listening when Haylee grumbled the night before that it would be nice to eat something other than raw vegetables every once in a while. Yes, it was early June and salad was refreshing, but it wasn't, in her opinion, a meal—even when her sister dressed it up with nuts and berries.

Lasagna was a meal.

Opening the refrigerator to snag a can of Coke, she asked, "Do you want one?"

Finley made a face. "You know I only drink diet."

"Fake sugar isn't good for you," Haylee said, even as she returned to the fridge to grab a can of diet cola for her sister.

"I know." Finley took the proffered can and popped the tab. "But real sugar won't help me squeeze into the Donna Karan dress I'm wearing for the Krieghoff wedding Friday night."

"You'll look fabulous no matter what you wear."

"Says the sister who could wear anything and yet chooses to live in jeans and T-shirts."

"Jeans and T-shirts are comfortable," Haylee pointed out in her own defense. "Not to mention appropriate for my job."

"For your job," Finley agreed. "But there's more to life than work—or there should be."

It was a familiar topic of conversation between them, because Finley was social and outgoing and, despite living with Haylee for her whole life, couldn't understand that her older-by-eleven-months sister was not.

Haylee ignored the comment and lowered herself into a seat at the table to riffle through the mail. She paused when she found a thick envelope with her name and address handwritten in fancy script. "What's this?"

Finley glanced over as she mixed ricotta in with the meat, noodles and sauce already in the skillet. "An invitation to Caleb and Brielle's wedding. I got one, too."

Caleb was a paternal cousin who lived in Haven, Nevada—along with most of the rest of the Gilmore family—and Brielle was the girl he'd been in love with since high school—and had apparently eloped with not long after their high school graduation eight years earlier.

"I thought they were already married," Haylee remarked, sliding a finger under the flap to open the envelope.

"They are, but they never actually had a wedding, so Brielle's grandfather is hosting a big reception to make things more official, show off their new baby and prove that the feud is over."

Haylee swallowed another mouthful of Coke. Though their father had left Haven, Nevada, some forty years earlier, he'd told his children about the Gilmore-Blake feud that dated back more than one hundred and fifty years to when Everett Gilmore, his great-great grandfather, discovered that the exact parcel of land he'd bought had also been sold to a man by the name of Samuel Blake. Rather than risk taking the matter to court and having one of them end up with nothing, the two men had decided to split the property down the middle, using Eighteen-Mile Creek—or Crooked Creek, as it was referred to by the locals—as the east and west dividing line between the two ranches.

Because the Gilmores had already started to build their home in the valley—on the west side of the creek, the Blakes were relegated to the higher elevation on the east—where the land was mostly comprised of rocky hills and ridges. The Gilmores' cattle immediately benefited from grazing on more hospitable terrain, while the Blakes struggled for a lot of years to keep their herd viable—until silver and gold were found in the hills on their side of the creek and they gave up ranching in favor of mining.

In addition, there was an ill-fated love affair between Everett Gilmore's daughter, Maggie, and Samuel Blake's youngest son, James, that ended with a stillborn child and further soured the relationship between the two families.

Haylee pulled the invitation out of the envelope and skimmed the details. "The wedding's in less than three weeks."

"A surefire way to keep the guest list down," Finley remarked, "is to wait until people have other plans to invite them."

"Obviously you have other plans," she noted.

"I'm an event planner—I always have other plans."

"And yet, you still manage to have a social life."

"You could have one, too, if you wanted one," her sister said.

It was true that Haylee had never worried too much about filling her after-work and weekend hours with parties and events. She was mostly content with her own company—and even happier with a good book in hand. It was enough for her to get together with a friend for lunch or meet a coworker for drinks every now and again. And for several years, that had been her routine. But over the past few months, she'd noticed an unsettling trend beginning to disrupt her comfortable routine.

Starting with Lisa, who'd had to reschedule their lunch date three times in order to squeeze it in between dress fittings and cake tastings and other appointments in preparation for her upcoming wedding; followed by Candace, who'd bailed on drinks one weekend because she hadn't been feeling well—and then confided that drinks would be out for the foreseeable future because she was pregnant; and, most recently, by Nancy, who'd simply been a no-show for Sunday brunch because her boyfriend had surprised her with a weekend getaway to Lake Tahoe, and she'd been so excited about the trip she hadn't thought to even send a quick text message to Haylee about the change of plans.

Haylee was sincerely happy for her friends, but she was also suddenly aware of the emptiness of her own life. Especially in light of the fact that get-togethers with Josslin had already dropped off her calendar because the first-time mom was understandably preoccupied with her new baby.

"It might be fun to catch up with the Haven relatives," she said now, thinking specifically of her cousin

Katelyn—an attorney married to the sheriff and mother to an adorable toddler—and Katelyn's sister, Skylar—who worked as a counselor with at-risk kids and tended bar at the local watering hole.

"It might be," Finley agreed.

"Do you know if Dad and Colleen are going to the wedding?"

"I doubt it, especially considering that they've already committed to making the trip at the end of August for Grandma and Grandpa's sixtieth anniversary."

"What about Logan?" she asked, naming their younger brother, a junior architect at a local firm.

Finley shook her head. "I called him yesterday, hoping to snag him as a plus-one for a recently jilted bridesmaid in the Krieghoff wedding party, but he said he's going to be working around the clock until the end of the month on a major design project."

"Well, I'm not going by myself," Haylee decided, tossing the invitation aside.

"Why not?" Finley scooped pasta into two bowls.

"Because I'd feel pathetic."

"More pathetic than sitting home alone?" her sister asked, not unkindly.

Haylee pushed away from the table to get cutlery and napkins. "I won't be alone. I'll be with Simon."

"Giving him a man's name doesn't change the fact that he's a cat—and if hanging out with your cat is the extent of your plans, that *is* pathetic."

"I know," she admitted.

And the truth was, she'd gone to the local SPCA and adopted Simon because, after numerous unsuccessful—and perhaps half-hearted—efforts to find companionship through online dating, she'd finally given up and acknowledged that if she didn't want to be alone, she was going to have to get a pet.

Finley sat at the table, across from her sister, and pulled her cell phone out of her pocket. "What's the email address on the invitation? I want to RSVP before I forget."

Her sister's thumbs flew over the keypad as Haylee read out the requested information.

"Thanks." Finley set her phone beside her can of soda. "Now Patrick at the Silver Star Vacation Ranch knows that I cannot attend, but my sister Haylee is very much looking forward to the event."

"What? You didn't—"

"I did," Finley confirmed, picking up her fork.

"But I never said I would go," she protested.

"No, you didn't," her sister agreed. "But I don't want you spending another Saturday night alone at home."

Haylee sighed. "Can I take Simon as my plus-one?"

"No." Finley pushed her noodles around in her bowl. "You're going to go with a mind open to the possibility that you might actually meet somebody."

"In Haven, Nevada?" She scooped up a forkful of pasta. "A town of…what? Maybe two hundred people?"

Finley tapped the screen of her phone again, performing a quick Google search. "Twenty-two hundred."

"Because I can't find a man in a city of half a million, but Mr. Right is going to be waiting for me in a town of twenty-two hundred," she remarked dryly.

"I don't expect you to find Mr. Right at the wedding—although Mr. Right *Now* would be a good start," her sister said with a wink.

Haylee sighed again. "I guess I'd better look into flights."

Because she had no intention of driving for seven hours in each direction when she was only going for a weekend.

"And hotels."

Was there even a hotel in Haven?

She thought she remembered hearing something about her cousin Liam renovating an old inn in town and made a mental note to look it up...after dinner. Because she'd worked through lunch and was starving.

"And you're going to need something to wear," Finley said.

"I'm sure I've got something in my closet that will work."

"I'm sure you don't," her sister countered. "Even a country wedding requires something dressier than steel-toed boots and a hard hat."

"How about Converse high-tops and a baseball cap?" she asked, joking.

Mostly.

Finley shook her head despairingly. "There are times when I sincerely question how we're related."

There were times when Haylee wondered the same thing.

And because there was no denying that her sister had much better fashion sense than Haylee, she swallowed her pride and said, "Will you go shopping with me?"

Now Finley grinned. "I thought you'd never ask."

Of course, it wasn't enough for her sister to ensure that Haylee had a new dress for the occasion. Finley had insisted that she also needed new shoes to go with the new dress, a purse to match the shoes and suitable undergarments to wear under the dress.

Now Haylee was standing in front of the mirror of her ground floor room at the Stagecoach Inn—the local boutique hotel indeed owned by her cousin Liam and managed by his wife, Macy—wearing a tiny pair of pink bikini panties and a matching lace bra that she had to concede was nothing less than an engineering marvel, as the garment somehow lifted and enhanced her body in a way that made it appear as if she actually had breasts.

Maybe Finley was right, she acknowledged, as she wiggled into the simple sheath-style dress in a pale shade of peachy-pink that her sister had called "coral." Maybe she'd never felt sexy because plain cotton wasn't sexy.

Or maybe she was deluding herself into thinking that some pretty clothes and pricey makeup could turn her into a different woman—a *confident* woman.

You've always been beautiful, even if you've never seen yourself that way, Finley had said. *But this outfit should give you a better understanding of the power that goes hand in hand with being a woman.*

With her sister's words echoing in her head, Haylee smoothed the front of her dress and reassessed.

Beautiful was a stretch, she decided.

On the other hand, she wasn't *un*attractive.

The sweep of mascara on her lashes made them look longer and thicker—and she didn't think anyone would guess that she'd needed three Q-tips to clean up around her eyes because putting mascara on her own lashes

was a lot more challenging than letting Finley do it.
The bronzer on her cheekbones added definition and
just a hint of color, and the peach-colored gloss on her
lips made them shine.

Peering into the mirror, she thought the overall result was pretty close to the transformation Finley had
effected.

So much so that Haylee doubted any of her coworkers would recognize her if they saw her now.

She slid her feet into the high-heeled sandals her sister had insisted were perfect for the dress, then picked
up the wristlet that coordinated with the shoes and
would hold her ID and keys (and the single condom
that she'd tucked inside, because even if she was skeptical about her odds of meeting someone, she didn't
believe in taking chances). Honestly, Haylee had spent
more money during that one shopping trip with her sister than she usually spent on clothes in a year—which
Finley assured her was *not* something she should be
proud of—and that was before they'd hit the cosmetics
department at Saks.

Trust me, it will all be worthwhile, Finley had promised.

So Haylee took a few cautious turns around her hotel
room, practicing so that she'd be steady on her feet. The
skinny heels did take some getting used to, but she figured she'd be okay as long as she didn't overindulge.

Although Haven didn't have an actual taxi service
and Uber hadn't yet found its way to the town, Jesse
Blake had hired a couple drivers so that none of the
wedding guests would need to worry about transporta-
tion to and from the event, especially if they had a few

drinks. The exaggerated wolf whistle of the driver who came for Haylee was more flattering than offensive— but maybe that was because the man was seventy years old if he was a day. Still, his reaction bolstered her confidence a little more and his steady chatter on the drive to the Silver Star helped loosen the knots of trepidation in her belly.

She arrived just as the guests were being ushered toward an outdoor seating area facing a gazebo decorated with vines and flowers. Haylee slipped into a vacant seat at the back and watched through misty eyes as Brielle and Caleb walked down the aisle hand in hand.

The bride wore a floor-length vintage lace wedding dress with cap sleeves, a wreath of flowers on her head and cowboy boots on her feet. Her groom was in a Western-style tux complete with cowboy hat and boots. As they renewed their vows in front of their families and friends—including their adorable infant son—there was no doubt in Haylee's mind that love had finally triumphed over the age-old feud between their respective families.

After the ceremony, she made her way through the crowd, stopping to chat with various relatives along the way, assuring her grandparents—who expressed pleasure at seeing Haylee but disappointment that her siblings and parents weren't in attendance—that the whole family would be making the trip in August for Jack and Evelyn's big anniversary party, and snapping photos of the decorations with her iPhone to share with her sister, who was always eager for new ideas that she might incorporate into her own events.

Everywhere Haylee looked, there were barrels and

buckets overflowing with greenery and white blooms. Fence rails had been draped with evergreen boughs trimmed with satin bows. Bistro lights were strung above the temporary dance floor, and the nearby food tent was filled with long tables heavy under the weight of hot and cold food servers, layered trays of sweets and cookies, a champagne fountain, kegs of beer, and coolers filled with sodas and juice pouches.

She lifted a glass of champagne from the tray of a passing waiter and sipped the cool, bubbly liquid as she made her way back outside again. Her gaze moved through the crowd, searching for someone—anyone—to talk to so she didn't look like the complete wallflower that she was.

Still, she was surprised when she caught the eye of a guy near the entrance of the tent—a guy so hot that her heart actually skipped a beat.

The chinos and button-down shirt he wore were appropriate for a country wedding; the cowboy hat and boots emphasized the country part. She guessed his height to be over six feet, though it was hard to be certain at a distance. Shaded somewhat by the brim of his Stetson were dark eyes, a narrow nose and perfectly shaped lips that, even as she watched, curved into a slow smile.

It was the kind of smile that a guy bestowed upon a girl to express his interest. Just because Haylee couldn't ever recall being the recipient of such a smile didn't prevent her from recognizing its meaning, and she wondered, with a small tug of envy, which lucky girl in the crowd was the subject of his attention.

Then her gaze lifted to his again—and she found his eyes focused on *her*!

No way, she decided, locking knees that had gone weak at the mere possibility. He had to be looking at someone else, someone standing close by or even behind her.

Usually that *someone* was Finley, but her sister was at home in Oakland, so Haylee turned her head to look. But her back was against the split-rail fence, and there was no one else around.

Which meant that he was looking *at her*.

Smiling *at her*.

And so she did what any self-respecting, socially inept girl would do when confronted by the attention of an incredibly hot guy.

She fled.

Chapter Two

Trevor Blake knew that inviting a woman to attend any kind of family event might give her the impression that their relationship meant something more than it really did, and inviting a woman to be his plus-one for a wedding seemed to imply that he was open to the possibility of a wedding in their future. So he'd decided that bringing a date to a family wedding seemed like a Very Bad Idea and resigned himself to attending Brielle and Caleb's reception on his own.

He'd had more than a few opportunities to second-guess his decision before the vows were even exchanged, as his solo attendance resulted in him being subjected to pitying glances and sympathetic slaps on the shoulder—not to mention the unwelcome and misguided matchmaking efforts of various aunts and cousins. But then he'd spotted the sexy brunette in the pink dress.

She'd disappeared into the crowd immediately after the nuptials, and he was scrutinizing the gathering, trying to catch another glimpse of her, when his brother joined him.

"I should've brought a date," Devin said, offering him one of the two glasses he carried.

Trevor swallowed a mouthful of beer before responding. "Has Aunt Millie offered to set you up with her bridge partner's granddaughter yet?"

"It was her bridge partner's second husband's granddaughter," Devin clarified.

"Oh, well, in that case," Trevor said, as he casually scanned the crowd again.

Apparently not casually enough, as his brother asked, "You looking for anyone in particular?"

"No," he lied.

"You once told me that weddings were a great place to meet single girls, but everyone seems to be paired up," Devin remarked, sounding disappointed.

"Not everyone," Trevor said. "Check out the one in the short green dress talking to Brielle right now—isn't that one of her roommates from New York?"

His brother nodded. "That's Grace. Lily's the one in the flowered sundress."

"Well, I'd put money on Grace being single and interested, because she's been sending furtive glances in your direction all afternoon."

"Really?" Devin asked.

"Really," Trevor confirmed.

Then his brother shook his head. "New York's a long

way away and I'm not interested in a long-distance relationship."

"Who said anything about a relationship?" he countered. "Why can't you just enjoy the company of an attractive female for a few hours?"

"Are you really so opposed to the possibility of falling in love again?" Devin asked, sounding worried.

"Love isn't all hearts and flowers," Trevor told him. "It's just the transitional stage between infatuation and heartbreak."

"And yet, despite that cynical perspective, you never have any trouble getting a date when you want one."

"I'm a Blake," he said, a simple statement of fact. "And so are you, so why don't you go on over there and ask Grace to dance?"

"Maybe later," Devin said, lifting his glass to indicate that he still had a drink to finish.

But Trevor knew the beer in his brother's hand was only an excuse. Devin was a whiz when it came to anything to do with computers, but he didn't have the first clue about how to interact with the female gender. He managed to hold his own with family members or work colleagues, but when it came to anyone with whom he experienced even a hint of a spark of attraction, his brilliant brother turned into a babbling idiot.

"Later might be too late," he felt compelled to warn. "Because Mitchell Gilmore looks like he's getting ready to make a move."

Devin frowned as he watched the other man make his way toward Grace, then his frown turned into a wince. "Don't look now, but Aunt Millie's heading in this direction."

Trevor heeded the warning, but mostly because his attention had been snagged by a flash of pink.

And there she was again—standing in front of the fence of a nearby paddock, sipping from a flute of champagne.

He would have bet his annual dividends that she was an out-of-town guest, because if she'd been a local resident, he would have met her long before now. He would have made a point of it.

She was on the skinny side of slender, and though he was generally attracted to a woman with more distinct curves, there was something about her that immediately appealed to him. She had dark hair tied up in some kind of twist that made him want to let it loose to tumble over her shoulders, to feel its softness in his hands. And she had long, shapely legs that he could easily imagine—

She caught him looking at him then, and her eyes went wide, as if she was privy to his innermost thoughts. Or maybe she was simply surprised by his blatant perusal.

He smiled, to assure her that he meant no offense by his attention, and waited for her to smile back—an acceptance of his wordless invitation.

Instead she turned her head, breaking the connection and snapping the thread of tension that had stretched between them across the distance, set her empty glass on top of a nearby barrel and walked away.

With a shrug, Trevor resumed his survey of the crowd.

There were plenty of other females in attendance, and he was certain he could find someone to flirt and dance with, if that's what he wanted.

But it was the one in pink who intrigued him.

And it had been a long time since anyone had done so.

He handed his half-empty glass to his brother. "Excuse me," he said. "There's someone I need to talk to."

Devin, following the direction of his gaze, asked, "Who is she?"

"I don't know, but I'm going to find out," Trevor vowed.

This was why she didn't wear fancy shoes, Haylee acknowledged, as she carefully made her way across the uneven ground. Sure, the sandals looked good with the dress, but they were more suited to a polished floor than country fields.

The skyscraper heels were out of place here, just like Haylee. And as she moved farther away from the gathering, she almost felt like a little girl again, playing dress up with her sister, pretending to be somebody that she wasn't.

At the end of the day, she knew the external trappings didn't matter. What mattered was the person inside—and that person didn't have the first clue about the rules of the games men and women played. But as she walked away from the smiling stranger, for the first time in her adult life Haylee found herself sincerely regretting that lack of knowledge and experience.

Just be yourself, Finley had urged. *Making conversation with a guy is no different than making conversation with anyone else.*

Haylee *knew* that, of course, because she talked to guys every day.

In fact, Monday through Friday, she spent more time in the company of men than women. But that was on the job and most of those guys were her coworkers. It wasn't easy for a female electrician to be accepted in what was predominantly still a male occupation, and it had taken some time—and a lot of hard work—to earn the respect and trust of her colleagues. The fact that they talked with their mouths full, didn't bother to censor their language and occasionally offered to buy her a beer after work proved that she'd done so. That, to them, she was just one of the guys. Certainly none of them had ever looked at her the way the gorgeous guy standing outside the food tent had looked at her.

Of course, he wasn't seeing the real Haylee Gilmore but rather the image that her sister had helped her create, to give her the confidence to put herself out there and meet new people. Finley would be so disappointed to know that her sister had run away from the first guy who'd made eye contact with her.

So focused was Haylee on her internal recriminations that she didn't notice the hole in the ground until she'd stepped in it. She immediately teetered, her arms windmilling as she fought to regain her balance. But it was no use—her heel was stuck and the rest of her was about to get up close and personal with the ground.

In fact, she had just about half a second to wonder if she'd ever be able to get the inevitable dirt and grass stains out of her dress before a pair of strong arms caught her.

"Oh," she said, breathless not from the stumble but the catch—and that was before she recognized the guy who'd done the catching.

"Are you okay?" he asked.

Of course, his voice was as perfect as the rest of him, and all her girl parts quivered in response to the sexy timbre.

"Um, yeah. I think so."

"Gopher hole," he told her, bending to retrieve the shoe that was still lodged in the ground. "A local hazard."

"I think the shoes are the hazard," she admitted.

"Maybe," he acknowledged, holding the sandal so that she could slide her foot back into it. "But they sure do look good on you."

He lifted the back strap over her heel, the pad of his thumb brushing against her skin, an unexpectedly sensual caress that raised goose bumps on her arms. Then he adjusted the straps that crossed over the top of her foot, to ensure they weren't twisted, and rubbed a spot of dirt off her shiny pink toenail.

"Nice color."

And she said a silent prayer of thanks to her sister for bullying her into a pedicure at the end of their marathon shopping session.

"Thanks," she said. "And for the rescue."

"It's what I do," he said as he straightened up again.

He topped her height by a good two or three inches, even with Haylee wearing heels, confirming that her original estimate of his height had been accurate. But his masculine good looks were even more potent at close range.

Making conversation with a guy is no different than making conversation with anyone else.

Finley was right—she *could* do this.

She *would* do this.

"Professional knight in shining armor?" she queried lightly.

"Strictly amateur," he said with a wink.

And her heart skipped again.

Damn he was potent.

But look at that, she mused. In a town of twenty-two hundred people, at a wedding with a significantly lesser number of guests in attendance, she was having a conversation—some might even say bantering—with a good-looking guy.

A *really good-looking guy*.

"So…are you a friend of the bride or groom?" he asked her now.

"Actually, I'm a cousin of the groom." She proffered her hand. "Haylee Gilmore."

He took her hand, but instead of shaking it, simply held it in his own. "No kidding," he said, sounding amused. "I'm a cousin of the bride."

"Do you have a name, cousin of the bride?"

"Trevor Blake."

"It's nice to meet you, Trevor Blake."

"The pleasure is mine, Haylee Gilmore."

She managed a smile and resisted the urge to press a hand to her stomach, where butterflies were fluttering just because she was standing close to him.

So close she could smell his aftershave—or maybe it was his soap. Either way, the scent clouded her brain, far more potent than the single glass of champagne she'd drunk.

"So where are you from, Haylee Gilmore? Because I know you're not from around here."

"Oakland, California."

"You must be close to your cousin, to have traveled so far to celebrate his wedding."

"Truthfully, I haven't seen Caleb—or any of my Haven cousins—in years," she confided. "This wedding was a good excuse to do just that."

"Did your boyfriend make the trip with you?"

Boyfriend?

She almost laughed out loud at the question, but of course that would ruin the image she was trying to project—apparently with some success, as this guy believed there might be someone with her. Or waiting for her back home.

Instead, she shook her head. "No boyfriend." And then, because the opening was too perfect to resist, she asked, "How about you?"

He shook his head. "Nope—no boyfriend."

She could feel the heat climb into her cheeks.

Then he grinned. "And no girlfriend, either."

"That's good," she said, and her face burned hotter. "I mean—"

He chuckled, saving her the effort of trying to fumble for the right words—or any words that didn't make her sound even more awkward and inept.

"It is good," he said. "Because it means there's no one to object if I ask you to dance."

She glanced back at the reception area and the mass of bodies crowded together on the dance floor.

"Are you asking me to dance?" she queried.

"I am," he confirmed and, without waiting for a response, drew her into his arms.

"Wait...you want to dance right here?"

"We can hear the music well enough, can't we?" he asked, swaying to the slow beat of Sam Smith's "Stay With Me."

The music wasn't very loud, but it was audible, and her body was already falling under the seductive spell of his movements.

"And by the time we made our way to the dance floor, this song would be over, likely to be followed by something like 'Twist and Shout' to get the crowd bouncing around again."

"You don't like 'Twist and Shout'?"

"It's a great song," he said. "But not one that would be conducive to me holding you—and I really wanted to hold you."

"It wasn't enough that I already fell into your arms—literally?"

"No." He held her gaze for a long moment. "It wasn't enough."

She could feel herself falling again—under his spell, this time, melting against him.

But how could she be expected to resist a guy who was as charming as he was good-looking?

And why should she even try?

What was wrong with indulging her own desires just a little, for just this one night?

"Tell me about yourself," he suggested, as they continued to dance under the stars. "What do you do in Oakland, California?"

One more piece of advice, Finley had said, as Haylee was zipping up her suitcase, ready to head out the door. *Don't talk about your job.*

Why not?

Because some guys are intimidated by a woman who wears a tool belt to work.

I wouldn't want to be with a guy who can't respect what I do.

Of course you wouldn't, her sister agreed. *But you're not looking for a life partner this weekend, just someone with whom to practice your flirting skills. And maybe your kissing skills.* Finley grinned then. *And maybe more.*

"I work for an electrical contracting company," Haylee finally said, in answer to his question. "What do you do?"

"I work for a local mining company."

"So you're not really a cowboy?" she asked, only the teensiest bit disappointed.

"Occasionally on weekends, I help out at the family ranch," he said, then winked. "But women really dig the hat."

She couldn't deny it was true. "And this local mining company...that would be Blake Mining?" she surmised. "The hugely successful silver and gold excavator that is Haven's single biggest employer and, I'd guess from your name, a family business?"

"And now that all my secrets have been revealed, you have to tell me something else about you," he said.

"Hmm..." She paused, as if considering what to reveal. The problem was, her life really wasn't very interesting. "How about a confession?"

"I'm listening," he assured her.

"This is the first time I've ever danced in a field of cows."

"The cows are on the other side of the fence, so we're actually dancing in a field beside a field of cows."

"I stand corrected," she said. "This is the first time I've ever danced in a field *beside* a field of cows."

He smiled then. "And if I kissed you now, would it be the first time you've ever been kissed in a field beside a field of cows?"

Her breath caught in her throat, but somehow she managed to respond. "It would be."

"Then let's make this a night of firsts," he said, and tipped the brim of his hat up before lowering his mouth to touch hers.

And then—

Oh.

My.

God.

—he *was* kissing her.

His lips were warm and firm and confident as they moved over hers, proving that he had not just experience but some serious skill, and Haylee's brain scrambled as she tried to keep up.

She'd been kissed before, of course, but never like this.

No one had ever made her feel so much—*want* so much—with just a kiss. When his tongue slid between her lips, her brain stopped trying to keep up and simply shut down, letting her instincts take over.

She lifted her hands to his shoulders, holding on to him for support as the ground seemed to shift beneath her feet. His hands skimmed up her back, not touching so much as teasing, stoking her desire, making her burn with want, with need. She pressed closer to him, marveling at his hardness, melting into his heat, wordlessly asking for more and offering everything that she had to give.

It was Trevor who finally ended the kiss, easing his mouth from hers only when they were both breathless.

"You are a dangerous woman, Haylee Gilmore," he said, whispering the words against her lips.

Dangerous?

He obviously didn't know her at all.

Or maybe she'd underestimated herself for a lot of years, because when she was with Trevor, she felt different.

Stronger. Sexier. Bolder.

And, if not dangerous, at least a little reckless.

"You started it," she reminded him.

"Yeah," he acknowledged. "And I was close to finishing it, too, in a field beside a field of cows."

The idea was more appealing than she wanted to admit. "That would have been another first for me," she said lightly.

"Me, too." He brushed his thumb over her bottom lip, still tingling from his kiss. "We should probably get back to the party."

"Okay," she agreed.

But he didn't step away from her. Not yet.

"How long are you going to be in town?" he asked instead.

"I have an early flight back to Oakland in the morning."

"That's not very long at all," he noted, sounding sincerely disappointed by this revelation. "I was hoping we could spend the day together and get to know one another a little better."

And then some kind of primal instinct took over, causing Haylee to throw caution—and common sense—to the wind. "Why don't we spend the night together instead?"

Chapter Three

Trevor lifted his bottle of beer to his lips, his gaze focused on the baseball game on the enormous television that covered most of one wall in the living room of his brother's town house. He enjoyed watching a good game, but this wasn't one—the Oakland A's were trailing the Houston Astros by several runs, and it was only the top of the fourth inning.

He swallowed another mouthful of beer as the batter connected with the next pitch and sent it flying over the right field fence, adding three more runs to the Astros' score.

"We should try to get to a game sometime soon," Trevor remarked, as the A's manager finally jogged to the mound and signaled a pitching change.

"I'm always up for a road trip," Devin readily agreed.

Trevor pulled his phone out of his pocket and tapped on the screen. "The A's are at home against the Rangers in a couple weeks."

His brother reached for the tablet on the coffee table in front of him and opened the calendar app. "I've got a conference in Montreal that weekend."

Trevor scrolled through the Athletics' schedule. "Two weeks after that, they're playing the Mets."

Devin wrinkled his nose. "Here's a better idea," he suggested as an alternative. "We fly to New York to see the Yankees."

"That wouldn't really be a road trip now, would it?"

"It could be, if we drove to New York."

"We're not driving to New York," Trevor told him.

"Yeah, considering how distracted you've been the last couple of weeks, that's probably not a good idea."

"I haven't been distracted," he denied. "I've just had a lot on my mind."

"A lot?" Devin echoed dubiously. "Or a woman?"

Trevor scowled.

"I was at the wedding," his brother reminded him. "I saw you dancing with that girl only a short while before both of you disappeared from the reception."

"So?"

"So it seems to me that you've been distracted since that night. What's the matter? Did you strike out?"

"No, I didn't strike out."

"But you didn't get very far," Devin surmised. "I'm guessing a single...maybe a double."

"I can't believe you're still using baseball analogies to describe sex."

"Baseball is timeless," his brother insisted. "Also, it seemed apropos to our original topic of conversation."

"Apropos, huh?"

"And you're deflecting," Devin noted.

"I'm not deflecting."

"Then tell me what happened with Haylee Gilmore."

Trevor lifted his brows, a silent question.

His brother shrugged. "I might have asked someone who she was when I saw you leave with her. And then I Googled her."

"Why?" he asked.

"Because you're my brother and I wanted to be sure you weren't being targeted—again—by a wannabe social media influencer who thought she could increase her number of followers by posting photos with hashtag Blake Mining Heir."

He frowned, not just at the possibility but the fact that he'd been so captivated by the sexy and solo wedding guest, it had never occurred to him to consider the potential risks of going home with someone he'd only just met—and it should have.

"Did you find anything interesting?" Trevor asked his brother now.

Devin shook his head. "She has almost no social media presence. In fact, she hasn't posted anything to her Facebook page since she adopted a cat a few months back.

"Her sister, on the other hand, is constantly tweeting or Instagramming, sharing pictures of various events that she's planned, hashtag Gilmore Galas."

Trevor hadn't known that Haylee had a cat—or a sister. Because they hadn't wasted a lot of time on conversation. In fact, once they'd gone back to her room at the Stagecoach Inn, they'd done very little talking. They'd been so hot for one another that they'd barely made it inside the door before they were tearing at one another's clothes.

His heart had almost stopped when he'd peeled that sexy dress off her and discovered the even sexier lace she'd been wearing beneath it. The Brazilian panties and plunge bra (yes, he'd spent enough time on the Victoria's Secret website when he was a curious teenager to recognize the styles) were constructed of an almost-sheer fabric with a few strategically placed floral lace appliques. Intrigued, aroused, he'd tumbled with her onto the mattress, then focused his attention on a closer perusal of her undergarments. He'd suckled her breasts through the barely there fabric, moving from one to the other, drawing her turgid nipples into his mouth, gently laving and pulling, making her writhe and moan.

As his mouth skimmed lower, his hands lifted to her breasts, his thumbs continuing to stroke and tease. When his tongue traced the low-cut front of her panty, her hips had lifted off the mattress, wordlessly encouraging him to continue his exploration. So he'd nudged her thighs farther apart and settled between them, eager to taste—

"What happened then?" Devin asked again, interrupting his erotic recollection.

What happened was that Trevor had spent the next several hours with an amazing and passionate woman who'd later disappeared from his life as suddenly and unexpectedly as she'd come into it.

But he didn't want to talk about Haylee—or even

think about her abrupt vanishing act—anymore. Instead he said, "What happened, according to the rumors I heard, is that you finally got up the courage to ask Grace to dance that night."

"Actually, she asked me," Devin admitted.

"And you said yes?" Trevor prompted.

"Yeah." The hint of a smile curved his brother's lips. "I did."

"Were her feet black-and-blue by the time the song was over?"

"If they were, she didn't complain," Devin said, just a little defensively. "And after we danced, we talked for a long time—"

"Probably because her feet couldn't handle any more dancing," Trevor interjected.

"And then," Devin continued, pointedly ignoring the interruption. "I kissed her…or maybe she kissed me. Either way—" his brother shrugged, his lips curving again "—we kissed."

"So maybe she's the reason you suggested a trip to New York," Trevor mused.

Now Devin shook his head. "I told you—and Grace—that I'm not looking for a long-distance relationship."

"Is the distance really the problem? Or is it that you've been alone with your computer for so long that you don't know how to interact with a female?"

He knew he shouldn't tease his brother about his lack of a social life. In fact, he should be grateful that Devin was a homebody because it meant that Trevor had somewhere to go when he didn't feel like hanging out at the bar. And the truth was, he'd been spending a lot more time at Devin's than Diggers' in recent years.

"Oakland isn't a quarter as far as New York," Devin pointed out now. "So what's your excuse?"

"I don't do relationships. Period," Trevor reminded him. But he did have a reputation to uphold, which was why he hung out at his brother's house rather than alone at home.

"You can't let one bad experience—"

"When you've had a fiancée throw a three-carat diamond back in your face and blame you for everything that's ever gone wrong in her life, you can talk to me about bad experiences," he said, abruptly cutting off what was sure to be another one of his brother's pep talks.

"Point taken," Devin said, sounding chagrined.

Trevor didn't feel guilty about using his broken engagement as a tool to shut down the conversation. Though his relationship with Alannis had ended more than four years earlier, only a few weeks after his fiancée had suffered a miscarriage, most of his friends and family continued to tiptoe around the subject. None of them knew the whole truth about what had happened, because Trevor would rather they believed he was still nursing a broken heart than acknowledge that he'd been played for a fool by his supposedly devoted fiancée.

He pushed himself up off the sofa now, eager to escape the direction of his thoughts. "I'm going to get another beer," he announced. "Do you want one?"

"Sure," Devin agreed. "Grab the chips and salsa while you're there, too."

"How many hands do you think I have?"

"As many as you have feet capable of making two trips," Devin said, but he rose, too, and followed his brother into the kitchen.

"Have you talked to Haylee since she went back to California?" he asked, reaching into the cupboard for a bowl.

"You're like a starving dog with a juicy bone, aren't you?"

"Have you?" Devin pressed.

Trevor opened the fridge and pulled out two bottles of beer. "No."

"So give her a call."

"Maybe I will," he said, because it seemed the most likely response to get his brother to drop the subject. And because he was unwilling to admit that he didn't have her number.

In any event, that was a minor impediment. He was confident that he'd be able to track her down, if he really wanted to. He just hadn't yet decided if he wanted to.

And maybe he was a little bit disappointed that she hadn't reached out to him, especially considering that she was the one who'd slipped out of the hotel room they'd shared without even saying goodbye.

He should be relieved.

He *was* relieved.

He was also frustrated and angry and spending far too much time thinking about a woman who'd clearly not spared him a single thought since she'd gone back to California.

He should put her out of his mind.

Instead, he took his beer back to the living room,

pulled up the Athletics' schedule on his phone again and bought two tickets to a baseball game.

Finley snagged a still-warm peanut butter cookie from the tray, sighing with pleasure as she bit into it. "I'm probably going to regret asking, but I have to know—what happened?"

Haylee paused in the act of transferring cookies from the baking sheet to the cooling rack to glance at her sister. "What do you mean?"

"I mean that you're stress baking."

"I'm not," she denied, returning her attention to her task.

"You always start measuring and mixing when you're upset or concerned about something," Finley pointed out. "Because it focuses your attention on something other than whatever is upsetting or concerning you.

"Not that I'm complaining," she assured her sister. "Why would I when I reap the delicious benefits? But since this is the third batch of cookies this week, I can't deny that I'm starting to worry."

"There's no reason for you to worry," Haylee told her.

Finley snagged another cookie. "I beg to differ. And now that I think about it...the baking started three weeks ago, after you got back from Haven."

"That's ridiculous," she said.

"And you've been sketchy with details about your weekend away," Finley continued in support of her argument.

"Sketchy with details?" Haylee echoed disbelievingly. "I took hundreds of pictures at the wedding and showed them all to you."

"And blushed like a schoolgirl when I asked you to point out all the sexy cowboys that you danced with."

"You know I'm more comfortable on the sidelines than the middle of a dance floor."

"Uh-huh," her sister agreed, popping the last bite of cookie into her mouth. "A fact that skirts around rather than answers the question."

"Since you brought up the subject of dancing," Haylee said, in a not-at-all subtle effort to shift the topic of conversation. "How was your date with Thomas last night?"

Finley sighed. "It was a disaster."

"That bad?" she asked, sincerely disappointed for her sibling. She knew how much Finley had been looking forward to the night out and how excited she'd been about spending more time with the guy she'd met a few weeks earlier.

Her sister nodded. "He actually flossed on the dance floor."

"Maybe he had something stuck in his teeth?" Haylee suggested hesitantly.

Finley chuckled. "I mean, he did the floss dance."

"I'm unfamiliar with that one," she admitted.

"You know the chicken dance?"

She nodded.

"Well the floss makes the chicken dance look like a well-choreographed ballet."

"I can't imagine," she admitted with a smile.

"But damn, he's a good kisser," Finley said, sounding sincerely regretful. "In fact, he's so good that when he was kissing me, I almost forgot about what an awful dancer he is."

"Are you going to see him again?"

"I haven't decided, though we're definitely *not* going out dancing again."

"But that's your favorite date night activity," Haylee noted.

"Second favorite," her sister said, with a grin. "And a guy who kisses so expertly and thoroughly most likely has serious skills in the bedroom."

Haylee had to admit that her own, albeit very limited, experience supported her sister's supposition.

Because Trevor Blake had been an amazing kisser.

And an amazing lover.

His mouth had been soft but firm as it moved over hers, coaxing more than demanding. His kiss had been so much more than that simple word entailed; it had been an unexpectedly sweet and irresistible seduction. And from the first brush of his lips against hers, she'd been under his spell. Not just willing but eager. Desperately yearning.

But yearning for what?

She hadn't been entirely sure—she'd only known that she wanted to take everything he offered.

More.

When his tongue had touched the seam of her lips, they'd parted instinctively. Desire had flooded her system, racing through her veins like a drug, making her heart pound and her knees weak. And when he'd drawn her closer, she'd melted against him, holding on to him as the world spun around her.

She'd wanted to blame the champagne, but the truth was, she'd had only one glass, so she knew it wasn't the bubbly alcohol that was responsible for her reaction but the man himself. And—

"And there you go again," Finley said, sounding exasperated.

Haylee snapped back to the present. "What?"

"What is going on with you?" her sister demanded.

"Nothing." She shook her head. "I'm sorry."

"I believe you're sorry. I don't believe it's nothing. So why won't you tell me what it is?" Finley asked, sounding hurt. "I thought we could talk to one another about anything."

"We can," Haylee assured her. "I'm just not sure it's worth talking about."

"Let me be the judge of that."

"Okay," she finally agreed, almost relieved to be able to share at least some of the details with her sister. "If I've been a little distracted since I got back, it's because… I met someone at the wedding."

"Someone tall, dark and handsome?" her sister asked, immediately intrigued and eager for details.

"Unbelievably handsome," she said, almost sighing as a mental picture of Trevor Blake filled her mind. "But I'd describe his hair as more sandy than dark, and his eyes are the color of semisweet chocolate."

"That's pretty specific," Finley noted, sounding amused. "And also, I happen to know, your favorite kind of chocolate."

Haylee couldn't deny it.

"Does this unbelievably handsome guy with chocolate-colored eyes happen to have a name?" her sister asked.

She nodded. "Trevor Blake."

Finley grinned. "Go big or go home, huh?"

"What?"

"Of all the guys to get you hot and bothered, it had to be a Blake."

"The feud is over," she reminded her sister. "And, in any event, it's not likely I'll ever see him again."

"Why would you say that?" Finley challenged. "Haven isn't so far. And you'll be back there again in August for Grandma and Grandpa's sixtieth anniversary."

"I'm sure he'll have forgotten about me long before then," Haylee said, already resigned to the fact.

But she knew that she wouldn't ever forget him and the one amazing night they'd spent together.

What am I doing?

The question nagged at the back of Trevor's mind throughout the seven-hour drive from Haven to Oakland.

Because he knew that the tickets to the baseball game were more a prop than a reason, that the true impetus for this trip was to see Haylee Gilmore.

The world was full of beautiful and interesting women, and he wasn't in the habit of chasing after any of them. But he wasn't chasing the unforgettable brunette from his cousin's wedding so much as he was chasing answers.

Dammit, he was *entitled* to answers.

And he was determined to get them.

But first he had to find her.

There were over a thousand Gilmores in Oakland, and he knew almost nothing about the woman he was looking for aside from her name.

Well, nothing that would help him track her down.

But he knew the scent of her hair, had combed his fingers through the long, silky strands. He knew the taste of her lips, had been intoxicated by her sweet, seductive flavor. He knew the softness of her skin, the sexy sounds she made low in her throat, and he knew how her body felt, wrapped around his.

But the one detail that was indelibly imprinted on his memory, the real reason he'd made this trip to California in search of answers, was that smart, sexy, irresistible Haylee Gilmore had neglected to share an important piece of information when she'd invited him back to her hotel room that night.

She'd failed to tell him that she was a virgin.

Chapter Four

Haylee's plan for Saturday afternoon was to do absolutely nothing. Unfortunately that plan was thwarted by her sister almost as soon as Haylee settled on the sofa with Simon.

She didn't need to pick up the phone to know it was Finley who was calling, because she'd assigned specific ringtones to her various family members and closest friends. She also knew that her sister was at an event, so she wasn't calling just to chat.

"What did you forget?" Haylee asked, as soon as she'd connected the call.

Finley had left early that morning to supervise the arrangement of flowers at the church for an afternoon wedding and ensure the bride's room was ready for her arrival. Though her sister was ruthlessly organized and kept a well-stocked emergency kit of essentials in the trunk of her car, this wouldn't be the first time she'd called Haylee to request something that wasn't in her emergency kit: Big Apple Red nail polish, a bottle of non-aerosol hairspray or Peach Bellini–flavored gourmet jelly beans to soothe an anxious bride.

Of course, Finley had two assistants who worked for her now, so it was rare that she tapped Haylee to run errands these days.

"A plus-one for the bride's brother," Finley said.

"You want me to find a date for some random stranger?"

"No, I want you to *be* his date," her sister clarified.

"I'm going to have to say 'no' to that," Haylee said.

"*Pleeease,*" Finley said, drawing out the word. "I'm desperate."

"It sounds to me like the bride's brother is desperate. And why is it your responsibility to find him a date, anyway?" she wondered. "Can't he enjoy his sister's wedding without a girl hanging off his arm?"

"That was the plan," her sister told her. "Until—at the rehearsal dinner last night—he found out that his former fiancée is going to be at the wedding with the groom's brother."

She rolled her eyes at the ceiling. "It sounds like the plotline of a poorly scripted soap opera."

"I know," Finley admitted. "But I promised the bride and groom that I would go above and beyond to make this day perfect for them."

"You make the same promise to everyone who hires you to plan an event," Haylee pointed out. "But you've never tried to pimp me out before."

"And because I make that promise," her sister continued, ignoring the latter part of Haylee's remark, "I'm booked solid for the next fifteen months."

"Yet you never considered the possibility that I might have plans for tonight."

"I considered it," Finley said. "But cuddling with Simon and bingeing on Netflix doesn't count."

"Simon and I beg to differ," she said, stroking a hand down the calico's back.

"Christopher's a really nice guy," her sister said, her tone cajoling. "And not hard to look at, either."

"I'm sure he is, but I don't know him—or anyone else who's going to be at this wedding," Haylee argued. "Plus, I have nothing to wear."

"The dress you bought for Caleb and Brielle's wedding would be perfect."

"It's at the cleaners."

"It was," Finley acknowledged. "I picked it up along with my dry cleaning yesterday. It's now hanging in the front closet."

Haylee sighed. "It's going to take me at least an hour and a half to shave my legs and do my hair and makeup."

"You've got sixty minutes."

Which was really all the time she needed, but she knew that if she'd told her sister she wanted an hour, Finley would have whittled that time down to forty-five minutes.

"Where am I going?" she asked now. "And how long is it going to take me to get there?"

"The reception is in the grand ballroom of the Courtland Hotel. He'll pick you up in an hour."

"Wouldn't it be easier if I met him there?"

"It might be easier, but if you don't show up with him, how will anyone know that you're together? Plus, if he's picking you up, I know you won't accidentally-on-purpose get lost on the way."

Haylee sighed. "Then say goodbye now so I can start getting ready."

"Goodbye," Finley dutifully echoed. "See you soon."

Fifty-five minutes later, Haylee tucked her phone, keys, ID and credit card into her purse and stepped outside to wait for Christopher.

She hadn't thought to ask what kind of car the bride's brother would be driving and was just about to text that question to her sister when a glossy black SUV slowed at the curb. Assuming it was her ride, she automatically started toward the end of the driveway.

Then the driver's side door opened and a familiar—albeit unexpected—figure emerged.

Her heart skipped a beat, then kicked hard against her ribs. "Trevor?"

The door slammed shut and he took a few steps closer, his gaze skimming over her, from the deliberately loose knot of hair to the pink dress and the strappy sandals on her feet. A smile curved his lips. "Déjà vu."

"What are you doing here?" she asked, determinedly ignoring the fluttery sensation in her belly.

"Looking for you," he said.

Her heart skipped another two beats, and all her girl parts sighed with longing.

"But I'm getting the feeling that I may have come at a bad time," he continued.

"Yeah," she admitted, deeply and sincerely regretful. "I'm on my way out…a favor for my sister."

She didn't want to call it a date, because it really wasn't. And though she hadn't seen or even spoken to Trevor since the night they'd spent together in her hotel room, she wasn't comfortable admitting that her plans included another guy.

"How about tomorrow then?" he asked.

"Tomorrow?" she echoed, her mind blank.

"Do you have any plans tomorrow? Because I've got an extra ticket to the baseball game, if you want to join me."

"You came all this way for a baseball game?"

"My brother and I usually make the trip a couple times a year, but he had to go out of town for a conference this weekend, so I'm on my own."

Obviously he enjoyed driving more than she did, as she'd chosen to fly to Haven for the wedding rather than spend almost seven hours behind the wheel of a car with no one for company.

"So…what do you say to catching a ball game tomorrow? The A's are playing the Rangers," he said, as if that additional bit of information might influence her response. "I'll even buy you a hot dog."

She managed a smile. "Now that's a tempting offer."

"Is that a *yes*?" he prompted hopefully.

Of course she wanted to say *yes*. She was thrilled to see him again, eager to believe that he'd sought her out because the night they'd spent together had meant as much to him as it had to her. Except that she wasn't the type of girl that a guy went out of his way to spend time with—and five hundred miles was definitely out of his way.

"Why are you really here, Trevor?"

He smiled again. "I'm a diehard A's fan." Then his expression turned serious. "But I also think there are some things that we need to talk about."

She swallowed uneasily. "You do?"

He pinned her with his gaze. "Don't you?"

Before she could respond, her phone buzzed inside her purse. "I need to check that."

Not surprisingly, it was a text message from her sister.

Christopher will be there in 2 min. Are you ready?

She tapped a quick reply.

Ready and waiting.

"Obviously our conversation will have to wait," Trevor noted.

"I'm sorry."

"No need to apologize. I should have realized that you'd have plans on a Saturday night."

She didn't tell him that it was a rare event, instead asking, "What time's the game tomorrow?"

"One-oh-five," he said. "How about if I swing by to pick you up around noon?"

"Actually, I've got to check in at a worksite not too far from the coliseum in the morning, so it probably makes more sense for me to meet you there."

He pulled his phone out of his back pocket. "I'll send

you the e-ticket so that we can meet at our seats rather than trying to connect outside."

"Sounds good," she said.

He swiped the screen, then looked at her. "I'm going to need your number."

"Oh, right." She felt her cheeks flush as she rattled off the digits.

A few seconds later, her phone pinged to indicate receipt of his message with the ticket attached. At the same time, a silver-colored sports car pulled up at the curb. "That's my ride."

Trevor took a step back, a slightly puzzled expression on his face. "I'll see you tomorrow then?"

She nodded, already looking forward to it.

The next morning, Trevor had breakfast at his hotel near the Oakland–Alameda County Coliseum, then checked out of his room and headed over to the ballpark. He still had a couple hours to kill before the game's official start time, and he didn't like to admit that he'd probably spend most of that time thinking about Haylee.

When he'd embarked on this road trip, he'd been looking forward to not just the baseball game but reconnecting with the woman who'd preoccupied his thoughts since the night they'd spent together. Yes, he wanted answers from her. But he also just wanted to see her and maybe, if the attraction between them was as strong as he remembered, get naked with her again and take his time teaching her to appreciate all the things he wouldn't have rushed through the first time if he'd known it was her first time.

It was obviously a testament to his own inflated

sense of self that he'd never considered that she might already have other plans—and not want to abandon them to be with him. He'd definitely never considered that those plans might be a date with another guy. Because notwithstanding what she'd said about a favor for her sister, it hadn't been her sister driving the silver sports car that picked her up—it had been a man.

Trevor might have thought it was an Uber or Lyft, except that drivers for hire didn't usually drive luxury vehicles. Plus this one had been wearing a suit, as he'd observed when the driver got out of the car to open the passenger-side door for Haylee.

She didn't glance in Trevor's direction as she lowered herself into the vehicle, so she didn't see him standing on the sidewalk with what was undoubtedly a *WTF* expression on his face and even more questions swirling in his mind.

The biggest one right now was: Would she use the ticket he gave her—or would the seat beside his remain empty throughout the game?

He scowled at the thought as his own ticket was scanned.

He could tell himself that he'd sought Haylee out not just for answers but because he felt guilty about taking her innocence. But the truth was, he'd been drawn to her from the start. From the first moment he'd set eyes on her at Brielle and Caleb's wedding, he'd been intrigued. By the time they'd danced together under the stars, in a field beside a field of cows, he'd been smitten.

And then he'd been dumped.

At least, it sure as hell felt that way.

So maybe his heart wasn't bruised so much as his pride was stung.

Except that even his brief interaction with Haylee the day before suggested there was more going on than a dent to his ego. There was definitely something between them—a spark that hadn't been extinguished despite the time and distance that had passed since they parted ways. So he really hoped she showed up today, because he knew that he wouldn't be going back to Nevada without seeing her again, and he was afraid he'd be venturing close to stalker territory if he showed up at her door a second time.

He shifted his attention to the field as the home team took their positions for warm-up. He still remembered his first major league game—an opening day contest at this very stadium when he was just ten years old. It had been a father-son trip, just Elijah Blake and Trevor, and one of his happiest early memories.

Devin had protested that he was a son, too, but their dad had remained firm. "Your turn will come," he'd promised his second-born. And it had, two years later, when Devin had reached the milestone of double digits.

After that, opening day had become an annual ritual for the three of them, and this park held a lot of wonderful memories: the sound of a ball coming off the sweet spot of a bat; a leaping over-the-wall catch that robbed a visiting hitter of a home run; a quick throw to pick off a base runner; an unexpected walk-off home run from the bottom of the lineup.

There were a lot of reasons that baseball was America's favorite pastime, and when Trevor and Devin were old enough to finance their own travels, the brothers started making additional trips to California to savor the glory of the game. They occasionally visited other parks, too, but the Athletics were their team—for better or for worse.

Thinking about his brother now, he pulled out his phone to check in with Devin.

How are things in Montreal?

Très occupé.

Trevor smiled at the response.

I just wanted you to know that while you're stuck in a conference room, I'm at the A's game and the sun is shining.

Tabarnak!

Trevor had no idea what that was supposed to mean, but the exclamation mark suggested that it was a curse of some kind.

Devin switched back to English then to ask:

Who's there with you? ;)

A stadium full of people I've never met before.

That got him an eye roll emoji, followed by:

Did you buy one ticket or two?

Trevor wasn't sure he wanted to answer that question—especially as the seat beside him was currently still unoccupied. Instead, he replied:

They're announcing the national anthem singer. I'll catch up with you later.

Enjoy the game.

He glanced at the time displayed on the top of his screen before he tucked his phone away and rose to his feet. The exchange with his brother had managed to divert his attention for a whole three minutes, which meant that it was now three minutes closer to the throwing out of the ceremonial first pitch—and there was still no sign of Haylee.

Chapter Five

She was late.

Haylee glanced at the electronic ticket on the screen of her phone again as she navigated through the thinning crowd in search of the entrance to Section 120. It had to be close to game time, as groups of spectators were moving away from the concession stands, carrying trays of food and drinks, toward their seats in the stadium.

The scents of grilled meat and greasy fries made her stomach growl, but she didn't stop. Not only because she worried that she was already late, but because her stomach—though empty—was also jittery about the prospect of seeing Trevor again.

Anticipation, yes, but a little bit of trepidation, too, as the echo of his words "we need to talk" reverberated inside her head. She was pretty sure she knew what the "some things" he wanted to talk about were—or at least *one* of the things. And it wasn't a topic that she was particularly eager to discuss.

She'd slipped out of her room at the Stagecoach Inn in the early hours of the morning without waking him because she was a coward, because she didn't want to answer the questions she knew he would ask. And though it still wasn't a conversation she was eager to have, she couldn't resist the opportunity to spend more time with him.

She showed her ticket to an usher, to ensure she was headed in the right direction. He nodded and smiled. "Enjoy the game."

"Thanks."

The crowd was restless, eager for the game to start— which meant that she wasn't actually late. Not yet.

She looked around, scanning the crowd. There were groups of men, couples, families, an elderly couple down by the third base line, decked out from head to toe in Athletics' gear. She'd never really understood the desire to display one's team allegiance, but she'd borrowed a T-shirt and baseball cap from her sister's closet—to blend in but also because she hadn't known what else to wear to a baseball game.

She could have asked Finley's advice, but then she'd have to admit that she had a date—if an invitation to a baseball game could be considered a date.

Which it probably wasn't.

Hopefully wasn't.

Because in addition to not knowing what to wear, she'd been so focused on getting to the job site that she hadn't thought to put on makeup before she'd left home earlier that morning. It wasn't until she was on her way to the coliseum that she wished she'd taken the time to brush some mascara onto her lashes and swipe some gloss on her lips.

Of course, most women carried those essentials in their purses so that they could freshen up their look at any point during the day, but Haylee wasn't most women. Her morning beauty routine consisted of slapping on some moisturizer with sunscreen, because she never knew when she might be working outside in the elements, and untinted lip balm.

Well, today Trevor Blake was going to meet the real Haylee Gilmore, and if he didn't like what he saw, he was going to be on his way back to Haven soon enough anyway.

She counted her way to Row 25, then looked for Seat 10. She spotted Trevor first, and the empty spot beside him.

"Excuse me," she said, sidling past the already seated spectators.

With every shuffling step, her heart began to beat just a little bit faster, until she finally reached the vacant seat beside him just as the crowd rose for the singing of the national anthem.

"Sorry I'm late," she said, after the anthem had concluded and they were settled into their seats.

"You weren't actually late," he pointed out.

"Then I'll apologize for cutting it close," she amended.

"No need," he said. "I'm just glad you made it. And

curious what you do for an electrical company that required you to work on a Sunday morning."

"We had to install a new breaker panel at a local law office, and they wanted it done before Monday."

"So you're an electrician," he realized.

She nodded.

"Why didn't you just say so in the first place?" he wondered.

"Because Finley told me that some guys are intimidated by women who work in what are traditionally viewed as male occupations," she admitted.

"Who's Finley? And why are you taking advice from her?"

"My sister," she said. "And because she's my sister."

"Even so, why would you want to be with a guy who felt threatened by your job?"

"I wouldn't," she assured him. "But it's hard to argue with a sister who has a lot more dating experience than I do."

"Well, speaking as a guy with a fair amount of dating experience, I have to confess a weakness for women who aren't just beautiful but interesting."

"Then you'd like my sister," Haylee noted.

Of course, all the guys she'd ever liked had liked Finley better. And she didn't doubt that if Finley had attended the wedding in Haven, Trevor wouldn't have looked at Haylee twice.

He shook his head, a slight smile curving his lips. "I like you, Haylee."

Her heart thumped against her ribs and heat rushed through her veins. "You do?"

"Yes, I do," he confirmed. "Why else would I give you my extra ticket?"

"Because you don't know anyone else in Oakland." Trevor couldn't help but chuckle at that.

"Because I wanted to see you," he clarified.

"And I didn't even put on any makeup today."

The blurted confession was immediately followed by a rush of color to her cheeks.

"Which only proves you don't need it. And as much as I like you in a dress and heels, this is a good look for you, too," he said, gesturing to the enormous gold-colored *A* emblazoned on the front of her dark green T-shirt and matching ball cap.

"I borrowed the T-shirt and hat from Finley's closet," she confided.

"Your sister's a fan?"

"She dated one of the players—Mark Nickel—a few years back. They broke up when he was traded to Baltimore."

"She couldn't bring herself to cheer for the Orioles?" he guessed.

"She didn't want a long-distance relationship."

"California to Maryland is quite a distance," he acknowledged, even as he wondered if Haylee was trying to make a point about the fact that they lived in different states.

Not that he was looking for a relationship, but he wouldn't view five hundred miles as an insurmountable barrier, and he didn't like to think that she'd already closed herself off to the possibility of something more between them. After all, most women thought he was quite a catch.

But that might be because he was a big fish in a small pond in Haven and Haylee was accustomed to more plentiful waters in Oakland. Except that she obviously hadn't done much fishing in those waters, as he'd discovered when he shared her bed.

Which was, of course, what he'd wanted to talk to her about. But listening to the buzz of the crowd around them, he realized that this wasn't the best time or place to get into a conversation about why she hadn't told him about her inexperience and then disappeared without even a goodbye the morning after.

He was still justifiably annoyed with her about that, but right now he was having trouble remembering his annoyance. Because he could smell just a hint of coconut in her shampoo, and he recalled that same scent lingering on the pillow where she'd lain her head. And he could see the sweet curve of her breasts beneath her T-shirt and was certain the scripted *A* had never looked so good. The hem of the shirt was tucked into slim-fitting jeans, and on her feet, she wore dark brown work boots—steel-toed, he'd bet, now that he knew what her job entailed. And while he appreciated a woman in sexy heels as much as the next guy, thinking about the contrast of Haylee's delicate feet with pink-painted toe-nails inside those heavy boots was a surprising turn-on.

She leaned forward in her seat as the batter's swing connected with the ball, sending it sailing through the air, deep into center field. But not quite deep enough, as the fielder's glove swallowed it on the warning track.

"Whew." She settled back again. "That was a little too close for comfort."

"Apparently the manager thought so, too," he noted,

as the man jogged out to the mound to talk to his pitcher, and only then realizing that he'd been paying more attention to the woman seated beside him than the action on the field.

"He can't call for a pitching change already," she protested. "That would put too much pressure on the bullpen."

"So much for thinking that I might impress you with my detailed knowledge of the game," he noted dryly.

"Sorry," she immediately apologized. "I'm not very good at sitting quiet and looking pretty."

"That isn't something you should ever apologize for," he assured her. "Although I'd have to disagree with the latter part of your claim."

"But now you've impressed me with your use of the word 'latter.' Most of the guys I work with only know it as a set of horizontal bars used for climbing up or down."

"I'll take points wherever I can get them," he said.

"You'd get bonus points for feeding me," Haylee told him.

"Are you hungry?"

"Starving," she admitted.

"You want a hot dog?"

"I'd love a hot dog."

"I'll head to the concession stand as soon as the top of the inning is over," he promised. "What do you like on your dog?"

"Ketchup and mustard. Please."

"And to drink?"

"A Coke would be great, thanks."

"I'll be right back," he promised.

Of course, he missed the better part of two innings waiting in line for their food, and the A's had taken a two-run lead by the time he returned, carrying a tray with two dogs, two Cokes, a heaping box of fries, a bag of roasted-in-the-shell peanuts and a package of licorice.

He put one of the cups in her cupholder, then handed her a foil-wrapped dog. "Thanks."

She eagerly unwrapped it, but paused when he set the bag of peanuts and the licorice in her lap. "What are those for?"

"Extra bonus points?" he suggested.

She chuckled as she lifted the hot dog to her mouth. When she finished chewing, she took a long swallow of soda. Watching her mouth close over the straw made him want to imagine those same lips closing around—

No. Not the time or place to indulge in prurient fantasies, he chastised himself, and turned his attention to his own lunch and the ball game.

It had been a couple of years since Haylee had last been at the coliseum for a baseball game. And while she occasionally caught the action on TV, the live experience was so much better. Sitting beside Trevor while watching the game was even better still.

But by the seventh inning stretch, the A's were holding a three-run edge over the Rangers, the food wrappers and beverage containers were empty and Haylee's stomach was feeling a little unsettled. It was her own fault, she knew, for racing out of the house without breakfast and then stuffing her face with everything Trevor had brought back from the concession stand.

Not that she'd eaten it all, but she'd consumed at least her fair share.

Still, she stood when everyone else did, eager to stretch her legs and restore some circulation to her bottom. But she must have moved too quickly, because the earth seemed to shift beneath her feet, forcing her to grab hold of the seatback in front of her for balance. Or she'd spent too much time in the sun. Or maybe too much time in close proximity to a hunky weekend cowboy who actually seemed to be interested in *her*.

Several times throughout the game, she'd glanced over to find his gaze on her rather than the action playing out on the field. But thankfully, he hadn't noticed her tilting off balance, and a few minutes later, they were seated again.

As the crowd roared in appreciation of the home team executing a textbook 4-6-3 play that put them within one out of the win, she glanced over at Trevor with a happy smile and found his attention focused on her.

"Why are you looking at me rather than the baseball game that you traveled five hundred miles to see?" she asked.

"Because you're a lot prettier than anyone on the field."

Unaccustomed to such compliments, she felt her cheeks flush. "You obviously missed the double play that just happened, because it was truly a thing of beauty."

"You obviously haven't considered that maybe the game was just an excuse to see you," he suggested.

She couldn't help but laugh at that.

"You don't think it's true?" he challenged.

"A few years back, I dated a guy who grumbled about having to drive from Chabot Park to Glenview to spend time with me," she told him. "So forgive me for not believing that you'd come all the way from Haven, Nevada, for the pleasure of my company."

"I have no idea how far Chabot Park is from Glenview—"

"About ten miles," she interjected.

"—but I'm sure the guy was an idiot," he continued.

"Or maybe he just wasn't that into me," she allowed, as the Rangers' potential final batter set up at the plate. "Although, in all fairness, I wasn't that into him, either."

"How long were you together?"

The first pitch was off the plate on the inside for a ball.

"We went out four or five times over the space of about three months."

"Four or five?" he asked, sounding amused. "You don't remember?"

The second pitch was high. Ball two.

"We ran into one another by chance one night when we were both waiting for a table at a new restaurant. We were both with friends and decided to eat together. I'm not sure that actually counts as a date."

"Did he drive you home after dinner?"

"No."

Trevor shifted his attention to the plate as the umpire finally called "stee-rike" on the third pitch. "Did he kiss you goodbye?"

"On the cheek."

He shook his head then. "Definitely not a date."

"Those are the criteria?" she asked. "Taking a girl home and kissing her goodbye?"

"At the very least."

After watching the first three pitches go by, the batter finally took a swing at the ball—and missed. Strike two.

"Then I've been on even fewer dates than I realized," she mused.

And when the batter swung again at an outside pitch for the third strike and final out, she was a little disappointed that this one—though not technically a date—was over.

"It's hard to complain when the home team wins," she remarked, as they shuffled toward the exit with the rest of the departing spectators. "But it sucked for Ramirez that he didn't get to bat in the ninth and have a chance to hit for the cycle."

"Most team players would say it's the win that matters."

"And they'd be lying," Haylee said, making him laugh.

"Seriously," she continued. "Giants fans who remember August 7, 2007, know it as the date that Barry Bonds hit home run number 756 to break Hank Aaron's record, but I bet most of them couldn't tell you the final score of that game—or even who won."

"Fair point," he acknowledged, guiding her toward the northside exits as the crowd began to disperse.

"The BART station is that way," she said, pointing.

"But the lot I'm parked in is this way," he said, nudging her forward.

"Then I guess we should say goodbye here."

"We'll say goodbye after I've taken you home," he said.

"There's no reason for you to go out of your way," she protested. "And I'm sure you're anxious to be getting back to your hotel."

"Actually, I've got a ten o'clock meeting tomorrow morning, so I'm heading back to Haven tonight."

"Then I definitely don't want to delay your departure."

"My father taught me to always see a girl safely to her door," he said.

"One of the criteria for a date," she noted, butterflies winging around inside her tummy at the thought that he might want to kiss her goodbye.

"And if you invited me to come inside for a cup of coffee—to help keep me awake for the long drive home—I could kiss you goodbye without any concerns about your neighbors watching."

"I could make you a cup of coffee," she agreed, as he walked her around to the passenger side of his vehicle. He clicked a button on the key fob to unlock the door, then reached for the handle, as if to open it for her.

"Is something wrong?" she asked when he paused.

"I'm definitely going to want a cup of coffee when we get to your place," he said, lifting a hand to tip the brim of her ball cap up as he lowered his head. "But I don't want to wait that long to kiss you."

Chapter Six

And just like the first time Trevor had kissed her, Haylee responded with a passion that roused his own. He wrapped his arms around her, to draw her closer, but she was already there, the soft curves of her body melting against him. He touched the tip of his tongue to the seam of her lips, and they parted willingly for him to deepen the kiss.

She lifted her arms and twined her hands behind his head, holding on to him as she kissed him back.

For the past several weeks, he'd been beating himself up over the fact that he'd taken her to bed—and taken her virginity—without ever guessing the extent of her inexperience.

No matter how often he told himself that he couldn't have known what she didn't tell him, he couldn't shake the feeling that he should have picked up on signs or signals. He had enough experience with women to rec- ognize inexperience, but Haylee's passionate responses to every kiss and touch had blinded him to all else.

Maybe she'd seemed a little overeager, but he'd chalked that up to the champagne, guessing that she was just a little bit tipsy. But not too tipsy—he would never have accepted the invitation to go back to her hotel if he'd suspected that she was drunk.

And he definitely wouldn't have accepted her invita- tion if he'd suspected that she was a virgin.

In retrospect, the pieces all fit together to form a clear picture. But in the moment, when she'd been pant- ing his name, her nails raking down his back, her body arching to meet his, he hadn't been thinking clearly. He'd barely been able to think at all.

He'd wanted her with a desperation he hadn't felt since he was a seventeen-year-old virgin eager to change that status. And when she'd lifted her hips off the mattress, he hadn't hesitated to accept the wordless invitation. He'd buried himself in her, ramming through the barrier of her virginity before his brain had a chance to register the unexpected resistance.

And by then, it was too late.

He'd heard her gasp of shock—or was it pain?—and immediately tried to withdraw. But she'd thwarted his best efforts, wrapping her arms and legs around him, drawing him even deeper inside her. And the glorious feeling of being deep inside her completely wiped from his mind any thought of pulling away.

But afterward, he didn't know what to say to her.

He'd been in shock. Stunned. Furious. Confused.

And so, when he'd returned to the bedroom after disposing of the condom marked with the evidence of her lost innocence and found her pretending to be asleep, he went along with the pretense, confident that he would get the answers he deserved in the morning.

Three weeks later, he still didn't have any answers. But he had Haylee in his arms, and right now, nothing else seemed to matter.

"Get a room." The suggestion was made in a derisive tone and from close proximity. "Or at least get out of my way."

Haylee had already pulled out of Trevor's arms, flattening herself against the passenger door of his SUV so the rude stranger could enter the adjacent vehicle.

Trevor resisted the urge to flip the guy off, acknowledging that he should be grateful for the interruption because he wasn't sure how far he would have gone in the middle of the afternoon in a busy parking lot—especially when Haylee had given no indication of wanting to stop him.

"I'll apologize for the poor choice of venue but not for the kiss," Trevor told her. "I've been wanting to do that all day."

Haylee blinked, surprised by the admission. "You have?"

"Actually, I've been thinking about it since I saw you yesterday," he confided, and lightly brushed his mouth over hers again. "Your lips are as soft and sweet as I remembered."

"And your kiss is as bone-melting as I remembered," she said, her head spinning and her knees weak.

He grinned. "I like that you say exactly what's on your mind."

"You do?" she asked dubiously.

"It's a refreshing change," he assured her. "A lot of girls like to make a guy guess what they're thinking—and then punish him for guessing wrong."

"I don't play those kinds of games," Haylee said. "Probably because I don't know the rules."

"Maybe not, but you have some serious skills."

"Do you think so?" she asked, pleased by his assessment.

"I also think it's lucky for we mortal men that you don't understand the true extent of your power," he said, and opened the passenger-side door for her.

As Trevor navigated the heavy flow of traffic leaving the coliseum, Haylee wasn't nervous about going back to her apartment with him because she knew they wouldn't be alone. Although Finley had planned all the minute details for a baptism celebration that afternoon, it was a small event and she'd put her assistant Julia in charge of the execution on-site.

She was, however, a little apprehensive about introducing Trevor to Finley, because no man had ever wanted to be with Haylee after meeting her sister. But maybe that was exactly the reality check Haylee needed. Being with Trevor—flirting with him and kissing him—made her want more. And despite her relative inexperience with men, she recognized that he wasn't the type to give more.

In any event, if he shifted his fickle attention to her sister—as members of the male species were apt to do—she should breathe a sigh of relief. Sure, it had been nice to be the sole focus of a guy's attention, at least for a while. But she knew that she was in way over her head and that Finley was much better equipped to deal with someone like Trevor Blake than Haylee would ever be.

"Nice place," he noted, following her down the flag-stone path that led to an old-fashioned carriage house behind a two-story stone-and-brick mansion.

"We like it," she said.

"You live with your sister?"

She nodded as she slid her key into the lock. "And Simon."

Speaking of, as soon as Trevor stepped into the foyer behind her, the silly animal streaked down the hall and disappeared into an open doorway.

"That was Simon," she told him.

"Cat?" he guessed.

Haylee nodded. "He's usually waiting for me at the door when I come home, but he's wary of strangers and will probably hide under my bed until you're gone."

As she headed to the kitchen, she heard the mur-mur of her sister's voice behind the closed door of her home office.

"You'll get to meet my sister when she's off the phone—if she gets off the phone. She has an event planning business, Gilmore Galas," she explained, as she examined the carousel of K-Cups. "Do you want regular or decaf?"

"Regular," he said. "I've got a long drive ahead of me."

"French roast, Colombian dark, breakfast blend or caramel vanilla?"

"Regular," he said again.

She smiled as she selected the French roast and popped it into the machine.

"Cream or sugar?"

"Yes. Please."

She opened the fridge to get out the cream and found a bag of sugar in the pantry. She set both on the table and grabbed a teaspoon from the drawer.

Finley walked into the kitchen then, looked at the condiments and gave a slight shake of her head.

"Haylee doesn't entertain very often," she said, opening the cupboard above the coffee maker and taking out a small ceramic pitcher and matching covered sugar bowl.

"You must be Finley," he said. "And really, this is fine. Don't get out the fancy dishes for me."

"They're not fancy," she denied. "And you are…"

"Trevor Blake."

She shook his proffered hand. "It's nice to meet you."

"Likewise," he said, smiling his thanks to Haylee when she set a mug of coffee in front of him.

"Cookies are always good with coffee," Finley hinted to her sister.

"Do you want a cookie?" Haylee asked Trevor.

"I think I ate more than enough at the ball game."

"So that's where you were," Finley noted. "Of course, the T-shirt and cap you stole from my closet should have been the giveaway."

"Borrowed," Haylee corrected.

Her sister, clearly undeterred by Trevor's insistence that he wasn't hungry, carefully arranged a handful of cookies on a plate.

"Peanut butter cup cookies," she said, setting the plate on the table with a couple of napkins.

"Homemade," he noted, sounding impressed.

"Haylee made them," Finley told him. "She can't boil water without scorching a pot—"

"That happened once," she interjected, rolling her eyes.

"—but her baked goods are the best. You'll think you've gone to sugar heaven."

"Now I have to try one," Trevor said, reaching for a cookie.

"If you believe the heaven part, you're going to be disappointed," Haylee warned.

He bit into the cookie and hummed a low sound of approval. "I'm not disappointed."

Finley winked. "Told you."

Her phone chimed with a text message. "Whoops! I forgot the guest book when I packed up at the reception last night. I'm going to run over to the hotel now to pick it up before it gets misplaced." She grabbed her purse off a hook by the door and tucked her phone in the side pocket. "It was nice meeting you, Trevor."

"You, too," he said.

But she was already gone, leaving Haylee and Trevor alone.

"Maybe running out without saying goodbye is a family trait," he mused.

Haylee paused with her mug halfway to her mouth.

"That is, after all, what you did the morning after we spent the night together."

"Because I had a plane to catch," she said. "And you were asleep."

"Or maybe because you didn't want to talk about what happened the night before?"

"I don't have a lot of experience with mornings after," she said.

"Or any?" he suggested.

"So it just seemed easier to avoid awkward and unnecessary conversation," she continued, ignoring his question as the answer was obvious.

"I'd argue that it was necessary."

"Why? Because you're accustomed to being the one who walks away in the morning?" she guessed.

He frowned at that. "No, because you were a virgin."

"Please don't make a big deal about that," she pleaded.

"Isn't it a big deal?" he asked.

"No," she responded.

He studied her for a long moment as he sipped his coffee. "How old are you, Haylee?"

"What does my age have to do with anything?" she wondered, baffled by the unexpected question.

"How old?" he asked again.

She huffed out a breath. "Twenty-nine."

"So you were a virgin for twenty-nine years, and then suddenly decided to get naked with a guy you'd met only a few hours earlier?"

"Trust me, that status wasn't deliberate. I wasn't saving it for someone special. I wasn't consciously saving it at all," she confided. "I guess I just…never met anyone that I wanted…to be…intimate with."

"So I should be flattered that you chose me?" he challenged.

"You don't have to be flattered. Just don't make a big deal out of it."

"I'm trying not to," he said. "But I can't understand how you got to be a twenty-nine-year-old virgin."

"By not having sex for twenty-nine years," she said, stating the obvious.

"Seriously," he said. "You can't expect me to believe that you didn't have boyfriends."

"I had a couple," she acknowledged. "I just didn't sleep with any of them."

"Not even the guy you were with last night?"

She frowned. "What are you talking about? Who?"

"The guy who picked you up in front of the house."

"That wasn't a date. It was a favor for my sister."

He lifted a brow.

"I told you she's an event planner," she reminded him. "Yesterday the bride was stressing because she found out that her brother's ex-fiancée was going to be at the wedding as the groom's cousin's plus-one, so Finley promised to find a date for the brother so that he wouldn't be alone."

His gaze narrowed. "You just made that up."

"I did not," she assured him.

"Does your sister often require your help at events?"

"Occasionally. But that was the first time I had to wear a dress and heels. Usually I just run errands. Although I did fill in as a server once, when the caterer was short-staffed."

"A woman of many talents," he mused. Then he shifted gears again to ask, "So…are you currently dating anyone?"

"Well, according to your definition, I had a date this afternoon."

"Nice guy?" he asked, obviously fishing for a compliment.

"Nice enough," she agreed.

"Good-looking?"

She reached for a cookie, fighting against a smile. "I'm sure most women would think so."

"What do *you* think?"

"I think he's way out of my league, and I'll probably never see him again after today."

He appeared to mull over that response as she nibbled on the edge of the cookie. Though they were usually her favorite, her stomach was already protesting the fact that she'd eaten more junk food in one afternoon than she usually consumed in a week.

She set down the cookie and picked up her mug, then put it down again without drinking.

"Excuse me," she said, abruptly pushing away from the table.

Trevor instinctively followed her down the hall, where the unmistakable sound of retching could be heard through the closed door of what he hoped was the bathroom.

He waited for the retching to stop, then tapped on the wood portal. "Haylee?"

She groaned. "Please. Go. Away."

He retreated a few steps but hesitated to go any farther until he heard the toilet flush, then the tap run. As he listened to the sound of what he guessed was her toothbrush, he found himself wondering about her sudden bout of nausea.

Maybe it was paranoia. Or maybe it was the fact that he'd been faced with an all-too-similar situation before. But Trevor suddenly found himself wondering...

Was it possible...could she be...pregnant?

He hadn't realized that he'd spoken aloud or that she'd come out of the bathroom until she responded with an immediate and vehement denial: "No! Of course not."

But he noted that her face had gone pale, as if she was only now considering the possibility.

"We used protection," she said, as if that would put the question to rest.

"A condom that you provided." And recalling that detail, deeply buried memories and ugly suspicions rose to the surface of his mind.

"Because even a girl who's never had sex knows the dangers of unprotected sex," she told him. "That's the only reason I've been carrying a condom with me since the night of my high school prom."

"Please tell me that's not the condom we used."

"Of course not," she denied. "That one's probably still in the purse I took to prom."

"Well, that's a relief," he said, following her back to the kitchen.

She seemed puzzled by his response. "Why does it matter where the condom came from?"

"Because a condom left over from high school would have expired a long time ago."

She swallowed as she sank into the chair she'd recently abandoned. "What do you mean—expired?"

He returned to his seat across from her. "I mean that condoms have a shelf life."

He wouldn't have thought it was possible, but her face got even whiter then.

"Why would you tell me something like that *now*?"

"I didn't realize it would be news to you."

"They shouldn't call it protection if it doesn't protect," she grumbled.

"Did we use an expired condom?" he asked her.

"I don't know…maybe." She nibbled on her bottom lip. "Probably."

He was trying really hard not to overreact, but he also wasn't going to pretend he wasn't pissed by this revelation. "I'm guessing that you're not on any other form of birth control?"

"No," she admitted.

"So it's not outside the realm of possibility that you could be pregnant," he noted.

She shook her head. "No," she said again, though not quite as vehemently this time as color filled her pale cheeks. "I got my period a couple of weeks ago."

"Was your flow normal?"

"Ohmygod." She dropped her face into her hands, clearly uncomfortable with the direction of their conversation. "Why are you doing this?"

"Because I need to know if there's any chance that you might be carrying my child."

"I just told you there's not."

"Sometimes the spotting that can occur early in pregnancy is mistaken for a period."

"How would you know something like that?" she challenged.

"I just do," he said, unwilling to get into the details of that particular history with her right now.

"It wasn't spotting," she said, the pink color in her cheeks deepening. "And I really don't want to talk about this anymore."

He nodded. "Okay. But just so we're clear—I'm not going to marry you."

Her eyes went wide and her jaw fell open, but she recovered quickly and replied, "I don't recall asking you to marry me."

"You didn't," he acknowledged coolly. "But I didn't want you holding on to false hope, in case your seduction at the wedding was all part of some elaborate plan to trap me."

"*My* seduction?" she echoed incredulously. "*You're* the one who followed me into the field."

"And *you're* the one who invited me back to your hotel."

"Obviously that night was a mistake," she snapped back at him now.

"I have no regrets about that night," he told her. "But I'm not going to be on the hook for the next eighteen years because of it."

"I didn't have any regrets, either," she said. "Until you started throwing around outrageous accusations."

"I'm sorry," he said. "But you wouldn't be the first woman who thought she could trap me into marriage."

"How many illegitimate Trevor Blakes are there running around in the world?" she wondered aloud.

"Not even one," he promised.

"And I can assure you, I have no interest in changing that number." She pushed away from the table again. "Since your coffee is obviously finished, you should go. You've got a long drive ahead of you."

Chapter Seven

He'd never been dismissed so completely—and angrily—by a woman.

Three days later, Trevor was still trying to figure out how an enjoyable afternoon at the ballpark had gone so spectacularly wrong. But maybe it wasn't such a mystery. Maybe a man accusing a woman of trying to get pregnant to trap him into marriage wasn't the best way to tell her that he'd like to see her again.

Of course, he hadn't acknowledged the truth of that desire even to himself until he was with her. Yes, he'd gone to California because he'd wanted answers. But he'd also wanted to know what it was about Haylee that had so completely captivated him from the start.

Her parting words suggested that she wasn't nearly as enamored of him, and he could hardly fault her for that. Not considering the things he'd said, the accusations he'd leveled.

Desperate for a reprieve from his own thoughts, Trevor picked up a six-pack and a pizza from Jo's and stopped by to see his brother.

"So tell me about the game," Devin said, as he lifted a slice of three-meat pizza from the box.

Trevor twisted the cap off a bottle and swallowed a mouthful of beer before responding. "The A's won."

"I got that much from the sports recap on the news," his brother said. "I was hoping you could supply a few more details."

"Ramirez almost hit for the cycle."

Devin waved a hand dismissively. "Almost doesn't count."

"He got on base with a double in the second and a triple in the fifth and homered in the seventh," Trevor continued anyway, because as long as he was talking about the game, he didn't have to think about the fact that the rest of his weekend had been a complete bust. "All he needed was a single in the ninth, but the A's didn't have to bat."

"That's an impressive almost," his brother acknowledged. "Remember when we saw Mark Nickel hit for the cycle?"

"Yeah, and then they traded Nickel in the off-season."

"Horrible trade." Devin reached into the box for another slice of pizza. "Did Haylee enjoy the game?"

Trevor froze with his beer halfway to his mouth. "What makes you think I saw Haylee?"

"Come on," his brother said. "We both know she's the real reason you went to California."

He scowled at that as he swallowed a mouthful of beer. "I didn't even realize she was the reason until I was halfway to California."

His brother shrugged. "Proof, yet again, that I've always been smarter than you."

"As if there was ever any doubt."

"Well, for what it's worth, I'm happy to see you showing a real interest in someone again."

"She lives in California," he reminded his brother.

"That's not so far," Devin said. "And it's long past time for you to start dating again."

"What are you talking about? I date."

"Picking up a woman in a bar, sleeping with her and never calling her again isn't really a date."

"I haven't done that in a long time," Trevor pointed out in his defense.

"And you haven't had a real relationship since…"

"Since Alannis?" he guessed, when his brother's words faded away.

"Yeah," Devin admitted.

"Sorry to disappoint you, but I don't have a real relationship—or any kind of relationship—with Haylee, either."

"And yet, you bought two tickets to a baseball game in Oakland despite knowing that I'd be in Montreal for the weekend."

"Maybe I forgot that you were going out of town."

"Or maybe you picked that weekend on purpose so that you'd have an excuse to offer the second ticket to Haylee…because you like her," his brother said in a teasing tone.

"Because I slept with her," he responded bluntly.

"Holy sh—" Devin clamped his jaw shut, censoring his own outburst. "You slept with Haylee Gilmore?"

"Yeah."

"After the ball game?"

He shook his head. "The night of Brielle and Caleb's wedding."

"I don't know whether to give you a high five or smack the back of your head."

"I didn't plan for it to happen," he said, aware that he sounded defensive.

"You're saying that you accidentally slept with a hot wedding guest?" his brother asked dubiously.

"I'm saying that I'm a simple guy who couldn't resist the invitation of a willing girl."

"Is that why you went to California—to see if she'd be willing again?"

"No," he said, then reconsidered. "Maybe."

"And?"

"She told me to have a safe drive back to Nevada."

Devin grinned. "Suddenly, I can't wait to meet her."

It was his fault for putting the idea in her mind, Haylee thought, as she clung to the sides of the toilet bowl late Wednesday night.

The possibility of a pregnancy hadn't even been a blip on her radar until Trevor mentioned it. But after he'd gone, she'd acknowledged—if only to herself— that her last period had not been usual. The flow had been surprisingly light and of short duration. Not that she'd given it a second thought at the time, but now she wondered...

Because it wasn't just the unusual period or even

the occasional bout of nausea, but for the past week or more, her breasts had felt heavy and tender. And she'd been tired—not just at the end of the day but first thing in the morning, hitting the snooze button rather than jumping out of bed at the sound of the alarm, as was her habit. And she knew, because she'd Googled "signs of pregnancy," that her symptoms checked too many of the boxes.

Of course, she also had a habit of scratching her head whenever she heard mention of head lice, so it was possible that the pregnancy symptoms she was experiencing were more imagined than real.

On the other hand, it was also possible that she *was* pregnant. Because she'd looked at the box of condoms after Trevor had gone and discovered that yes, they were out of date.

Way out of date.

That fact, combined with the reality of her light period, had her starting to feel a little panicky. Because having a baby wasn't anywhere in her short-term plans.

She could be happy for Josslin, because her friend was in a committed relationship and she and Rob had actually wanted to have a baby. And for Candace, because she and Derek had tried for almost three years before she finally got pregnant. And considering what her friends had been through to start their families, it seemed ridiculous to imagine that Haylee might be pregnant after the first time she'd slept with someone, especially when they'd taken precautions to avoid such an outcome.

Condoms have a shelf life.

Okay, yes, she was aware of that now. But she stubbornly refused to believe that one night with Trevor Blake had created a baby. It was far more likely that throwing up a hot dog was her stomach's way of protesting the consumption of tube meat while sitting in the sun watching a ball game.

What about the beef and green peppers with rice the following night?

Obviously her stomach was still unsettled after its rejection of the hot dog.

And the chicken parm the night after that?

Clearly her stomach had a long memory.

It couldn't be morning sickness—because she felt fine in the mornings.

Thinking it through rationally, Haylee almost managed to convince herself there was nothing to worry about. Until the next morning, when her alarm went off and she felt so exhausted she didn't want to get out of bed. Then she remembered the message she'd got from her boss the night before, asking her to meet him in his office first thing instead of heading directly to the site, and forced herself to get into gear.

She'd worked for Henry Warren for almost eight years now. The owner of Bay Electric had reluctantly taken her on as an apprentice when she was still in school—as a favor to her father, who he'd known for a lot of years. Henry had expressed more than a few doubts about her ability to succeed in the profession and was certain she'd give up long before she had the required number of hours to take her licensing exam. He'd been surprised and impressed when she graduated near the top of her class, and immediately added her to his staff.

Since then, Haylee was usually the first on-site in the morning and the last to leave at night. And she was gratified to know that her hard work and dedication were finally going to be rewarded. Right now, the crew was in the last stages on the retrofit of an old canning factory that was being converted into apartments. And when the final inspection was done, they would be moving on to another retrofit of an older and even bigger building, which Henry had promised to put Haylee in charge of because he'd be busy overseeing work at the new community center in Piedmont.

"How's the Weston project coming?" Henry asked, referring to the canning factory project by the name of the owner.

"We'll be finished today," she assured him. "The final inspection's scheduled for three o'clock tomorrow."

"That's good, because we'll need all hands on deck for the Shearing project on Monday."

"I didn't realize it was starting so soon," she said. "When did you want to meet to go over the plans? Or is that why I'm here now?"

"You're here because I wanted to tell you that Wade has the plans." Though he was speaking to her, he kept himself busy shuffling through papers on his desk to avoid meeting her gaze.

"I don't understand," she said, though she was afraid she was starting to. "Why does your nephew have the plans when you said that you were going to name me the project manager?"

"That was my intention," Henry confirmed. "But Wade's wife is pregnant again."

"What does that have to do with anything?" she asked, sincerely baffled.

"He's going to need the extra money that he'll make as project manager to support his family."

"I've worked for you longer than Wade has, and I've had my license longer," she pointed out. "I've *earned* this opportunity."

"That's all true," her boss acknowledged. "It's also true that you live in an apartment on your parents' property."

"Which is about as relevant as Wade's wife's pregnancy," she said.

"It *is* relevant," Henry insisted. "Because if I have to make cuts, at least I know I don't have to worry that you'll be homeless."

"Cuts?" she echoed, feeling numb. "Not only am I not getting the promotion you promised, but now you're telling me that I'm going to be laid off?"

"No," he denied. Then he sighed and scrubbed his hands over his face. "I mean, I hope not."

She sank down onto the edge of the chair facing his desk.

"We didn't get the community center."

"I'm sorry, Henry," she said, knowing that the loss of the contract wasn't just a blow to the company but to her boss personally.

"Me, too," he said, sounding sincerely regretful. "As soon as I've got another project, you'll be the one."

"That's what you said last time," she reminded him.

He flushed. "And I meant it. But you know Wade is my wife's sister's son and—"

"There's always a but, isn't there, Henry?"

She didn't stick around to hear his response.

Though she wanted to bury her disappointment in a pint of chocolate chip cookie dough ice cream, she still had a job to do—at least for the present.

As she made her way to the site, she found herself alternately railing against the injustice of Henry's decision and reluctantly understanding his rationale. He wasn't a bad guy. He just lived according to outdated standards and believed that Wade, being a man, needed to provide for his wife and children. Or maybe it was that Henry, being married to Wade's mom's sister, needed to keep peace in his own home.

She'd been tempted to challenge his decision, to demand to know if he might have made a different choice if she was the one who was pregnant and needed to support a child. But she knew her boss well enough to understand that he already struggled with the concept of a woman on his crew—despite her proven qualifications and competency—and the idea of a pregnant woman doing the job would be too much for him.

So it was a good thing she wasn't pregnant.

But later that day, on her way home, she stopped at the pharmacy to pick up a test.

Just to be sure.

"I really appreciate you coming early to help with the setup for the party," Brielle said, when Haylee showed up at the Circle G early the following Thursday afternoon. "When we first started planning, it seemed as if there was plenty of time to do everything that needed done, but now the party is in two days and I still have a list of errands as long as my arm."

"I'm happy to help," Haylee assured her. "And I'll no doubt be able to run your errands faster because I'm not carting a three-and-a-half-month-old baby around with me."

"It's not Colton that slows me down but all his stuff," the new mom said. "I swear, I've traveled out of the country for a week-long holiday with less than what's crammed in his diaper bag every time I walk out the door. And the bag weighs at least as much as his baby seat—with him in it."

"Just think of the biceps you'll have built up by the time he's walking," she teased.

"That might be a plus," Brie acknowledged. "And speaking of bags, where are yours?"

"I dropped them off at the Stagecoach Inn on my way over."

Her cousin's wife frowned. "I thought you were going to stay here."

Haylee shook her head. "I appreciate the invitation, really, but you've got enough going on, with the party coming up and a baby waking you at all hours of the night."

"Now we're getting to the real reason you'd rather stay at the hotel," Brie surmised.

"Actually, the real reason is that Finley had already booked the room for both of us, so when I decided to fly in early, I just bumped the check-in date forward by a few days."

"It's silly to pay for a hotel when we've got empty bedrooms here."

"Liam gave us the friends and family rate."

"I should hope so," Brie said. "But Caleb and I were

really hoping we'd get to spend more time with you, especially considering that you came all this way for our wedding and we hardly saw you that weekend."

"It was a short trip," she acknowledged. "And you were kind of busy, being the bride and all."

"I hope you had a good time at least."

"I had a great time," Haylee said. And then, as memories of that night played back in her mind, she felt the telltale flush of warm heat filling her cheeks.

"Oh. My. God." The other woman's eyes grew wide. "You hooked up with someone at the wedding."

Haylee's cheeks burned hotter. "I wouldn't call it a hookup," she denied, though of course she knew it hadn't been anything more.

"Tell me all the juicy details," Brie urged.

"There's really not much to tell." Aside from the fact that it had been the most amazing experience in her life—but of course she could hardly admit that to her cousin's wife.

"Does he live in Haven or was he an out-of-town guest?"

"He's local," she admitted.

Brie grinned. "And are you going to invite him to the anniversary party?"

"No," she immediately said again.

"Why not?"

"Because then I'd have to introduce him to my family."

"And you don't think they'd approve of him?" the other woman guessed.

"Actually, I'm more worried that they'd make a big

deal out of it. I haven't introduced them to many—" or *any* "—guys," she confided.

"As long as he's not a Blake," Brie teased.

"Why would you say that?" Haylee asked cautiously.

"Oh. My. God. He *is*."

"Would that be a problem?" she wondered, unwilling to confirm or deny the truth of the other woman's claim.

"I know you've lived your whole life in California, so you may be unaware of the history between the Blakes and the Gilmores," Brie acknowledged. "But it's been fraught with conflict."

"I've heard the stories," Haylee assured her. "I also know that the animosity between the two families is a big part of the reason that you and Caleb were apart for eight years."

Her cousin's wife nodded.

"But you're together now, and both families were there to celebrate your marriage. In fact, I heard that your grandfather made that cradle—" she nodded toward the handcrafted piece of furniture in which the baby was currently sleeping "—for Colton."

"All true," Brie agreed. "But the roots of the feud are deep in this town, and I'd hate for there to be a renewal as a result of another Blake-Gilmore romance gone wrong."

"Then you have nothing to worry about," Haylee told her. "Because there's no romance at all."

"I don't know if I'm relieved or disappointed, but I know you've somehow managed to distract me from the most important question."

"The party?" Haylee guessed.

Brie shook her head. "Which one of my Blake cousins caught your eye at the wedding?"

Chapter Eight

In addition to the multitude of errands to be done before the party, Haylee had a task of her own to complete. But first she'd have to summon enough courage to drive over to the corporate offices of Blake Mining and ask to see Trevor.

Maybe it would be better to call him and set up a meeting on neutral ground. She had his number now, though she hadn't heard from him since he'd left Oakland after the ball game. Not surprising, considering that she'd essentially shoved him out the door of her apartment that day.

So after delivering the cake topper—from the original wedding cake that Evelyn Gilmore had carefully packed and kept in a box in the attic for nearly sixty years—to Sweet Caroline's so the baker could use it on the enormous cake that had been ordered for the anniversary celebration, she intended to head over to Trevor's office. But as she exited the bakery, her empty stomach growled. Loudly.

She considered returning to the shop where there had been no shortage of tempting treats on display: cakes and cookies and muffins and doughnuts. But she knew the errands she had to run would keep her busy for much of the day—not to mention needing fuel for her conversation with Trevor—so she decided to detour to Diggers' Bar & Grill to grab something a little more substantial to eat.

And maybe she was procrastinating, too.

Putting off that inevitable meeting just a little while longer.

Or so she believed until she walked into the restaurant.

It was late for lunch, and there were several empty tables to choose from. Following the instructions on the sign to Please Seat Yourself, she started toward a narrow booth, her steps faltering when she realized Trevor was there—with a woman.

She felt a sharp pang of something that might have been disappointment and immediately chided herself for the emotional response.

She hadn't seen or heard from him in more than three weeks. Of course he hadn't been sitting around, thinking about her, and she shouldn't be surprised—never mind disappointed—that he'd obviously moved on to flirting, dating and probably even sleeping with other women.

Though she was tempted to turn back around and

walk out again, her empty stomach wouldn't allow her to retreat. Instead, she slid into the booth and picked up the laminated menu tucked behind the tray of condiments, peeking past the edge of it for a closer look at Trevor's dining companion.

It wasn't a surprise to Haylee that she was beautiful, with long blond hair that fell in loose curls to the middle of her back. She wore a sleeveless sheath-style dress in a shade of blue somewhere between royal and navy with perfectly matched high-heeled pumps on her feet. She laughed at something Trevor said, the sound neither girly nor harsh but almost musical. No doubt she was one of those women who even cried pretty, Haylee thought resentfully, all too aware that tears tended to turn her face into a splotchy red mess.

Was this a sign? she wondered. Proof that his reputation as a player was well-founded and that she should consider herself lucky that she hadn't heard from him since he'd walked out of her apartment three weeks earlier?

The server delivered Haylee's drink on her way to dropping the check at Trevor's table. His dining companion started to reach for the paper slip, but he caught her hand and shook his head, then said something that made her laugh again.

Haylee sipped her ginger ale and checked her phone for messages. There was one from Brielle, asking her to pick up an additional fifty plastic wineglasses from the party store in Battle Mountain.

She sent a quick reply, to let Brie know that she'd take care of it, then set her phone aside again.

"Haylee?"

She glanced up to find Trevor standing by her table, the blonde—even more beautiful up close—at his side. "Trevor," she said, feigning surprise. "Hi."

He didn't introduce his companion and the woman didn't offer her hand or her name, though she did smile as Trevor asked, "What are you doing here?"

"Just grabbing a quick bite before I get back to the mile-long list of errands I'm running for Brielle," she told him, playing it casual.

He grinned, and a whole kaleidoscope of butterflies spread their wings and took flight in her belly. "I meant, what brings you back to Haven this time?"

Duh. Of course that's what he meant.

"Oh. My grandparents' sixtieth wedding anniversary. They're having an open house at the Circle G to celebrate."

The blonde, apparently bored with their conversation, spoke up to say, "It sounds as if you two have things to catch up on, and I have to get back to the office." She touched her lips to Trevor's cheek. "Thanks for lunch."

"Anytime," he said.

As she walked away, Trevor slid onto the empty bench across from Haylee without waiting for an invitation.

"Don't you have to get back to work, too?" she asked.

He answered her question with one of his own. "Why does it seem as if you're always trying to get rid of me?"

"I'm not trying to get rid of you," she denied.

"Then you don't mind if I keep you company while you have your lunch?"

"I don't mind," she lied. "But your girlfriend might feel differently."

His brows drew together. "My girl—oh, you mean Jenna?"

"Is that her name?"

"It is," he confirmed. "And she's my cousin."

Her skepticism must have been evident, because he immediately offered more details, as if to convince her.

"My father's brother's daughter," he said. "And Jenna's brother, Patrick, is the owner and operator of the local Silver Star Vacation Ranch, where Brielle and Caleb had their wedding."

The server brought Haylee's soup and sandwich—and a cup of coffee for Trevor.

"Thanks, Deanna," he said.

"You're very welcome."

Haylee dipped her spoon into her soup while Trevor emptied two packages of sugar and two creamers into his cup.

"So when is this big anniversary celebration for your grandparents?"

"Saturday."

"Do you have a date?" he asked. And then, before she could respond, he continued, "Because it turns out that I'm free on Saturday."

She swallowed another mouthful of soup. "Are you angling for an invitation?"

"Actually, I'm more interested in spending time with you, but since you're going to be at the party—" he shrugged "—two birds, one stone."

"I'm going to be pretty busy, pouring drinks and serving cake, so you wouldn't really see me," she hedged. "Not to mention that the whole place is going to be overrun with Gilmores."

"You're brushing me off."

"I'm not." She nibbled on the edge of her sandwich. "I just don't want you to think that we're going to pick up where we left off."

"You mean with you throwing up and then throwing me out of your apartment?"

"No," she denied. "I meant the last time I was in Haven." But now that he mentioned it, considering how they'd parted ways that day, she was surprised that he'd want to spend time with her.

"Ahh…" His lips curved in a slow and decidedly smug smile. "You're referring to when we were naked in bed together."

She was certain the rush of color to her cheeks was answer enough that she didn't need to respond verbally.

"I'd be lying if I said I wasn't interested in the possibility of getting naked with you again," he told her. "But I wasn't presuming anything."

"Good to know," she said, and turned her attention to her sandwich.

"But since you mentioned that night…this might be a good time for me to say what I meant to say when I was in Oakland."

"What's that?" she asked, a little warily.

"That I'm sorry I didn't know it was your first time when we went back to your hotel room."

"It's all good," she said. "Really. I don't want to talk about that night."

Except that she knew they had to talk about it—not

to recap the details of their lovemaking but to discuss the repercussions of it.

Just not now. She wasn't ready to have that conversation right now.

"I just wanted you to know that if I'd known it was your first time, I would have taken more time with you."

"It's all good," she said again, silently begging him to take the hint.

Finally, he nodded.

When she'd finished eating and paid her check, Trevor walked her out to her car.

"Is your whole family going to be in town for the anniversary celebration?" he asked.

She nodded. "My dad and stepmother are driving through tomorrow, and my sister and brother are flying in Saturday morning."

"So everyone else is coming on the weekend, but you're here now," he mused.

She shrugged. "There was an unexpected lull at work, so I offered to lend a hand with some of the last-minute details."

"Hence your mile-long list of errands."

She lifted a brow. "Did you just use *hence* in a sentence?"

"Is that along the same lines as *latter*—not meaning a climbing apparatus?"

"It is," she confirmed.

"My mother made us read all the time when we were kids," he confided. "Apparently you learn things that way."

"Who knew?"

He smiled then, and though she was relieved to discover that he didn't apparently harbor any hard feelings, she knew that wasn't going to make it any easier to tell him what she needed to tell him.

"So was helping with the party really your only reason for coming to town early?" he pressed.

"You think there's another reason?"

"I do." He set his hands on her hips and moved in closer. "And I think I know what it is."

"No." As he started to lower his head toward hers, she put a hand on his chest, holding him at a distance. "You don't."

"Then tell me," he urged.

"Okay, I did come to Haven to see you," she admitted.

His lips curved, his smile just a little bit smug.

"But only because I wanted to tell you..."

"Tell me what?" he prompted, when her words trailed off.

She drew in a breath, bracing herself to say the words out loud for the very first time.

"I'm pregnant."

Trevor felt his smile slip and his stomach drop.

"What did you say?" he asked, certain he must have misheard.

"I'm pregnant," Haylee said again.

And it sounded again like she said she was pregnant, but not three weeks earlier, she'd assured him that wasn't possible. "But you said—"

"I know what I said," she interjected. "I was wrong."

He shook his head, unwilling to believe it.

This couldn't be happening to him.

Not again.

She was watching him closely, waiting for some kind of reaction or response.

"Okay," he said, and took another minute to try and organize the thoughts spinning around in his head into some semblance of order.

"You're pregnant," he finally acknowledged, because that didn't necessarily have anything to do with him. "But why are you telling me?"

"Why am I telling you?" she echoed, sounding confused. "Because it's your baby."

He swallowed the panic that was rising inside him. "Is it?"

"Are you suggesting...you think I slept with someone else?"

"I'd be an idiot not to consider the possibility that you hooked up with someone else after we were together," he told her, desperately searching for an alternative explanation to her revelation.

She drew back, as if stricken by his response. And maybe, if the widening of her eyes was sincere and not part of a deliberate deception, a little bit hurt by the accusation.

But he didn't stop there. No, despite all the warning signs of danger ahead, he forged on.

"You wouldn't be the first woman to try to trap a man with another man's baby," he said.

Now her eyes flashed with anger. "I can't tell if you have a really high opinion of yourself or a really low opinion of me."

"I'm just trying to figure out your angle," he told her.

She straightened her shoulders and lifted her chin.

"And you did," she said. "You're right. I've had several other lovers since the night we were together. So many, in fact, that I don't really have a clue who's the father of my baby, so it would probably be best if you just forgot I even said anything to you about it."

Trevor wished that he could, but the word "pregnant" was flashing like a neon sign inside his head, and he knew that forgetting wouldn't be possible.

Obviously this bombshell revelation required further discussion, but before he could think of anything to say, she was driving away.

As a result, he laid awake through the darkness of night trying to figure out what it all meant, what he was supposed to do, and with long-buried memories playing out in his mind.

"I can't be seven weeks pregnant," Alannis said to the doctor. "I got my period last month."

Dr. Perry smiled. "You wouldn't be the first expectant mom to mistake implantation bleeding for menstruation."

"Implantation bleeding?" she echoed uncertainly.

"It's what sometimes happens when the fertilized egg attaches to the lining of the uterus," the doctor explained.

"Seven weeks," Alannis said softly, her gaze on the screen showing the grainy ultrasound image of the tiny blob that would grow into their baby.

"Seven weeks and two days, to be precise."

"So the baby will be due in August?"

The doctor nodded. "August fourteenth."

But Trevor wasn't really listening anymore. He was remembering the argument he'd had with Alannis eight weeks earlier over a business trip that would require him to be out of the country for the two-year anniversary of their first date. She'd wanted to celebrate in a big way—and he knew she was hoping he'd get down on one knee—so he'd actually been relieved when his uncle had tapped him to attend the conference in Toronto.

He'd invited Alannis to go with him, thinking she might want to do some shopping or indulge in pampering at the spa, and then when he was done with work they could do some sightseeing together. But she'd turned her nose up at the invitation.

So he'd gone to the conference and she'd stayed in Haven.

She'd been waiting for him—naked in his bed—when he got back from his five-day trip, seven weeks ago today.

They'd used protection when they made love, as they always did. She'd opened the package and put the condom on him—a chore she usually disdained—and he let himself believe it was her way of apologizing for picking a fight before he went away. Or maybe a thank-you for the diamond earrings he'd brought back for her.

In any event, she'd seemed as surprised and dismayed as he when the condom broke...

And now she was seven weeks and two days pregnant.

He asked her about the date discrepancy when they left the doctor's office, but she'd waved off his questions, insisting that the doctor's estimate was only that and that she obviously couldn't be any more than seven weeks along in her pregnancy—and wasn't it exciting that they were going to have a baby?

She'd been persuasive and he'd been willing to be persuaded, and on the way home, they stopped at The Goldmine to get Alannis the ring she'd always wanted.

For the next four weeks, he'd let himself get caught up in the excitement and anticipation. Maybe he hadn't believed he was ready to settle down, but the realization that he was going to be a dad changed everything. He was happy to step up, eager to make plans for their future and the arrival of their little bundle of joy.

Then Alannis lost the baby and she blamed him, because he wasn't there for her. Because he was never there for her...

So many mistakes that he wouldn't make again.

Haylee spent Friday with her grandmother, taking her to various appointments to be primped and pampered in preparation for the big party. Of course, Evelyn Gilmore insisted on spoiling her granddaughter, too, treating her to a mani-pedi at Serenity Spa and a hair trim at Clip 'N' Curl. After that, they went to pick up the dress Evelyn had ordered from Bonnie's Boutique. The proprietor was in the process of changing the window display when they arrived, and Evelyn requested that she strip down the mannequin she'd just finished dressing so that Haylee could try the dress on.

By the time she returned to the Stagecoach Inn after dropping her grandmother off at the end of the day, Haylee was exhausted and weighted down with packages. Still, it had been a good day—and Evelyn had kept her so busy, she'd barely given Trevor Blake a passing thought.

Then she walked into the lobby and saw him.

He was dressed in a shirt and tie, as he'd been the day before, but today his tie was loosened, the top button of his shirt was undone and the cuffs of his sleeves rolled back to reveal strongly muscled forearms. His fingers jabbed at the keyboard of the laptop open on the coffee table in front of him.

She didn't know why he was there and she wasn't going to assume it was for her, so she prepared to walk by, as if she didn't even see him.

But she'd only taken a few steps when he glanced up, and he immediately jumped up to intercept her path. "I was beginning to wonder if you were ever coming back."

"Is there something you wanted? Because I think we said everything we needed to say yesterday."

"Actually, I wanted to take you for lunch."

She glanced pointedly at the oversize clock on the wall above the check-in desk. "It's four thirty."

He followed her gaze. "No wonder I'm so hungry."

Her lips twitched, but she refused to smile. She was still too angry and hurt to let herself be charmed by him.

"I've been here since eleven thirty," he confided.

"You're kidding."

"You can ask Macy if you don't believe me, but she left at three to pick up her kids and Rose came on duty. She's setting up the wine and cheese in the library now, but she can tell you that I've been here since she arrived. Thankfully, the hotel has decent Wi-Fi."

"For guests of the hotel," she pointed out.

He shrugged. "Macy gave me the password."

She set down the bags that she carried, to give her arms a momentary respite. "Why are you really here, Trevor?"

"I wanted to apologize...for the way I reacted to your news yesterday."

"Are you referring to the implication that I sleep with a different guy every weekend?"

Though her tone was cool, Trevor could see the lingering hurt in her eyes. "I didn't mean it. I know it's not true," he assured her. "But my mind was reeling and clearly not communicating with my mouth."

"I guess I can understand that," she acknowledged. "It took a long time for my head to stop spinning after I saw the plus sign on the pregnancy test."

"So what are your plans?"

"Plans?" she echoed uncertainly.

His gaze shifted away, as if he was uncomfortable asking his next question, "Are you going to have the baby?"

She tried not to react, so he wouldn't see that the question stung more than a little. After all, he didn't know her well enough to know that she would never choose to terminate a pregnancy. "Yes, I'm going to have—and keep—the baby."

"Have you seen a doctor?" he asked.

She nodded. "My family doctor confirmed the results. I have an appointment with an ob-gyn in a couple weeks."

"Let me know when and where and I'll be there."

"I didn't tell you because I expect anything from you. I just thought you had a right to know."

"And now that I know, I want to be involved."

"But that's not really practical, is it?"

"Practical or not, we need to figure out a way to make it work, because I'm going to be a part of my child's life."

Haylee wasn't sure if the words were a threat or a promise.

Chapter Nine

Having grown up in Oakland, with no extended family around, Haylee wasn't accustomed to big family gatherings. And when all of the Gilmores were together, it was a *very* big family gathering. Of course, there were other guests in attendance, too, for the celebration of her grandparents' sixtieth wedding anniversary. Friends and neighbors, young and old, and it seemed to Haylee that everyone knew everyone else. As food was eaten and beverages were drunk, groups gathered and splintered and babies were passed around.

Right now, her fourteen-year-old cousin Ashley was playing pat-a-cake with toddlers Ava, Max and Sam, while the triplets' parents enjoyed the rare opportunity to eat dinner without little ones tugging at them and demanding attention. Haylee spotted her recently engaged cousin Skylar and Skylar's fiancé, a hunky former Marine named Jake Kelly, over by the paddock with Sky's three-year-old niece Tessa, who was proudly telling everyone she met that she was getting a baby sister for Christmas. The little girl's parents, Katelyn and Reid, were setting out plates and napkins for the cutting of the cake.

"Can you watch Colton for a few minutes?" Brie asked, already passing the baby off to Haylee. "Valerie can't find her cake knife so I'm going to run home to get mine."

"Of course," she agreed, trusting that the "few minutes" wouldn't be much more than that as Caleb and Brie's house wasn't too far away on the western boundary of Circle G Ranch.

"His diaper bag's in the kitchen, if you need it, and there's a bottle in the fridge, but I fed him—" she glanced at her watch "—just about an hour ago, so—"

"Go," Haylee interjected. "Colton and I will figure things out."

"Thanks." Brie dropped a quick kiss on top of the baby's head. "Mommy will be right back."

Someone had rigged speakers up outside, and Haylee swayed from side to side with the baby along to the music. The guests of honor had been making the rounds, saying hello to all the well-wishers, when the music changed and Elvis Presley started to sing "Can't Help Falling in Love." The song must have had some significance to Jack and Evelyn, because he reached for his wife's hand and drew her into his arms. They danced right there on the grass, smiling at one another as if there was no one else around.

Watching them together, so obviously in love after sixty years together, Haylee felt her throat tighten with emotion. Their devotion to one another was a rare and precious gift, proof that happily-ever-after could happen, if only for a lucky few. Her gaze moved around the crowd, noting all the other couples in attendance.

Her dad and Colleen had been happily married for fifteen years now. (Of course, they'd only found one another after Robert Gilmore survived the implosion of his first marriage, leading Haylee to wonder if—the example of her grandparents aside—real happiness was only possible after heartbreak.) Next to her parents was her uncle Dave, also remarried after being widowed a lot of years earlier. His second wife, Valerie, was standing at his side, their hands linked together.

It was only since celebrating her twenty-ninth birthday in January and learning that various friends were getting married or having babies that Haylee had started to think about her own future and wonder if she'd ever find a partner to share her life. Not that she was in a hurry, but she'd always thought she had plenty of time. Now that she was going to have a baby, she realized that her window of opportunity wasn't only rapidly shrinking but likely already gone.

She felt a vibration against her arm and looked down at the baby in her arms, who gave her a wide, toothless grin.

"Was that gas that rumbled out of your tummy? Or did you just fill your diaper?"

Of course, he didn't respond—but the not-so-fresh scent coming from his bottom told her to prepare for the worst.

"Let's go find that diaper bag," she suggested.

It was her first time in Dave and Valerie's house, but the back door opened into a mudroom that led to the kitchen, so it didn't take her long to find the diaper bag and dig out the supplies that she needed. There was a family room off the kitchen, and she decided to change the baby in there, to afford him a little more privacy.

"It's been a lot of years since I've done this," she confided to Colton as she laid him down on the change pad. "So you might have to bear with me while I figure this out."

Of course, changing a diaper was probably the simplest of all the things she had to figure out over the next seven months or so. Messy, she acknowledged, as she wiped his bottom, but simple.

And while being a mom wasn't anything that she'd planned for this stage of her life, as she affixed the tabs on the new diaper, she already knew that she was going to love her baby more than anything.

Then she refastened the snaps on Colton's denim overalls and lifted him into her arms again.

He gurgled happily. And why wouldn't he be happy? He had a full belly, a dry diaper and a mommy and daddy who loved one another as much as they loved him.

Maybe she couldn't give her baby that kind of family, but as she tidied up the changing area, Haylee vowed to be the best mom that she could be.

Of course, she was going to have to make some compromises. She'd have to look into day care, and she wasn't sure she was comfortable with the idea of letting a stranger take care of her baby. But she was getting way ahead of herself. She had a lot of time to figure out day care—and significantly less time to figure out how and when she was going to tell her family that she was pregnant.

Maybe it would be easier if she'd ever introduced them to a boyfriend—or if the father of her baby had ever been her boyfriend. Instead, he was practically a stranger and their baby was the product of a single night together.

Yeah, she was definitely going to need some time to figure out how to explain the situation to her father. Maybe Finley would have some ideas, but she hadn't even told her sister, and as a general rule, she told her sister everything. But Finley didn't even know that she'd slept with Trevor on her previous trip to Haven, though her sister likely suspected something had happened, based on her comment about the sexual tension she'd sensed between Haylee and Trevor when he'd been at their apartment.

Of course, Finley also had no idea that Haylee had still been a virgin prior to that night with Trevor. Her always popular sister had shared all kinds of details about her romantic relationships when they were in high school, while Haylee had remained on the outside look-ing in. And when Haylee had headed off to college in pursuit of her liberal arts degree (which her father had insisted would help her figure out what she wanted to do and turned out to be of absolutely no other use to her as an electrician), Finley had teased her about finally having the opportunity to lose her virginity. Later she'd obviously assumed that her sister had done so at some point during her four years away, and Haylee had never corrected her mistaken assumption because she couldn't help but feel it was a little bit pathetic that she hadn't ever hooked up with anyone in all that time.

She tucked Colton's supplies back into his diaper bag.

"Are you ready to rejoin the party?" she asked him.

The baby responded with another gummy smile.

"I'll take that as a yes," she said, pushing open the door to carry him outside—and finding herself face-to-face with Trevor Blake.

He was dressed in a similar outfit to what he'd worn the night they first met, right down to the cowboy hat and boots, and her heart skipped a beat again.

His lips curved in an easy smile, then he looked from her to the baby in her arms and raised a brow. "That was fast."

"This is Colton," she told him.

"Ah, Brielle and Caleb's little guy," he realized.

She nodded.

"He's grown since the wedding."

"That was almost two months ago," she pointed out to him. But she didn't want to talk about the wedding or babies—and she especially didn't want to talk about the baby they'd made together the night of the wedding—so instead she asked, "Why are you here, Trevor?"

"I'm your date."

"I don't recall inviting you," she said. "In fact, I specifically recall *not* inviting you."

"But it occurred to me, assuming that all of these people are going to find out you're carrying my baby at some point, that it might come as less of a shock if they've actually seen us together."

"Except I wasn't planning on telling anyone that it's your baby."

"You were planning on keeping the father's identity a secret for the next seven months?"

"More like the next eighteen years," she admitted.

"Well, change of plans," he said.

"Why do you get to decide?"

"I'd prefer for us to make decisions together, but that would require you being willing to listen to my input."

"Fine," she agreed, eager to terminate the conversation before they were interrupted.

"Now that wasn't so hard, was it?" he asked, as Brielle swooped in to steal Colton out of Haylee's arms.

"And now I have my baby and my answer," she said, her gaze moving between Haylee and Trevor. And though her tone was light, her expression was worried.

"Your answer to what?" Trevor asked curiously.

"*Nothing,*" Haylee said firmly, fingers mentally crossed that his cousin wouldn't say anything to reveal the subject of their previous conversation.

"Which one of my Blake cousins was most likely to crash a Gilmore party," Brie said, granting her a temporary reprieve.

"I'm not crashing," he denied. "I'm Haylee's date."

"Is that so?" Brie murmured.

"It is," Haylee confirmed, her smile tight.

"Then I'll leave you to enjoy the party," Brie said, then turned and dashed off, leaving Haylee alone with Trevor.

Trevor didn't stay long.

Just long enough to ensure everyone was talking

about the fact that he'd been there and had been very attentive to Haylee, so that when her pregnancy was revealed, people would add one plus one to come up with the requisite two—or three, adding their baby to the equation. He'd even brushed a light kiss against her lips before he left. And though she knew it was all part of his act, the fleeting touch of his mouth had stirred her up inside.

It had also stirred up a hornets' nest, as she heard several of her Gilmore relatives grumble about "those damn Blakes"—conveniently forgetting, or maybe not caring, that they'd recently danced at the wedding of a Gilmore and a Blake.

Of course, when she got back to the hotel room she was now sharing with her sister, Finley had wanted to know all the details about what she believed was a blossoming romance between her sister and the weekend cowboy. And the late night meant that Haylee was dragging the next morning.

"I'm going to run over to The Daily Grind to grab a latte and a cruller," Finley said, when Haylee got out of the shower. "What can I get for you?"

Haylee considered as she rubbed a towel over her wet hair.

"A chocolate glazed," she decided, her mouth watering at the prospect of biting into the sweet treat. Her stomach, though, seemed a little uneasy about the fried dough. "On second thought, change the doughnut to peppermint tea."

"Are you okay?" Finley asked, concerned.

"Yeah. I just haven't completely bounced back from that stomach bug I had." Which, of course, hadn't really been a stomach bug at all but merely the explanation she'd given her sister to explain why she'd had her head in the toilet.

Her sister frowned. "That was three weeks ago."

"I know."

"And you're still not feeling one hundred percent?"

"I'm feeling a lot better," she said. "I'm just not sure I'm ready for a doughnut, but tea sounds good."

"Tea instead of coffee? I'm stunned."

"I think I OD'd on caffeine yesterday," she fibbed. "I'm still feeling a little jittery."

"Okay, tea it is," Finley said with a shrug.

Haylee exhaled a sigh of relief when her sister had gone. Though Finley had mostly accepted the excuses and explanations she'd offered for her queasiness, tiredness and recent dietary changes, she knew she wouldn't be able to keep her pregnancy a secret for very much longer. And it wasn't really that she wanted to keep it a secret so much as she needed to figure things out on her own before everyone else started chiming in with well-meaning advice.

She busied herself packing while her sister was out, eager to get on the road to the airport when Finley returned. She was just zipping up her suitcase when a knock sounded at the door.

Assuming her sister couldn't get to her key because her hands were full, she automatically pulled opened the door—and found herself face-to-face with Trevor again.

"This is getting to be a habit," she said.

"Good morning to you, too," he said cheerily.

"Sorry—I got a late start this morning and I have to finish packing before Finley gets back."

"Packing?" He frowned. "Where are you going?"

"Home."

"You can't go back to California," he protested. "You're having my baby."

"Baby?" Finley echoed from the hallway.

Haylee looked past the man to her sister standing on the other side of the open door with a takeout bag and tray of hot drinks in her hands and her jaw on the floor.

She glared at Trevor, furious that he'd outed their secret to her sister without any preparation or warning.

"Oh. My. God." Finley pushed past him into the room. She set the tray and bag on the dresser and turned to face her sister, hands on her hips. "You didn't have a stomach bug, did you? You're pregnant."

"Yes, I'm pregnant," she admitted.

"Why didn't you tell me?" her sister demanded, sounding hurt.

"I didn't tell anyone until I told Trevor, three days ago."

"You should have told *me*," Finley insisted.

"You're right, and I'm sorry," Haylee said, attempting to appease her. "And you can yell at me all you want later, but right now, can you give us a few minutes?"

"Five minutes," Finley reluctantly agreed.

"Thank you."

Trevor didn't waste any time. As soon as the door had closed behind her sister, he said, "I think we should get married."

Haylee stared at him as though he'd grown a second head. "You've got to be kidding me."

"I'm not," he assured her.

"Aren't you the same man who bluntly told me, only three weeks ago, that you wouldn't marry me?"

"Because I had no intention of being trapped into marriage, if that was your endgame when you invited me back to your room."

"I didn't have an endgame. There was no plan to seduce you—or anyone—when I came to Haven for the wedding. In fact, I didn't even want to come."

"That's all water under the bridge," he said. "What matters now is moving forward."

"And how are we supposed to do that?"

"You could start by responding to my proposal."

"I'm not sure 'we should get married' counts as a proposal," she remarked dryly. "And even if it does, my answer is *no*."

He scowled. "What do you mean, *no*?"

"I mean that I'm not going to marry you."

"But…you're pregnant with my baby," he said again.

"Maybe you should put a billboard up on Main Street to ensure everyone in town knows."

"I haven't told anyone—aside from your sister," he said.

"That's exactly my point," she said.

"You weren't planning to tell her?"

"Yes, *I* was planning to tell her. When *I* was ready."

"I'm sorry," he said, sounding sincerely regretful. "But I bet all would be forgiven if you asked her to be your maid of honor at our wedding."

Haylee shook her head. "Do you even listen when other people talk?"

"Getting married is the right thing to do."

"Says who?" she challenged.

"Says me."

"Well, I don't happen to think that an unplanned pregnancy is a good reason to exchange vows," she argued.

He folded his arms over his chest. "Can you think of a better reason?"

Love, she wanted to say.

But, of course, they weren't in love. They'd shared nothing more than a moment of lust and now they were dealing with the consequences of that weakness.

She mentally winced at the thought, refusing to think of her pregnancy as a punishment. Maybe she wouldn't have chosen to have a baby right now—or with a guy she barely knew—but she regretted only the circumstances of her child's conception, not the tiny being growing inside her.

"Obviously you need some time to think about my proposal," he decided.

She huffed out a breath. "I don't need time—I need you to go away."

"Then I guess neither one of us is going to get what we want," he told her.

Haylee knew that her sister would have questions. She also knew that Finley would respect her desire to keep the news of her pregnancy quiet and not ask those questions in front of Logan, and since they were all flying back to Oakland together, she had a few more hours to sort out her thoughts before the interrogation began.

Or so she believed until Logan's flirtation with the airline attendant at the check-in counter resulted in him being upgraded to first class—leaving his sisters in coach with no barrier between them. She did, however, wait until the beverage service had passed their row before she began.

"When I asked you why you were stress baking, three weeks after Caleb and Brielle's wedding, you told me that you'd *met* somebody there," Finley said, sounding hurt. "You never told me that you'd *slept* with him."

"I didn't know how to tell you," Haylee said.

"How about—'Hey, Fin. I met this really hot guy and banged his brains out'?"

Heat crept up Haylee's neck and into her cheeks. "I'll try to remember that for next time, but it was a first for me."

"What was a first? Sleeping with someone you just met—or having a one-night stand?"

"Both," Haylee admitted.

It was a simple one-word answer, but something in her tone must have given her away, because Finley's gaze narrowed suspiciously. "But you'd had sex before, right?"

"Not...no," she admitted.

Her sister looked stunned. Her mouth opened and then closed again before she finally asked, "What did you do when you were at college?" Then she shook her head. "Never mind. Obviously nothing worth talking about."

"And that's why I didn't tell you," Haylee said. "It was embarrassing enough to be a twenty-nine-year-old virgin without having to confess that fact to my much more beautiful and ever popular sister."

"I'm not more beautiful," Finley denied. "And I was only more popular because I was more outgoing. People

asked me to go out and do things because I said yes—
I didn't realize it was an issue for you."

"Of course it was an issue," she said. "How could
it not be an issue when every boy I ever liked in high
school liked you better?

"And maybe that's why I didn't say anything about
what happened with Trevor," she admitted now. "Because deep down inside, I knew it wouldn't have happened—he wouldn't have looked at me twice—if you'd
been there."

"If you really believe that, you haven't been paying attention when the guy looks at you," Finley said.

"He only looks at me because I'm pregnant with
his baby."

"Did he know that when he was in Oakland?"

"*I* didn't even know it then."

"Which proves my point," Finley said smugly.

Haylee didn't think it proved anything—and she had
more pressing concerns anyway. "What am I supposed
to do?"

"What do you want to do?"

She sighed. "Travel back in time two months and
buy a new box of condoms."

"You do know there are options…"

"I know," she said. "But I do want the baby—that's
the one thing I do know. But I'm scared, too, and I can't
help wondering what if…"

"What if you change your mind about wanting your
child—like mom did about us?" Finley guessed.

"Yeah," Haylee admitted. "Maybe there's some kind
of maternal deficiency in her genes—and maybe I've
got it, too."

"Or maybe Sandra Burke is just a selfish woman who wanted more than the life she had with our dad," her sister suggested as an alternative. "After all, she hasn't abandoned Sebastian," she added, referring to their half brother from their mother's second marriage.

Haylee considered that as she nibbled the complimentary pretzels and sipped her ginger ale.

After a few minutes, Finley spoke again, saying gently, "I'm sorry."

"Why are *you* sorry?" Haylee asked.

"I was upset because I thought you were holding out on me, but I realize now that you were dealing with a boatload of stuff. I still wish you'd confided in me rather than dealing with it alone, but I can understand that the whole situation must have seemed overwhelming."

"I'm sorry, too," Haylee said now. "You've always been there for me and I shouldn't have expected that this time would be any different."

"Thank you," her sister said.

"And I promise, the next time I'm dealing with a boatload of stuff, I'm dragging you onboard with me."

Finley nudged her arm. "I'll be the one with the life jackets."

Because she'd always been there to buoy her sister's spirits, and Haylee knew that she always would be.

Trevor was scowling at the papers on his desk when his brother walked into his office Monday morning.

"Hazel warned me that you were in a mood," Devin said from the doorway.

"Even happy is a mood," he noted.

"Which you are clearly not."

"I've just got a lot on my mind."

"A lot—or a woman?" his brother queried.

Trevor ignored the question to ask one of his own. "Why are you here? You always say you like doing tech support for the company because you can do it from home."

"Most of the time that's true, but there was a hardware issue I had to look into and I thought I'd stop by to see if you wanted to grab coffee before I head out."

"Sure, coffee sounds good," Trevor decided, since he wasn't able to concentrate on much of anything anyway.

"The Daily Grind or Sweet Caroline's?"

"Tough choice," he admitted. The Daily Grind had better coffee, but Sweet Caroline's had the best pastries.

They opted for Sweet Caroline's, because it was a little closer to the office.

"I meant to tell you—I met Haylee Gilmore here Saturday morning," Devin said, when they were seated with their drinks and sweets—a chocolate croissant for Trevor and cherry Danish for Devin.

"She was in town for her grandparents' sixtieth anniversary celebration on the weekend," Trevor said.

"That would explain the huge cake that I helped load into her car," his brother noted. "So…you knew she was here?"

He nodded. "I ran into her at Diggers' on Thursday. And at the hotel on Friday."

"What were you doing at the hotel?" Devin wondered.

"Waiting for Haylee," he admitted.

"You turning into a stalker?" his brother asked worriedly.

He scowled. "Of course not. I'm just trying to figure out how to convince her to marry me."

Devin choked on his coffee. "You want to marry her?"

"I'm going to marry her," he clarified.

"But you've known her all of—" his brother did a quick calculation his head "—eight weeks. And for most of those weeks, she's been in California." Then realization dawned. "She's pregnant, isn't she?"

He nodded. "And before you say anything else, let me assure you that I learned my lesson about the dangers of unprotected sex a long time ago, but apparently the disclaimer on the condom box is there for a valid reason."

Devin considered this for a long minute before asking, "You're sure it's your—"

"I'm sure," he cut in. He might have implied otherwise to Haylee, but that had been a knee-jerk reaction borne of panic. When he was able to think clearly again, he'd known there was no way she'd lost her virginity to him the night of the wedding and then taken another lover a short while later.

"Wow." Devin cleared his throat. "I'm not quite sure what else to say."

"'Wow' about sums it up," Trevor acknowledged.

"You don't seem to be freaking out," his brother noted.

"I freaked out when she told me."

"A reasonable reaction under the circumstances, I'd say." Devin swallowed a mouthful of coffee, then mused, "So...you're going to be a dad."

Trevor's fingers tightened on the handle of his mug. "That's the plan."

His brother cursed, belatedly remembering that Trevor had been down this same road once before. "Damn. Sorry."

"No need to be," he said. "But I will ask you to keep this to yourself. It's early days yet and Haylee isn't ready to share the news."

"Of course," Devin agreed. "But you said something about needing to convince Haylee to marry you—are you telling me that you proposed and she said no?"

He nodded.

Devin started to chuckle, then faked a cough to cover it up.

"I'm glad you're amused," Trevor remarked dryly. "But I fail to see any humor in the situation."

"Of course you do," his brother acknowledged. "Because you're so accustomed to women falling at your feet that you don't know how to woo one."

"Woo one?" Trevor echoed, shaking his head. "Jesus, Dev. No one talks like that anymore."

His brother just shrugged. "Maybe that's the problem. Wooing a woman has become a lost art."

"And what do you know about wooing women?" he challenged.

"A fair amount, I'd say, after having read extensively on the subject."

Trevor resisted the urge to roll his eyes. "And has all that knowledge actually gotten you a date?"

"It will, when I find the right woman," Devin insisted.

"The world is full of women. How will you know the right one if you don't go out with any of them?" he asked.

"Is Haylee the right one for you?"

"She's having my baby," he reminded his brother.

"And that's why she turned down your proposal," Devin deduced.

Trevor frowned. "What's why?"

"You don't want to marry Haylee. You only want to do the right thing."

It was exactly what Haylee had said, and he was a little uncomfortable to realize that his motivation was so obvious.

"Not five minutes ago, you seemed to agree that I should marry her," he reminded his brother.

"But she has to *want* to marry you," Devin said. "Which means that you need to take action and not just rely on the fact that you're Trevor Blake and any woman should feel lucky to wear your ring on her finger."

"I think taking action is what got us into this situation."

"Try to think outside the bedroom," Devin suggested dryly.

Trevor knew that he should heed his brother's advice, but he couldn't help thinking that even if seducing Haylee wasn't guaranteed to get her on board with his marriage plan, it would certainly be enjoyable.

Chapter Ten

Haylee booked half a day off work for a dental appointment the Thursday after the anniversary party. Though it was only a little white lie, she still felt guilty about the deception. Not that she believed she owed her boss the truth, but her family was a different matter.

Several of the online resources she'd consulted had noted that many expectant women chose not to share their happy news until after the first trimester because of the fifteen to twenty-five percent of pregnancies that ended in miscarriage, eighty percent of those happened within the first three months. And despite her pregnancy being unplanned, she knew she'd be devastated if anything happened to her baby.

She also knew it wasn't fear of losing her baby that

was the reason for her silence—it was fear of her father's disappointment and disapproval.

Finley had been surprisingly silent on the subject of her sister's pregnancy since their return from Haven. Though Haylee suspected there was much she wanted to say, so far she'd kept her opinions to herself.

As the date of her ob-gyn appointment drew nearer, she considered asking Finley to go with her. Partly to show her sister that she'd never intended to exclude her and partly because she was a little nervous about going on her own. In the end, though, she decided not to say anything, because she didn't want to put Finley in the position of keeping any more information from the rest of the family.

The only person who knew of her plans was Trevor. Since her return from Haven, he'd kept in not just regular but frequent communication. They talked almost daily and exchanged text messages even more often. She was surprised to realize that she enjoyed their conversations and actually looked forward to chatting with him every day.

Maybe because the distance allowed her to talk to him as the father of her baby and forget that she melted into a puddle of hormones whenever she was in close proximity to him. But they didn't only talk about her pregnancy—they talked about all manner of topics, the kind of getting-to-know-one-another conversations that usually happened on first and second dates—before a man and woman ended up in bed together.

During their conversation a few days earlier, Haylee had told him about her appointment. He'd asked her about the when and where, but she hadn't expected him to make note of the details. But now it was Thursday at one o'clock, and he was standing at her door.

"Is there another baseball game today?" she asked, ignoring the way her heart bumped against her ribs.

He grinned, as if he could see right through her feigned indifference—and maybe he could.

"As a matter of fact, there is," he said. "The A's are playing in Kansas City today."

"Then you obviously made a wrong turn somewhere."

He shrugged. "Since I did, maybe you wouldn't mind if I went to see the doctor with you?"

"I don't mind," she allowed. "But I didn't expect that you'd actually come all this way for a prenatal checkup."

"It's my baby, too," he said.

"I'm not likely to forget that fact," she assured him.

"And, as I told you before, I want to be involved in my child's life."

"I assumed that meant *after* the baby was born," she admitted.

"Maybe I want to be there for you, too."

Her gaze narrowed suspiciously. "Why?"

"Because I know you haven't told anyone else about your pregnancy, aside from your sister—"

"Actually, *you* told my sister."

"—and I didn't want you to have to go through this on your own," he continued, ignoring her interjection.

It was a sweet—and surprising—gesture. And not an impulsive one. Working for a family-owned business, he obviously had a great deal of flexibility, but she'd never anticipated that he'd travel so far to take her to a doctor's appointment.

"So…are you ready to go?"

"The appointment isn't until three o'clock," she reminded him.

"Great. That means we have time for lunch first."

Haylee had been prepared to go to the clinic on her own, but she was glad Trevor was there. Maybe their relationship was untraditional—if it could even be called a relationship—but despite having been taken aback by the news of her pregnancy, he'd stepped up.

She'd been admittedly skeptical when he'd told her that he would be there for her and the baby. It seemed like a lot of talk from a man who lived in a different state, but now he was here, proving that he was willing to make the effort.

"Hi, Haylee." The doctor offered her hand and a warm smile when she walked into the exam room. "I'm Kelly Robertson."

"It's nice to meet you," Haylee said.

"I see you brought a friend," the doctor noted, glancing at the man standing beside her patient.

"Trevor Blake," he said, shaking her hand in turn. "I'm the baby's father."

"I'm glad you're here," Dr. Robertson said. "It's always easier for the expectant mom if she has support during her pregnancy—and after, of course."

"Trevor lives in Nevada," Haylee felt compelled to point out.

"He should get bonus points then, for coming all this way for a prenatal checkup."

"You hear that?" Trevor nudged his shoulder against hers. "I should get bonus points."

Haylee rolled her eyes as the doctor chuckled.

"Of course, it's the expectant mom who has to do all the really hard work," Dr. Robertson said, "so we're going to focus on her right now."

She turned to Haylee and continued. "Today, we're going to check your vital signs—heart rate, breathing and blood pressure, which we'll continue to monitor throughout your pregnancy. We're going to review your personal and family medical history, talk about your menstrual cycle, birth control usage and reproductive history. Then we're going to conduct a physical exam, calculate your estimated due date, and confirm the date with an ultrasound scan, which will also give you a first peek at your baby. Any questions about any of that?"

Haylee shook her head.

"Having the dad here means we can get his family medical history, too," the doctor said. "But I will ask him to step out of the room while you have your physical exam and invite him to come back for the ultrasound, okay?"

"Okay," she agreed.

Trevor nodded.

"Great." She reached for a blood pressure cuff. "Let's get started."

The doctor asked a steady stream of questions and made notes directly into the computer on her desk as she went along.

"Any abdominal pain, nausea or vomiting?"

"I've had some morning sickness," Haylee acknowledged.

"But not just in the morning," Trevor chimed in.

"I know it can be disruptive and unpleasant, but

it will pass," the doctor promised. "Though it varies from one expectant mother to the next—and even from one pregnancy to the next—it generally starts to let up around week ten and is usually resolved by week fourteen.

"In the meantime, I'd advise eating smaller meals more frequently and sticking to bland foods as much as possible. And if you lose a few pounds in the first trimester, don't panic—you'll gain them back again soon enough."

"What if I'm throwing up but still gaining weight?" Haylee asked. Most of the articles she'd read on pregnancy suggested that a lot of expectant moms lost weight in the first trimester, but despite the intense—and thankfully short-lived—bouts of nausea, her appetite had returned and her clothes were already starting to feel snug.

"That's less common but not an obvious cause for concern, either, especially for a mom who's young and healthy and fit," Dr. Robertson said. "Do you feel as if you've put on a couple extra pounds?"

She nodded. "Four pounds."

The doctor smiled but made a note in the computer.

She asked Trevor to step outside while she performed the physical exam, but invited him back in again for the ultrasound, so that they could actually see their baby.

"Are you nervous?" he asked, as they waited for the doctor to return with the portable scan machine.

"Nervous and scared," she admitted. "And maybe just a little bit excited."

He took her hand and linked their fingers together.

It felt like an oddly intimate act, despite the fact that

their bodies had been joined even more intimately, but she held on, grateful for his presence.

"How about you?" she asked.

"I'm flat-out terrified," he admitted.

"Why are *you* terrified? There isn't a baby growing inside you, getting ready to push all your internal organs out of place."

He winced at the thought. "I'm terrified because, up until this point, this has been more of a concept than a reality—for me," he acknowledged. "Seeing our baby will make everything real."

"I'm the one who decided to have this baby," she reminded him. "You don't have to stick around if it's not what you want."

"You want to have and raise a baby on your own?" His tone was skeptical.

"It wouldn't be my first choice, but getting pregnant by the first guy I ever slept with wasn't a lifelong ambition, either."

"Maybe it was meant to be," he said.

"You don't believe that," she chided.

"I'm not sure what I believe anymore, but I do want to stick around. I want to be there for you and our baby."

He sounded sincere, and the fact that he was here certainly added weight to his claim, but it was early days yet. The prospect of parenthood was novel, maybe even exciting. But how long would it hold his attention? What would happen when he started to date someone who objected to him spending time with the woman who was pregnant with his child? And what would it mean for their child when he decided to start a family with someone else? Would their child be neglected? Forgotten?

"Haylee…"

"Yeah?"

"You're cutting off the circulation in my fingers."

"What? Oh." She immediately loosened her grip. "Sorry."

"Maybe you're a little bit scared, too," he suggested.

She was, but not for the reasons he assumed. She was afraid of making the same mistakes her parents had made—and of her child paying the price.

The brisk tap on the door cut off this uncomfortable introspection.

"Are you ready for the fun part?" Dr. Robertson asked, as she wheeled the portable machine into the room.

"Ready," Haylee confirmed.

"That's the spirit." The doctor took a seat on the swiveling stool and tapped a few keys on the computer. "Dad, why don't you stand behind Mom so that you can see what's happening?"

Trevor obediently moved to the other side of the table.

The doctor peeled back the paper sheet over Haylee's abdomen and took a bottle of gel from the warming tray, squirting it on the expectant mom's belly.

"I just need to take some measurements first, to help verify your estimated due date, and then we'll let you take a peek at your little one," she promised.

"Shouldn't my due date be thirty-eight weeks after the date of conception?" Haylee asked.

"It should," the doctor agreed. "But unless a woman

is tracking her ovulation, it's not possible to accurately pinpoint the date of conception. And even if there's a specific event—an oops, we forgot birth control or the condom broke—there's no way to be certain that ovulation and fertilization coincided on that date. Because the egg might only be viable between twelve and twenty-four hours, but a woman can get pregnant from an act of intercourse occurring up to five days prior to ovulation and even two days after."

"I didn't realize there were so many variables," Haylee admitted.

"Believe it or not, ultrasound measurement of the fetus in the first trimester is the most accurate method to establish gestational age."

"In that case, I'll stop talking and let you get to it."

Dr. Robertson chuckled as she began to move the wand over the patient's abdomen. "I'm happy to answer any and all questions that either of you might have, at any time... Oh, this is a surprise."

Haylee squeezed Trevor's hand tighter. "What do you mean? Is something wrong with the baby?"

"No, nothing's wrong," the doctor hastened to assure them. "Everything looks good... Here, why don't I let you take a closer look at this." She turned the monitor so they could see what she was looking at. "As I was saying, everything looks good—" she smiled then "—with both babies."

"I'm sorry—*what*?"

"There's the first baby—" Dr. Robertson pointed to a small blob on the screen, then moved the wand and her finger "—and there's the second one."

"Two babies?" Trevor said, sounding stunned.

"Twins?" Haylee said at the same time, in a similar tone.

"Twins," the doctor confirmed.

Trevor didn't remember much of what happened after that.

The doctor continued to do her thing, but he couldn't really focus on anything she'd said after confirming that Haylee was pregnant with twins.

Due March 25. Somehow the date had penetrated the fog that had descended on his brain. And the warning that it wasn't unusual for multiples to come early. Which meant that he and Haylee had less than six-and-a-half months to get ready for the arrival of two babies.

Two babies.

He glanced at Haylee as they exited the clinic.

She appeared as shell-shocked as he felt.

"Do you want to sit down?" he asked. "You look like you're going to pass out."

"I'm fine. I'm just…" She lowered herself onto the edge of one of the benches that flanked the doors. "I guess my head is spinning a little."

"Mine, too," he admitted.

"I'm not sure I'd completely wrapped my head around the idea of one baby and now…"

He nodded his agreement.

"Twins." She tipped her head to look up at him, her expression just a little bit panicked. "What am I going to do?"

He sat down beside her. "I think you mean, what are *we* going to do?"

"I figured you'd be on your way back to Haven—as fast as possible."

"The thought did cross my mind," he confided. Then he shrugged. "But you know where I live."

She managed a smile, but it wobbled around the edges and her eyes filled with tears.

"Obviously this changes things," he said.

She nodded slowly.

"Now there are twice as many reasons to get married."

"Still not good reasons," she argued.

"Twice as many midnight feedings and dirty diapers," he pointed out.

She closed her eyes. "Thanks. You're helping me feel so much better."

"I'm trying to help you see that we need to do this together."

"How are we supposed to do anything together when we live five hundred miles apart?"

"You could move to Haven and move in with me," he suggested.

"That's a great idea," she said, her voice dripping with sarcasm. "Except that my job and my family—*my entire life*—is in Oakland."

"You want me to move here?"

"No!" Then, in a curious tone, she asked, "Would you?"

He shrugged. "I'm willing to consider all options, including the most obvious solution to this situation—marriage," he added, in case it wasn't obvious.

"Marriage only seems like the obvious solution right now," she said. "But a legal union based on a shaky foundation is destined to fail, and then we'd end up fighting over custody and access and a wagon wheel Roy Rogers garage sale coffee table."

He looked at her blankly. "A *what kind* of coffee table?"

"See?" she said. "That proves it. If you knew me, you'd know that *When Harry Met Sally* is my favorite movie."

"If you move to Haven—or I move here, we'll have plenty of time to get to know one another," he pointed out. "And even watch cheesy movies together."

"It's not a cheesy movie," she denied. "It's a classic."

"*Casablanca* is a classic," he told her.

She narrowed her gaze. "Are you sure you haven't seen *When Harry Met Sally*?"

"I don't think so, but I'd be happy to watch it if it means that much to you."

She closed her eyes then and sighed. "What are we going to do?"

"We don't need to make any decisions right now," he reassured her. "What we need is ice cream."

Haylee offered a tremulous smile. "You read my mind."

Trevor went back to Haven that night, but he called Haylee the next day, just to check in. And again the day after that, to see how she was doing. Their phone conversations had already become a regular part of her nightly routine, and it was one she looked forward to.

But when he called the following Wednesday night, she was tempted not to answer because she knew he'd immediately suspect something was wrong and she wasn't ready to talk about it. So she let his first call go to voice mail, and the second one, too.

Next came a text message:

If you don't answer your phone, I'm going to call emergency services to request a welfare check.

The third time he called, she answered.

"What's going on?" he asked, immediately concerned.

"I'm just feeling a little overwhelmed about everything."

"I'd say that's understandable, considering the recent revelation that you're going to have two babies in about six months," he noted.

"True," she agreed. And maybe she should have left it at that, but he'd proven to be a really good listener and, since Finley was out, she really needed someone to talk to right now. "But it's not only the pregnancy."

"Is there anything I can do to help?"

The sincere concern in his voice nearly undid her, but she drew in a deep breath and slowly let it out again, determined to hold it together—to pretend her whole life wasn't falling apart. "Do you know anyone who's looking to hire an electrician?"

"What? Why?"

She sniffled. "I kind of lost my job today."

"Because you're pregnant?" he guessed.

She shook her head, then realized he couldn't see her. "No. I didn't even have a chance to tell my boss the news before he called me into his office to explain that the company was experiencing an unexpected downturn and there wasn't enough work to keep everyone on."

"I'm sorry, Haylee."

"I'm not even the most junior employee, but I was the first one to get cut." And though she could probably make a case that she was let go because she was a woman, in violation of California labor laws, what would be the point?

"Did you lose your medical insurance, too?"

She groaned softly. "I didn't even think about that."

"I'll have you added to my plan," he promised.

She knew the out-of-pocket costs for prenatal care and hospital delivery could be daunting, so it would be foolish to refuse. "Can you do that?"

"It would be easier if we were married," he said. "But yes, I can and I will."

"Thank you," she said sincerely.

"But since you've got some time on your hands, why don't you come back to Haven for a while?"

"Do you have any rewiring that you need done?"

He chuckled. "Unfortunately, no. But I did hear that the mayor was putting out a tender for someone to do the holiday installations."

"For real?" she asked, her curiosity piqued.

"For real," he assured her. "Terry James has been lighting up Main Street for the past thirty-five years, but he and his wife retired to Arizona in May and apparently nobody gave a passing thought to who might take over the work he usually did."

"There can't only be one electrician in town," she said.

"Of course not," he agreed. "But Sparky is busy with

the new housing development and most of his guys are already working overtime there."

"There's an electrician in town whose name is Sparky?"

"It's a nickname—if not an original one," he told her. "His real name is Rohan. I went to school with his younger brother, so I could use that connection to reach out and ask if he's hiring and then pass your information along, if you think you might be interested in a change of scenery for a few weeks."

"I can't imagine twiddling my thumbs until Henry calls me back," she said. "And I've worked on holiday installations in the past."

"Is that a yes?"

"Yes," she said. After all, there was no harm in getting more details. A decision about the job wouldn't have to be made until it was actually offered to her.

"I'll call Sparky first thing in the morning," he promised.

"Thanks." She knew there were no guarantees, that Sparky might be as reluctant to hire a woman as Henry had initially been. But if he was willing to take a chance on her, it might not be a bad idea to get out of Oakland for a while—or at least until she figured out how to tell her father that he was going to be a grandfather.

Chapter Eleven

Sparky was more than happy to look at Haylee's résumé and, after a brief telephone interview confirmed that she was eligible to work in Nevada, he offered her an eight-week contract to help with the town's holiday lighting and, in his words, "get the mayor off my back."

Three days later, she said a tearful goodbye to her family and was on her way to Haven.

Her sister had packed a cooler with healthy snacks and drinks, probably not so much for Haylee as for the babies. Finley had been thrilled to learn that she would have not just one but two babies to cuddle and spoil before the end of March, and she was practically bursting to share the news with someone—anyone. But Haylee knew she could trust her sister to keep her secret.

She was driving to Nevada this time, so that she

wouldn't have to rent a vehicle when she got there. Driving also meant that if she decided this was a bad idea while she was en route, she had the option of turning around—as she considered doing every sixty minutes or one hundred miles—whichever came first.

She didn't have any concerns about the job she would be doing—she was looking forward to the opportunity to be busy and productive again. No, it was the proximity to Trevor that worried her.

Not that she was going to move in with him. He'd immediately offered, assuring her that he had plenty of space, but she'd declined. Not just because it would raise the eyebrows of every Gilmore and Blake in Haven, or even because she didn't want news of such an arrangement to make its way back to her father, but because she didn't trust herself not to fall under Trevor Blake's spell.

In any event, when word got around that she would be working temporarily in Haven, Haylee fielded several calls from family members with offers of empty rooms. She accepted Caleb and Brielle's offer.

"This is great," Haylee said, turning around in the middle of the spacious and beautifully decorated guest room. "I don't know how I can ever thank you guys enough."

"You might not be so thankful when Colton wakes you up several times in the middle of the night," Brie warned.

"I'm happy to help with the baby in any way that I can."

"We'll see if you're so willing at 3:00 a.m.," Caleb said dryly.

"We'll see if I hear him," Haylee said. "I'm a pretty deep sleeper."

"Colton's screams could wake the dead."

"Stop that," Brie scolded her husband. "You're going to have her calling the Stagecoach Inn for a room before she's even unpacked."

"Here's a better idea," Caleb suggested, grabbing his wife around the waist and nuzzling her throat. "We'll let Haylee stay with the banshee baby and we'll get a room at the hotel."

"Now that's a tempting proposition," Brie agreed. "Regan said the Wild Bill suite was incredible."

"Make the reservation," Haylee said. "Me and Colton can hang for a weekend while you get busy making him a little brother or sister."

"Oh no," her cousin immediately protested. "No way."

"He means 'not yet,'" Brie said.

"Could you imagine?" Caleb asked his wife. "If you got pregnant now, we'd have another baby not long after Colton's first birthday. It would almost be like having twins." He shuddered at the thought.

"My sister and her husband have twin girls," Brie explained to Haylee. "They're absolutely adorable, but there's no denying that Regan and Connor have their hands full."

Haylee managed a stiff smile. "I can't imagine."

"I don't want to," Caleb said. "Now, if you don't need me for anything else here, I'm going to head out to feed the horses."

"Go ahead," Brie said. "I'll keep Haylee company while she unpacks."

Her husband nodded. "I won't be long."

But still he brushed a soft, lingering kiss on his wife's lips before he slipped out the door.

"Married eight years and you still act like newly-weds," Haylee teased.

Her cousin's wife laughed. "Maybe the secret to keeping the romance alive is living apart for the first seven-and-a-half of those years."

"I think the secret is love," Haylee said, a little wistfully. "That's obviously what brought you back to one another after so much time apart."

"It was love—and a little bit of luck."

"Luck?"

"I guess you haven't heard the whole story," Brie said.

And while Haylee transferred her clothes from suitcase to dresser, the other woman told her about her chance encounter with Caleb at a hotel in Vegas during a girls' weekend getaway and how her impulsive decision to spend one last night with the only man she'd ever loved had created not only their son but their second chance.

"So how far along are you?" Brie asked, as Haylee zipped up her empty suitcase after her packing was undone.

"What?"

"I just had a baby," Brie reminded her. "I'm familiar with the early signs of pregnancy."

Haylee sighed and sank onto the edge of the mattress. "Ten weeks. But you have to promise not to tell *anyone*. I'm still trying to figure out how to tell my parents."

"Of course. Wait, is that why you wanted to get away

from Oakland for a while?" Brie asked, sounding concerned. "Because you haven't told the father, either?"

"No. The father knows," Haylee said. "But…he isn't in Oakland. He's here."

"Oh." The other woman obviously put enough pieces together then to see the big picture, because her eyes went wide. *"Oh."*

Haylee nodded.

"Just when the dust was starting to settle," Brie mused. "How did Trevor react to the news?"

"He was understandably surprised," Haylee said. "Because we were impulsive but not careless."

"I know he has a reputation as a player," Brie said. "But I hope you won't judge him for it. I think he deliberately cultivated that persona because he didn't want people feeling sorry for him."

"Why would anyone feel sorry for him?" Haylee wondered.

Trevor's cousin hesitated, as if she was uncertain about how much to say—or had perhaps already said too much.

"Come on, Brie, he's handsome and popular and a Blake—why would anyone feel sorry for him?" she asked again.

"Because he was engaged a few years ago," Brie finally confided. "And…his fiancée was pregnant."

She swallowed. "What happened?"

"She lost the baby."

Haylee's eyes filled with tears. "I can't imagine how horrible that must have been for both of them."

Trevor's cousin nodded. "And made even worse by the fact that Alannis blamed Trevor."

"Why?" she wondered, her heart aching for his loss.

"Because he wasn't there when it happened. And so of course he blamed himself, too."

"How long ago was this?"

"I was living in New York at the time, but I think it was four—or maybe five—years ago," Brielle said. "They broke up a short while later and, as far as I know, he hasn't been in a serious or exclusive relationship since then."

"Well, our relationship is neither serious nor exclusive—if it can even be called a relationship," Haylee said.

"I'll bet he proposed."

"Which only proves he has a strong sense of responsibility."

"He did." Brie's grin quickly faded. "But the absence of a huge diamond on your finger suggests that you turned him down."

"I don't think a baby—or even two babies—is a reason for two people who barely know each other to get married."

"Did you say two babies?"

Haylee nodded.

Her cousin's wife chortled. "No wonder your face went white when Caleb mentioned the idea of twins."

Rohan Sullivan, aka "Sparky," was about six-and-a-half-feet tall with frizzy red hair and a quick smile. But it wasn't only his physical appearance that distinguished him so completely from Haylee's former boss—Rohan was more than happy to add a female electrician to his crew. Or any electrician, as there was a definite shortage of qualified tradespeople willing to live and work in a small town in northern Nevada.

As he'd said during their telephone interview, "It doesn't bother me if you pee sitting down or standing up as long as you know how to use a Megger."

Haylee did and she was hired.

She started work at 8:00 a.m. and clocked out at 4:00 p.m. But living with Caleb and Brielle at the Circle G meant that she had to be out of the house shortly after seven each morning to ensure she made it to work on time. And then she got to do the forty-minute drive again at the end of the day.

She'd anticipated that living and working in Haven would make it easier to get together with Trevor, but she didn't see him at all the first week. The second week, he was out of town at a trade show for three days, but they agreed to meet at Diggers' for dinner Friday night.

Of course, having dinner in town required Haylee to make another trip back and forth to the ranch so that she could wash off the sweat from her day and make herself pretty—or at least presentable—for a date with the father of her babies. After her shower, she sat on the edge of the bed to put on her socks and closed her eyes for just a minute.

Dr. Robertson had assured her that tiredness was a common problem for many expectant moms in the first trimester. She'd also warned that many of the usual signs and symptoms might be amplified due to the fact that Haylee was carrying two babies, but that she should start to feel a little more energetic by the second semester.

She couldn't wait…

* * *

"Are you ready to order?" Deanna asked.

Trevor glanced at the time displayed on his phone. "Yeah. I'll take a southwest burger with a side of waffle fries, to go."

"Good choice," she said, collecting the two menus that had been set on the table and moving away to punch in his request at the order station.

He tried calling Haylee again, but the call went directly to voice mail. So he texted, again, but there was no response.

They'd agreed to meet at seven o'clock, and it was now almost eight. Obviously she wasn't just running a few minutes behind schedule—in which case she most likely would have called or texted him to say so—she'd stood him up.

When Deanna brought his check along with his meal packaged to go, he paid for the food and left a generous tip in the hope that she wouldn't tell all her coworkers that he'd been stood up.

He wasn't just annoyed that Haylee was a no-show, he was sincerely disappointed. And worried. If she'd changed her mind about meeting him for dinner, why didn't she let him know?

And why wasn't she answering her phone?

That was the question at the forefront of his mind when he knocked on his cousin's door.

"Trevor, this is a surprise." Brielle stepped away from the door, inviting him in.

"Is Haylee here?"

Of course, he knew that she was, because he'd parked behind her car in the driveway.

"She is, but she's upstairs. Sleeping."

"Sleeping?"

"When she came in after work, she said she was going to take a shower and then head back into town for dinner, but—oh, she was supposed to meet you," his cousin realized.

He nodded.

"I'm sorry," Brie said. "I saw her sprawled out on top of the covers, fast asleep, when I went upstairs to give Colton his bath, and I figured she'd just changed her mind about going out. If I'd realized you had plans, I would have woken her."

"I'm glad you didn't," he said. "She obviously needed sleep more than food."

"The first trimester is hard," Brie said sympathetically. "And more so, I imagine, carrying two babies."

He sighed. "She told you?"

"I don't think she really meant to," his cousin admitted. "But my pregnancy wasn't so long ago that I couldn't recognize the signs."

"Can you do me a favor?" he asked.

"Sure," she agreed readily.

"Can you check her phone and maybe plug it in? I think the battery probably died."

"I did wonder why you'd driven all the way out here instead of calling," Brie said.

"And if it's not password protected, maybe delete the twenty-seven text messages I sent?"

She bit her lip, hiding a smile. "I'll see what I can do."

Trevor said goodbye and walked out, still disappointed that he hadn't got to see Haylee but no longer worried that something had happened to her.

On his way to his truck, he crossed paths with Caleb, returning to the house.

"It'd be easier for me to pretend I didn't know you hooked up with my cousin if you didn't come sniffin' around her while she's staying here," the rancher said.

"So you know, too," Trevor realized.

"I wish I didn't. And I can't imagine—I don't want to imagine—how it happened. Haylee is hardly your usual type."

"You don't think I'm attracted to beautiful, smart, sexy women?" he challenged.

Now the other man looked thoughtful. "Not many people see Haylee that way. Of course, not many people have seen her dressed up like she was at the wedding. *I* almost didn't even recognize her."

Trevor couldn't deny that it was the dress with the short skirt that first snagged his attention. But then, when she'd looked at him, it was her eyes that had held him captive. And later, it was her smile that further entranced him. And the more time he spent with her, the more he liked her.

"Well, I'll be damned," Caleb mused, taking in his expression. "You really do have a thing for her, don't you, Blake?"

"You stay out of my business, Gilmore, and I'll stay out of yours," Trevor told him.

"Deal."

Trevor reached out to slap the snooze button on his alarm, but the damn thing wouldn't stop ringing. Because it wasn't his alarm, he finally realized, it was his phone.

He peeled open his eyes to glance at the clock as he swiped to connect the call.

"'lo?"

"I'm *so* sorry."

"Haylee?"

"Ohmygod—did I wake you?"

"It's 7:00 a.m. on a Saturday."

"I didn't realize it was so early. I woke up and saw your text message and wanted to call right away to tell you that I was sorry."

"Did you say *message* or *messages*?"

"Message," she said again.

Thank you, Brielle.

"And I am. Sorry, I mean."

"It's okay," he said. "It was my fault for making plans at the end of the week."

"Maybe we could reschedule for tonight," she suggested. "If you don't have other plans."

"I'm heading over to Crooked Creek for a few hours this afternoon, to help my grandfather bale hay, but tonight sounds good."

"Seven o'clock at Diggers'?"

"Actually, I've got a better idea."

"Are you going to tell me what it is?"

"No," he said. "But I'll pick you up at seven."

"I bet he's taking you to that fancy restaurant in the hotel," Finley said, when Haylee was Skyping with her later that afternoon.

Though she missed seeing her sister—and Simon—

every day, it seemed to Haylee as if they'd talked more in the two weeks since she'd been gone than they had when they were actually living together. She talked to her dad and Colleen, too—on Sundays and Wednesdays, because Robert Gilmore liked to have a schedule and stick to it. And he didn't like to video chat, instead calling Haylee from his landline phone on predetermined times and dates.

"Do you think so?" she asked Finley now.

"Well, he said it was a better plan than Diggers', and the only other restaurants in town are Jo's Pizza and Sunnyside Diner."

"How fancy is fancy?" Haylee wondered. "And what am I supposed to wear?"

"The dress you wore to the anniversary party would be perfect."

Maybe. *If* it still fit over the growing curve of her belly without announcing her pregnancy to the world. "Do I have to wear heels with the dress?"

"Yes, you have to wear heels with the dress," her sister confirmed. "It's an implicit part of the agreement between a man and a woman when he takes her out for a nice meal."

"You might be wrong about where we're going," Haylee pointed out. "Maybe all-day breakfast is the new dinner trend."

"I'm not wrong," Finley said. "But right now, I have to run to a major fundraiser for an up-and-coming political candidate—big names and bigger dollars."

"Have fun," Haylee said.

"Not likely," her sister said. "But we'll talk tomorrow. I want to hear all the details about dinner with the daddy of your babies."

"We'll talk tomorrow," she confirmed.

"One more thing," Finley said, before she signed off.

"What's that?"

"Wear sexy underwear, just in case."

Chapter Twelve

Finley wasn't wrong, Haylee acknowledged, as she looked around the restaurant.

Trevor had managed to wrangle an eight o'clock reservation at The Home Station, and it absolutely lived up to the "fancy" descriptor.

"This is really nice," she said.

"Wait until you try the food."

"That good?"

"The chef, Kyle Landry, studied at the School of Artisan Food in England."

"How'd he end up here?" she wondered.

"He grew up here," he told her. "In fact, his mom is Jolene Landry, of Jo's Pizza."

"For future reference, I would have been just as happy with pizza."

"There's nothing that compares to Jo's," he agreed. "But the menu here uses locally sourced ingredients to create hearty meals to satisfy the hungry rancher and impress the sophisticated traveler."

"Why does that sound as if you're reading it from somewhere?"

He turned his menu around, to show her the restaurant's mission statement on the first page.

"Which I would have seen if I'd actually opened the cover of mine," she noted, and did so now.

"Everything sounds good," she said, her gaze skimming over the offerings a second time.

"Then order one of everything," he suggested.

"I'm hungry," she acknowledged. "But I'm not *that* hungry."

"But you're eating for three," he reminded her.

"If only that were true," she said. "According to the doctor, I should only be consuming an extra three hundred calories a day in the first trimester—although I get to bump that up to almost seven hundred in the second and nine hundred in the third."

"But what are you going to have tonight?" he asked, as the server, who'd introduced herself as Erin, approached their table again.

"I think I want to start with the arugula and pear salad with Gorgonzola dressing."

"One of my favorites," Erin said.

"And then—" she looked at the menu again "—the chicken breast stuffed with spinach and mushrooms served on a bed of risotto."

Trevor made a face. "Sounds like a lot of green stuff to me."

"Green vegetables are good for you," she said.

"And for you, sir?" the server prompted.

"I'll start with the shrimp and pork wontons followed by the prime rib au jus with fingerling potatoes and baby carrots."

"Can I make a recommendation?" Erin asked.

"Of course," Trevor said.

"Save room for dessert," she said with a wink, then went to place their orders.

"I'm glad I saved room for dessert," Haylee said, as she pushed the parfait glass away.

"You liked the mousse?"

"It was white chocolate mousse with dark chocolate something-or-other garnish—what's not to like?"

"Then why did you only eat half of it?"

"Because even half was probably more than three hundred calories."

"Do you want to try my banana cake with caramel ice cream? It's amazing."

"You are the devil, aren't you?"

He grinned and nudged his plate toward her.

She retrieved her dessert spoon from the parfait glass and scooped up some of his dessert. Sliding the spoon between her lips, she closed her eyes, humming in appreciation of the rum-roasted bananas with the spongy cake and sweet ice cream.

"Yeah, that's good, too. Really good."

He liked watching her eat. She didn't pick at her meal, pretending she wasn't hungry, as other women he'd dated had sometimes done. No, Haylee ate like a person who enjoyed good food, although the sounds she made to express her enjoyment stoked in him a different kind of appetite.

She opened her eyes then and found him staring at her. "Do I have something on my face?"

She didn't wait for his answer, but lifted her napkin to her mouth.

He reached across the table to touch her arm, halting her scrubbing. "There's nothing on your face."

"Then why are you staring at me?"

"I sometimes forget how beautiful you are," he admitted. "And then I look at you and you actually take my breath away."

"Did the bartender maybe slip some rum into that glass of Coke?"

"You're a smart, capable woman who has plenty of self-confidence when it comes to your professional capabilities, but you shy away from personal compliments," he noted. "Why is that?"

"Maybe because I don't get a lot of personal compliments," she said.

"I can't be the first man who's told you that you're beautiful."

"And if I said that you were?"

"I'd say that there's something wrong with all the guys in California."

"Or maybe all the charm was taken by the guys in Nevada."

"Maybe," he agreed, as he handed his credit card to Erin to settle up their bill.

* * *

"I've been thinking about it," Trevor said, as he drove her back to the Circle G. "And I think you should move in with me."

"Whoa!" She twisted in her seat to look at him. "Where did *that* come from?"

"You've been in Haven for two weeks now, and tonight is the first chance we've had to get together."

"I came to Haven to work," she reminded him.

"I know," he admitted. "But I didn't think the job—and all the back-and-forth—was going to be such a time-suck. It's obvious that it's wearing you out."

"You work as much as I do," she pointed out.

"You're right," he acknowledged. "But you said that one of the reasons you decided to take the job in Haven was so that we'd have the opportunity to spend time together and get to know one another better."

"Which is what we were doing tonight."

"And now, we've got a half-hour drive back to the Circle G. A drive that you have to do every morning to get to work and every afternoon to get back again—but that you wouldn't have to do twice each day if you were living in town with me."

It was actually closer to a forty-minute drive, which she didn't point out to Trevor as it would only add weight to his argument. And it was true that, by the time she made the drive back to her cousin's house at the end of every day, she was usually ready to fall into bed exhausted. But of course, she didn't, because Brielle was always eager for adult company after being alone with her adorable—and undeniably demanding—infant son all day. So Haylee would hang out in the kitchen with her for a while, keeping an eye on Colton while the little guy's mom was busy getting dinner ready.

Haylee felt guilty that she was living under their roof and didn't do more, but Brielle insisted that cooking for three people was no more work than cooking for two. Plus, she told her houseguest with a wink, Finley had called ahead to warn her that Haylee was a hazard in the kitchen.

"You're not saying anything," Trevor noted, when she remained silent for a long moment.

"I'm trying to process this unexpected invitation," she admitted. "You know I don't cook, right?"

"I didn't know," he said. "But I didn't ask you to move in with me so that you could cook for me. Although now that you mention it, I'm wondering how you can claim not to cook when I've eaten your peanut butter cup cookies."

"That's baking, not cooking."

"How is it different?" he challenged. "You combine ingredients, put them in the oven for a specified amount of time, and take them out again when they're transformed into something else."

"Technically, baking is a type of cooking," she allowed. "But it's the only kind I do."

"It doesn't matter," he said. "Because I'm not asking you to cook. Or clean. I have a service that comes in every Thursday to dust and vacuum."

"What about scrub toilets?" she asked. "I hate scrubbing toilets."

"They do that, too," he assured her.

"Do you have a spare bedroom?"

"Three of them," he said. "You can take your pick—or you can share mine."

She ignored the deliberately provocative suggestion—and the "yes, please" clamoring of her hormones. "Why do you have a four-bedroom house?"

"Because the price was right and real estate is always a good investment."

"So they say," she agreed.

"What do *you* say? About moving in, I mean," he clarified.

"It would be convenient to live in town," she acknowledged. "I'm just not sure it's a good idea."

"I was joking about sharing my bedroom, if that's your concern."

"Were you?" she challenged.

"No," he admitted. "I mean, if you were interested in sharing my bed, I wouldn't say no. But if you're concerned that I'd take advantage of you staying with me to try to seduce you, I promise you that I won't."

"So we'd just be...roommates?"

"And maybe friends."

"You want to be friends?" she asked dubiously.

"It seems like a good place to start," he pointed out reasonably. "Since eventually we're going to be parents together."

She didn't know if she could be friends with him when she couldn't be around him without thinking about what had happened that night in her hotel room. When he smiled, she remembered the feel of those lips against hers. When he touched her arm, she remembered the feel of those hands caressing other parts of her body.

It wasn't just that she couldn't stop thinking about the fact that she'd been naked with him, but that her traitorous body wanted her to get naked with him again. She wanted to feel the way she'd felt when she was in his arms. Desirable. Desired.

"So...what do you say?" Trevor asked, as he pulled into the long, winding lane that led to the Circle G.

There were all kinds of reasons that she should say no. So many things that could go wrong. But when she opened her mouth to respond, she didn't express any of those concerns.

"I say 'thanks for dinner, Roomie.'"

Haylee missed her family.

Though she was enjoying her work and especially the time she was spending with Trevor, she was conscious of the five-hundred-mile distance between Haven and Oakland. Between her and her siblings and her dad and stepmom.

She FaceTimed with Finley almost every day and talked to her dad and or Colleen a couple of times a week, on a predetermined schedule. So when her phone rang at precisely 8:00 p.m. Sunday night, she couldn't help but smile as she connected the call.

"What's this I hear about you renting a room in town now?" her dad asked, after their usual exchange of pleasantries was complete.

"I'm renting a room in town now," she said.

"What was wrong with the room you had at your cousin's house at the Circle G?"

"I loved spending time with Caleb and Brielle and

Colton, but it was a forty-minute commute to and from my job."

"If the job isn't working out, then you should come home," Robert said.

"The job's working out fine," Haylee told him. "In fact, I'm really enjoying it. I just wasn't enjoying the long drive at the beginning and end of every day."

"I don't like the idea of you living alone in town. It's not safe."

"Haven's a lot safer than Oakland. Colder, too," she said, in a deliberate effort to shift the topic of their conversation.

"One of the things I definitely *don't* miss about Nevada," he said.

And she breathed a sigh of relief that the topic of her living arrangements had been abandoned—at least for the moment.

"Are there things that you do miss?" she asked him now.

"Family," he admitted. "Sometimes I forget how much until I go back for a visit and then have to say goodbye again." Then he paused, and she could picture him shrugging. "But ranching wasn't in my blood the way it is in my brothers'—I'm happier near the ocean, running my company."

He said it casually, as if Gilmore Logistics was a neighborhood shop when it was actually an international shipping conglomerate.

"But you seemed to enjoy catching up with them when you were in town for Grandma and Grandpa's anniversary party."

"Sure," he agreed. "Just because we have different

interests doesn't mean we don't get along. But speaking of people who were at the party—have you seen any more of that Blake boy who crashed it?"

"His name is Trevor, Dad. And it's not crashing if you're invited."

Of course, she hadn't actually invited Trevor, but there was reason to let her father know that.

"I'll take that as a yes," he grumbled.

"I don't understand how you can dislike him when you don't even know him."

"He's a Blake—that's all I need to know."

Haylee wanted to put her head down and bang it against the desk.

Instead, she tried logic and reason. "The land dispute between the Gilmores and Blakes happened long before you were born," she pointed out. "Don't you think it's kind of silly to be holding a grudge over something that had nothing to do with you?"

"It is what it is," he said stubbornly.

And her father being her father, she knew she wasn't going to change his mind tonight, so she steered the conversation to another topic again.

"You have to tell them," Devin said, when Trevor stopped by the following Tuesday afternoon to pick up the laptop he'd rebuilt for him.

The "them" was obviously their parents, and Trevor knew he was right, but it still wasn't a conversation he was eager to have.

"I know," he admitted. "But Haylee and I agreed to keep the news quiet until after the first trimester."

"I'm not talking about the babies—although yes, that, too."

Trevor frowned. "Then what are you talking about?"

"Haylee living with you."

"How the hell do you know that?"

"It's a small town," his brother reminded him.

"And she only moved in two days ago," he pointed out.

"So...how's it going so far?"

"Quietly," Trevor said.

"Huh?"

"We're mostly tiptoeing around one another."

"Living together is a big step," Devin said.

"I know, but it seemed...expedient," he decided.

"Expedient?" His brother laughed. "Oh, please tell me that's the word you used when you asked her to move in."

"Of course not. I'm not a complete idiot."

"That's debatable."

"So who told you?" he asked now.

"No one would ever gossip directly to me about you, but I overheard the news at The Daily Grind, The Trading Post and the library."

"The library?"

Devin shrugged. "There's a new librarian who's kind of cute. Anyway, the point is that it won't be long before the news makes its way to Miners' Pass."

"You're right," Trevor acknowledged. "I just wanted to give Haylee a chance to settle in and hopefully decide she likes me before I subject her to Lorraine and Elijah."

"Your call," his brother said. "But don't say I didn't warn you."

* * *

Their first disagreement had been about the payment of rent. Trevor didn't even want to discuss the matter, assuring her that he didn't need or want her money, but Haylee had insisted so she could honestly tell her father that she was renting a room in town in order to be closer to work.

Just another white lie, she'd assured herself, but she knew it was only a matter of time before the collective weight of all those lies brought down the house of cards she was living in.

Still, her argument at least persuaded Trevor, who agreed to accept a nominal sum—which he planned to put into a savings account for their babies. In exchange, he gave her a key and the code to the alarm system, then carried her suitcase up to the room she'd chosen.

It was the second smallest of the three guest rooms on the upper level, but she told him she liked the soft periwinkle blue color on the walls. Truthfully, she'd chosen the room because it was the farthest from his— because why tempt fate? Her hormones already rioted whenever he was in the same room with her, and she wasn't sure she'd be able to control them if there was only one thin wall between her and the father of her babies.

If Trevor experienced any residual feelings of attraction toward her, he did an admirable job of controlling them. He didn't kiss her or touch her, except inadvertently, or even flirt with her. And he certainly didn't say or do anything that suggested he laid awake in his bed at night, thinking of her just down the hall in her bed.

She was relieved, of course.

And maybe just the teensiest bit disappointed.

Living with Haylee was torture—and it was only the end of week one! How was he ever going to survive the next five weeks without losing his mind? And a lot of help he'd be to her in the second half of her pregnancy if he was in a padded room.

It shouldn't have been a big deal. Having lived with Alannis for nearly a year, he figured he knew what he was getting himself into when he suggested that Haylee move in.

He was wrong.

On the positive side, Haylee was surprisingly low maintenance. She didn't fuss with her hair or obsess about her clothes. In fact, she rarely even bothered to put on makeup. But she always smelled good, and just a whiff of her body wash in the morning was enough to have him walking around in a semi-aroused state for the rest of the day. And the way her eyes lit up when he walked in the kitchen, as if she was happy to see him, well, what man wouldn't respond to that? Not to mention her smile, which never failed to make him crave the sweet taste of that perfectly shaped mouth.

And just this morning, he'd walked into the laundry room to find her pink bra and matching panties draped over the drying rack. Which, of course, brought back vivid and erotic memories of the night he'd had the pleasure of peeling the sexy garments from her sexier body and—

"Trevor?"

He snapped back to the present. "Did you say something?"

"Just that I don't want my being here to interfere with your plans," she told him.

"What plans?" he asked, certain that he'd missed part of the conversation while he'd taken his mental detour.

But she lifted a shoulder. "How am I supposed to know? But I'm guessing that you don't usually spend every Friday and Saturday night at home."

"Not every Friday and Saturday," he acknowledged. "Although my social calendar has a lot more empty pages than most people would believe."

"I'm only saying that you shouldn't feel compelled to curtail your...usual activities just because I'm living here temporarily."

He stared at her now, torn between bafflement and amusement. "Are you talking about sex?"

She averted her gaze. "Not necessarily," she hedged. "Although I recognize that's probably part of your usual extracurricular routine, I was talking about dating or... whatever."

"And you're saying that you'd be okay with me bringing other women back here for...whatever?" he pressed.

She shrugged again as she played with a loose thread on the sleeve of her sweater. "It's your house, though the women might appreciate if you focused on them one at a time rather than as a plurality."

There had to be something wrong with him that he found himself turned on by her convoluted words and prim tone, but there was no denying that he was. Or maybe it was just that they were talking about sex, albeit in abstract terms.

"Since you brought up the subject," he said, "I feel compelled to confess that I have been focused on one woman."

"Well, then… I'll be sure to stay out of your way if you want to bring her here."

"Haylee…" He paused, waiting for her to look at him. When she finally did, he smiled. "I'm talking about you."

She swallowed. "Me?"

He nodded. "I haven't wanted anyone else since the night we spent together."

"Is it because…do you feel…responsible…for taking my virginity?"

"When I think about that night, responsible is the very least of what I feel," he assured her.

"What do you feel?"

"Answering that question might venture into dangerous territory," he warned. "So I'm just going to say that you're an amazing, intriguing and unforgettable woman."

Haylee was too guileless to heed his implicit warning, instead asking, "Then why haven't you kissed me, even once, since I've been here?"

"Because I promised you that, if you moved in here, I wouldn't try to seduce you." A promise that was increasingly testing the limits of his self-control.

"I only asked about kissing," she said, her cheeks turning pink. "Not…seduction."

"They're not so very different, when the kissing is done right," he told her. "And the next time I kiss you, you can be sure that I'll do it right."

Chapter Thirteen

Haylee was *freezing*.

An unexpected cold front had swept through the area, dropping temperatures well below seasonal norms, and she clamped her jaw tight to prevent her teeth from chattering as she stepped into the bucket. She didn't ordinarily mind working outdoors, but she was quickly realizing that she didn't have the wardrobe to work outside in twenty-degree weather.

"You going to be okay up there?" Sparky asked.

"I'll be fine," she said, as she flexed her fingers to maintain blood flow to the frigid digits.

"You need to get some Hot Mitts," he told her.

"What?"

He grinned and shook his head. "California girl."

"And proud of it. Shivering," she acknowledged. "But proud."

"Hot Mitts are activated hand warmers," he explained. "You take them out of the package, pop them inside your gloves and then they keep your hands warm all day."

"Whoever invented those is a genius," she decided. "Is there a whole body version?"

"Unfortunately not. You'll have to talk to your boyfriend about keeping the rest of you warm," he said, with a wink.

"Let's just get this job done so we can break for lunch and I can wrap my hands around a hot bowl of soup."

There were plenty of assistants scurrying around the offices of Blake Mining, any one of whom Trevor could have tapped to run paperwork over to the courthouse. But Haylee had mentioned that she was going to be working in town square this week, so he decided to make the trip himself and maybe steal her away for lunch.

After he'd finished in the clerk's office, he headed back outside. A white panel van with the familiar Sparky's Electric logo was parked on the side of the road and the man himself was pacing the sidewalk with a phone to his ear.

He finished up the call as Trevor approached and then tucked the phone into his pocket. "What's up?"

"I thought I might take Haylee to lunch, if she's around."

"She's around but she's busy," Sparky said, pointing. Trevor, following the direction indicated, nearly had a heart attack when he saw the bucket perched at least twenty-five feet in the air, and a figure in dark overalls securing lights to the peaked roof.

"That's Haylee up there?"

"Yep. She's making good progress, but I'd guess it's going to be at least an hour before she's done."

"Maybe another day then," he decided, suddenly no longer hungry.

He'd thought he understood what her job entailed. But he realized now that he'd chosen to focus on the fact that she looked sexy as hell with a tool belt slung around her hips and a hard hat on her head rather than the potential dangers she faced when she went to work every day.

Sure, there were all kinds of codes and regulations designed to keep her safe, but still, equipment could fail or malfunction, accidents could happen.

And he knew from experience, sometimes bad things happened for no reason at all.

A long hot shower helped Haylee thaw out at the end of the day. Even better, after she was dry and dressed again, she walked into the kitchen and found Trevor standing at the stove, stirring something in a pot. The sweet scent of chocolate filled the air.

She looked at the array of ingredients on the counter. "You made hot chocolate from scratch?"

"I'm more than just a pretty face, you know."

She was beginning to realize that he was so much more than she'd imagined. And the more she got to know him, the more she realized he was a man she could seriously fall for—if she was foolish enough to let herself fall.

Which, of course, she wasn't.

"Actually, it was your hot body that first caught my eye," she said lightly.

"Was it?"

"Apparently I'm shallow that way."

"And yet that hot body is here, every day, and you haven't once taken advantage of it," he noted.

"You said you wanted to be friends," she reminded him.

"I say a lot of stupid things," he said, making her laugh.

"Whipped cream or marshmallows?" he asked.

"Whipped cream," she said.

He piled a mountain of whipped cream onto the cocoa, then grated chocolate on top of the whipped cream.

"What did I do to deserve this?"

"You were stuck outside all day."

"That's the job," she reminded him, as she sat at the table and wrapped her hands around the mug.

"I know," he said. "But I didn't know that you'd be the one in the bucket twenty-five feet in the air."

"What did you think—that I just flipped the switch on a breaker when all the work was done?"

"I guess I didn't think about it enough," he admitted.

"Do you have a problem with my job?" she asked, seeming to brace for his response.

"Of course not," he denied. "I just didn't expect that I'd worry about you every morning when you walked out the door to go to your job."

"You don't have to worry," she told him. "I would never jeopardize our babies."

"I'm not worried about our babies."

"You're not?"

"No," he said. "Because I know you're taking care of them. I worry about you, because you won't let anyone take care of you. Because you won't let me take care of you."

"I don't need anyone to take care of me," she insisted. "But I appreciate that you want to. And—" she lifted her mug to her lips again "—I appreciate the hot chocolate."

Haylee sat cross-legged on top of her bed with her laptop open.

"How's my favorite guy?" she asked, trying not to think about the one down the hall who, despite all his sexy talk, still—three days later—had not kissed her.

The sound of contented purring came through her speaker, making her smile.

Of course, Simon wasn't responding to her question as much as the behind-the-ears scratch he was getting from Finley, on whose lap he was perched while Haylee and her sister Skyped.

"I think he's maybe finally starting to forgive you for ditching him to run off and live with some guy in Nevada."

"I came here to work," Haylee reminded her sister. "And Simon knows that I wanted to bring him with me."

"Does he?" Finley teased, shifting the cat so he was centered in front of the camera. "Does this look like a cat that knows—or even cares? He only cares that he's got food and water in his bowls, and a clean litter box."

Which was the reason Finley had insisted that Haylee leave her beloved feline in California with her, because she didn't want her pregnant sister to risk toxoplasmosis through exposure to soiled kitty litter.

"Well, you could tell him that I love him and miss him," Haylee said.

"I do," Finley promised. "Every day."

"I love you and miss you, too."

"Don't," her sister said firmly.

Haylee nodded, appreciating that the single word warning was intended to steer them away from a path that would end up with both of them in tears. But at least she had pregnancy hormones as an excuse for her turbulent emotions.

"How are Dad and Colleen doing?" she asked now, because she missed them, too.

"Didn't you talk to them last night?"

"Just Dad, and you know he doesn't say too much."

"Then you don't know that Colleen's niece and her husband are expecting," Finley guessed. "The baby's not due until April, but they're so excited, they couldn't resist sharing the news. I stopped by the warehouse the other day and caught Colleen shopping online for baby stuff."

Haylee sighed. "I already feel guilty enough because I haven't told them."

"So *tell them*," Finley urged.

"I will," she promised, because she knew that she had to—even if she had yet to figure out the how and when.

Thankfully, Finley didn't press for specific details, asking instead, "How are things in Haven?"

"A lot colder than I anticipated," Haylee confided.

"The temperature really dropped this week, so my Saturday is probably going to be wasted shopping for warmer—and bigger—clothes."

Her sister sighed. "Only you would think shopping is a waste of time."

"It's certainly not my idea of fun."

"Obviously I need to make another trip to Nevada."

"I need clothes for work and leisure. Not party dresses or palazzo pants and sequined tops."

"Those palazzo pants look great on you," Finley said. "But I bet you didn't even take them with you."

"There was a finite amount of space in my suitcase—and they probably wouldn't fit me right now, anyway," she grumbled. "All my clothes are starting to feel snug, and I've completely given up even trying to button my favorite jeans."

"That's because you're growing my nieces or nephews inside of you. And I promise, if even one of your babies is a girl, I'll teach her everything you don't know about fashion."

"Because you're going to be the best auntie ever."

"I will," Finley promised. "Of course, if you have a daughter who is anything like you, she might only accessorize with hard hats and tool belts."

"And my son might be a clothes horse."

"And since you're obviously not, I'll be there on Friday."

"Don't you have a big event this weekend?" Haylee asked, because her sister's weekends were always booked.

"The Forrester-Osborne wedding," Finley said. "Canceled."

"Oh, no." Haylee could imagine her sister's disappointment and frustration to have an event canceled after she'd put in so much hard work—as Finley always did—to prepare for it.

"The stress of the wedding just got to be too much for the bride and groom, so they ran off to Vegas and eloped."

"Did they really?"

Finley nodded. "The bride's parents were livid, but they paid the full tab for the five hundred–plus guests, arranged to have the flowers distributed to nearby hospitals, donated the meal to a local food kitchen and sent me a case of champagne—really good stuff.

"Plus I now have the whole weekend off," she continued. "Because there's no rehearsal dinner on Friday or wedding brunch on Sunday. And before you tell me that I can't abandon Simon, I know Colleen will be happy to watch him for a few days."

"In that case, I'll see you on Friday," Haylee said, not just because she'd be foolish to decline her sister's offer to help her shop, but because she missed her like crazy already.

"Will you be able to pick me up at the airport, or should I make other arrangements?"

"Send me your flight details when you have them, and I'll figure something out."

Finley didn't look particularly pleased when she saw Trevor waiting for her at the airport.

"I guess Haylee couldn't make it," she said.

"My schedule's more flexible than hers," he said, reaching for her bag.

"I've got it," she said, extending the handle of the wheeled carry-on to pull it behind her.

He shrugged and led the way through the double doors to the parking lot.

Finley followed, sucking in a breath as she stepped outside. "Haylee was right," she muttered. "It's cold here."

"Welcome to October in northern Nevada," he said. "Although this recent cold snap is a little colder than usual."

She didn't respond, but he suspected that Haylee's sister had clamped her teeth together to prevent them from chattering.

He opened the passenger door so that she could get out of the wind, and this time, she didn't protest when he reached for her bag to toss it onto the back seat.

He climbed behind the wheel, turned the key and cranked up the heat. Finley rubbed her hands together as he pulled out of the parking lot and headed toward Haven.

Twenty minutes later he broke the silence to say, "You were a lot chattier when I met you in Oakland."

"That was before I knew you'd knocked up my sister," she told him.

"It was a joint effort."

She didn't look amused.

"What about raising the babies—is that going to be a joint effort, too?" Finley challenged.

"Absolutely," he confirmed.

She seemed taken aback by his ready agreement.

"It would be a lot easier for both of you if you were married."

"I agree."

Finley frowned. "Well, that wasn't as hard as I expected."

"The hard part is convincing your sister," he told her.

"You've discussed this with her?"

"Tried to. She thinks that a baby—or even two babies—isn't a good enough reason to get married."

"Are you telling me that you asked her to marry you?"

He nodded. "More than once."

"Hmm."

"What does that mean?"

"I'm considering the possibility that I might have misjudged you."

"Maybe you could consider nudging your sister toward the idea of marriage," he suggested.

"Maybe I will," she said.

"Other than that, do you have any specific plans while you're in town?"

"We're going to some place called Battle Mountain to go shopping tomorrow."

"You're likely to be disappointed by the offerings in the shops compared to California," he warned.

"Haylee's only interest is in winterizing her wardrobe," Finley said. "I'm here to ensure that 'warm' doesn't look like a fashion disaster."

"Your sister always looks good."

"You're right. Her style is different than mine, but it mostly works for her. But the dress she wore to Caleb and Brielle's wedding…"

She paused then, as if to give him a moment to remember.

As if he would ever forget.

"…I picked that out. And the underwear, too."

"Thank you," he said sincerely. "And please take my credit card when you go shopping tomorrow."

"Are you suffering from baby brain already?" Finley asked, as she unclipped a pair of leggings from the hanger and handed them to her sister.

Haylee wiggled into the pants. "Why would you think that?"

"Because you're obviously distracted—you've tried on every single item of clothing that I've handed to you without question or complaint."

"That's why we're here," she reminded her sister.

"And I can see now that you weren't exaggerating about needing not just warmer but bigger clothes." Finley splayed a hand on the curve of her sister's belly. "Your babies have already grown so much."

"I'm not going to be able to hide my pregnancy for very much longer, am I?"

"Not much," Finley agreed. "So you might want to tell Dad before everyone in Haven figures it out and he hears it through the grapevine."

"They're already talking about that Gilmore girl from California moving to town and right in with Trevor Blake."

"No doubt it's all the single girls in town gossiping— or their disappointed mothers," Finley said. "Jealous that you snapped up one of the sexiest men in town."

"I haven't snapped up anyone. Trevor only suggested that I move in with him so that I don't have to commute so far to work."

"I wouldn't be so sure about that."

"Anyway—" Haylee turned around to face the mirror again "—I'm sorry if I've seemed preoccupied."

"Don't apologize—tell me what's on your mind."

Haylee sighed. "I think I'm falling in love with him."

"And why wouldn't you?" her sister said. "He's seriously hot and totally into you, and you guys are going to have the most beautiful babies."

The mention of the babies made her smile, but it didn't eliminate the worry that niggled at the back of her mind.

"And yet, for some reason, you seem to think that falling in love with him would be a problem," Finley realized.

"Of course it would. Because I don't have any experience with stuff like this, and I really don't like not having control of my emotions."

"Have you never been in love before?" her sister asked curiously, as she handed Haylee another sweater to try on.

She shook her head.

"I guess I shouldn't be surprised," Finley said. "You always were so much smarter than me."

"That's not true," Haylee protested, as she studied her reflection in the full-length mirror.

"I like the style but not the color," her sister said. "It washes you out."

She tugged the sweater over her head again and folded it before adding it to the discard pile. "So how many times have you been in love?"

"Probably not as many as I believed in the moment," Finley acknowledged.

"Then it's possible that I'm wrong—that what I'm feeling isn't love at all?" she asked hopefully.

"Anything's possible," her sister agreed. "But in this case, I'm leaning toward your feelings for Trevor being the real deal."

Haylee sighed. "I don't want my heart broken. More important, I don't want my babies' hearts broken."

"This is about Mom again, isn't it?"

"I don't know. Maybe."

"You've got to get her out of your head," Finley said. "I'm not denying that her walking out screwed us all up to some extent, but Trevor seems like a really great guy. So maybe, instead of being afraid of what might go wrong, you should consider all the things that could go right."

"He *is* a really great guy," she agreed.

"And yet you turned down his proposal," her sister noted.

"He told you about that?"

Finley nodded. "What I want to know is—why?"

"He only wants to marry me because he believes it's the right thing to do, and I want him to *want* to be with me."

Now her sister shook her head. "I think the baby hormones are messing with your brain."

"No doubt," Haylee agreed.

"Because I've seen the way the man looks at you, and I can assure you, he isn't thinking about duties or responsibilities—he's thinking of you naked."

"That's just sex, and don't guys think about sex all the time?"

"Nineteen times a day," Finley told her. "On average."

"I'm not going to ask how you know that."

"I read a lot," her sister said, answering anyway. "My point is, there's nothing wrong with building a relationship on a foundation of physical attraction."

"That ship might have sailed," Haylee said, touching a hand to her belly.

"I don't think you need to worry about that." Finley gathered up the clothes her sister was buying. "Now let's go check out the lingerie department."

Chapter Fourteen

Trevor knew it had been hard for Haylee to say good-bye to her sister when Finley left. While it was true that she had a lot of family in Haven—more than in Oakland, even—she missed her parents and her siblings.

"What do you think about making a trip to California at the end of the month?" he suggested after they'd returned home from the airport Sunday afternoon.

"Why?" she asked.

"To see your parents—and tell them that they're going to be grandparents."

"Have you told your parents?" she challenged.

"Not yet," he admitted, though he knew that he needed to do so soon. "But you're almost fifteen weeks along now, so it should be safe to share the news."

"You're right," she agreed. "I was originally thinking I'd tell my dad when I went home for Thanksgiving, but I'll be more than five months pregnant by then and, considering how my waistline is expanding already, there might not be any hiding my condition."

"We could take advantage of Nevada Day and go to California for a long weekend," he offered.

"What's Nevada Day?"

"It's celebrated on the last Friday of October each year to commemorate the state's 1864 admission to the union. The main festivities take place in Carson City, with various events through the day, including military flyovers and a parade."

"I had no idea," she said. "Do you celebrate with your family?"

"We used to go to the capital when me and Devin were kids, but not since then. Haven has its own celebration, on a smaller scale, at Prospect Park with fireworks in the evening."

"Well, I don't want you to miss out on that," she said.

"If you're going to Oakland, I'm going with you," he said.

"It's really not necessary."

"They're my babies, too."

"Are you sure?"

"Yes, I'm sure," he told her. "But I do have one question—should I borrow a bulletproof vest?"

"My dad doesn't own a shotgun," she assured him. "Although he was on the wrestling team in high school. Or maybe it was college."

"That would be a funny story to tell at our wedding," he mused. "How I was pinned to the mat by my father-in-law."

"There isn't going to be a—"

He touched a finger to her lips, silencing her in mid-sentence. "Don't dig your heels in," he cautioned. "It will only be harder for you to pull them out when you change your mind later."

"I'm not going to change my mind."

He just smiled. "We'll see." Then he turned his attention to the calendar app on his phone. "I've got a meeting Thursday morning, but we could leave right after that, if you can get away from work a little early, too."

"I'll email Rohan right now," she said, refusing to call her boss Sparky, as everyone else did. She reached for her phone and scrolled through her contacts. "What's the actual date?"

"Thursday's the twenty-ninth."

"Which is my stepmother's birthday," she said, suddenly remembering.

"Does that mean there'll be cake?" he asked hopefully.

She shook her head as she began tapping her screen, typing a message.

"It was your job to order the cake and that's what you're doing now?" he guessed.

She managed a smile then. "No. It's her sixtieth birthday this year."

"And you're not allowed to have cake when you're sixty?"

She sent him a look. "My dad planned a surprise trip to Hawaii to celebrate the occasion."

"So the cake will be in Hawaii?"

"What is your obsession with cake?" she wanted to know.

"I'm not obsessed," he denied. "I just happen to like cake. Especially devil's food cake with raspberry buttercream frosting."

"Nope, not obsessed at all," she said dryly.

"It's what my mom always orders from Sweet Caroline's for my birthday," he confided.

"When is your birthday?" she asked, only now realizing that she didn't have a clue.

"March fifteenth."

"Maybe our babies will be born on your birthday," she said.

"Our babies aren't due until the twenty-fifth," he reminded her.

"But less than half of all twin pregnancies go to term."

"It might be fun to share my birthday," he decided, then winked. "As long as I don't have to share my cake."

She smiled at that, then her phone chimed, indicating receipt of a text message. She swiped the screen and sighed. "And this year, Colleen's cake will be in Hawaii."

"Which means there's no point in us going to Oakland for the Nevada Day weekend," he realized.

Now she nodded.

"You want to go to Hawaii?"

She smiled at that. "Who wouldn't? But no, we're not going to crash their private holiday."

"So when are we going to share our happy news?"

"I guess it will have to wait until Thanksgiving."

"You don't ever Skype or FaceTime?"

"Not with my dad," she said. "He's technology

averse. Besides, I really think this is something that needs to be shared not just face-to-face but in person."

"Your call," he assured her.

She just hoped she hadn't already left it too late.

"You're pretty good at that," Trevor noted, watching with some surprise as Haylee whisked away the wet diaper and slid a dry one beneath Colton's bottom.

Because why wouldn't he want to spend his Friday night babysitting someone else's child in preparation for all those future Friday nights when he'd be home with his own?

But he didn't really mind. Not as long as he was with Haylee.

"I changed a lot of my brother's diapers when he was a baby," she told him. "Apparently it's one of those things—like riding a bike—that you never really forget."

"I thought Logan was only four years younger than you."

"Almost four years," she clarified. "But I was actually referring to my half brother, Sebastian, from my mom's second marriage."

"I didn't realize your mom was still alive," he admitted. "You don't ever talk about her."

She shrugged. "There's nothing to say. We don't really have much of a relationship anymore."

"Why's that?" he asked curiously.

"Because the children from her first, failed marriage don't fit into the narrative of her new, perfect life. Not that I'm bitter," she said, all too aware of the sharp edge in her tone.

"When did your parents split up?"

"The summer after Finley and I finished fifth grade."

"You and your sister were in the same grade?"

She nodded. "My birthday's in January and hers is in December."

"Busy year for your parents," he noted. "Almost as if they had twins."

"Almost," she agreed. "Anyway, for the next few years, we were shuttled back and forth between our dad's house and our mom's apartment."

"So your mom lives in California, too?"

"Not anymore. She moved to Florida with her new husband after the wedding."

"That's…far." He wasn't sure what to say. He suddenly felt…privileged? Guilty? Just for living in a town where his entire family was little more than a stone's throw away. "How often did you see her?"

"We used to go every other Easter, Thanksgiving and Christmas and for two weeks every summer."

"And now?"

Haylee shrugged. "Maybe once every couple of years."

"Do you talk?"

"Occasionally. Between the time difference and her very busy schedule of charity events and country club lunches, it's hard to set up a call. But we keep in touch via email, regularly if not frequently."

"When are you going to tell her that she's going to be a grandmother?"

She seemed startled by the question. "I hadn't given it a single thought."

"Why not?"

"I guess because she hasn't been part of my life in so long, I can't imagine her as part of our babies' lives."

"She still needs to know."

"You're right," she acknowledged. "But let me get through breaking the news to my dad first."

"Your call," he said.

"But since we're on the subject—why haven't you told your parents?"

"Because I was hoping to be able to tell them that we were getting married first."

"The babies will be coming in March whether or not there's a ring on my finger," she reminded him.

"I know," he admitted. "But the 'whether or not' gives me hope that you haven't completely ruled out the possibility."

Haylee was teaching herself to cook.

It hadn't been a conscious decision, it just kind of happened one day that she arrived home before Trevor and saw the Mmm… Meals kit in the refrigerator. He'd apparently tried the local service a few months earlier and discovered that it greatly simplified not just meal planning and preparation but grocery shopping, too. With the ingredients assembled and step-by-step instructions provided, she considered the point he'd made about cooking not being so much different from baking and decided to give it a try.

He'd seemed pleasantly surprised to arrive home a short while later and find dinner was almost ready to go on the table. Perhaps the chicken had been a little overcooked, but he'd been so sincere in his appreciation that she was encouraged to try again. Her subsequent efforts had shown some improvement, though Trevor was usually the first one home at the end of the day and already prepping the meal when she came in.

On Wednesday, though, she found him staring at the ingredients when she walked into the kitchen.

"Is something wrong?"

"I don't remember ordering lamb and lentil stew."

"So maybe they sent the wrong kit," she suggested.

"I'm not a fan of lamb—it's too chewy," he told her. "Or stew—it's too…soupy."

She laughed at that. "We could order pizza."

"That sounds like a good plan. We haven't had pizza in…wow—has it really been *three days*?"

"I'm sensing sarcasm," she noted.

"When I walked into Jo's the other night, Kendra teased that I should ask about the frequent diner rewards."

"Is there such a thing?" Haylee asked.

"Apparently not," he said. "Because when I mentioned it to Jo, she said the reward was getting to eat her pizza."

"And she's right."

"You want pepperoni and mushrooms again?"

She wrinkled her nose. "Actually, mushrooms aren't really appealing to me these days."

"You mean since Sunday?"

"I can't help it if my taste buds are out of whack."

"So what does appeal to you these days?" he asked.

"Hmm…sausage and peppers?"

"Sweet or hot?"

"Hot," she decided.

He called Jo's to place the order.

"Do you want anything else while I'm out?" he asked Haylee.

"I don't want you to go out of your way, but we're out of chocolate milk."

"You want chocolate milk with your pizza?"

"No," she immediately denied, then reconsidered. "Probably not."

He smiled, no longer surprised by her unusual food choices. "How's our ice cream supply holding up?"

"Maybe I should go to the store with you."

"Good idea."

He grabbed a basket instead of a cart, since Haylee insisted she only wanted a few things. Ten minutes later, the basket was almost full when she said, "We missed the snack food aisle."

"What do we need from there?"

"We don't *need* anything," she admitted. "But I've been craving dill pickle potato chips."

His distaste must have been revealed in his expression, because she laughed.

"I'm guessing I won't have to share them?"

"Only if you open the bag when Devin's over," he told her.

"Hmm, maybe I better grab two bags."

"You better grab them quick if you don't want our pizza to get cold."

"I'll be right back," she promised.

He added a tub of fudge brownie ice cream to the basket, using the bag of mini marshmallows as an insulator between the frozen foods and fresh, then turned around and found himself face-to-face with Lorraine Blake.

"Hello, Mother." He was more than a little surprised to run into her here because he knew that Greta—his parents' cook—was responsible for the weekly shopping. He also knew that Wednesday was the cook's day off. "What brings you here in the middle of the week?"

"We're having friends over for drinks later and your father wanted some charcuterie," she said.

He had to fight back a smile, thinking about how Haylee had responded to his use of the word "hence" and wondering how she'd react to his mother's mention of "charcuterie" in casual conversation when most people would say cold meats and cheeses.

"That's an unusual assortment of items," she noted, looking at the contents of his basket. "Even if you were a ten-year-old."

He shrugged, unaffected by her disapproval.

Of course, he had thirty-one years of experience to condition him to her exceedingly high standards and demanding nature. Nothing less than one hundred and ten percent was ever good enough for his mother, and even then, that effort had better be reflected in the results.

But Haylee didn't have that experience, and though he was sure she had to be wondering why he hadn't yet introduced the future mother of his children to his own parents, she hadn't pressed him to do so. Maybe Brielle had given her a heads-up that his parents—much like his cousin's—were too busy making money to concern themselves with supportive familial relationships.

Even so, he should have warned Haylee. He should have said something to prepare her for this moment—

and probably better prepared himself, too. Instead, she was happily oblivious as she made her way down the frozen food aisle toward him, a lamb to the slaughter.

"I found them," she said, holding the bags of dill pickle chips together over her head as if she was hoisting a trophy.

He couldn't help but smile at her enthusiasm as he waved her over.

"And who is this?" Lorraine demanded to know.

If his mother's tone had been cool before, it was downright frigid now, and her gaze—as it raked over Haylee, from the purple Converse high-tops on her feet to the denim that hugged her legs and tunic-style sweater that didn't completely conceal the swell of her fifteen-and-a-half-weeks baby bump—was icy.

His mother was, of course, dressed in a designer suit and high heels and somehow managed to look fresh after ten hours at the office.

Haylee's smile slipped and she hugged the chips against her.

"This is Haylee." Trevor slid a supportive arm across her shoulders. "Haylee, this is my mom, Lorraine Blake."

"Oh." Perhaps sensing it might be bitten off, Haylee didn't offer her hand. Instead, she nodded. "It's nice to meet you, Mrs. Blake."

"I'm sure it is," she responded.

"Is Dad here with you?" Trevor asked, attempting to deflect her attention.

"That would be convenient, wouldn't it? Then you could introduce us both to your…friend…in the middle of the grocery store."

"I'll take that as a no," he said.

"He was on a call with China when I left the office," Lorraine finally responded to his original question. "But I'm sure he'll be disappointed to know that he missed…this."

"No doubt," Trevor agreed.

"But I'm glad I ran into you," she continued, as if she didn't have the opportunity to see him every day at the office. "I've been meaning to invite you—" her gaze slid over to Haylee again "—both of you—to dinner Saturday night."

"For Devin's birthday," he guessed. He'd anticipated that there would be a family meal to celebrate the occasion, because there always was, but he hadn't decided whether or not he should subject Haylee to the event.

His mother nodded. "I do hope you can make it."

When Trevor didn't immediately respond, Haylee made the decision for both of them.

"We wouldn't miss it," she said.

Because she had no idea what she was getting herself into.

Chapter Fifteen

"Why didn't you say something?" Haylee asked, pausing in the act of applying gloss to her lips. "When your mother said we were invited for dinner—why didn't you say something?"

"Because I was trying to come up with a believable excuse as to why we couldn't make it."

She recapped the gloss and dropped it into her purse. "And how was I supposed to know that?"

"Maybe because I wasn't saying anything."

"I'm not good with silence," she admitted.

"I know," he said, teasing to lighten the mood. "I live with you."

She adjusted the skirt of her purple dress, then turned to look at her profile in the mirror. "This isn't so bad," she decided. "I look chubby more than pregnant, don't you think?"

"I think you look gorgeous," he said. "And just a little bit scared."

"Your mom is…intimidating."

"You've had three days to come up with an excuse to get out of it, if you don't want to go," Trevor pointed out.

"And I considered several," she confided. "But backing out at the last minute would be rude, and your mother already doesn't like me."

"That's not true," he denied.

"Please—we both know she wasn't happy to meet me when we ran into her at The Trading Post."

"That was my fault," he said. "I should have told her that I'd asked you to move in."

"And that I'm pregnant."

"Let's save that revelation for another day," he suggested.

"I don't see how that's possible when your mother already knows."

"Why would you think that?"

"Her disapproving tone combined with the way her gaze kept dropping to my midsection."

"That's my mother's usual tone. And she was probably focused on the potato chips. She doesn't approve of junk food."

"She doesn't approve of *me*."

"Even if that's true now, her opinion will change when she learns that you're carrying her first *and* second grandchild."

"Do you really think so?" she asked dubiously.

"Hope springs eternal," he said, though truthfully,

he'd learned a long time ago to temper his expectations whenever his parents were involved.

She picked up a square box wrapped in brightly colored paper and topped with a red bow.

"What's in the package?" he asked.

"Your brother's birthday present."

"You didn't have to get him anything."

"I wanted to," she said. "What are you giving him?"

"A six-month subscription to Mmm… Meals."

"That's the meal kit delivery service you use, isn't it?"

He nodded. "It was a gift from Devin for my birthday."

"You're kidding."

Now he shook his head.

"Bet he likes my gift better," she said.

"What is it?"

She smiled. "You'll have to wait and see."

"Relax," Trevor said, as he walked beside Haylee toward the front door of his parents' house. "You look like you're getting ready to face a firing squad."

"Maybe because that's how I feel," she told him.

"You like my brother," he pointed out.

"Are you suggesting that if I like your brother, I'll like your parents?"

"No," he said. "I'm just reminding you that you like my brother—and he adores you."

And the fact that it was Devin's birthday was the only reason that Haylee was there.

As they stepped up to the door, her hands tightened around the gift she carried. She already sensed that

Trevor's mom didn't approve of her, and she didn't hold out much hope that she'd make a better impression on his father. But she'd made an effort, dressing for the occasion in a plum-colored wrap-style dress that she'd bought on her recent shopping trip with Finley.

Trevor looked as handsome as always, casually attired in dark jeans and heather-gray fisherman knit sweater.

A uniformed housekeeper met them at the door to hang their coats and then escort them to the parlor where Mr. and Mrs. Blake were having predinner cocktails.

Haylee tried not to gawk as she walked alongside Trevor to the designated sitting room at the front of the house.

Trevor briefly made the introductions, and Lorraine was gracious enough to pretend that they were meeting for the first time. Drinks were poured—a beer for Trevor and sparkling water for Haylee—and conversation flowed, albeit not very smoothly.

"While we're waiting for your brother, why don't you help me choose a bottle of wine for dinner?" Lorraine suggested to her elder son.

"You know a lot more about wine than I do," Trevor said.

"I'm not sure that's true," she said, linking her arm through his so that he had no choice but to follow her out of the room, leaving Haylee alone with Elijah Blake.

She sipped her water and searched for something to say, finally settling on, "Your house is lovely."

"Have you been given a tour?" Trevor's dad asked.

"Just between the foyer and here."

"Come on," he said. "I'll show you around."

Haylee couldn't deny that she was curious about the house, so she fell into step beside him. He might have been in the business of mining, but he knew a lot about architecture and regaled her with details about the construction and various features of the home.

"And this is the library," Elijah said, opening a set of classic French doors into a gorgeously appointed room with a trio of arched windows and built-in floor-to-ceiling bookcases.

"It's beautiful." She ventured farther into the room, pausing when she spotted the single book on display on the middle shelf of one of the enclosed cases. The dust jacket was faded and slightly worn around the edges, but in good condition otherwise.

"Is that a first edition of *The Hobbit*?" she asked.

"It is," he confirmed.

"That was one of my all-time favorite books when I was growing up. I didn't enjoy *Lord of the Rings* as much, but I was probably just too young to appreciate it. That and the Ringwraiths gave me nightmares."

"It took me a while to track down that copy," Elijah said. "And it cost me forty thousand dollars at auction when I did."

"Wow." She appreciated literature and understood that original printings were works of art as much as books, but she was still taken aback to learn the value of it.

"Outbid a Rockefeller and an unidentified billionaire hedge fund manager from New York," he said proudly. "And when I brought it home, I couldn't imagine ever parting with it."

"I wouldn't want to give it up, either, if it was mine," she said.

"And it could be."

"Excuse me?" she said, taken aback by his suggestion.

"It wouldn't take up much room in your suitcase when you pack to go back to California," Elijah said.

"No, it wouldn't," she agreed, starting to get an idea of where the conversation was going—and desperately hoping he'd prove her wrong.

"Or I could write you a check, if you prefer."

Nope, not wrong.

"You want me to leave," she realized, feeling sick inside.

"Not just pretty but quick," he said approvingly, as he opened the top drawer of the glossy antique desk to retrieve his checkbook. "So how much do you want? What's your magic number?"

Because in his world, everything was for sale.

Everyone had a price.

"If and when I decide to go back to California, it will be because it's what Trevor and I decide," she said. "Not because you paid me."

"Trevor isn't thinking straight right now," his father argued. "He's trying to do the right thing, because that's the kind of man he is, but I'm not going to let him be taken advantage of by another girl who got knocked up—especially one named Gilmore."

So much for Trevor's theory that his mom hadn't been looking at Haylee's midsection—and her hope that the age-old feud wouldn't be a factor in her relationship with Trevor.

She took a deep breath and forced herself to count to three inside her head before she responded. "I'm going to overlook your insulting assumptions about me because you don't know me," she said, when she could finally speak calmly. "I'm even going to give you credit for looking out for your son because I haven't yet held my babies in my arms and already there isn't anything I wouldn't do for them. But I can't understand your willingness to push those babies—your grandchildren—out of your life."

"Bab*ies*?"

She nodded. "Trevor and I are having twins."

Though Elijah was apparently surprised by that revelation, he recovered quickly. "Just because you claim they're my son's babies doesn't make it true."

"It's not a claim, it's a fact," Trevor said from the doorway.

Though his tone was level, there was no mistaking the fury simmering beneath the surface.

His father dropped the checkbook back into the drawer and hastily shoved it closed. "Trevor. Son—"

"Unless the next words out of your mouth are a sincere apology to Haylee, I don't want to hear them."

"I think you've misunder—"

"Nope," Trevor said, cutting him off. "Not an apology. And not a misunderstanding, either." He shoved the bottle of wine in his hand toward his mother, who was standing beside him, then strode across the floor to grab Haylee's hand. "Let's go."

Though her stomach growled in protest of the fact that they were leaving before dinner, she didn't say anything as she slid her feet into her boots.

Devin walked through the front door as Trevor was helping with her coat. "Where are you going?" he asked, oblivious to the drama that had played out before his arrival. "You didn't eat without me, did you?"

"We're not hungry," Trevor said, at the same time Haylee's stomach growled again.

Devin's brows lifted.

"We'll pick up something from Diggers' on the way home," Trevor promised her.

She nodded, then to his brother said, "I'm sorry."

"I don't know what happened," Devin told her. "But I'm willing to bet you didn't do anything wrong."

"How much money are you willing to pony up?" she wondered, and immediately wished she could take back the question.

"So that's the direction he went," Devin realized, shaking his head and sending a worried glance toward his brother. "Now I have to say that *I'm* sorry—and promise that I'll bring you a piece of cake later." Then he winked. "If there is any leftover cake."

She smiled at that and kissed his cheek. "Your gift is on the sideboard in the parlor. Happy birthday."

Trevor had never been more furious with his parents. He wouldn't have been surprised if they'd expressed disappointment because "whoops! I did it again." But he'd never anticipated that they'd attempt to interfere in such a bold and insulting manner.

Haylee had called Diggers' to place their order while he drove, not able to get away from his parents' house fast enough. Now they were parked behind the restaurant to wait the requisite "twenty to twenty-five minutes" until their food was ready.

He didn't know what to say to Haylee, how to apologize. She had to be feeling hurt and angry, and because he'd taken her to Miners' Pass, he couldn't help but feel complicit in her emotions.

After several moments of silence, she reached over the console and touched a hand to his arm. "Are you okay?"

He turned his head to stare at her, baffled. "You're worried about *me*?"

"You're obviously upset."

"I'm seriously pissed," he said, his tone clipped.

"Okay," she agreed cautiously.

"And more sorry than you can imagine," he added, in a quieter voice.

"I was grateful for your spirited defense, but I don't blame your parents for looking out for you. And of course they'd be skeptical about paternity. You haven't asked for a DNA test, and you haven't told them that I was a virgin when we slept together."

"Because that's none of anyone's business but ours," he told her.

"And I appreciate your discretion, but they don't know me and, from their perspective—from any perspective," she acknowledged, "our relationship is moving pretty fast."

"You're right that they don't know you. But instead of trying to get to know you, my father tried to buy you off."

Haylee nodded, unable to deny that fact.

And he continued to seethe for several more minutes before she spoke again, saying, "Can I ask…about your fiancée?"

Trevor blew out a breath. "Of course he told you about Alannis."

"He only mentioned that you'd found yourself in a similar situation before," she said. "But I heard about your engagement—and the baby—from Brie."

"Then what more do you need to know?" he asked.

"For starters, why you didn't tell me."

"Because it's ancient history."

"Five years is hardly ancient history."

He shrugged. "Well, it feels like it."

He thought—*hoped*—that would put an end to the topic of his ex-girlfriend, but Haylee's next question proved him wrong.

"Were you and Alannis together for a long time?"

"A couple of years."

"I'm guessing your parents got to know her pretty well during that time."

"Not really," he said. "Regular Sunday night dinners aren't really a thing with Lorraine and Elijah—unless someone's birthday happens to fall on a Sunday. So if you're worried that they're comparing you to Alannis—don't."

"Because they didn't like her, either?" she guessed.

"They thought she got pregnant on purpose because she wanted the Blake name and money." And to this day, he couldn't be sure they were wrong. "But they agreed that getting married was the right thing to do, under the circumstances."

"Because even if she was a gold-digger at least she wasn't a Gilmore?"

"The feud has nothing to do with us," he insisted.

"If only that were true."

"Here's an idea—if we have a boy, we'll name him Gilmore, then he'll be Gilmore Blake."

"Or both the babies could have Gilmore-Blake as their hyphenated surname," she suggested.

She could see he wasn't thrilled by that suggestion, because she followed it up by saying, "But we've still got time to figure out those details."

"Yeah, I guess we shouldn't get too far ahead of ourselves," he agreed.

"I'm sorry...about the baby you lost," she said gently.

It was the first time in a very long time that anyone had mentioned the child he'd never known. The pain had faded...even the dull ache was mostly gone now. Maybe that's why he was able to confide to Haylee something he'd never told anyone else before.

"The truth is... I'm not even one hundred percent sure it was my baby."

She considered this revelation for a minute before responding, "But that didn't matter to you...did it?"

"No," he said. "It didn't matter."

His feelings for Alannis might have changed when he suspected she'd been unfaithful, but his love for the baby they were going to have together had been unwavering. The fact that Haylee had realized that, possibly before even he did, proved she was more attuned to his feelings than he'd given her credit for. "I've noticed that you catch yourself sometimes, when you start to talk about a future event with the babies—almost as if you're afraid to make plans."

"Alannis was still in her first trimester when she

lost the baby," he told her. "But we'd already ordered a crib and change table and all the other paraphernalia a baby needs."

"You were excited about being a dad."

And devastated when that dream didn't come to fruition.

But maybe a little relieved, too. Because as much as he'd been determined to be a good husband and an even better daddy, he knew that a baby wouldn't magically fix the problems that had become apparent in his relationship with Alannis in the months before her pregnancy.

"I *am* excited about being a dad," he said now, because it was true. "And I'm really glad I'm having these babies with you."

Then he leaned across the console and lightly touched his mouth to hers.

"I have to admit, I'm not really disappointed to be sitting on the sofa in your living room watching a game on TV and eating burgers and fries from Diggers'. Those ladderback chairs I saw in your parents' dining room didn't look all that comfortable. Plus I overheard your mom say something to you about osso buco—" She shuddered.

"This is much better," he agreed, grateful that she was looking on the bright side of their change of plans. "But I thought we might watch a movie instead of a game tonight."

"A movie sounds good," she agreed, lifting her cheeseburger to her mouth as he pressed a button on the remote.

Her attention was snagged by the first few bars of music even before the names Billy Crystal and Meg Ryan popped up on the screen.

"Really? This is what you want to watch?" But she was smiling now, too, pleased not just with his choice but that he'd remembered.

He shrugged. "You said it was your favorite."

"Maybe I should have warned you that it's a chick flick."

"I figured as much," he admitted.

Her gaze narrowed speculatively. "Is this a trap? We're going to watch this and then you're going to make me watch your favorite movie, and it's going to be some awful slasher film?"

He propped his feet up on the coffee table. "I don't have a favorite movie."

"Really?" She popped the tab on her soda can and sipped. "There isn't any one movie that you've seen multiple times but still can't resist watching again when you're scrolling through the channel guide and see it's on TV?"

He thought about it for a minute. "I usually can't resist the *Star Wars* movies. Except Episode One—I can skip that one."

"I liked Episode One when I first saw it," she said. "Until I realized that little Anakin Skywalker grows up to become Darth Vader."

"You don't know the power of the dark side."

She rolled her eyes. "Shut up and watch the movie."

He shut up and watched the movie.

But during the scene in the bookstore, he leaned

closer, squinting at the image on the screen. "Why does Sally's friend look familiar?"

"I should have guessed that you'd recognize her," she noted.

"But from what?"

"Picture her with side buns," she said, referencing Carrie Fisher's iconic hairstyle in the first *Star Wars* movie.

"It's Princess Leia," he realized.

She nodded.

"I have to confess, when I think of Princess Leia, I don't think about her hairstyle in Episode Four but the gold bikini in Episode Six."

"Of course you do," she noted dryly.

He just grinned.

She didn't know if he grinned when the deli scene played out, because she didn't dare look in his direction. But when the director's mother spoke what was undoubtedly the movie's most famous line, he chuckled.

Haylee kept her gaze on the screen.

The final credits had just started to roll when the doorbell rang. "I'll get it," Trevor said, gathering up the empty food and beverage containers on his way to the door—and returning with his brother.

Haylee's smile widened when she saw the plate in Devin's hand. "Is that leftover cake?"

"It is," the birthday boy confirmed, setting it on the table.

"Thanks," she said.

"No, thank *you*."

She smiled again. "I take it you liked your gift?"

"Best birthday present ever," he told her.

"I knew you'd appreciate a gift certificate for Mmm... Meals," Trevor chimed in.

"I do," Devin agreed, winking at Haylee. "But I was referring to Haylee's gift—and wondering how she managed to get her hands on a baseball signed by Mark Nickel."

"So that's what was in the box," Trevor said, because of course they hadn't been there to see his brother open it.

"I know people who know people," she said.

"And her sister Finley dated Mark when he played for the A's," Trevor said, explaining the cryptic remark to his brother.

"Did you ever get to see him play?" Devin asked.

"A few times."

"Me and Trev were at the game, three years ago, when he completed a natural cycle."

"Me and Fin were at that game, too," Haylee said.

"No kidding," Devin mused. "Just think, the two of you might have met at the coliseum three years ago."

"Somehow, in a crowd of fifty thousand–plus people," Trevor noted dryly.

"Why not? Out of all the guests at the wedding, Haylee's the one who caught your eye. An admittedly smaller gathering," Devin said. "But still, I've never seen you so quickly and completely smitten."

"Smitten?" she echoed, amused.

"Why do you think he bought those tickets to the baseball game?"

"Because the two of you were planning to go, but then you had to go out of town for business."

"You actually bought that story?"

She looked at Trevor quizzically. "It's not true?"

"It's true," he insisted. "Devin was in Montreal that weekend."

"Which you knew when you bought the tickets," his brother pointed out.

"I'll get plates for the cake," Trevor said.

Devin chuckled at his brother's hasty escape.

"Is it true?" Haylee asked, after the cake had been eaten and Devin was gone.

"Is what true?"

"Did you come to Oakland to see me?"

"Yeah," he reluctantly admitted.

"But that was before you even had a reason to suspect I might be pregnant," she realized.

He nodded.

"But…why?"

He shrugged. "Because I couldn't stop thinking about you."

"Maybe you really were smitten," she mused.

"And I'm becoming more and more each day," he told her.

She wasn't entirely sure he wasn't just teasing her, but it was something to think about.

Chapter Sixteen

"**Y**ou better not be calling to say that you can't make it home for Thanksgiving," Colleen said, when she answered the phone on the Tuesday before the holiday.

"Of course I'm coming home," Haylee assured her. "I'm only calling to let you know that I'm not coming alone."

"You're bringing a guest to dinner?"

"If that's okay."

"Of course it's okay. I'm just…surprised," her step-mother said. "Is it anyone I know?"

"You met him at the anniversary party," she confided.

"The one everyone was whispering about crashing the party?" Colleen guessed.

"That's him," Haylee confirmed. "Trevor Blake."

"He seemed like a nice man—and handsome," Colleen acknowledged. "Though your father might have mumbled something about 'lying, scheming Blakes.'"

Which wasn't really a surprise, in light of the comments he'd made on the phone to Haylee, and confirmed that the Blakes weren't the only ones still holding onto a grudge.

"You've known him a while then?" her stepmother guessed.

"Yeah." Haylee glanced down at the swell of her belly.

About five months, in fact.

But, of course, she kept that to herself.

"How long have you been dating?"

If she told Colleen that they were just friends and then she showed up pregnant, her stepmother would have a million questions about the identity of the baby's father. But was it accurate to describe their relationship as dating? Or maybe accuracy wasn't as important right now as setting the stage for the big reveal.

"We've been together for a while," she acknowledged.

"And you want to introduce him to your family." Her stepmother sounded delighted at the prospect of meeting Haylee's new boyfriend.

Her first boyfriend.

"Maybe it is too soon," she decided.

"No, it's not," Colleen denied. "We'd be happy to have him join us for Thanksgiving."

"Will you promise not to give him the third degree?" she asked hopefully.

"I will, but I don't pretend to have any control over your father," her stepmother warned.

"Do you think he'll play nice if I bake a pecan pie for him?"

"I have no doubt that it will go a long way toward softening his disposition," Colleen said.

"Something smells good," Trevor noted, as he walked into the kitchen.

"Pecan pie." Haylee set the baking tray on top of the stove and closed the oven door before turning to face him.

They'd been living together for almost four weeks now, and he still made her heart pound whenever he walked into the room.

"For dessert?" he asked hopefully.

She shook her head. "For Thanksgiving."

"Because you're sucking up to your father because you haven't yet told him that he's going to be a grand-father in less than four months."

"Okay, maybe I am struggling a little to come up with the right words," she acknowledged.

"Maybe you shouldn't worry so much about the right words and just tell him. On the other hand, maybe you shouldn't say anything at all."

She stared at him incredulously. "You think I should wait until a later date to share the news? Like maybe after the babies are born?"

He chuckled. "No, I'm suggesting that your dad might realize you're pregnant when he sees you."

Now she looked down at the front of her sweater, already stretched over the swell of her belly and sighed. "I'm not going to be able to hide it much longer, am I?"

"Honey, you only think you're hiding it now."

"If I wear a bulky sweater, no one will notice."

"Maybe," he said, though his tone was dubious. "But it would have to be a really bulky sweater."

"And I'll carry the pie in front of me."

"Because that was such an effective strategy with the chips," he remarked dryly.

She sighed again. "I waited too long, didn't I? Now Thanksgiving is going to be a disaster."

"Look on the bright side."

"What's that?"

"It will have blown over by Christmas."

"I can only hope," she said.

"But since you've still got that line between your brows that you always get when you're worried about something, why don't you tell me what it is."

"I don't want our babies to be pulled in different directions at every holiday. Easter with Mom, Thanksgiving with Dad, Christmas with Mom. Then the reverse order the following year."

He tiptoed carefully, aware that he was inching onto treacherous ground. "If you married me, there wouldn't be any question about where our kids would spend Christmas, because they'd be with both of us."

"For how long?" she challenged. "How long do you think it would take until you realized it was a mistake to marry a woman you don't love?"

He tipped her chin up, forcing her to meet his gaze. "I promise you, when we get married, I will do everything in my power to make our marriage work."

"Don't you mean, *if* we get married?"

"I'm trying to think positive." He took her hand and guided her over to a chair. "And I'm positive that there's something more going on here that you're not telling me. This part I'm less sure about, but I'm guessing it has something to do with your mother."

"Why would you say that?" she asked, sinking into the seat.

He sat down beside her. "Because you don't talk about her. You happily volunteer information about your dad and stepmom, but aside from telling me that your mom's remarried and lives in Florida, you haven't told me anything about her."

"Maybe because I'm ashamed of what she did...and worried that I might turn out to be just like her."

"What did she do that was so terrible?" he asked.

"She walked out and never came back. I don't mean that we never saw her again," she clarified, though he already knew that she and her siblings had been shuffled from one home to another for some time after the separation. "But our family was never the same after that.

"She claimed that she left us with our dad because it would be less disruptive for us to stay in the house we'd always lived in. And maybe she was right, but at the time...how could we not feel as if we'd been abandoned?"

"I can't imagine what that must have been like," he admitted. He had his own issues with his parents, but at least they'd always been there.

"My dad was as confused as we were," she continued. "He had no idea there was anything wrong before she announced that she didn't want to be married anymore."

"Was there someone else?"

Haylee shook her head. "No. Not then. She said it wasn't that she didn't want to be married to my dad, but that she was taking a stand against the institution in general. That marriage was designed to oppress women, making them responsible for cooking and cleaning and raising the kids."

"I'm sorry," he said sincerely.

"My grandmother came to stay with us for a while, until my dad figured out a more long-term arrangement. Meanwhile, my mom was living in an apartment that he was paying for. But only until she could support herself, or so she claimed."

Which was probably why Haylee was so determined to earn her own income, to not be dependent on her family or—God forbid—a husband for financial support.

"She didn't have a college degree or a lot of work experience, but she eventually got a job as a hostess at the new Black & Blue Steakhouse when it opened up in town."

He recognized the name of the high-end restaurant chain and had, in fact, dined at a Black & Blue on his last trip to Vegas.

"Three years later, Dalton Burke walked into the restaurant."

"Of Burke Food Group?" he guessed, naming the company that owned and operated Black & Blue as well as a few other national restaurant chains.

She nodded again. "And suddenly marriage wasn't a

trap but a celebration. Or maybe it was an opportunity for her to get out of Oakland.

"She always had dreams of traveling the world and resented that my dad wouldn't take her all the places she wanted to go, because he doesn't like to be away from his shipping business for too long. In fact, the trip he took to Hawaii for Colleen's birthday is the first real vacation he's probably had in five years.

"Dalton's business is different. He's constantly on planes, crisscrossing the country to check on various interests here and there, or—when he's not working—jetting off to ski in Switzerland or sail the Mediterranean, and my mom's happy to go with him. Of course, they have a tutor for Sebastian, because why would he waste his time in a classroom when he could celebrate his tenth birthday at the original Legoland in Denmark?"

"That's the age you were when they separated," he remembered.

She nodded. "Coincidentally, that was the same year I learned that Santa wasn't any more real than wedded bliss."

"A tough age to have your family—and childhood illusions—fall apart," he noted sympathetically.

"Is there ever a good age?" she wondered aloud.

"Probably not," he acknowledged. "But just because your parents' marriage didn't work isn't reason to diss the whole institution."

"How about the fact that forty-five percent of all marriages end in divorce?" she said.

"I think that's a flawed statistic. And in any event, marriage shouldn't be about statistics but about sharing your life with someone you care about."

"What about love?" she challenged.

"Love?" He didn't quite manage to mask the derision in his tone.

"'To love, honor and cherish' is a keystone of the traditional vows," she pointed out.

"So we'll exchange nontraditional vows," he suggested. "Because I can promise to be a faithful husband and attentive father, but there's no way I'm ever going to fall in love with you."

His words only confirmed what Haylee already knew, but that knowledge failed to lessen the sting of his assertion.

"Thank you for that unique offer," she said coolly. "But I'm going to have to decline."

"Be reasonable, Haylee."

"This is me being reasonable," she told him, pleased that she'd managed to tamp down on her instinctive—and admittedly less rational—response, which was to tell him that there was *no way in hell* she'd ever say "yes" to such an insulting proposal.

Well, he'd blown that in spectacular fashion, Trevor realized, as he watched her storm out of the room.

Two steps forward, three steps back.

Over the past few weeks, they'd made real progress in their relationship. During that time, he'd been surprised to discover how much he enjoyed being with her. She was easy to talk to, not only knowledgeable on a wide variety of subjects but interested in learning more. She had strong beliefs and opinions, but she wasn't at all close-minded.

Except, perhaps, on the matter of marriage—that

was the one topic of discussion about which they continued to butt heads.

Half an hour later, he knocked on her open bedroom door.

"I made dinner," he said, peeking around the portal. "Are you going to come down to eat? Or do you want me to bring you a plate?"

She looked up from the book she was reading. "What's for dinner?"

"Baked chicken, scalloped potatoes and steamed broccoli."

After a brief hesitation, Haylee slid her bookmark between the pages and closed the cover. "I'll come down."

"Are you still mad?" he asked, when she ventured into the kitchen as he was dishing up the food.

"I was never mad." But she didn't look at him as he set a plate in front of her.

He wanted to take her at her word and let the matter drop, but something in her tone warned that she was hurting, and the last thing he'd ever wanted to do was hurt her. So instead he said, "You sounded mad."

She stabbed her fork into a broccoli spear. "Pregnancy hormones are running rampant in my body. You shouldn't pay too much attention to how I sound."

"I'd like to apologize anyway."

Finally she lifted her gaze to his. "What exactly are you apologizing for?"

"For letting you think that my inability to fall in love with you has anything to do with you when the truth is, I'm never going to fall in love with anyone. Ever."

She picked up her knife and sliced into the chicken. "Don't you mean 'ever again'?"

"You think I'm still heartbroken over Alannis," he realized.

"Aren't you?"

"No." He pushed his potatoes around on his plate. "But sometimes I wonder if something inside me died when the baby did. I don't mean to sound melodramatic, but it's true. Afterward, I went on with my life, but... I was mostly just going through the motions."

"I know something about that," she told him.

"Because you lost your family, too, when your mom walked out."

She nodded.

"So maybe this is a second chance for both of us," he said. "But you have to be willing to give us a chance."

"I'm here, aren't I?"

He wasn't sure if she was referring to her presence in Haven or, more specifically, at the dinner table.

Either way, he had to figure it was a step in the right direction.

"There's my pecan pie," Robert Gilmore said, when he opened the door to greet his guests—or maybe just Haylee, who stood on the porch with the promised treat in hand.

"And pumpkin," she said, referring to the pie that Trevor, standing slightly behind her, was carrying.

"Well, let pumpkin come in," Colleen said, winking at Trevor as she opened the door wider to allow them entry.

"You remember Trevor?" she asked.

"Sure," her dad said. "The party crasher."

"Rob," his wife chided.

"Yeah, yeah. Best behavior," he remembered.

Trevor grinned, unoffended. "It's nice to see you both again."

"Finley's not here yet?" Haylee asked, wondering how they'd manage to arrive before her sister, who only had to walk across the yard.

"Logan's car's in the shop, so she went to pick him up."

Which was nice of her sister but undermined Haylee's hope that their father would be less likely to blow a gasket in front of the whole family.

"Take off your coats and stay awhile," Colleen urged. "I'm just going to take these pies to the kitchen. Robert, why don't you get the kids something to drink?"

"What do you like, Blake? Beer? Wine? Whiskey?"

"A beer would be good," he said. "Thanks."

"Haylee? We've got a bottle of that Riesling you like."

"Actually, just water for me, thanks." She lowered herself onto the edge of the sofa. Trevor sat beside her and took her hand, giving it a gentle squeeze for moral support.

Her dad started out of the room, then abruptly turned around again. "Before I forget, Henry stopped by the warehouse the other day. He said business is starting to pick up again and he'll for sure have work for you early in the new year."

"Did he?" Haylee wasn't sure what else to say.

"I thought you'd be a more excited about the news— about coming home."

"It is good news," she said, as Colleen returned from

the kitchen. "It's just that Trevor and I have some news to share, too."

Her father took a few steps closer, the promised drinks forgotten. "What kind of news?" he demanded.

"I'm—"

"*We're,*" Trevor interjected.

"—pregnant."

There was a moment of complete and stunned silence, followed by Colleen exclaiming, "Oh, that's wonderful news!" Then she turned to her husband, to prompt him. "Isn't it wonderful, Rob?"

The lack of an immediate reply told Haylee that he wasn't nearly as thrilled as his wife. And when he finally did respond, he was looking at Trevor.

"I wouldn't expect a Blake to know what's the right thing," he said, "so I'll tell you—it's marrying the girl you got pregnant."

"Dad—"

He silenced his daughter with a sharp glance, then shifted his attention back to her future groom.

Trevor wasn't easily intimidated, but the intensity of the older man's stare caused a bead of sweat to slowly snake down his spine. Still, he felt compelled to say, "Haylee hasn't decided if that's what she wants."

Robert's eyebrows drew together over his narrowed gaze. "*Haylee* hasn't decided?" he echoed, before turning to her again.

She lifted her chin. "Yes, Dad. It's the twenty-first century and a woman actually does get a say in such matters."

"A woman who doesn't say 'no' when a man invites

her to his bed shouldn't say 'no' when he wants to do the right thing," her father insisted stubbornly.

"Maybe we could table this discussion for another time?" Colleen suggested, starting toward the door in response to the ring of the bell.

"This discussion has waited long enough already," Robert argued.

His wife gave the expectant parents a sympathetic glance as she went to answer the summons.

"How far along are you?" the Gilmore patriarch asked his daughter.

"Twenty-one weeks."

"Five months," her father said, converting the response. "You didn't say a single word to me about this for *five months*."

"I didn't know how to tell you, and I knew you'd have strong opinions about what we should do—"

"Damn right I do."

"And I know we have some decisions to make," Haylee continued, her tone placating. "But you have to let me and Trevor make them."

"How could you let this happen?" her father demanded, shaking his head. "You're a Gilmore and he's a Blake."

"What does that have to do with anything?"

"Everything, because the news that Trevor Blake knocked up Haylee Gilmore is going to get things all stirred up again."

"The only one getting stirred up is *you*," Haylee said.

"Speaking of stirring," Colleen said, returning with Finley and Logan in tow. "I need Haylee to help me in the kitchen with the gravy."

"Why are you asking her for help?" Logan teased. "She can't cook."

Haylee glared at her brother even as she rose to her feet to give him a hug. Of course, she hadn't told him about her pregnancy, either, and his eyes practically popped out of his head when he felt the roundness of her belly press against him.

"Whoa," he said. "Maybe you have learned to cook—and eat—because you've packed on more than a few pounds since I last saw you."

She smacked the back of his head playfully. "I'm pregnant, you moron."

"Wow. Um…" His gaze darted cautiously between his sister, their father and their guest. "Congratulations?"

"Thank you." She kissed his cheek. "I'm going to help Colleen in the kitchen."

He made a pained face. "And I was really looking forward to a delicious meal."

"I'll help, too," Finley said, grabbing her sister's arm as she lifted her hand to smack Logan again.

Haylee mouthed *sorry* to Trevor as she was dragged toward the kitchen.

Though he wished he could follow her, he held his ground and offered his hand to Haylee's brother. "I'm Trevor."

The younger man's gaze narrowed on him. "You're the baby's father?"

He nodded.

Logan's grip tightened painfully. "So when's the wedding?"

"We were just discussing that," Robert said.

And Trevor realized it was going to be a very long three days.

Chapter Seventeen

"I think that went pretty well," Trevor remarked, after they'd finished their meal and retreated to the carriage house, where he and Haylee were spending the weekend.

"Were we at the same table?" she asked incredulously.

"The meal was delicious."

"Colleen's a good cook," she agreed.

"And dessert was even better."

She smiled then. "Thanks. Though I noticed that you opted for pumpkin despite telling me you were dying to try the pecan."

"I saw the way your dad glowered at Logan when he asked for a slice of pecan, and I figured he already had enough reasons to want to kill me in my sleep."

"I'll make another pecan pie when we get back to Haven, just for you," she promised.

"I'll hold you to that," he said. "Now tell me what our plans are for tomorrow."

"I figured you'd be ready to leave at sunrise."

"I want you to enjoy this weekend with your family," he assured her.

"I'm not sure how much enjoyment is going to be had considering my dad's mood." She sighed. "Did you notice that he hardly spoke two words to me during dinner?"

"I'm sorry," he said sincerely.

She shrugged, ignoring the tears burning the backs of her eyes. "It's not your fault."

"Isn't it?"

"It takes two to tango," she pointed out.

"But I'm the one who asked you to dance."

She managed a smile. "Only literally," she said. "I'm the one who invited you back to my hotel room."

"You did," he confirmed. "And I don't regret a single minute of that night."

"Do you really mean that?" she asked dubiously.

"I really do," he said. "I know my initial reaction to the pregnancy left a lot to be desired, but that was just because it caught me completely off guard. Once I had some time to wrap my head around the idea that I was going to be a father, I realized it was something that I wanted. That our babies are wanted."

The sincerity in his tone had fresh tears welling in her eyes. "I was terrified by the idea of having to go through all of this on my own," she confided. "I'm so grateful to you for stepping up." Then she sighed. "And sorry that my dad can't be happy for us."

"He'll come around," Trevor said. "Though truthfully, I can understand why he's upset. If we have a girl—or girls—you can bet that she or they will be locked up until they're thirty."

"Thirty seems a little extreme."

"Look what happened to you at twenty-nine," he teased.

"Look what happened," she agreed, touching a hand to the curve of her belly.

He placed his hand over hers. "Colleen will bring your dad around," he said, hoping to reassure her. "She seems to have a way with him."

"She does," Haylee agreed with a nod. "But who's going to bring Elijah and Lorraine around?"

"That's a good question," he admitted. "Of course, getting married would likely help smooth things over with both sets of parents."

"Can we include that oh-so-romantic sentiment in our vows?"

"Sure," he agreed, ignoring her sarcasm. "Along with noting that we enjoy spending time together, we're both committed to being good parents and we share off-the-charts chemistry in the bedroom."

"We had sex *once*," she said dismissively. "You can't make a claim like that after only one night."

"I'm willing to put my claim to the test—anytime," he told her.

She shook her head. "You can't be the least bit attracted to me right now."

"Not the least bit," he agreed. "A whole lot."

"Are you one of those guys who's turned on by pregnant women?"

"I'm one of those guys who's turned on by *you*."

"You say things like that, and yet…"

"And yet?" he prompted.

She shook her head.

"And yet we've been living together for almost five weeks and I still haven't kissed you?" he guessed.

"That isn't what I was going to say," she told him, but her refusal to meet his gaze suggested that he'd hit pretty close to the truth. "You were pretty clear about the rules when I moved in with you."

"I said I wouldn't try to seduce you while you were living under my roof," he acknowledged, taking her face gently in his hands. "But we're not under my roof now, are we?"

And then he kissed her.

Finally, Haylee thought, as his mouth settled over hers.

But that was as far as things went before her sister walked into the room.

"Whoops!"

Of course, Haylee knew that if her sister hadn't wanted to interrupt, she would have turned back around and walked out of the room again without saying anything at all.

"Of course, annoying sisters wouldn't barge in under my roof," Trevor mock-whispered to her now.

"But this is *my* roof," Finley said unapologetically. "And I'm just getting a drink and then going back to my office—but please don't do anything that's going to traumatize Simon."

"When are we going home?" he asked, after Finley had gone.

Not soon enough.

"Sunday," she reminded him.

"If we'd thought about it, we could have made an appointment to see Dr. Robertson while we're here this weekend."

"Not likely."

"Why not?"

"Because it's not just a weekend, it's a holiday weekend."

"So when is your next appointment?" he asked.

"Actually, I'm not going to see Dr. Robertson again."

"You haven't decided to give birth at home with a midwife or something crazy like that, have you?"

She laughed. "For your information, midwives can deliver babies in hospitals, too. But no, I've only decided to continue my prenatal care with Dr. Amaro in Battle Mountain."

"Are you telling me…are you planning to stay in Haven?"

"Rohan said that he has work for me at least through January, if I want it. And by that time, I'll probably be ready for some time off to get ready for the babies' arrival," she explained. "Plus, I know you really want to be there for the delivery, and this seemed the most logical way to make it happen."

"I don't know what to say," he admitted. "So I'll start with thank you."

"Well, it's not just for you," she said. "I'd kind of like

you to be there, too, so that I have someone to swear at when I'm sweating through labor."

He grinned. "I'm your man."

The first time that Trevor proposed to Haylee, he was only trying to do the right thing. She'd been absolutely right about that. He hadn't given any real thought to what it would be like to marry a woman he didn't even know; he'd only been thinking that he had to step up and take responsibility for the consequences of his actions.

Beyond that, he also wanted his children to have the benefit of growing up with two parents. And he wanted to be a dad who was there for all the big and little milestones in their lives. He didn't want to be a weekend dad or—far worse, if Haylee decided to go back to California—an occasional-holiday-and-two-weeks-in-the-summer dad.

But now that she'd decided to stay in Haven at least until the babies were born, he was determined to take advantage of every minute to show her the kind of life they could have together as a family. And the upcoming holiday season fit perfectly into his plans.

"Tell me about your first high school crush," Trevor suggested, as they made their way to town square for the tree lighting ceremony the following Wednesday night.

"That seems like an oddly random request," she noted.

"The program of events for tonight said that the high school band would be there, which got me thinking about my own high school days and wondering about yours."

"Why do you assume I had a high school crush?"

"Because everyone does," he said matter-of-factly.

"Who was yours?" she asked.

He smiled at the memory. "Skylar Gilmore."

"You had a crush on my cousin?"

"Westmount High isn't a very big school and—" he shrugged "—her last name notwithstanding, she's really hot."

"She's also engaged to a Marine," Haylee pointed out to him.

"I saw the ring—and her fiancé—at your grandparents' anniversary party." He lifted his arm to flex his biceps. "Lucky for him, I got over my crush on his fiancée a long time ago."

"I'm sure he'd be shaking in his combat boots otherwise," she said, fighting against a smile.

"Now tell me about your crush," he urged.

"His name was Cory Ransom," she finally said. "He had shaggy blond hair that was always falling into his eyes and the sweetest smile."

"Was he a jock, stoner or geek?"

She frowned at the labels. "He played bass clarinet in the band and served as treasurer on student council."

"Definitely a geek," Trevor decided.

"If he was, then so was I."

"Did he ever find out about your crush? Was he secretly crushing on you, too?"

"Yes and no," she said. "Although, for almost two full weeks in my senior year, I was foolish enough to believe that he liked me, too."

"What happened?"

"He asked me to be his date for the spring formal."

"Sounds like a pretty good reason to believe he liked you," Trevor noted.

"I was so excited," she confided. "Especially since he'd always seemed more interested in my sister than me. But I didn't clue in, not even when he suggested that we share a limo with Finley and her date—" Her brow furrowed. "I can't even remember who she went to prom with that year. Damon? Calvin? Brian?" Then she nodded. "It was Brian Nardone."

Of course, the name meant nothing to Trevor, so she continued. "Anyway, I found out later that Cory only asked me to go with him because Finley had already agreed to go with Brian, and he figured that double-dating with them meant he'd still get to spend the evening with her."

"Ouch."

She nodded.

"How'd you find out?"

"I saw my date putting the moves on my sister. Of course, Finley had some moves of her own and dropped him with a quick jab to his nose."

"For real?"

She nodded. "He fell to his knees, apologizing to her. She told him that he should be apologizing to me."

"Did he?"

"If you consider 'I'm-sorry-but-you-should-have-known-that-I-really-wanted-to-be-with-your-sister' an apology," she said.

"Were you heartbroken?"

"Less than I thought I'd be, because I think I always knew he wasn't interested in me. But I was disappointed. And embarrassed."

"Where's this guy now? What's he doing with his life?"

"I have no idea."

"Then how am I supposed to find him and punch him in the nose?"

"Finley already took care of that," she reminded him.

"That doesn't make me feel any better."

"While I appreciate your Neanderthal instincts, I got over my crush on Cory a long time ago."

"That helps," he decided, as they joined the crowd gathered around the big tree in the center of the square.

It seemed as if most of the town had turned out for the big event, including the high school band, as Trevor had noted, playing classic holiday tunes, and the children's choir, singing along. The Rotary Club was selling hot chocolate in support of Toys for Tots and accepting canned food donations on behalf of the local food bank.

Trevor stood behind her, his arms around her to insulate her from the biting wind, while the mayor gave a thankfully brief speech that talked about the spirit of the season and the importance of helping others—not just during the holidays but throughout the year. He finished by wishing a "Merry Christmas" to all and lighting the tree.

The crowd gasped as the tree was illuminated, red and green and blue lights shining brightly against the darkness of night, and Trevor whispered, "Good job," close to Haylee's ear.

She tipped her head back to smile at him then. "I cursed that tree the whole while that I was fumbling with tangled lights, but now, yeah, I can agree that it was all worthwhile."

The frigid air had turned her cheeks and nose pink, but her lips were curved and her eyes sparkled, and looking at her, Trevor felt something shift inside his heart. And in that moment, the man who'd been certain he wasn't capable of experiencing love again, knew he was in serious danger of falling for this woman.

"Can we go home now?" she asked.

It pleased him that she'd started referring to his house as "home," but he knew better than to draw her attention to the fact.

"Yes," he said. "We can go home now."

When they got there, he took her coat to hang it in the closet, his hand brushing against hers in the exchange.

"Your hands are like ice," he noted.

"Because it's freezing outside."

He sandwiched her cold hands between his much larger and warmer ones.

"You need better gloves," he decided.

"Or hot chocolate?" she suggested hopefully.

"I can make hot chocolate," he said. "But why don't we try something else first?"

He slid his arms around her and drew her close—or as close as her growing belly would allow, then lowered his head and touched his mouth to hers.

His lips moved over hers softly, fleetingly, savoring the moment. He loved kissing her, loved the way her lips yielded and her body melted. He loved the quiet sounds she made deep in her throat.

But he wanted more than a few stolen kisses. He wanted to make love with her again, to enjoy not just the taste of her lips but the mating of their bodies. But he was trying to take things slow this time—trying to show some of the patience and finesse that had been lacking the first time he'd taken her to bed.

Her first time ever with a man.

He couldn't make up for the mistakes he'd made, but he could ensure that the next time was better. And he would, if he ever got the chance.

"I think that did the trick," she said, when he eased his lips from hers.

"I'm glad," he said, and brushed his mouth over hers again. "Do you still want hot chocolate?"

She lifted her gaze to his. "What are my other options?"

"Anything you want."

"I want you," she admitted.

"That's convenient," he said. "Because I want you, too."

"I don't understand why," she admitted softly. "Especially now—"

He touched a finger to her lips, silencing her doubts. He didn't know the root of her insecurity, but he knew it ran deep. Perhaps it had started with the abandonment by her mother and been exacerbated by the popularity of her more outgoing sister. Whatever the reason, he couldn't go back in time and change any of that for her, he could only assure her that right now, she was everything he wanted.

"I want you because you're smart and beautiful, strong and sexy, compassionate and stubborn, kind and generous, and every day that I spend with you, I only want you more."

"Show me that you want me," she said. "Take me to bed."

"Your wish is my command," he said, and lifted her effortlessly into his arms to carry her to his bedroom.

He set her on her feet beside the bed, then kissed her again. His tongue swept into her mouth, tasting, teasing. His hands slid under her top, touching, tempting.

She wasn't sure what to do with her own hands. She wanted to touch him, too, but considering the way the world was tilting beneath her feet, she was afraid that if she let go of his shoulders, she'd tumble to the floor.

He eased his mouth from hers to whisk her sweater over her head. Her long-sleeved undershirt and bra followed. She shivered as the cool air brushed over her skin.

"I'll keep you warm," he promised, as he eased her back onto the mattress and tugged her leggings and panties over her hips, down her legs, and tossed them aside with the other discarded garments.

"I'm not cold anymore," she told him.

Because she wasn't.

Because how could she be cold when there was so much heat flooding her system?

He got rid of his own clothes, then straddled her naked body, his knees bracketing her hips, holding her in position while his hands and mouth moved over her, exploring and exciting her with every touch.

"Your breasts are fuller," he noted, cupping them almost reverently in his palms. "Are they more sensitive?"

"*Everything* is more sensitive."

He smiled at that. "This might be even more fun than I anticipated."

"Have you been anticipating this?"

"Every night since you moved in," he said, then he

shook his head. "No. Every night since we first made love."

He knew just where to focus his attention to maximize her pleasure, and though she understood that his knowledge was the result of a wealth of experience, she refused to dwell on that now. She refused to compare herself to the undoubtedly numerous women who'd shared his bed before her.

She was only going to focus on the here and now.

And here and now, her body was quivering with wanting.

Since she didn't have the same wealth of experience, she let her instincts guide her as she reached between their bodies and wrapped her fingers around him. She felt him jerk in her hand, and immediately released her grip.

"I'm sorry."

"No." His fingers circled her wrist, drawing her hand back to him, encouraging her exploration. "It's good." His eyes closed on a groan as she stroked him. "Really good."

Then he lowered his head and kissed her again, long and slow and deep. His hands continued to move over her, stoking the fire that burned deep inside her.

She'd always been a sucker for romantic books and movies, but as much as she'd enjoyed watching or reading about a couple finding their way toward a happily-ever-after, she'd been suspicious of the love scenes. Heroines who'd never truly known physical satisfaction until they gave themselves to the fictional heroes.

She'd had no great expectations when she'd invited Trevor back to her hotel room after the wedding. She'd just wanted to know what all the hype was about, but she hadn't expected to feel the earth move. She hadn't anticipated that her body would be capable of feeling so much—and somehow still yearn for more.

He'd given her everything she wanted—and more.

She'd been stunned and breathless and perhaps a little bit scared. She wasn't accustomed to being out of control, but from the first kiss, the first touch, there was no denying that he was in command.

It was no different this time. From the first brush of his hands, the first touch of his lips, she was at his mercy. But at least she knew what to expect this time, or so she thought until he shifted his position on the mattress as his hands stroked her body and his mouth moved lower, trailing kisses over the swell of her abdomen, nibbling the inside of her thighs.

Her breath caught in her throat when he gently nudged her knees farther apart and settled between them. He parted the soft folds of flesh at the apex of her thighs, and everything inside her tensed and tightened. Then his tongue flicked over the nub at her center, a playful stroke that made her gasp even as her hips instinctively lifted off the mattress.

He responded to the wordless request, continuing to lick and nibble and suck until she was sure she couldn't take any more.

Still, he gave more.

"Please," she said. "I can't…"

She didn't know what she intended to say, but he wasn't listening to her, anyway.

She flew apart—shattering into a million jagged little pieces like the explosion of a light bulb that had absorbed too much current.

He held her as she came back to earth, her body quivering and trembling. And he brushed his lips gently over hers then. "Okay?"

She could only nod as he finally moved into position between her thighs, filling and fulfilling her. The tension immediately began to build inside her again, even before he started to move, long and steady strokes that caused the pressure to build ever higher. Then deeper. Harder. Faster.

Her fingers dug into his shoulders, holding on to him as the world tilted and spun. She could tell that he was close to his release. She could hear it in the shallowness of his breathing, feel it in the tense muscles of his arms as he held himself over her.

He seemed to be holding himself back, waiting for something…waiting for her? But he'd already given her so much pleasure. So much more than she'd expected or anticipated.

And still there was more yet again.

When he finally let himself go, she knew that he'd taken more than just her body this time—he'd taken her heart.

Chapter Eighteen

Trevor fell asleep with Haylee in his arms, and she was still there when he awakened the next morning. He wasn't accustomed to sharing his bed, and he was surprised to realize that he didn't mind her being there. No, it was more than that—he wanted her there. Not just this morning but every morning, for the rest of their lives together.

He'd already thought about making the room directly across the hall into a nursery, so it would be easy for them to hear and tend to the babies when they needed anything. Though she hadn't said anything about staying in Haven long-term, he refused to consider any other possibility. And he hoped that, after last night, she'd realize their babies were only one of the many reasons she should stay.

She shifted in her sleep, sliding her leg over top of his, snuggling so that her breasts were pressed against his chest. Yeah, he could definitely get used to falling asleep with Haylee in his arms and waking up with her beside him. And because she was there, and conveniently naked, he let his hand skim from her thigh to her hip to her breast. He loved the softness of her skin, the curves of her body, the roundness of her belly where their twin babies nestled in her womb. He found her breast, brushed his thumb over her nipple. She sighed softly, then her eyelids flickered and slowly lifted.

"Good morning," he said.

"Good morning," she echoed, a little shyly.

"Did you sleep well?"

"Very well," she said. "And you?"

"Same." He dipped his head to brush his mouth over hers.

Her eyelids drifted shut again as he deepened the kiss. And when he shifted so that she was beneath him, she opened for him not just willingly but eagerly, and their bodies began to move, finding their rhythm and release together.

"You had sex," Finley said, during a Skype call with her sister the following afternoon.

"I'm almost six months pregnant and it wasn't an immaculate conception, so why do you sound surprised?" Haylee wondered.

"I mean you had sex recently," her sister clarified.

"How could you possibly know something like that?" she demanded.

"You have a definite glow, and before you remind me again that you're six months pregnant, I'll point out that you weren't glowing quite so much when we chatted just a few days ago."

"Okay, yes. I had sex."

"Now hold up your hands."

"What? Why?"

"Because I want to see the ring."

Haylee sighed and shook her head. "You're almost as pushy as he is."

"So there's no ring?" her sister asked, sounding disappointed.

"There's no ring."

"I don't understand," Finley said. "Why are you still refusing to make wedding plans when it's obvious that you're head over heels in love with the guy?"

She didn't bother to deny it. Her sister had always been able to read her like an open book. "It's not my feelings that are in question," she said.

"You doubt his feelings for you?"

No, she had no reason to doubt his feelings. She knew exactly what they were and what they weren't. He cared about her, but he didn't love her, and he'd made it clear that he never would.

And she couldn't marry a man who didn't love her.

"Take a leap," Finley urged. "Tell him how you feel."

"I'll think about it," Haylee said, but only to get her sister off her back.

Because the truth was, she had no intention of leaping and going splat.

* * *

"Hey," Haylee immediately protested, when Trevor pulled back the heavy curtains, filling the room with bright sunlight. "It's Saturday."

"It is," he agreed.

"I get to sleep in on Saturday."

"And you did."

She reluctantly opened one eye even as she pulled the covers up under her chin. "What time is it?"

"Eleven thirty."

She jolted upright. "It is not. It can't be."

He pointed to the clock beside the bed.

"I honestly don't remember the last time I slept so late," she told him.

"I didn't want to wake you, but the farm closes at three o'clock."

"Farm?" she echoed dubiously. "Like with cows and pigs and stuff?"

He smiled. "Like with Christmas trees."

"Really?" There was joy in that single word and light in her eyes.

"Really," he confirmed. "If you can be ready in half an hour, we'll even stop for lunch on the way."

"I can be ready," she promised.

True to her word, twenty-nine minutes later she was tucking her feet into her boots. Trevor was more interested in the rest of her and noted with appreciation the denim leggings and knit turtleneck sweater that hugged her curves.

He'd never been one of those guys who thought all pregnant women were beautiful or that they glowed from the marvel of life growing inside them. Maybe it was because Haylee was carrying his babies, but Trevor thought she looked stunning.

They grabbed a quick bite at the Sunnyside Diner, because despite it being lunchtime, Haylee wanted breakfast. After they'd fueled up with pancakes and sausage, they headed toward Comet's Christmas Tree Farm, fifteen miles past the Dusty Boots Motel on the highway leading out of town.

"Did your family come here to get Christmas trees when you were a kid?" Haylee asked, as he helped her out of the truck.

"Nah. We usually just chopped one down at Crooked Creek," he told her. "But this is the top-rated local Christmas tree farm on Yelp."

"Out of how many?" she wondered.

"One," he admitted. "But the reviews were all positive."

She started toward a fenced-in area beneath a banner that advertised Precut Trees arranged in groups by height. But Trevor caught her shoulders and turned her in the opposite direction.

"If we're going to get a tree, we're going to get the whole tree experience."

She glanced at the signs that guided visitors toward the Cut Your Own Tree section.

"Did you bring anything to cut a tree with?"

"Didn't have to." He pointed toward a covered market-style stand, the back wall of which was hung with saws of various sizes. "We can borrow what we need, including a sled to haul the tree back with us."

"Then what are we waiting for? Let's go get a tree," she said.

After he'd signed out the required tools, they headed toward the self-serve section of the farm. There were several other couples and families wandering through the trees, discussing and debating options. Despite some heated disagreements about color and size, it was readily apparent to Haylee that this was a happy tradition for everyone there.

She paused when she spotted a man and woman with a couple of little boys who might have been twins—seven or eight years old, she guessed. The mom stood on the sidelines, her mitten-clad hands wrapped around a travel mug, watching as the dad helped the boys saw through the trunk of the tree they'd selected.

"Look, Mom!" the boy in the dark blue coat called out. "We're doing it."

"We're cutting the tree," his brother, wearing a matching gray coat, added.

"I'm looking," she promised. "You're doing a great job."

"When we go see Santa, can we tell him we cut the tree?"

"Of course."

"And then we can tell him what we want for Christmas, right?"

"You can tell him about *one* thing on your wish list," she said. "But remember, he's got a lot of gifts to deliver to a lot of kids, so there are no guarantees."

"But we were *really* good this year."

"Except when you were fighting," the boys' dad chimed in.

"Yeah. 'Cept when we were fighting."

"Haylee?"

Still smiling at the exchange, she hurried to catch up with Trevor again.

"Did your family go out into the woods hunting for the perfect tree when you were a kid?" he asked, as they walked around the lot, examining various specimens.

She shook her head. "We went to the local hardware store and picked a tree from the lot."

"Well, it's kind of the same thing," he said. "So take a look around and tell me which tree you think will look best in the living room."

"Where, in the living room, are you planning to put it?"

He shrugged. "Beside the sofa, maybe."

She wrinkled her nose.

"Or a much better location that you're going to suggest," he said dryly.

"I was just thinking, if you put it beside the fireplace, you'd be able to see it when you're sitting on the sofa," she pointed out.

"Okay, we'll put it beside the fireplace," he agreed.

She liked the way he said "we," as if she and Trevor really were a "we"—even if it was only a temporary situation.

"But then you'll have to move the recliner."

"So I'll move the recliner," he said. "No one ever sits there anyway."

"True," she acknowledged.

"Now we know where it's going, but we still have to pick the tree." He pointed to one nearby. "How about that one?"

She looked at the tree, then at him. "It's perfect...

if you're looking for a prop to stage a production of *A Charlie Brown Christmas*."

He perused the tree more closely. "I guess it is a little sparse," he acknowledged.

"And crooked."

"What about this one?" he asked, moving on to the next evergreen.

She did a slow walk around the specimen. "I think it could work."

He retrieved the saw from the sled.

"Is there anything I can do to help?" Haylee asked.

"Stay out of the way, so the tree doesn't fall on top of you."

"I can do that," she agreed.

She could also appreciate the scenery—and she indulged herself in doing just that. Whether he was wearing chinos with a shirt and tie to go to the office or jeans and flannel to hang out at home, Trevor always looked good. Today, in deference to their outdoor venture, he was wearing a leather jacket over a chunky knit sweater and well-worn jeans that hugged his thighs and butt. Even through the various layers of clothing, she couldn't help but appreciate the breadth of his shoulders and the power of his muscles as he sawed through the trunk of the tree they'd chosen.

And yet despite his obvious strength, he'd been a patient and selfless lover, ensuring that she experienced a pleasure she hadn't even known existed. Which was definitely something she should *not* be thinking about right now, she realized, as her blood warmed and her body temperature began to rise.

She unzipped her coat and loosened the soft wool

scarf she'd wrapped around her throat in an effort to cool the heat in her veins.

When the tree was strapped down on the sled, they retraced their steps toward the sales office to finalize their purchase.

The young man working at the toolshed measured their tree and gave them a slip, directing them to the barn to complete their purchase.

Haylee had been so focused on finding a tree that she hadn't even glanced toward the barn when they arrived. But she did so now, and noted that the wide doors were flanked by potted fir trees wrapped in red ribbon and decorated with shiny red balls. Evergreen boughs were tacked over the entranceway and similarly decked out.

The inside didn't look much like a shelter for livestock. The space was open and brightly lit, with signs hanging from the rafters to identify designated areas, such as Craft Corner and Cookies & Cider.

Curious, she took a few steps toward the Craft Corner where a teenager, dressed like an elf, was sitting at a child-sized picnic table with a couple of young children, helping them decorate paper plate wreaths. At another table, a trio of preschoolers were occupied with fat crayons and holiday-themed coloring pages. The on-site activity center was obviously designed to keep kids occupied while their parents browsed in the gift shop at the back.

Looking around, she noticed that all the employees of Comet's Christmas Tree Farm were dressed like Santa's helpers, complete with jingle bells on their shoes and pointy hats on their heads.

Haylee breathed in the scent of pine and… "Do I smell apples?"

"Hot apple cider," he said, nudging her toward the area designated Cookies & Cider. "Do you want a cup?"

"Yes, please."

He held up two fingers to the young woman—also dressed like an elf—who was stirring the spiced cider in an enormous pot. She ladled a portion into each of two cups, then passed them across the counter.

"Enjoy," she said, with a smile. "And make sure you try the cookies, too. They're made fresh every day."

"Try the cookies," Trevor repeated to Haylee.

She surveyed the artfully arranged assortment. "I shouldn't."

"Why not?"

"Because I've already gained twenty pounds."

"Those twenty pounds look good on you."

"You're only saying that because half of them are spilling out of my bra."

He had to fight the smile that wanted to tug at his lips. "Are they? I hadn't noticed."

"Liar."

He was chuckling as an older woman with gray hair neatly secured in a bun at the nape of her neck and wire-rimmed glasses perched on her nose came over to re-plenish the display of cookies.

"Mrs. Claus?" Haylee guessed.

"Oh no, dear," she said, with a conspiratorial wink. "Mrs. Claus is at the North Pole, helping Santa get ready for Christmas. We're just some of Santa's happy help-ers here." She tapped the tag fastened to her red vest. "I'm Meg."

"Did you make these cookies, Meg?" Trevor asked, selecting another from the tray. "Because they're delicious."

She nodded. "I did."

"Spritz cookies are one of my holiday favorites," Haylee said, giving in to temptation and reaching for one in the shape of a snowflake sprinkled with blue sugar. "But the shapes never hold for me when I make them."

"Because no one ever told you the secret trick," Meg guessed. Then she dropped her voice to a whisper and said, "Chilled cookie sheets."

"Really?"

The older woman nodded. "I promise, it makes all the difference."

"I'll give it a try," Haylee said.

"But right now, we need to pay for our tree," Trevor said, brushing cookie crumbs off his fingers.

"Did you get a receipt from Lewis at the toolshed?"

Trevor pulled it out of his jacket pocket.

"The cash register's in the gift shop," Meg said.

"Of course," he said. "Just like at Disneyland—exit through the gift shop."

The older woman smiled. "In addition to trees, we've got everything you need to decorate them and your home. We also have a variety of personalized ornaments, handcrafted gifts and toys."

"I'm going to take another cookie and go do some shopping."

But as they made their way around the gift shop, it was Trevor who seemed to be on a mission.

"What are you planning to do with all those lights?"

Haylee asked, as he dropped several packages into his basket.

"Put them on the tree."

"You don't think you have enough at home?"

"I don't actually have any," he admitted. "I've never put up a tree or decorated for the holidays before."

"Why not?"

"Because I usually spend Christmas Day at my parents' house."

"But what about all the days and nights before the holidays?" she asked.

He shrugged. "It just always seemed like more bother than it was worth."

"So why is this year different?"

"Because I want our first Christmas together to be perfect."

Our first Christmas.

Haylee liked the sound of that.

But still, she was afraid to hope.

"Look at these," he said, holding up two knitted stockings in traditional Nordic designs. One was blue with snowflakes and mittens and the other was red with Christmas trees and reindeer.

"For the babies?" she guessed.

He nodded.

"They're certainly big enough for Santa to fill with lots of goodies."

He grinned. "That's what I was thinking. There are green and gray ones, too," he told her. "Maybe we should get one in each color."

Of course they'd need four stockings for their babies, she realized. One set for Christmas at Mommy's house and one set for Christmas at Daddy's. And though she knew he was only being practical—maybe even thoughtful—the reality of their situation put a sudden pall on what had been, up to that point, a near-perfect day.

"Haylee?" he prompted.

She had to clear the tightness from her throat before she could reply. "Sure. One of each would be good."

Then she turned away, feigning an interest in the pine cone ornaments displayed on one of the many tabletop trees set up around the shop.

"What do you think?" Trevor asked, after he'd finished securing the trunk into the base that they'd also bought at the Christmas tree farm. He tilted his head. "Is it crooked?"

"It's perfect. Or it will be, when you put all the lights and ornaments on it that you bought at the tree farm."

"What was in all those packages you bought?" he asked.

"I got handmade ornaments for Colleen, Finley, my grandmother and—because it was irresistible, a dated 'Baby's First Christmas' ornament for Colton."

"You obviously believe in getting an early start on your shopping," he noted.

"You think this is early?" she asked incredulously. "It's barely December."

"It *is* December," she said. "And Christmas is less than three weeks away."

He shrugged, obviously unconcerned. "It doesn't take long to buy gift cards."

"That's the extent of your Christmas shopping? Gift cards?"

"What's wrong with gift cards?" he wanted to know.

"Nothing," she said, though her tone suggested otherwise. "They're a perfectly acceptable gift for a co-worker or pet sitter or mail carrier, but not your parents or brother or grandfather."

Or girlfriend-slash-fiancée-slash-wife, he guessed, though she didn't mention any of those.

"I've never heard any complaints."

She shook her head. "Why don't you skip the card purchase and just wrap the cash? Better yet, save the wrapping and use Venmo."

"This seems to be a hot button for you," he noted. "Did your ex-boyfriend give you a gift card last Christmas?"

"No," she denied. "Although that would be a valid reason for the shift of status from boyfriend to ex."

"Note to self—buy Haylee an actual present."

"That's not what I meant," she protested.

"You don't want a gift?"

She huffed out a breath. "Can we get back to focusing on the tree?"

"Sure," he agreed. "I'll start with the lights while you pop the corn."

"No one actually strings popcorn anymore," she told him.

He chuckled. "It's not for stringing. It's for eating. Decorating is hungry work."

He was right, and the big bowl of popcorn she made was empty long before they'd hung the last ornament on the tree. But still there were more holiday decorations to be put up, including the stockings Trevor had bought.

"Which one do you want?" he asked, holding them up for her inspection again.

"You're letting me choose?"

"Sure."

"I'll take the red and the green, if you don't mind."

"The traditional Christmas colors," he noted. "I always suspected that you were a traditional girl at heart, but you only get one—so is it red or green?"

She frowned at that. "Why do I only get one?"

"Why do you need more than one?"

She sensed that there was a miscommunication happening and was eager to clarify. "Didn't you get four so that we'd each have a set for the babies?"

He dropped his arms. "That's what you thought?" he asked, sounding surprised—and maybe a little bit disappointed.

"What else was I supposed to think?" she said.

"That there will be four of *us*—you, me and two babies."

"Oh."

He shook his head. "Apparently I'm the only one of us who hopes that our first Christmas together isn't also our last."

She didn't know what to say to that—she had no experience with relationships. She knew she'd hurt him, however inadvertently, but she didn't know how to make it right. And before she could come up with a reply, she heard the back door slam.

He was gone.

And she was left behind. Again.

Chapter Nineteen

Haylee halted abruptly in midstride when she walked into the kitchen the following morning and spotted Trevor leaning against the counter, drinking a cup of coffee.

She looked tired, he noted, as if she hadn't slept well—or maybe not much at all.

If so, that made two of them.

Recovering her composure, she moved to the cupboard to retrieve a mug. He automatically flipped the switch on the electric kettle, to heat the water for the peppermint tea she liked to drink in the morning.

"I didn't realize you were here," she finally said.

"I do live here," he reminded her.

"You walked out," she said, accusation in her tone.

"I was mad," he pointed out in his defense. "And I didn't want to say something I would regret later."

"You walked out," she repeated.

The way she said it reminded him of the words she'd used to describe the circumstances of her parents' separation: *She walked out and never came back.*

And he realized how deeply scarred she'd been by her mother's abandonment.

"But I came back," he said gently. "And no matter how upset or angry I might get when we argue about something, I'll always come back."

"How can you be so sure?" The question was barely more than a whisper.

And he realized that what she really wanted to know was how could *she* be sure.

"Because I can't imagine my life without you in it," he said sincerely.

Inexplicably her eyes filled with tears.

"Hey," he said, gently brushing her hair away from her face.

"I don't want our first Christmas together to be our last," she told him, the words pouring out in a rush. "But I don't want to get my hopes up, either."

He took her hands and gently pulled her into his arms. "Then maybe we should agree to take it one day at a time," he suggested.

"I can do that." She leaned her forehead against his chest. "I don't like to fight."

"Me, neither, but the making up could be fun. And look at that—you're standing under the mistletoe."

She tipped her head back to see a sprig of holiday

greenery hanging from the ceiling. "When did you put that up there?"

"The *when* doesn't matter," he told her. "All that matters is that you're under it and now I have to kiss you."

"I don't think that's actually a rule," she said.

"Maybe it's not a rule, but it *is* considered bad luck to refuse a kiss under the mistletoe."

"Well, I certainly don't want bad luck."

"Then let's make sure you don't get it," he said, and lowered his mouth to touch hers.

It felt as if it had been weeks instead of hours since she'd been in his arms, and Haylee immediately realized that there was nowhere else she wanted to be. But she didn't just love the way he made her feel—she loved *him*.

He was handsome and kind and interesting and funny and an amazing lover. Plus he didn't seem to mind that she was a lousy cook, or that she didn't bother with makeup or even that she was more comfortable in steel-toed boots than high-heeled shoes.

He accepted her just the way she was. And that was everything she'd never known she was looking for.

"Hungry?" he asked, when he finally eased his mouth from hers.

And bonus—he liked to feed her.

"Starving," she admitted, with a smile.

"Go get dressed while I start breakfast."

"Or...you could help me get dressed and we could eat breakfast later?" she suggested hopefully.

"A much better plan," he decided.

* * *

Haylee knew that if she walked back to her car and drove away now, no one would ever need to know that she'd been here. Except maybe whoever was monitoring the half a dozen security cameras that were focused on the front door. Instead she drew in a deep breath and splayed a hand on her belly.

"I'm doing this for you guys. Because I want you to have a good relationship with both sides of your family."

And because she knew that wouldn't happen unless someone took a first step, she lifted a hand and knocked on the heavy wood.

When the door opened, she was taken aback to see Lorraine Blake on the other side of the threshold.

"Haylee…this is a surprise." Trevor's mom sounded not just surprised but pleased to see her.

"I should have called first," she acknowledged. In fact, she'd thought about doing so but had opted for a spontaneous visit—in case she chickened out at the last minute.

"Don't be silly," Lorraine said. "You're welcome to drop by anytime."

Haylee couldn't imagine this would ever become a habit, but she appreciated the sentiment. "I won't take much of your time," she promised.

"But you will come in for a cup of tea, won't you? I just put the kettle on and it would be nice to have some company."

"Oh. Um. Sure."

Lorraine smiled and stepped away from the door so that she could enter. "Let me take your coat."

So much for making a quick getaway, Haylee thought, as she unbuttoned the garment.

"Thank you," she said, as Lorraine hung it in the closet.

"What kind of tea do you like?" Trevor's mom was already on her way to the kitchen, leaving Haylee with no choice but to follow. "I've heard that Rooibos is good during pregnancy, because of its antioxidant properties."

"Please don't go to any trouble on my account."

"It's no trouble at all. And that's the kettle starting to whistle now."

So Haylee took a seat at the granite island in the spacious kitchen while Lorraine made tea.

"There should be some cookies here, too," Trevor's mom said, opening and closing cupboards. "But Greta's out running errands and I have no idea where she keeps— oh, there they are." She opened a snap-lock container. "Do you like oatmeal chocolate chip?"

Haylee nodded.

"They're Trevor's favorite," Lorraine noted, as she arranged several cookies on a plate.

She set the plate near Haylee, then poured the tea. "Milk or sugar?"

"No, black is fine, thanks."

"I like mine the same way," Lorraine said. "Lots of cream and sugar in my coffee, but nothing in my tea." She sat down beside Haylee and offered a weak smile. "I'm babbling—I do that when I'm excited or nervous, and I have to confess to feeling a little of both because I don't know why you're here but I'm so glad that you are."

"You are?" Haylee asked cautiously.

"Let me start with an apology," Trevor's mom said. "I was rude and dismissive the first time I met you, partly because I was hurt and annoyed to hear through the office grapevine that my son was living with a woman he'd never even introduced to me, and partly because, well, even if you had royal blood rather than Gilmore blood in your veins, you still wouldn't be good enough for my son. And I know that sounds harsh, but when your children are old enough to date, you'll understand."

Haylee took a tentative sip of her tea as Lorraine continued to talk.

"Then I followed up by inviting you to our home but doing nothing to make you feel welcome." She took a cookie from the plate and broke it in half over a napkin. "I didn't know that Elijah was going to offer you money to go back to California…but I'm not sure I would have tried to talk him out of it if I did. And while I know his offer was crass and offensive, we both needed to know that you were with Trevor for the right reasons."

"I might have been able to appreciate the rationale if not for the execution," Haylee said. "Because while I was the target of the ambush, Trevor got caught up in it, too, and we both got hurt."

"I know, and I *am* sorry," Lorraine said now. "We both are. And you certainly don't owe us anything, but…we'd really like a chance to get to know you."

Haylee honestly didn't know what had happened to change Trevor's mom's attitude toward her, but there was no denying that she sounded sincere. And maybe the reasons weren't as important as the results, anyway. "I'd like that, too."

Lorraine smiled, obviously relieved. "Now that I got that off my chest, why don't you tell me why you stopped by?"

Haylee reached into the side pocket of her purse and pulled out a black-and-white photo. "I wanted to drop this off for you."

"What is—oh." The other woman's eyes got misty as she realized: "It's a picture of the babies."

She nodded. "Dr. Amaro wanted to do another ultrasound, just to double-check that both babies are developing on schedule—and they are," she assured the soon-to-be grandmother.

"How are you doing? Are you feeling good?"

"Mostly." To anyone else, she might have confessed that it was tiring to cart around an extra twenty pounds and frustrating to not be able to sleep on her back anymore, but she couldn't imagine she'd ever be comfortable sharing those kinds of personal details with Trevor's mom—and definitely not yet.

As the back door opened, Lorraine said, "That sounds like Elijah coming home."

Haylee forced a smile as she lifted her cup to her lips again.

Her plan had been to drop off the photo and leave— a gesture to hopefully open the lines of communication. She hadn't anticipated a tête-à-tête with Trevor's mom, and she certainly didn't want another confrontation with his dad. But she could hardly rush off when she still had half a cup of tea to drink.

"Who's car is…" Elijah's words trailed off when he saw Haylee sitting in his kitchen.

"Hello, Mr. Blake."

He nodded, an acknowledgment more than a greeting. But he didn't seem aloof so much as chastened, as if whatever had swayed Lorraine's attitude had similarly affected her husband, too.

"Look what Haylee brought for us, Elijah." Lorraine slid the picture across the counter for his perusal.

His face softened as he examined the image, the babies labeled Twin A and Twin B. He cleared his throat. "Did you find out if they're boys or girls or one of each?"

"We did," Haylee confirmed. "But Trevor isn't ready to tell anyone else yet."

"Are you going to do one of those gender reveal parties?" Lorraine asked hopefully. "We could host a little get-together here, if you wanted."

She shook her head. "Thanks, but we're not going to have a party."

"Maybe a baby shower? Babies need a lot of stuff, and two babies will need twice as much."

"We're going furniture shopping tomorrow," Haylee said. "Now that we've picked out the paint, Trevor's eager to get the room ready for the babies' arrival."

"Then it's good you stopped by today," Elijah said. "Because I've got something for you, too."

He wasn't gone more than half a minute before returning with a check that he set beside Haylee's cup.

"Déjà vu," she murmured.

"No," he said. "It's not—" He blew out a breath and looked helplessly at his wife.

"Elijah's trying to say he's sorry, too," Lorraine said.

"Then what's this?" Haylee asked.

But the answer was right there, on the memo line where her finger was pointing: to decorate the nursery.

It was a ridiculous amount of money, no doubt enough to decorate and furnish a whole house.

But Haylee realized that it was also an olive branch, so she took it—for Trevor's sake and for their babies.

A few days later, Trevor was assembling the cribs they'd bought for the nursery when Devin stopped by.

"Great—you can give me a hand," he said, gesturing for his brother to hold the end panel. "This is definitely a two-person job."

"Where's Haylee today?"

"At the spa with Brie and Regan. She claims she can't reach her feet anymore so she needs someone else to paint her toenails for her."

"Her belly does seem bigger every time I see her," Devin remarked.

"Do me a favor? Don't mention that to Haylee."

His brother chuckled. "She's been spending a fair amount of time with our cousins recently."

"And her own," Trevor said. "I know she misses Finley, but I think she's enjoying being here and getting to know her extended family better."

"I heard you guys had an appointment with her new doctor in Battle Mountain."

Trevor nodded. "Dr. Amaro who, coincidentally, delivered Regan's twins. But how did you hear about that?"

"Actually, Mom showed me a copy of the last ultrasound photo."

Trevor swore as the screwdriver slipped in his hand. "How did she get a copy of the photo?"

"Haylee dropped it off yesterday."

"So that's where she went," he realized. "She said she had some errands to run, but she didn't mention stopping by Mom and Dad's place." He shook his head. "I don't know if she's incredibly brave or incredibly foolish."

"I don't know, either," Devin admitted. "But I'd say you're incredibly lucky to have a woman who's willing to walk into the lion's den to make peace with your family."

"Yeah," Trevor agreed. "So is that why you stopped by—to tell me how lucky I am?"

Devin picked up the other end panel and held it in place so his brother could connect it to the sides.

"No. I wanted to let you know that I've got a couple of tickets to the Golden Knights game next Saturday night."

"Where'd you get your hands on those?"

"I did some work for a guy down there and, as a bonus, he gave me the tickets. I thought maybe we could make a weekend of it, if you're available."

"Sounds good," Trevor said.

"Just like that? You don't want to check with Haylee first?"

"She's not my wife," he reminded his brother.

"I hit a sore spot," Devin realized.

"Nope," he denied. "If she doesn't want to get married, I can hardly force her."

"I'm a little surprised to hear that she's still resisting. The last time I saw you guys together, you seemed totally in sync."

"I thought so, too, but apparently having a great relationship and wanting to raise our kids together isn't enough without love."

"So tell her that you love her," his brother urged.

"I'm not going to lie to her so that she'll let me put a ring on her finger."

"Now I see the problem," Devin said, shaking his head.

"Want to share?" he asked.

"You're an idiot."

"On second thought, you can keep your not-so-insightful opinions to yourself," Trevor decided.

"I didn't suggest that you lie to Haylee. I told you to tell her you love her because you do," his brother continued, not keeping his opinion to himself.

"But I don't."

"And the fact that you actually believe that is why you're an idiot."

"Look, Haylee's great. We get along well and I enjoy being with her, but I'm not stupid enough to open up my heart and fall in love again."

"Yeah, because that's something you can totally control," his brother said dryly.

"It is," he insisted.

"And so, when Haylee decides it's time to pack up and move back to California, you'll just wish her a safe journey and wave goodbye? Maybe you'll even be relieved, because then you can go back to spending your Saturday nights at Diggers', buying drinks for any pretty young thing who smiles at you. Because variety is the spice of life, right? A man would have to be a fool to settle down with one woman when there are so many who want to be with him."

"She's staying in Haven until after the babies are born."

"And then what?" Devin pressed.

"We haven't talked about anything beyond that," he admitted, ignoring the growing sense of unease inside him.

"Give her a reason to stay," his brother urged.

"I've already given her two."

Devin shook his head. "If you lose the most amazing woman you've ever known because you can't forgive your ex for her manipulations, then maybe you don't deserve her."

Haylee had no objection to Trevor going to Las Vegas with his brother. It felt strange being alone in his house, but she didn't worry about keeping herself busy. She had holiday baking to do, a couple of seasonal favorites to watch on the Hallmark Channel and *Beth & Amy*, a new release by her favorite author.

But still, keeping busy didn't keep her from missing him, so she decided to plan and prepare a special meal for his homecoming on Sunday. Nothing too fancy— she was still cautiously dipping her toe in the water when it came to actual cooking—but she found a fairly simple recipe for stir-fried chicken and vegetables and decided to give it a go.

Although The Trading Post wasn't too far to walk, she was still a California girl not just at heart but in her blood, so she opted to drive the short distance.

There was one light on Main Street, and of course it turned red as she approached. She applied her brakes carefully, in case the road was icy, and stopped at the line. She watched the green pickup truck in her rearview mirror as it stopped behind her, but the darker SUV-type vehicle was coming up fast behind it.

She heard the squeal of brakes as the SUV tried to stop, but it was too late.

Trevor didn't intend to wake her, but he needed to touch her, to reassure himself that she was okay. As he lifted his hand to lay it on top of hers, he saw that it was shaking—just like everything inside him.

Haylee's eyelids flickered, then opened.

"Hey," he said softly.

"Trevor? What are you doing here?"

"Where else should I be?"

"In Las Vegas with your brother."

"We turned around as soon as I got Sky's message that you were here."

"You didn't have to do that," she protested. "I'm fine. Sky should have told you that I was fine."

"She did," Trevor admitted. "But you were in a car accident and—" God, just saying it aloud made him feel sick.

"I wasn't really involved in the accident," she told him. "I was just at the end of a chain reaction caused by a distracted driver rear-ending the vehicle behind me."

"And yet you're at the urgent care clinic," he pointed out.

"The paramedics overreacted," she said. "They took one look at my belly and were worried that I was about to give birth on the side of the road and insisted I get checked out by a doctor."

"I'm glad they did," he said.

"But I'm fine," she said. "And our babies are fine."

"I'll believe it when the doctor springs you from this place."

"Consider her sprung," Dr. Foss said from the doorway.

"Really?" Haylee asked hopefully.

"Really," the clinic doctor confirmed.

"See?" she said to Trevor, just a little bit smugly.

"You might have some soreness and bruising from the seat belt," the doctor warned. "But there's nothing we can do about that. You can alternate hot and cold compresses on your back and neck, if you start to stiffen up. Otherwise just relax and let Mr. Blake take care of you."

"I can do that," Haylee said.

"I'll make sure of it," Trevor promised.

Despite her insistence that she could do it herself, he helped her dress. As he did so, he skimmed his hands over her torso, gently searching for any tender areas, and she rolled her eyes when he lingered in some of his favorite spots—the newest one being the round curve of her belly.

But aside from a red mark on her shoulder that would likely turn into a bruise in the next day or two, she didn't appear to be any the worse for wear. He helped her on with her coat, then her hat and mittens, reminding her that it was cold outside. "I know," she admitted. "That's why I was driving to the grocery store instead of walking."

"I should have been here for you," he said, feeling guilty that he wasn't and relieved that she hadn't been injured and terrified to think that she might have lost their babies—and he might have lost her.

"You're not responsible for what happened."

"I should have been here," he insisted, as they exited the clinic.

"You can't be with me every minute of every day."

"Says who?"

"Let me rephrase—I don't want you with me every minute of every day," she told him, softening the words with a smile. "You have to trust that I can take care of myself and our babies."

"How about every night?" he asked. "Can I be with you every night?"

Her smile widened. "I can't think of any reason that I'd object to that."

They were almost at the parking lot when she suddenly stopped, in the middle of the sidewalk, and tipped her head back. "Trevor...look."

He was looking—at her—as she held out her mittened hands, palms up, to catch the fluffy white flakes.

"Have you never seen snow before?" he asked, amused by her childlike wonder.

"Of course I've seen snow," she told him. "But it doesn't snow in Oakland. Ever." She watched a snowflake melt into the knitted fabric. "Actually, that's not true. I think it snowed once, maybe nine or ten years ago."

"We don't get a lot of snow here, either. Of course, this is the desert, so we don't get a lot of any kind of precipitation."

"Maybe the snow is a Christmas miracle," she suggested.

"Then it must be a year for miracles," he said, sliding his arms around her middle. "Because this is already the fourth."

"The fourth?" she echoed curiously.

He nodded. "You were the first." Then he splayed his hands on the curve of her belly. "Our son and daughter are the second and third, so this is the fourth."

Haylee felt her throat grow tight. "You really think our babies are a miracle?"

"Don't you?"

"I do," she agreed. "But I was afraid you'd think they were a mistake."

"Unplanned doesn't mean unwelcome," he said.

"That isn't quite what you were saying a few months ago."

"A few months ago, I was still reeling from the news of your pregnancy. And maybe afraid to let myself hope that this time…"

She placed her hands over his, a wordless gesture of understanding.

They stood silently for a moment, then Haylee felt a gentle nudge on the left side of her belly.

She heard his breath catch. "Was that…one of our babies?"

"It was. And that—" she said, when she felt another movement on the right side "—was the other one."

He turned her around then, so that she was facing him, and kissed her softly. "I love you, Haylee."

She hadn't expected to ever hear those words come from his lips, and though she desperately wanted to believe them now, she feared his declaration was an emotional reaction to the events of the day rather than a true reflection of his feelings.

"I'm sorry you were scared when you heard about the accident," she said cautiously. "But I think maybe you're twisting that fear into something else."

"I'm not," he denied. "Maybe I shouldn't have said the words for the first time standing outside of a medical clinic, but that doesn't make the feelings any less real. It's just that when I realized the truth of my feelings, I didn't want to wait a minute longer to share them with you.

"I'm not going to ask you to marry me again—not right now," he said. "Because I don't want you to think the words are tied up with expectations, but I want you to know that I'm sincere about wanting to be not just a father to our babies but a husband to you. A husband who will love and honor and cherish you every day of our life together. And when you're ready, I will happily get down on one knee and ask you to be my bride."

She didn't know how to respond, what to say. Then she heard the echo of her sister's words in her head— "take a leap"—and she did. "I love you, too." And it felt so good to finally release the feelings that she'd kept buried deep in her heart, she couldn't resist saying it again. "I love you, Trevor."

He kissed her then, on the grassy slope beside the urgent care clinic, while the snow continued to fall around them.

"And I want a Christmas Eve wedding," Haylee said, when he eased his mouth away from hers.

His brows lifted. "You want to get married?"

She nodded.

"*This* Christmas Eve?"

"Unless you think that's too soon," she said.

"Are you kidding? I would have married you three months ago," he reminded her.

"But you didn't love me three months ago."

"Or maybe I just didn't know that I did."

"Either way, I think we both needed some time to be sure what we wanted."

"Are you sure?"

"I'm sure," she said. "You made me believe that happily-ever-after is possible. You made me believe in us."

He touched his lips to hers again. "Then let's go home—we've got a wedding to plan."

Epilogue

Christmas Eve

"This was a ridiculous idea." Haylee frowned at her reflection in the full-length mirror. "I look like a beluga whale."

"You do not," Finley protested. "You look like a radiant bride."

"A very pregnant bride."

"Was your pregnancy supposed to be a secret?" her sister teased. "Because I doubt there's a hoop skirt anywhere in this world that would hide your babies bump, but I would have tried to find one for you."

"I just never imagined myself waddling down the aisle." She picked up her bouquet and held it in front of her, but the simple hand-tied arrangement of red roses with holly, ivy and mistletoe didn't hide anything, either. "Although truthfully, I'm not sure I ever imagined myself getting married at all."

"What are you talking about? Every little girl dreams about her wedding day," Finley said. "Doesn't she?"

"Maybe I did when I was a little girl," she acknowledged. "But as I grew up and rarely dated and never fell in love, I resigned myself to the fact that it wouldn't ever happen for me."

"And then you met Trevor."

Haylee smiled. "And then I met Trevor."

"And the Gilmores and Blakes drew battle lines."

She could laugh about it now—and did—but there had been a few moments when she'd wondered if the two families might come to blows. Most recently at the rehearsal dinner at The Home Station.

But her stepmother must have been a diplomat in a previous life, because somehow Colleen managed to smooth things over so that by the end of the night, Robert Gilmore and Elijah Blake were actually doing shots of whiskey together in honor of the happy couple.

"Seriously, though, I'm happy for you, sis." Finley's eyes filled with tears. "I'm going to miss you like crazy, but I'm happy for you."

"You're welcome to visit whenever you want."

"And I will," her sister promised. "But I'm still keeping Simon."

"I figured that out when we were in Oakland for Thanksgiving," she acknowledged. It didn't seem to matter to Simon that she was the one who'd taken him from the shelter; he'd quickly shifted his allegiance to the one who filled his food and water bowls every morning.

"Do you mind?" Finley asked.

She shook her head as a light knock sounded. "I know you'll take good care of one another."

"That better not be Trevor," Finley said, making her way to the door. "Because I told your soon-to-be husband, in no uncertain terms, that he was not allowed to see you before the ceremony."

She wrapped her hand around the knob and opened it just a crack, clearly prepared to send her future brother-in-law on his way if he'd dared to ignore her instructions.

"Oh," Finley said, and took a step back as she opened the door a little wider. "It's you."

Haylee stopped fussing with her flowers and glanced over her shoulder, wondering who it could be.

Then Sandra Burke stepped into the room.

"Mom." It was an effort to get the single word out through a throat that suddenly felt too tight.

"Look at you," Sandra murmured, her eyes shiny as she looked from one daughter to the other. "Both of you. My beautiful girls."

Haylee managed a wry smile. "Finley's beautiful. I'm pregnant."

"You're both beautiful," their mom insisted.

"I'll give you two a minute," Finley said, giving Sandra a quick hug before slipping through the still-open door and closing it firmly behind her.

"I didn't know you were coming," Haylee said, when her sister had gone.

"Your fiancé said he wanted it to be a surprise—

though I suspect he didn't say anything to you in case I didn't show up," Sandra admitted. "I missed far too many important events in your life.

"My fault, I know," she hastened to acknowledge. "But I couldn't let your wedding day be another one."

"I'm glad you're here," she said, surprised to realize it was true.

"Me, too," her mom said. Then, a little uncertainly, "Can I hug you—or will I wrinkle your dress?"

Haylee answered by stepping into her arms.

There had been a lot of debate and discussion about where Haylee and Trevor should get married. The bride's father thought the wedding should take place in her hometown; the groom's parents wanted to host it at Miners' Pass; Haylee had suggested the Silver Star, because it was where they'd first met; Trevor hadn't cared where the wedding happened—he just wanted Haylee to be his wife.

In the end, they'd decided to exchange vows in front of the Christmas tree they'd decorated together inside the home where they'd fallen in love.

"Nervous?" Devin asked, as he took his position beside his brother.

"Nope."

"Not even a little bit?"

Trevor shook his head. "I feel as if I've been waiting for this moment—for Haylee—my whole life."

"It seemed to take you that long to admit your feelings for her," his brother teased.

"True enough," he acknowledged. But now that he'd finally admitted what was in his heart, he'd vowed to tell her every day so that she'd never have cause to doubt his commitment to her and the family they were making together.

He wasn't nervous, but his heart did start to beat a little bit faster when the music started. Then Finley, dressed in festive red taffeta, made her way down the narrow aisle between the rows of chairs. A moment later, Haylee was there, looking more beautiful than he'd ever seen her, and his heart swelled with so much love for her, he felt as if his ribs might crack.

"Dear friends and family, we are gathered here today..."

The minister spoke about the sanctity of marriage and then guided the bride and groom through the exchange of vows, and then finally said, "I now pronounce you husband and wife."

He didn't conclude with an invitation for the newly-weds to kiss, but Trevor was prepared to take matters into his own hands. He pulled a sprig of a familiar green plant out of his pocket and held it over Haylee's head.

And smiling, he kissed his bride under the mistletoe.

* * * * *

MILLS & BOON

Coming next month

AWAKENING HIS SHY CINDERELLA
Sophie Pembroke

"Trust me," Damon said, with feeling, "it's drawing exactly the right amount of attention to your figure. You look incredible." And he really had to stop looking at his big sister's best friend that way. Not least because she'd never given him even the slightest hint that she wanted him to.

There was that one night, his brain reminded him. That one night when you could have kissed her, if you'd wanted to.

But he hadn't. Because she was Celeste's best friend. Because she wasn't the sort of girl you messed around with, and he hadn't known how to do anything else.

Because she'd seen deeper than he liked, and it had scared him.

Her smile turned shy and she went back to studying the creatures on her dress, thankfully oblivious to his thoughts. "It is like my windows, isn't it?"

Somewhere someone clapped their hands again, and bellowed for them to take their places.

"Come on. We're starting." Damon took her arm and led her towards the bar. He needed another drink, and she hadn't even had one yet. "Let's grab a glass of something bubbly, and you can tell me more about your windows and your work until it's time to shout out the countdown, or whatever we need to do."

"You really want to know more about the windows?" She sounded astonished at the prospect.

"As it happens, I really, really do." And not just because of the way she lit up when she spoke about the things that mattered to her. Or because it would give him a chance to listen to her melodious voice. Those things weren't important to him. Or shouldn't be, anyway.

No, he wanted to know more because he had the inklings of an idea that could help both of them get what they needed in life. If he could persuade her to take a chance on him.

It was just business. That was all.

He just needed to keep reminding himself of that.

Continue reading
AWAKENING HIS SHY CINDERELLA
Sophie Pembroke

Available next month
www.millsandboon.co.uk